SALVATION

Legends of Graham Mansion
Book Four

Rosa Lee Jude

Mary Lin Brewer

10/16

This is a work of fiction.

All of the characters, organizations, and events portrayed in this novel

are either products of the authors' imaginations

or are used as fictional characters.

Two Southern Belles Publishing

Cover Photos: Mary Lin Brewer, Robin Lewis, Justin Plaster

ISBN-13: 978-0-9882094-3-5
ISBN-10: 0-9882094-3-8

Printed in the United States of America.

DEDICATION

To Our Mothers
They are our True Salvation

The Keys to Our Success

The ghosts of our past walk with us today. Listen closely. You will hear them. Look closely. You will see them. Read closely, for they are here within these pages. Our ghosts speak to us as we create these stories, as we imagine these characters, and as we blend this fiction with the powerful histories of the Graham families and this great country. Thus it is the voices and faces of our past that come alive in our present day, and we are forever connected.

There are many people who have played key roles in assisting to make this, our fourth book, possible. While this list is not all-encompassing, we hope it will show our heartfelt gratitude to those who have been extra special in the process.

To Our Readers – our extended family, we love you. You have welcomed us, nurtured us, and encouraged us beyond our wildest dreams, and we thank you. You have made all the difference in how we view writing.

To Our Editor, Donna Leedy Stroupe – you, my dear, have been our salvation from the beginning. You know our embedded clauses better than anyone. We celebrate your incredible gifts of grammar and syntax but what is more, we are blessed to call you our friend.

To Our Ex-Officio Editors – Pam Newberry, Marcella Taylor, and Carole Bybee – a true sisterhood of wordsmiths if there ever was one! Your devotion to our content, presentation, and accuracy is only surpassed by your own excellence with the written word. Word warriors! Yes! That is you!

To Our Graphic Designer, Julie Newberry – your talents transform our words into a visual language for the web, for promotions, and for our book covers. Thank you, Jules! You color our world!

To Our Layout Designer, Julie Titus – yours are the last eyes on the book, yet it is your gifted fingers that create the final, magical balance of space and text in each book. Thank you, Julie!

To Our Vendors – Thank you to our local and regional brick and mortar stores! We are grateful for your showcasing our series and nurturing it as if it were your own baby. You are a rare breed indeed, resilient and strong, not unlike a few of our favorite *Legends* characters.

And, finally, and most importantly,

To Our Significant Others and Families – Love conquers all. We are so very thankful for your cocoon of love...it has carried us when we could not carry ourselves.

Our utmost thanks to all of the above and to all the others who have inspired and empowered us. And, most of all, our gratitude goes to all those who will read these pages and travel with us to another time.

The Story Behind The Story

The five-volume *Legends of Graham Mansion* series is set in the beautiful Blue Ridge Mountains of Southwest Virginia on the historic Major Graham Mansion property and surrounding area. Rosa Lee Jude, writer, and Mary Lin Brewer, researcher and historian, teamed up to create Mary Lin's dream of a Graham Mansion book series that would take historical information about the people and events of the Graham Mansion's 200-plus year history and weave a story to explain the property's most interesting mysteries.

Redemption was the first installment and focused on the 1786 murder of Joseph Joel Baker. Central heroine, Grae White, traveled back in time to meet the property's first family and discover the unwritten story behind Baker's grizzly murder.

In the second book, *Ambition,* Grae traveled back to 1830 and met the young David Graham. Later known as Squire David, this ambitiously driven man was the patriarch of the massive Graham estate. On this adventure, Grae discovered the secret behind the tragedy that changed this man forever.

Deception, the third volume in the series, takes Grae to 1859 where she became intimately acquainted with the mistress of Graham Mansion, Martha Bell Peirce Graham. On her third journey through time Grae unravels the conflicting facts and unexpected truths of Martha's "madness," her misery, and ultimately, her sheer might.

Salvation is the fourth and longest book in the *Legends of Graham Mansion* series. Compelled to understand and reconcile the mysteries surrounding Graham Mansion, Grae travels back to 1864, arriving during the cataclysmic peak of Civil War hostilities in southwestern Virginia. During this dangerous journey, Grae is shocked and her very existence is threatened as she explores and uncovers long-hidden Graham family secrets.

The *Legends of Graham Mansion* series is a work of historical fiction. History has been used in the creation of this story, but the majority of what will be found within these pages is pure fiction, a speculative look at what might have occurred. The authors have endeavored to be true to the time period and respectful to those persons who are fictionally portrayed. The story also has the twist of time travel and a glimmer of paranormal. The latter aspects are due, in part, to some of the accounts that the many ghost hunters, clairvoyants, and paranormal experts have relayed to Mary Lin over the past ten years.

Major Graham Mansion is a very real place. It is located in Wythe County, just a few miles from the historic Great Wagon Road and the New River, as well as, modern-day interstates I-77 and I-81. The property has been owned, renovated, and maintained since the late 1980s by Virginia native, Josiah Cephas Weaver. The Mansion is often open seasonally for a variety of special events, including GrahamFest, haunted history tours, paranormal investigations, and the wildly popular fall event, Haunted Graham Mansion™.

PRESENT DAY

ONE

Rap, rap, rap—Grae wasn't prepared to have to knock to get out of the closet. It was an ominous feeling, like being trapped between time periods in a dark, musty box. Grae wondered if the floor would fall beneath her feet and she would slide down the stairs to nowhere like Alice going down the rabbit hole. She tried the knob once more. Slowly, the door opened. Jay's face was peeking at her from the other side.

"Why did you close the door?" Grae pushed the door open the rest of the way as she looked behind Jay to see if anyone else was around. No matter how many times she went on her journeys through time, she still forgot that only an instant passed for those who stayed in the present.

"I didn't close the door," Jay whispered. "It closed itself. It scared me to death."

"What do you mean 'it closed itself'?"

"You were standing there, and then you disappeared and the door immediately closed." Jay rubbed the back of his neck.

"But, you were standing in the doorway. It should have knocked you into the closet."

"Yes, it should have."

"But?" Grae didn't understand why it was taking him so long to tell the story.

"It should have knocked me in there. Instead, it went right through me. I thought that time had closed the door on you."

"What are you two whispering about?" Jay's sister, Madison, came around the corner.

"Ah, Grae was showing me this, ah, unusual old closet." Jay kept rubbing his head as he tried to steer his sister toward the round side. Grae stood just over the doorway in the foyer and looked back into the closet.

"Yes, a round closet is indeed unusual. But this was once a very grand home; you would expect it to have some eccentricities." Madison commented, as she touched the side of the closet. "Well, I came to find you, Jay. Go get your coat. Mack and Perry are going to take us for a walk around the property." Jay glanced briefly at Grae before he followed Madison.

"Do you need help changing out of the dress?" Grae jumped when she realized that her mother was behind her.

"No, I think I can do it by myself." Grae turned as she began to climb the steps and looked intently at her mother. The age had returned to the young face that she had spent so much time with in 1859. She wondered if her mother's memory of her time as Loretta would now include a young woman who she had worked with named Maria. For an instant, Grae thought she saw a glimmer of recollection in her mother's eyes, but then it was gone.

"Carrie and her mother have practically taken over the cleanup in the kitchen." Kat laughed and ran her fingers through her hair. "Lucy is making a special version of hot chocolate. I have a feeling that it may have peppermint schnapps in it."

"That sounds nice. I'll be back down in a few minutes." Grae continued going up the steps. Her mind was racing. It was still Thanksgiving. They had a houseful of guests.

"Are you okay? Something seems different about you."

"I'm fine. I guess all the excitement has just caught up with me." Grae turned back around. "Mom, where did you put that box that I found in the wall upstairs?"

"Your grandfather was the last one to have it. You'll have to ask him. Why?"

"Oh, I just was wondering about something I saw in it." Grae turned and began walking up the steps again.

"Grae, what's happened?" Kat was still standing at the bottom of the steps. "Don't try to hide it from me. Fifteen minutes ago, you were cheerful and energetic. Now you seem tired and sullen. In my experience, that can only mean one thing."

Grae stopped in her tracks. She didn't want to turn and face her mother. She couldn't hide the truth. She couldn't hide how this last journey had changed her.

"Grae, look at me."

Slowly, Grae turned and faced her mother. For a moment, it felt as if they were transported back to 1859, back to the home of Squire David and Martha Graham. Grae saw a young girl, named Loretta, standing before her, reaching, reaching for someone who Grae could not see. There were tears streaming down her face and a key in her hand—an identical key to the one that was around Grae's neck.

"No! No! It couldn't have happened. No, I would have remembered. It wasn't you!" Kat began to sway. Grae raced to reach her, but she fell backwards before Grae could grasp her arm.

"Mom! Mom! Are you okay?"

"You were that girl, the girl who designed dresses. Martha adored you. Squire David despised you. After you disappeared, he said he would kill you if you ever came into the house again. This house!" Kat rose to her feet, just as Lucy hollered from the kitchen.

"Kat! Come try my very special hot chocolate."

"I'll be there in a minute." Kat turned back to her daughter and grabbed her by the arm. "You will not, I repeat, will not travel back in time again. I will not have you make the same mistakes that I have. I have had enough of this." Grae jerked her arm out of her mother's grasp.

"You don't understand. I have to go back. I have to…"

"You don't have to do anything. You cannot imagine the heartache that can be caused by time travel."

"I think I have seen enough heartache back there to understand it."

"I'm not talking about back there. I am talking about the heartache that can result in the present when you mock the past, when you think that it is all a grand adventure. You cannot undo what happens. You can never make up for the loss." Kat's tone was stern and her look was dangerous. It was a side of her mother that Grae had never seen.

"Why can't you tell me…"

"We don't talk about it. We don't ever talk about it. You just listen. You heed my words. I am not kidding around. I forbid you to time travel again!" Kat turned and began to walk toward the back of the house.

The words rattled Grae. She was exhausted from her journey to 1859. As she walked up the stairs to her room, all she could think about was taking a nice long hot shower. But that wasn't possible. She had to change back into the clothes she wore during Thanksgiving dinner and act as if only a few moments had passed.

As she entered her room, she was again struck with how different it looked to her. Being in the house during its early years was a stark contrast to the Graham Mansion of the present. It was an elegant mansion in 1859 with fresh paint and wallpaper. Everything glistened from daily cleaning due to hours of slave labor. It was a young house then. In the present, it showed the age of almost two hundred years of history behind it. The paint was faded; the floors were worn and creaked like old bones. What little wallpaper was left was from different eras and mismatched at best. While Kat and Grae tried, it was almost impossible to keep it clean. Dust and dirt seemed to seep from the walls during the night. The slave quarters to the rear no longer housed workers to keep the residence spotless. Grae thought about all of this as she took off the beautiful purple dress and returned it to the long bag that Missus Akers had brought it in. From the corner of her eye, she saw a small blue ball roll across the floor.

"Clara, I guess I still haven't visited your time yet. I do wish that I could meet you." The blue ball moved again in the opposite direction.

"You decent in there?" Gav's voice at the door brought Grae back to the reality of the day.

"Yes, come on in."

"I can't believe we actually have a few minutes by ourselves." Gav pulled Grae into a hug landing on her bed. "I've missed you."

"I've been right here." Grae tried to laugh off the awkward feeling that existed between them. It was hard for her mind not to wander to all of the strange things that happened. Earlier in the fall, Gav was stalked at college by a girl named Eve. She was actually a woman from 1786 that was seeking revenge on Grae because of Patrick McGavock's love for a girl named Arabella. It was an identity that Grae had assumed on her first journey back in time. Patrick's love had followed her to the present.

"I realize everything that happened with Eve was scary, but it's not just that. Each time you go on a journey, you seem a little different. It seems like you just change each time I see you." Gav gently kissed her. "You even seem different since dinner." Grae put on a smile and tried to hide what she now knew that Gav could see all too well.

"We'll just have to go downstairs and watch football and have some fun. I bet that Grandpa and Perry will be fighting over the calls that the officials make." Grae reached for her socks and began to put them on, looking away from Gav.

"Wait a minute." Gav pulled her back to him. "That's it, isn't it?" He searched her eyes. "You've been gone again. Today. When was it? Just now, after you showed us that dress?" Grae took a deep sigh. She couldn't keep anything from him. "That's why your mother came back into the kitchen so upset. She drank a whole cup of those spiked hot chocolates that Lucy made. It's a wonder it didn't scald her throat."

Grae stood up and walked toward the front window, remembering the conflict with her mother just a few minutes ago.

"She doesn't want me travelling any more. She'd kill me if she knew that I almost didn't make it back this time."

"WHAT? You almost didn't come back? Well, she has a right to be upset, and I think I agree with her."

Grae turned around and saw that Gav was now standing behind her. He looked mad.

"How can you agree with her? I thought you understood why I had to take these journeys."

"I thought I did too, but now I am not so sure. I don't understand why you would jeopardize your life here with us for some people who have been dead for over a hundred years."

"But they need me. I am helping them."

"Listen to yourself. These people are dead, Grae. They were rotting in the ground long before our grandparents were even born."

"Gav! That's an awful thing to say." Grae turned away from him and looked back out the window.

"But it's the truth. You have built this life for yourself in this world that doesn't exist anymore."

"I am helping them find the truth. I am helping reveal the truth behind the mysteries of their lives. I want to set the record straight!"

"And what good will that do? Will it stop them from dying? Will it make them live again?"

Grae turned and faced him. She no longer saw the understanding in Gav's eyes that she once did. "Gav, just think about this for a minute. Imagine if history portrayed you as someone you weren't or said you had done things you hadn't. Wouldn't you want someone to set the record straight, if they could, even if it was long after you were gone? Don't you see the value in that? The importance of righting a wrong?"

"If it could change things, then maybe. But I don't see what has changed by you finding out the truth. You went back to the time of the Bakers and found out that his death was an accident instead of a murder. Did that change anything for Mister Baker? He still died with an ax in his head. Those two slaves were still hung. And from what you've told me, you came mighty close to sharing part of the guilt with them."

"Well, I can't change what happened. It's against the rules. But, I was helpful to Ama; I was her friend. I learned why Squire David became so hard and mean."

"And in exchange he probably has a bounty on your head." Gav looked Grae squarely in the eyes. "It's like you are searching for something there. Like you have some mission. It's like you are seeking your own salvation in someone else's life." The words stung Grae, like a slap in the face. Gav didn't understand, perhaps he never did. "And this love affair you are having with one of my ancestors. I don't understand that either. I am right here, standing in front of you, but you would rather be with a McGavock that died a hundred years ago." There it was; the real issue. Gav was jealous.

"It's not like that at all. Patrick is just special to me. He saved my life so many times." Grae reached out to Gav, but he backed away.

"He wouldn't have to be saving you if you were where you were supposed to be. If you were here, with me. What's really happened between you two? What have you given him that you've not given me? Why does he have such a hold on you?"

Gav wouldn't say the words, but she knew what he was asking. They had danced around the topic all summer. She thought that he was being patient and understanding because so much was changing in her life. But, now, she realized that he was suspicious. He didn't trust her.

"Well? What's your answer?"

"I thought you knew me better than that." Grae frowned and shook her head.

"I am beginning to think that I don't know you at all." Gav paused at the doorway. "Maybe, maybe we should take a break." He didn't look at her as he said it.

Grae remained silent. A sob was lodged in her throat. He left the room, closing the door behind him. She let out the sob and all those she had held tightly within for many months came out of her like an ocean. Her whole body shook. She knew that this day would come, deep down she knew. Her mother was right. The journeys do harm to the present.

A few minutes passed, and she went to the window and gazed out. There was no evidence of where she had been, only the same horizon that had marked the land for centuries. She saw Gav walk off the porch. His parents walked beside him to their vehicle. Gav got into the back seat. He didn't look back at the house. Again, Grae began to cry. She watched as they drove away. A soft knock came at her door. Grae turned to see her mother peeking in. All anger on her face was gone.

"Grae, Shasta is leaving. She's got to go to work." Kat stopped and looked closely at her daughter. "There's something wrong, isn't there? Something happened between you and Gav. Are you okay?" Kat's answer came in the form of a new round of crying. Liquid seemed to be coming out of every opening of Grae's face. Kat pulled her into a strong hug and gently stroked her daughter's hair.

"He doesn't trust me." Grae said between sobs. "He doesn't understand why I feel like I have to go."

"Darling, I understand how you feel. But, I also know what the outcome can be. These journeys are not worth it. If things aren't working out for all the normal reasons between you and Gav, so be it. But don't lose him this way. These journeys are not worth what is lost because of them. They were the biggest mistake of my life."

Grae pulled away from her mother and looked her in the eyes.

"You keep saying that. You keep warning me. You never tell me what happened to you. I met you in 1859. I was with you for quite a while. I didn't see anything bad happen to you."

"Just because you didn't see it, doesn't mean that it didn't happen."

"Then tell me. Maybe I'll be able to understand why I should stop going back."

"I am not going to say this again, Graham Belle. You are not to go back to the past again. Not ever."

"You've got to give me a better reason than that."

"Don't you defy me, Grae. Reckless behavior leads to circumstances that are dire and disastrous." Kat walked out of the room and slammed the door.

"Dire and disastrous. That's it. There is some connection between my mother and who The General once was. I felt that he had to have a connection to her. What in the world could it be?" Grae plopped down on her bed and wiped the tears from her face. "Maybe, if I can take just one more journey, maybe then I can uncover the truth that will mean something to someone in the present. I've got to find a way to make Gav understand that my time travel isn't about Patrick."

Grae watched from the window later as Jay and Madison left after their tour of the property. Jay looked back at the house toward Grae's window, but she backed away so he couldn't see her. She thought that everyone had left the house until she heard a soft knock at her door. Carrie's red hair was the first thing Grae saw peering in her doorway.

"Can I come in?" Gav's sister quietly walked into the room and closed the door behind her. "Are you okay? Your mom told me that you and Gav had a fight."

"You might as well know. We broke up." Grae didn't think she had any more tears, but some began to escape her eyes anyway.

"Oh, no. Oh, that can't be. He adores you." Carrie's words should have been comforting to Grae, but they only made the ache in her heart more profound.

"Well, that may have been true, but he doesn't right now. He doesn't trust me anymore."

"Why? How can he not trust you?" Carrie sat on an oversized pillow that was on the floor. She absentmindedly rolled the blue ball toward the fireplace. She didn't seem to notice the ball rolled back to her. Grae smiled as she thought of the sweet little girl who was probably delighted to have someone play with her.

"Oh, Carrie, it's a long story. It's hard to explain."

"Does this have to do with your time travel?"

Grae gave Carrie a shocked look as she asked the question. "How? What?" Grae was afraid to say too much.

"Your mother told me about it last month while we were doing the funnel cakes. She explained the whole process to me and how the women in your family have this unique ability."

"Just exactly how did this come up?" Grae's eyes narrowed as she thought about the lengths that her mother would go to in order to keep tabs on Grae's journeys.

"Well, let me think. I'm not really sure." Carrie paused. As she was thinking, she once again rolled the ball back toward the fireplace. This time, two came back to her. She rolled both of them back. "I think that it was when she was teaching me how to make the batters. We got to talking about the kitchen and how weird it was that all those modern appliances were in this old house. Somehow, we got to talking about how many different time periods this house has seen and the different families who have lived here. I guess she just thought that was a good opportunity to tell me about it. I was just so thrilled that she trusted me with your family secret."

"Did she ask you to do anything with this information?" Grae's mind raced with this new revelation. Her mother's tactics were rising to a new level if she was willing to reveal the time travel secret to someone outside the family. Even Perry didn't know, but now Carrie did. Kat was making the girl into a spy.

"Yes, she asked me not to tell Perry. She said that men didn't understand it." Carrie laughed. "Mostly, she asked me to keep an eye on you and to be your friend. Like that is hard."

Carrie was her friend, no doubt. Her mother knew that Grae would not suspect Carrie's watchful eye or the amount of time that she was around. As Perry's girlfriend, too, Carrie had plenty of reasons to be at Graham Mansion.

"Gav is just being stubborn. Even if he is on the Hokie football team, he is now a small fish in a big pond. He is probably missing the worship. I know that he is hopelessly devoted to you."

"Well, I don't know. He's pretty mad, and I don't know how to make him feel otherwise. You see, Carrie, there is this ancestor of yours that was very devoted to me as well. In his younger days, he is the spitting image of Gav, or I guess it is really the other way around. He has saved my life more than once and is a very good friend. It's kind of like having Gav there with me."

"Wow! That is so cool! It gives me chills just thinking about it. Have you told Gav that?"

"Sort of, it's kind of hard to talk to him about it. It seems to irritate him to hear about Patrick."

"Patrick," Carrie sighed. "That is such a nice name. Oh, I wish I could meet him."

"I don't think that will be possible. But, honestly, he and Gav have many of the same characteristics. I feel like I have met the older Gav." Grae paused and thought about Gav for a moment. "Oh, what I am going to do if Gav finds someone else?" Grae began to cry again.

"Oh, he won't. I know it. He's just letting off steam." Carrie rolled the ball again. "Grae, can you tell me who I am rolling this ball to? This is all feeling very weird. But, at the same time, I am not scared."

Grae laughed through her tears. "You figured that out, huh, after only rolling it about twenty times. Her name is Clara."

"Perry has mentioned her; I just couldn't remember her name. He and I went to the store to buy this blue ball. Perry said that the balls keep getting damaged somehow. Does she do it?"

"No, Clara is a very gentle child. Squire David is destroying the balls. He gets angry with me and destroys Clara's toys. Because he is nothing but a bully." Grae said the last part loudly.

"Squire David? As in the man who built this house?"

"Yes, that's the one."

"He's here?" Carrie whispered.

"It doesn't matter how low you say it, if he is around, he can hear you. And, yes, I don't think he likes anyone in his house. When Clara was living here, Squire David's daughters had to hide her in this very room. He didn't want a poor orphan living with his family. If he had been a little kinder, Clara might not have died." Grae was talking loudly again.

"Really?" Carrie's eyes were wide with amazement. Grae smiled as Carrie looked over her shoulders.

"Well, I don't know that for a certainty, but that is what I suspect. I think that her parents were dying of something like smallpox or some other awful disease of the time, and they wanted her to get away from the sickness. Perhaps Clara's father worked here in some way for Squire David. Maybe Martha, Squire's wife, took pity on the situation and took the little girl in. We shall probably never know, but, for some reason, Clara cannot leave this house. It's our job to be her friend." Grae sat down on the floor next to Carrie and rolled the blue ball.

TWO

Sleep overcame her just after nightfall. Her dreams were fitful and full of snippets of time. The present, the past, all mixed up in a nightmare. Gav was shot in 1786. Martha was one of her professors at college. Mister Abbey managed Squire David's General Store. The General was a dog. Everything was screwed up.

The following morning, Grae rose early to go to work on Black Friday. She wondered what each journey might be doing to her physically. "I feel like I am several years older each time I come back," Grae said to her reflection in her bathroom mirror. She almost thought she saw gray hair and some wrinkles around her eyes. "Stress lines, no doubt. I'll have to get some special face crème for that." Grae sighed. "I bet the store will be hopping today."

Grae's part-time job at Big Walker Lookout was an adventure in itself. The owner, Mister Abbey, was a real character and had indulged her interest in coffee bean roasting. Making Big Walker Brews was now a regular part of her job. "I sure hope that I have enough of all the flavors ready for today. As cold as it is, they are likely to sell like hotcakes."

"I hope you are talking to yourself in there." Grandpa Mack's voice came through the crack between the door and the frame. Grae opened the door and saw her sweet grandfather dressed and ready to take on the day.

"I sure am, Grandpa. You know, it just might be the most intelligent conversation I will have all day." Grae gave him a wink as she continued to brush her teeth.

"Oh, we are feisty this morning, little girl. I hope those crazy shoppers appreciate your personal brand of humor. You know, there are many things about this old body that I didn't take care of as good as I should, but my teeth aren't one of them." Grandpa stood behind Grae and smiled into the mirror. "I'm seventy-six years young and I still have all my pearly whites. Let that be a lesson to you. Take care of your teeth. You can't make new ones."

"I will, Grandpa. It smells like Mom is up and making breakfast."

"Yep, that's what I came up here to tell you. We better get down there before that smell wakes up Perry."

Grae returned to her room and put the final touches on her outfit. A quick glance at her cell phone showed no messages from Gav. Grae felt a tug at her heart. "I guess I have to give him some time."

There weren't too many words exchanged at the breakfast table. Grandpa was deep into his newspaper. Kat continued to cook as Perry appeared, groggy and wrinkled, shortly after Grae began to eat. She appreciated the silence. She knew that it would be a rare commodity during the busiest shopping day of the year. As she walked out the back door to her car, her mother followed her.

"Grae, I'm sorry that I was so hard on you yesterday. I should have been a little more understanding since you were so tired and mixed up from returning. But that doesn't diminish my strong desire for you not to travel anymore. Surely, now with what happened with you and Gav, you must see the seriousness of all this."

"Mom, Gav is just jealous. He thinks I have a love back in time." Grae opened the door of her car.

"Well, do you?"

"Mom, it's complicated. Yes, a part of me does love Patrick. He has come to my rescue many times. The Patrick I met in 1786 was so much like Gav. It was like having him there with me. It was comforting. But, the Patrick I met in 1830 was an old man, and I didn't see him at all in 1859. He was still living then, but his age limited his travels. I do not imagine that I will ever see him again."

"But, how does all this affect your feelings about Gav? And, more importantly, how does it affect how you act toward Gav? Are you making him jealous by the way you talk about Patrick? Or the way that you treat Gav? Maybe you are not giving him enough devotion. Even young love is a fire that needs stoking now and then."

"I will think about that, but, for now, I need to just leave him alone. He needs to think about what he did, too." Grae got into her car.

"Perhaps, but I wouldn't take too long. I'm sure there is some girl at Tech who is waiting to take your place.

Someone who isn't distracted by time travel." Kat closed the door of Grae's car.

As Grae watched her mother walk back to the house, she thought about her last statement. "There's probably a long line waiting to take my place. But, they are only a threat if he wants them to be."

Grae could not make the coffee and hot chocolate fast enough. Black Friday brought a crowd of eager shoppers who not only were ready to purchase, but also take photos of the beautiful blanket of snow that had graced the mountain overnight. She was amazed at the number of families that were all dressed in red and green and taking family photos.

"Mark and I were talking earlier in the week when we saw the forecast," Mister Abbey said as he filled his mug with his third cup of Jingle Bells. "Mark said that we could offer the service of uploading the photos for people and show them how they could make a quick and easy Christmas card."

"Oh, so that's why he is sitting over there in the corner with his laptop. I was getting a little perturbed at him. I thought he was just goofing off." Mark was another part-time employee at the store. He was a little younger than Grae, but he had a neat personality. It was like he was an old man in a young man's body.

"No, it was his idea for us to post on Facebook that we would help with the picture taking and the uploading. I think that has brought some extra business in today. The families are buying lots of presents while they are here."

Grae swore that she could see a twinkle in Mister Abbey's eyes. His resemblance to Old Saint Nick was very apparent in this Christmas atmosphere.

"Grae, I think that you better let me relieve you of coffee making duty so that you can go in the back and bag up some more of those coffee beans. They are flying off the shelves."

"Sure, Mister Abbey, I was just getting ready to brew a batch of Peppermint Kiss. We have full pots of Jingle Bells and Blue Christmas."

"Excellent!" Grae and Mister Abbey traded places behind the counter. "Grae, I don't mean to pry, but have you heard anything about your father?" Grae bowed her head.

"Mom tried reaching the doctor last night, but I guess with the holiday they were short staffed. I hope that she reaches him today. We are hoping that he will have some news about how the experimental treatment is working."

"He has been in my prayers. You all have been. I know that the circumstances make it extra difficult."

"Yes, Perry and I weren't on the best of terms with him when he was put in prison. But, we are trying to put that behind us and focus on hoping that he will get well. The prognosis is pretty bleak."

"We spend a lot of time talking about miracles this time of year. We will continue to hope for one." Grae watched as Mister Abbey turned to a waiting customer. "I saw you all shivering out there. It looks like you got a wonderful and marvelous photo of your beautiful family. Does that little darling there like hot chocolate?"

Grae made her way through the many people huddled throughout the store to the back room. As she began to fill the bags with the beans she had roasted earlier in the week, she thought about her father. She imagined that his Thanksgiving had not been very special. Being in prison was bad enough, but being in the prison hospital had to be the worst. It was strange; all the thoughts she was having about her father's illness seemed to be making her feel sick.

"It's really hot back here," Grae said out loud to herself. The room started tilting a little. "Ouch!" Grae grabbed her head. "I don't feel too well..."

"Does she have any allergies?"

Grae could hear a man's voice asking questions. She knew that she should open her eyes, but they felt so heavy.

"She had a reaction to penicillin as a child, but I am not aware of anything else."

Grae heard the voice of her mother. It seemed to be very far way. Where in the world was she? The last thing she remembered she was bagging coffee beans in the back of the store. Wait, she also remembered hearing a siren, or did she dream that?

"We'd like for her to be conscious before we do the MRI, but if she doesn't wake up soon, we will go ahead and perform the test."

Grae wondered who they were talking about.

"Grae, Grae, can you hear me?" Kat gently squeezed her daughter's hand. Slowly, Grae tried to open her eyes. "Doctor, I think she's responding." Grae squinted her eyes as she opened them. The light above her was very bright.

"What happened?"

"You passed out at work, Grae. You wouldn't wake up so they called an ambulance. Do you know what happened to you? Did you fall and hit your head?"

Grae reached for her head. It felt like it weighed a hundred pounds. "I don't think so. I remember feeling really hot."

"Grae, I'm Doctor Ashton."

Grae tried to focus on where the voice was coming from, but he looked a little blurry.

"We are going to take you to radiology now and do a test." Grae shook her head. The small movement made her head hurt even more.

"My head really hurts."

"Let's get the MRI out of the way, and then we will give you some medication to help with the pain." The doctor nodded to her mother as he left the room.

"Grae, have you ever felt this way before?"

Grae thought about the question her mother asked, searching her memory.

"There's been a time or two when I have had sharp pains in my head. But, it was sort of like the pain you get from a sinus infection."

"Have you passed out before?" There was silence after Kat's question. She took hold of Grae's hand. "You have, haven't you? Why didn't you tell me?"

"I was away."

"Oh, no, Grae." Kat shook her head and looked around to see if they were alone. "Something like this happened to you...back there?"

"I don't think like this. I mean I didn't have to go to the emergency room."

"Of course, you didn't." Kat paused, waiting for Grae to realize what she had said. "Grae, there aren't emergency rooms back there."

"Oh, yeah, that's right." Grae's voice told the truth. She sounded exhausted.

"We're ready to take her to radiology." Two technicians came in and wheeled Grae away on the gurney. Kat followed.

Several hours and many tests later, Grae found herself lying down in the back of her mother's old black Jeep going home.

"Yes, Mister Abbey, we are going home now." Kat was talking on her cell phone as Grandpa Mack drove. "I think that she does feel better…No, I don't think that they figured out what happened, but they did rule several things out. Our family doctor will schedule an appointment with a neurologist…I appreciate all that you did today. Please thank everyone that helped…I will tell her that…You have a good night."

"He's a talker, isn't he?" Grandpa Mack laughed as Kat tucked her phone into her purse.

"He is that indeed. But, he also is very devoted to our Grae." Kat turned around and faced Grae in the backseat. "Once Mark found you, Mister Abbey tried to awaken you, and then immediately called 911. He said that the rescue squad made it up the mountain in record time."

Grae shook her head and closed her eyes again.

Grae slept through Friday night and most of Saturday. When she would have brief times of wakefulness, there was always something going on in her room. Her mother was bringing her food or fluffing her pillow. Her grandfather was peeking in the door and giving her a big smile and thumbs up. She even opened her eyes once to find Perry sitting in the middle of the floor rolling a ball back and forth with Clara.

"What happened to Shasta? Did she go home?" Grae had dreamed that her best friend had been standing over her in a white nurse's uniform, hat and all. She was taking Grae's pulse and shaking her head. The dream made Grae giggle.

Shasta was supposed to be staying for the entire Thanksgiving weekend.

"Yes, she went home this morning. Mom tried to get her to stay, but she said that Mom had enough to do taking care of you. She's a really good friend, you know. She left work and got right to the hospital and stayed with Mom until Grandpa and I got there. I think she must know someone there that knew you two were friends. She will make a great nurse one day. You look like you are dozing again. Get some rest, sis."

When Sunday morning arrived, all of the snow had melted and the temperature had risen to an unseasonable fifty-nine degrees. Her head felt better, but she had a strange feeling that something was going on inside of her.

She raised herself up in bed and rubbed her eyes. The sun was shining brightly through the old glass panes of the window. There was something about the light that reminded her of Martha. The more she looked at the light, the more she felt the presence of her dear friend. Grae thought about her last moments with Martha in 1859. She wondered if the purple broach brought her joy. A knock at her door caused her to look away from the light.

"Are you awake?" It was the soft voice of Carrie.

Grae looked back at the light and a cloud had passed over. Grae sat up in the bed. "Yeah, Carrie, come in."

Carrie's red hair seemed to enter the room before the rest of her did. Grae thought how this physical attribute really paralleled her personality.

"We've been so worried about you." Carrie sat down on the side of her bed. She put a basket, filled with many of Grae's favorite snacks and a paperback book, down next to Grae.

"Oh, I will be okay." Her voice sounded convincing, but Grae bet that how she looked told a different version. "It's just something minor, I'm sure." Grae looked down at the quilt that was covering her. She absentmindedly pulled at a loose string

"You know, Gav has been worried about you, too." Carrie paused. "He's just…well…he has to go back to Tech today."

"Sure, I know." Grae gave Carrie a little smile. She had expected that Gav might text her when he learned that she was sick, but she hadn't received any messages from him.

"Will you be able to go back to school tomorrow?"

"Yes, I think so. The doctor doesn't want me to drive for a little while, but I can ride in with Mom and either wait for her or catch a ride home with someone else." Grae looked at Carrie. She seemed very fidgety. "Is something wrong?"

"Oh, no." Carrie forced a smile, which wasn't very convincing. She let out a deep sigh. "Yes, I can't hide much from you, can I? Well, I just don't understand what has happened between you and Gav. This might sound selfish, but I am afraid that something might happen between me and Perry." Grae gave her friend an understanding smile. How could she explain the difference in the two situations?

"Perry adores you. Don't worry. Gav and I aren't seeing things the same way right now. It's a really long story and…"

A knock at the door was soon followed by Kat walking in with a large bouquet of flowers in one of her grandmother's beautiful blue glass vases. There was something about that blue that drew Grae's eyes even more than the flowers.

"Aren't these just lovely, Grae?" Kat's worry lines were now replaced by smiling ones.

Grae forced her eyes to leave the vase and look at the flowers within, which were a multi-colored assortment of daisies, some natural colors, some not. It was bright and cheerful, and kind of psychedelic. It matched Grae's bedspread.

"Where did they come from?"

"Well, a handsome young man came to the door a few minutes ago and handed them to me. I thought at first they were mine." Kat laughed. She looked at the confused looks on Grae's and Carrie's faces and continued. "It was Gav. He is on his way back to Tech and left these for you."

Grae jumped out of the bed and, in the process, almost knocked Carrie to the floor. She rushed toward the window, but Gav's car was nowhere in sight.

"Oh, darling, he left about ten minutes ago. It took me a while to find this vase. He seemed like he was in a hurry." Kat exchanged glances with Carrie. "Carrie, why don't you come downstairs with me? I am going to make Grae some brunch. She slept through breakfast. Why don't you help me, and we can let Grae get dressed?"

Carrie nodded and headed out the door. Kat lingered a moment in the doorway as Grae sat back down on the bed. "He looked very concerned. He seemed uncomfortable. Give him some time."

Grae smiled at her mother's choice of words. Time. That was the problem.

THREE

The week began and Grae seemed better. No pains in her head or strange feelings, just an incredible weight of tiredness. Mister Abbey insisted that she take the week off. She agreed. It would be difficult to get to work without being able to drive anyway. So, Grae spent her free time in the library on campus until her mother got off work. It gave her lots of time to work ahead on some end-of-the-semester assignments and log some extra volunteer hours in the genealogy library for her scholarship.

"Grae! I am so glad to see you. How are you feeling?" Alice was Grae's library supervisor and had grown up with Kat. There was a story there that Grae had never quite known how to approach.

"I am feeling better. It was scary, but, hopefully, the doctors can figure it out. It might have just been an isolated thing." Grae set her book bag down on the chair in front of Alice's desk. There was something different about her. Alice seemed brighter.

"I have been so worried. Your mother called me yesterday and filled me in on what had happened." Alice put a lock of hair behind her ear. Then, it hit Grae what the difference was. Alice's normally mousy brown hair was highlighted and her long locks were now cut just below her shoulder.

"Your hair looks great." Grae said, studying her further. She then noticed that Alice also had on heavier makeup, gold hoop earrings where studs usually resided, and her clothes seemed to fit better. Alice had undergone a makeover.

"Well, thank you, Grae." Alice nervously touched her hair.

"You've made a lot of changes this past week, huh?"

"Yes, well, I thought it was time for a different look."

Grae waited for Alice to continue talking. If you left enough silence, someone would fill it. Alice sat down at her desk, and Grae sat down across from her. She fiddled with some papers before looking back at Grae again.

"Well, you're not going to go to work until I tell you the real reason, are you?" Grae smiled. "I have had two dates with Mister Gibbs. It's been forever since I have dated anyone. I thought maybe a new look would give me some confidence."

"You look fabulous. Is it working?"

"Not really, I am just a nervous wreck. I just don't know how to do this."

Grae thought about what Alice had just said. Alice had never been married. Grae wondered how many relationships she had been in. As if she could read Grae's mind, Alice began to tell her.

"The most serious relationship that I have ever had was in high school. He was the love of my life. I have had a couple of brief relationships since then, but they never seemed right." Alice got a faraway look in her eyes. "I guess; I just kept hoping that…" The phone rang and Alice stopped to answer it.

While she was conversing with a customer about what records the library had on the Newberry family, Grae began looking at the list of requests that she needed to begin working on. There seemed to be something about the holiday season that made people more interested in their heritage.

"That sounded like a long one." Grae said, as Alice hung up the phone and began to type the information into their database system where they logged all of the requests for information that were received.

"Yes, this lady's husband is a descendant of the Newberry family and has traced them back to Wythe County. She wants everything that we can find. This will keep you busy for a while."

"I guess it is like that tourism lady who came to visit Mister Abbey the other day said, all roads do lead to Wytheville." Grae laughed. "So, this high school love of yours, what happened to him?"

Alice dropped her coffee cup and a big brown stain began growing on the grey carpet.

"I'm sorry. I didn't mean to upset you. That is none of my business. I shouldn't have asked."

"No, it's okay…I just thought you would have…well, I mean, it's been a long time ago and I'm not used to talking about it. It's very difficult to explain, because I really don't..."

The awkward conversation ceased as Mister Gibbs walked into the room. He had started teaching at the college in early October, when the previous Chemistry professor had made a sudden decision to retire.

Grae wasn't currently taking chemistry, but several of her friends had the class and talked about "dreamy" Mister Gibbs. His first name was Murphy. It was an unusual first name, but somehow it seemed to fit him. His eyes were the color of coffee beans and they had the same rich look as the beverage. His dark hair and complexion complimented his tall muscular build. He was a model for tall, dark, and handsome. Grae estimated that he was about the same age as Alice, give or take a year or two. Grae watched as her supervisor's face lit up as the gentleman began to speak.

"Hello, Alice." Mister Gibb's voice sounded smooth as silk. He noticed that Grae was standing to the side. "I'm sorry, I have interrupted something."

"No, Murphy, that's fine. This is Grae White. She volunteers for her scholarship."

"Ah, nice to meet you, Grae White." Mister Gibb's teeth gleamed like a model's in a toothpaste commercial. "Your parents must have had a sense of humor."

"It's short for Graham, my mother's maiden name."

"Now, that makes sense. We are notorious for shortening people's given names and giving them a whole new meaning. I was stricken with Murph at a very young age." Mister Gibbs smiled again and returned his attention to Alice. "I am free until three. I was wondering if you might like to grab some lunch?"

"Oh, that would be great." Alice glanced at Grae.

42

"I can hold down the fort, no problem. You go and have a nice lunch." Grae picked up the list of assignments and began to walk to the back room.

"Can we bring you some lunch?" Alice called to Grae as they were leaving.

"Beat you to it!" Grae could hear Jay answering Alice.

"Oh, hello, Jay. I hope that you and Madison had a lovely Thanksgiving."

"We did. We had a wonderful meal at the Graham Mansion."

"Oh, I bet it was delightful. Kat is a fabulous cook." Alice turned and waved. "I've got to run."

"Have fun!" Grae said, as she waved back.

"Who's the model guy?" Jay asked, after Alice had left.

"You saw it, too, huh? He is rather dreamy. That is Mister Gibbs, Murphy Gibbs. He is the new Chemistry professor. It seems that he may be turning Alice's world around."

"Alice's world could use some turning."

"Jay! That's not nice!"

"I didn't mean anything bad by it. It's just that Alice has that mousy librarian look. Isn't she about your mom's age? Now your mother, she's got it going on." Jay set down a bag of Chinese takeout on the long table where they usually worked.

"Really? You've been checking out my mom." Grae rolled her eyes.

"No, that's not what I meant. I am just making an observation that your mother has an updated modern young look. Alice does not." Jay began opening a container of food.

"Okay, I will let you by with that. But, I am watching you. So, what did you get me and what are you doing here?" Grae began nosing around in the brown paper bags that were on the table. The smell was intoxicating.

"I brought you San Sen Lo Mein," Jay said, as he smacked Grae's hand out of the way. "And, I am here to see how you are doing. You gave us all a scare." Jay handed Grae a container of food. "Besides, I haven't heard anything about your journey."

"Now, the truth comes out!" Grae laughed as she sat down and dug into her meal.

"Grae, that's not fair. I really was worried about you. Worried about what was wrong and what may have caused it."

"You're concerned that it might be because of the time travel."

"Yes, aren't you? I've not told you about what happened to me." Jay moved the food around in the box with his chopsticks. "For months, after I came back, I couldn't sleep. I was lucky to get two or three hours a night. I would wake up in a cold sweat and smell the musty odor of Doctor Minson's bag. I felt like I was being transported back each time I closed my eyes."

"Why haven't you told me this before?" Grae's head began to hurt slightly as the conversation continued.

"Well, Grae, we haven't had a lot of time to get to the intimate details of our lives. We spent so much time investigating Martha before your last journey that we really didn't talk about ourselves much."

"That's true. Maybe we should." Grae smiled as she went back to eating her meal. "You are one of the few who really understands what I have been through. And, I should listen to your story. We might both learn something."

"Okay, friend. Let's start with that visit to the hospital. Why did you decide to scare us?" Jay began eating his food in big bites. "Wow! This is really good."

"Chewing helps the process a lot there." Grae laughed as duck sauce dribbled down Jay's chin.

"Stop it." Jay said, wiping his face with a napkin. "Not everyone has Martha Stewart cooking meals for them."

"Your sister can't cook?"

"That's an understatement. My sister can't boil water. We eat a lot of frozen dinners, sandwiches, and takeout." Grae noticed that Jay was about to begin on his second lunch serving. "Our mother is a wonderful cook. I think Madison is adopted."

"Well, what's wrong with you? Maybe you are the one who inherited the cooking gene." Grae hadn't realized how hungry she was until she began eating. She was certainly partial to Asian food and Peking's was top-notch; but, somehow, her taste buds seemed extra happy with the selection.

"Actually, that's not a bad idea. It may have been passed down to the men of the family. Rock owns a restaurant in Baltimore."

Grae wasn't sure she had ever seen anyone eat an eggroll in three bites. He was putting Perry to shame.

"Your real name is Jewel and your brother is Rock. How come Madison didn't get stuck with Pebbles or something?" Grae giggled.

"Yeah, the only reason Madison lucked out is because that is our mother's maiden name." Jay took a large drink of bottled water. His appetite appeared to be slowing down. "So, when do you go back to the doctor?"

"I think I am supposed to go to a neurologist this week if we can get an appointment. My family physician, Doctor Griffin, is out of town, but she is trying to get a neurology appointment for me at UVA Medical Center." Grae twirled a shrimp between her chopsticks. "The more I think about it, the more I wonder if it really might be related to time travel. I actually had some smaller episodes when I visited 1830. I thought at first it was the shock of seeing Patrick again, but maybe it was something else. Did you do any research about illness after time travel? Did any of the journals of the travelers that you read mention anything about their health changing?"

"Actually, now that you mention it, several of them had headaches. I was looking more for insomnia since that was what I was experiencing. I did a flow chart about their symptoms after travel though, so I will go back and study that."

"A flow chart about symptoms? What were you planning to do with that data?"

"I was planning to use it for a doctorate thesis." The casualness of the way that Jay made the statement shocked Grae as much as the knowledge.

"Really? What happened? Why aren't you working toward that?"

"I had to come here and find you." Grae then realized how much Jay had sacrificed to find her and to help her on these journeys. The Graham family had them both suspended in time, so to speak. They were troubled with mysteries that needed to be solved.

"Okay, so you don't seem to want to talk about your visit to the hospital. Why don't you tell me then about your visit back in time?"

"Oh, now, that is a long story." Grae yawned as she stood up to collect the remains of their lunch and take it to the trash. "I'll be right back."

As Grae walked through the rows of file cabinets to go to the back area, she noticed that Shasta and some of her nursing class friends were at a table in the far corner of the library. Grae hadn't seen Shasta since Thanksgiving Day, and she couldn't actually remember talking to her after she came back from her journey. She made a mental note to text her later. Maybe they could have lunch one day or spend some time together.

As she walked by the storage room, Grae casually glanced inside. It appeared that Alice had used some of her spare time during the days before Thanksgiving break to straighten the room up.

"Hey, there you are. I got to worrying that you had passed out again."

Grae turned around quickly in the doorway of the storage room to find Jay standing right behind her. He was so close to her that he grabbed Grae's arms to keep her from falling backward. The feeling that came over her was shocking. In her mind, flashed an image of him dressed in a dark blue wool suit, and a small round hat, similar to the kind worn by Charlie Chaplin, was on his head. A thin bow tie was tightly positioned at the collar of his white shirt. He looked younger; his usual five o'clock shadow at two in the afternoon was not visible. But, there was something else, the pain in her head ceased. She felt better than she had in days.

"Are you okay?" Her mind kept holding on to the relaxed feeling. Jay shook her. "Grae, speak to me, you're scaring me!"

"I'm fine. Just fine. You startled me."

She looked down and realized that she had hold of his arms as well. She released her grasp. He did the same. Their close proximity must have made him feel uncomfortable as he stepped back. The pain in her head returned. He cleared his throat.

"I imagined that the storage room might have either been all in disarray or might be behind glass." Jay's nervous laugh did little to ease the awkwardness. Grae knew that he had felt something, too.

"Yes, well, this is the neatest I have seen it. Alice must have had some time on her hands before Thanksgiving."

Grae looked at the shelves in the small space. Most all of the boxes that had been scattered on the floor were now on shelves. Some had been labeled with their contents. In the back of the room sat the box that contained some of her grandmother's research. The sight of it reminded Grae that she had not returned the files she had taken home during that snowy weekend in early November. She must remember to bring them back, but she knew that they probably contained more information that she needed.

"Are any of the files back here about the Graham family?" Jay had a box labeled "Umberger" tilted on the shelf. He had slid off the top and was looking through the files.

"I think the only one is there on the floor in the back. It contains some of my grandmother's research. I just remembered that I still have some of the files at home. I begged Alice to let me take them on the weekend that we had the big snow. I obviously cannot be trusted. They are still at home on my desk."

Jay put the lid back on the box he was looking in and slid it back on the shelf. He started to walk to the back of the room, but Grae was in his way.

"We better get back out front. There might be customers." Jay furrowed his brow and turned to walk back to the doorway.

"Listen, I'm sorry if I made you uncomfortable. I was afraid something was wrong. You had a faraway look in your eyes, almost like you were in a trance. Your fingertips felt like they were on fire. I could almost see what it felt like." Jay walked out of the room with Grae closely on his heels.

"What did you see?" She passed him in the hallway and faced him as they arrived back in the public area.

"Oh, I just think my mind was reacting to what I thought was happening to you."

"What did you see?" Grae stood firm in front of him and looked Jay straight in the eyes.

"You saw something, too, didn't you? What did you see?"

"I asked you first. Now, tell me, Jay."

"I saw the color purple, bright, glowing, like it was on fire." Jay waited for some reaction. "What does it mean?"

"Was it purple like the broach I had? The one that I took off Eve?"

"Yes...yes, it was. It was just like that."

Jay followed as Grae went back to the tables where they were working. Grae picked up the clipboard that contained the list of research assignments that she needed to work on for the genealogy clients. Out of the corner of her eye, she could see Jay. He watched her, but his eyes were darting back and forth as if he was thinking about something complex.

"Wait! I don't think you had the broach on when you returned…Actually, I am positive that you didn't. What happened to it?"

"I gave it to Martha." Grae began searching for files regarding the first name on the list.

"Why did you do that? Didn't you need it to return to the present?"

"No, I obviously did not." Grae pulled out a file and began leafing through its contents.

"So, why did you give it to her?"

"Because, I thought she needed it. It had belonged to someone that she loved." Grae could see that a very confused look was now crossing Jay's face.

"Eve? Martha loved Eve? I didn't know that they even knew each other."

Grae paused to think about what Jay had said. "I don't know if they really did or not. But the broach didn't really belong to Eve. It belonged to Elizabeth. Eve stole it from her when she killed her."

"Okay, now I am really confused. Who is Elizabeth?"

Grae finally gave up and stopped what she was doing. "Elizabeth was Martha's sister-in-law. She was married to Martha's brother, Alexander. He is the one who had so many wives. She is the one whose name was scratched off of her tombstone."

"That tombstone part sounds familiar, but why did Eve kill her?"

"Elizabeth was the witch who Eve went to in order to try and get Patrick back. Elizabeth was a time traveler. She escaped to the late 1700s in order to keep from being murdered by her husband."

"And the broach belonged to her?"

"It was a gift from Martha to Elizabeth on Elizabeth's wedding day."

"So you gave it back to Martha, because...?"

"Because, I thought it would bring her joy. I thought it would bring her peace."

"Did it?"

"I think it brought her some joy. Peace? I am not sure. I didn't stay around long enough to find out."

"Why?"

"When I put the broach on Martha, she almost simultaneously grabbed hold of the key around my neck. Something about those two things happening together sent me back here." Grae thought back to that moment. "It was almost like you could feel it in the room, feel the departure getting ready to take place. It was the first time that I didn't have to physically use the key in some way."

"If Elizabeth was a witch, maybe the broach had power."

"Oh, I am sure it was a token that held power."

"Well, I think some of that power is in you now. When I took hold of your arms, it was almost blinding it was so bright."

"That's a very interesting idea."

"Listen, I've got to go. I promised that I would help Madison with something. We will have to continue this conversation later." Jay gathered up his belongings and began to head for the door

Grae could see in the distance that Alice had just returned. She was standing at the desk in the main part of the library talking to two members of the staff. She looked radiant.

"Grae, what did you see?"

"What? When?"

"When you had hold of my arms?"

Grae paused, debating whether she should reveal the truth. "I saw you."

Jay didn't have time to respond before Alice came up behind him.

"Oh, you are leaving, Jay? I hope you and Grae had a nice lunch. Mine was wonderful. We went to this new little café that just opened downtown…"

As Alice chattered on, Grae watched as Jay stood there for a moment taking in what Grae had said. Alice was moving Grae toward her desk as she continued talking. She turned back just in time to see him smile briefly and leave.

"How did today go?" Kat barely allowed Grae to get into the Jeep before she began asking her questions.

"Fine."

"Did you get very tired? Does your head still hurt?"

Grae thought about her answer before she replied. There was a point when it hadn't hurt, but she didn't dare tell her mother when it occurred. Kat would not want anyone else who had time travelled to be hanging around Grae.

"Yes, it still hurts some, but, you know, the lights in the library are very bright." Even as it was coming out of Grae's mouth, she thought about how lame it sounded. Her mother wouldn't buy that.

"You know, you are right. That florescent lighting is almost blinding at times. Maybe you should take some sunglasses with you tomorrow."

Grae couldn't believe her ears. "Yes, that might work." She had to change the subject. "Did you know that Alice was dating that new professor, Mister Gibbs? He's quite the cutie."

"Ah, no. I didn't know that she was dating anyone."

"She's totally changed her look. She's lightened her hair and is wearing more makeup. She looks so happy. She started telling me about this first love of hers in high school..."

Grae felt the car lurch as Kat slammed on the brakes. She looked up and saw that they were at a stop light and that it was green. "Mom! Are you okay?"

Kat looked at Grae, then back at the light, and began driving again. "Yes, I'm fine. I just thought I saw something in the road." Her voice didn't sound too convincing.

"Yeah, well, anyway, Alice is dating this new professor and she seems really happy."

"I'm glad. You know, I think we should call the warden and postpone our visit to see your father this weekend." It was obvious that Kat was trying to change the subject, but Grae would go along with it. "Doctor Griffin's office called. They have made an appointment for you with a neurologist at the UVA Medical Center on Wednesday."

"No. Why? Don't make this about me. I am fine. This doctor I will go see on Wednesday will say the same thing. We have got to go see Dad."

"Grae, I am just not sure that the long drive will be good for you. What if you have another episode?"

"We will stop at a hospital. I was on top of Big Walker Mountain the last time and everything was fine. I am still not convinced that I just didn't have some sort of strange bug or something."

"But, you said yourself that your head still hurts."

"Yes, but maybe I am just developing headaches. People do that you know. Remember Kelsey Winterborne at my old school? She started having headaches when we were freshmen; they said she would probably grow out of it once she reached her twenties."

"Graham, I do not think that your headaches are the same as Kelsey's. You cannot take this lightly. This might be all connected to your time travelling and you know it."

Traffic was unusually busy on the interstate. Grae wondered if the tractor-trailers had begun to move more potential gifts to replace those that were wiped out on Black Friday. That term would now have a new meaning for Grae since she ended up in the hospital.

"Don't change our appointment to see Dad, at least, not until we go to the doctor. Perry will be so disappointed."

"Okay, we will wait until Wednesday to decide. But, if the doctor says you shouldn't travel, then you will not."

Grae started to say something, but her mother held up her hand.

"I mean it. Your father wouldn't want you to jeopardize your health."

As they exited off the interstate, Grae thought about her father. Tom White had been the picture of health before he was incarcerated. She wondered if his time in prison, for his creative accounting, was what made the horrible cancer that was now attacking his body manifest itself. His whole life changed in a little over a year. He went from being the man who had everything to one who lost everything. It was another one of those moments when it seemed like Kat could read her daughter's thoughts.

"I know that you want to spend as much time with your father as possible. I haven't told Perry this, but I spoke with your father's doctor over the weekend. I called because I wasn't sure what was going to happen to you, and I wondered if your father was strong enough to hear about you. The doctor told me that Tom is responding to the treatment. He has hardly been sick at all."

"Well, that is hopeful, a little." Grae looked at her mother. It was already beginning to get dark and the low light made Kat look younger. Grae smiled as she saw what almost looked like the silhouette of her friend, Loretta, beside her. She wondered what else happened to her friend after she made her sudden departure. Grae longed to talk to her mother about the experience. "I'm glad that it at least isn't making him sicker."

"I've always thought that it is a strange thing that we use poison to kill poison. It would seem to me that we would need good to counteract evil, even within our bodies."

As the paved road turned to gravel, Grae began looking at the woods that surrounded the road. She could barely make out a couple of deer about twenty feet away. They had managed to escape the sites of the many hunters who loved to hunt on the vast property. Grandpa Mack rose early many mornings during the late fall to escort hunters from far away over the hundreds of acres of land. They continued the drive in silence and were soon at Graham Mansion. Grandpa was sitting on the front porch waiting. He waved as they drove around to the back. He climbed down off the porch and followed them. Grae noticed that his once straight stride now had a slight limp to it. His arthritic knees did not like the falling temperatures.

"It's mighty cold for Dad to be sitting outside." Kat got out of the Jeep and walked toward the back of the house where Grandpa stood waiting.

"Before you go inside, I need to tell you something, Katie."

"What's wrong? What's happened?"

"Your son has been in a fight at school." Grae swore that Grandpa was trying hard not to smile. "Now, before you go getting all riled up, he is fine. But, he's going to have shiners, and you have to go to the school tomorrow and talk to the principal."

"What in the world? Why didn't the school call me?"

"They said they tried to but were told you were in a meeting for the rest of the day. So the secretary called here, and I went and retrieved him."

"Perry is going to be grounded until he graduates."

Grae hadn't seen her mother so mad at Perry since he took Easter egg dye and made their miniature white poodle, Choo-Choo, look like a multi-colored egg.

"Hold on, daughter, you need to hear why he was in a fight first." Grandpa raised his hand to stop Kat from interrupting. "I'm not condoning fighting, but the fellow had his reasons. It seems that there is a new boy in the senior class that has been friendly with Carrie. I think Carrie had just been ignoring him, but, you know, sometimes that can just make a boy even more interested." Grandpa gave Grae a pointed look to be sure she was listening. "It seems that after lunch, this boy, I believe his name is Ethan, came up behind Carrie at her locker and picked her up from behind. Perry was a few feet away at his own locker. He heard Carrie screaming, turned around and saw this boy swinging her around in the air. About the time Perry got to them, Ethan put the girl down and kissed her. Well, that's all it took, and Perry and his friends were on top of him."

"Oh, dear; how I am going to punish him for that?" Kat looked at Grae and smiled.

Grandpa and Grae followed Kat into the kitchen. Perry was sitting at the kitchen table with a glass of milk. He gradually raised his head up, and Grae could see the beginnings of two full-fledged black eyes.

"Oh, Perry, not both of your eyes!" Kat dropped her purse on the table and pushed Perry's hair back from his forehead to get a better look. As Kat turned her son's head to see better in the kitchen light, Grae noticed that Perry's lip was also swollen.

"That guy must have been on the boxing team at his old school." Grae couldn't resist teasing him a little. Perry gave her a smirk as Kat went to the freezer and retrieved two bags of frozen peas.

"Put these on your eyes. Did you see the school nurse?"

"Yes, that's where he was when I got to the school." Grandpa had poured himself a cup of coffee. From the smell of the kitchen, he had just brewed a pot. "The nurse cleaned the blood off him and bandaged up his hands. She said that she didn't think anything was broken, but it might be good to take him to the eye doctor just in case. I went ahead and called my eye doc and made him an appointment for tomorrow morning. I will take him so you don't have to miss work."

"Thanks, Dad, I appreciate that." Kat turned her attention back to Perry. "You know that I do not approve of fighting."

Perry lowered his head. He looked pitiful sitting at the kitchen table holding a bag of peas on each side of his face. Grae winced thinking about how much being hit in the eye must hurt.

"But, your grandfather's told me about the circumstances, and I don't really see that you had much choice. You had to defend Carrie." Perry's head came up in a flash. A big smile crossed his face. "Are you facing any school punishment?"

"No, I don't think so. One of the teachers actually saw what happened and told the principal what Ethan did to Carrie. I actually just shoved him. He pounded me. My friends pounded him." Perry had a big smile. "Gav would have loved it." Perry looked at Grae, and then realized what he had said. "Oh, I'm sorry, sis, I forgot."

"It's okay. You are right. He would have loved it, and he would have been right in the middle of it with you." Grae paused and smiled. "He would be proud of you. How's Carrie doing?"

"She's worried about me. She's called me like a hundred times. She's scared to death that Mom will ground me or something."

"You go upstairs and rest. We've got to get some dinner going."

"Let me take my stuff upstairs, and I will be right back down to help you."

Grae walked past the closet and briefly touched the rounded side. Blue light flashed before her eyes and she started to feel the room move. She immediately removed her hand from the wall and the feeling instantly stopped.

"I won't do that again." Grae said to herself.

"What's wrong, Grae?" Perry was right behind her and took hold of her arm. "Ouch! I forgot about these bandages."

Grae looked at Perry's hands. They were both bound. "Shhh, I'm fine. We don't need Mom rushing in here."

"You looked like you were passing out."

"Just a little dizzy. You're the one who should be laying down, Rocky." Grae grinned. This time, Perry pushed her arm, again forgetting about his bandaged hands.

"Okay, I give. Let's just stay away from each other for a little while." They were both heading upstairs as they heard a knock on the front door.

"I'll get it, Mom." Grae set her backpack and coat down on the steps. She opened the door and saw Carrie's scared face and behind Carrie stood her parents. They were both holding what appeared to be bags of food.

"Hello, Grae," Mister McGavock said. "We're here to see how everyone is doing this evening."

"Jason! Lesley! Please come in." Kat was behind Grae before she had a chance to respond.

"We are sorry to intrude, but we wanted to see how Grae and Perry were doing." Lesley McGavock gave Grae a small hug. Catching sight of Perry, a painful expression crossed her face. "Oh, my dear, look what that horrible boy did to you! Jason, we must go visit that boy's parents. Look what he did to our Perry."

Grae stepped back out of the way. Shaking her head, Perry was now a hero.

"My goodness, son, you are going to have to learn to duck." Jason slapped Perry on the back. "I hope this young man isn't in trouble with his mother for defending our daughter's honor."

"Well, Jason, I don't approve of the fighting, but I do understand why Perry felt like he needed to. I will not punish him for defending this sweet girl." Kat engulfed Carrie in a big hug. Grae noticed that the coloring immediately came back to Carrie's face. She beamed at Perry.

"Kat, the least we could do was to bring you dinner tonight. We know how Perry loves Italian food." Lesley smiled at Perry. "So, I called in a big order of food to our favorite Italian restaurant, Mickey G's, and Jason picked it up on his way home. How does that sound to everyone?"

"That sounds delicious and so very thoughtful." Kat gave Lesley a quick hug. "But, I have one condition, you've got to stay and eat with us."

"We were hoping so! Lesley ordered enough food to feed an army."

Grae smiled as she watched Mister McGavock laugh.

"I only wish Gav was here to enjoy it with us."

Her smile vanished and she quietly stepped towards the stairs as everyone else headed to the kitchen and dining room.

"Grae, I'm sorry if that upset you." Gav's father stopped her as she picked up her things. "He will come to his senses in a little while."

"I'm not sure that it's that simple, sir."

"I've seen how he looks at you. The mere mention of your name brings a smile to his face. I know you must be tired, but you come back down and get some of this good food."

"I will." Grae climbed the stairs and walked into her room of blue. She heard a beeping from within her backpack. "I haven't even thought about my cell phone." Retrieving her phone from deep within the bag, she saw that she had several messages. She quickly scanned the texts. One was from Shasta asking her to call. Another message was from someone in her history class about a group project that was due the following week. As she began to listen to her voicemail messages, she saw one of the balls move across the room.

"Hello, Grae, this is Mister Abbey. We are all hoping that you are having a wonderful and marvelous day. Give us a call on Tuesday and fill us in on your progress. Bye-bye now."

Grae smiled as she hit the delete button and moved on to the next message.

"Hey, Grae, your brother was just in a massive fight. Some new kid tried to step into his shoes with Carrie. He rocked it." Aaron was a sophomore who had a crush on Grae during her senior year. Now he called her every once in a while with random bits of high school news. There was one more message.

"Grae, its Gav. Carrie called me about the fight. I hope Perry is okay. I tried to call his cell, but his mailbox is full. Tell him, I'm proud of him…hope you are feeling better. Bye." His voice sounded so formal. Grae listened to the message a second time, clicked the delete button, and began to cry.

FOUR

Physically, Grae felt stronger every day. Most of the headache pain had passed. She was anxious for her visit to the neurologist. Maybe the doctor would convince her mother that it was just a random occurrence. Mentally, it was another story. The phone message from Gav had hit her hard. She was glad she deleted it; otherwise, she would have listened to it over and over again.

"Grae, what is wrong?" When Jay found out that she was spending most of her extra time on campus at the library, he had set up residence there.

"What do you mean?" Grae looked up from a huge stack of files. Alice had given her a complicated research project for a lady in Oregon whose great-great-grandfather was born in Wytheville.

"You just seem preoccupied, like your mind is far away."

"Oh, maybe it's the meds that they have me on. I will be glad to go to the neurologist and find out that everything is okay."

"No, I don't think it is that. You seem sad, like you are trying to hide your sadness. You know, I'm a good listener."

"I guess I might as well tell you." Grae sighed and faced Jay. "Gav and I broke up."

"Oh, I'm sorry, I didn't know. Do you want to talk about it?"

"Actually, you are one of the few people who I can tell the real reason it happened. He's jealous of Patrick."

"What?!"

"He is jealous of Patrick. He thinks that I am in love with him."

"You have got to be kidding me. Patrick McGavock has been dead for a hundred years."

Even though Grae knew the words to be true, it still caused a feeling of sadness to wash over her. It was hard to imagine that the wonderful man she knew who had, so many times, come to her gallant aid had spent over one hundred years in a grave somewhere. She hoped that she would be able to find that location and pay homage to him one day.

"I suppose that I should have considered Gav's reaction before I told him about Patrick."

"Gav needs to grow up!" He picked up his coffee mug and headed to the coffee maker in the back of the offices. Grae could hear him making a lot more noise than usual. When he returned he was still speaking loudly. "Can he not grasp the concept that every male-female relationship doesn't automatically equal love and sex?" Jay began pacing in front of the windows that looked out into the main part of the library. His movement reminded her of The General's pacing. As he slurped down his coffee, Grae looked past him and saw Shasta sitting alone at a table in the corner.

"I'm going to go talk to Shasta for a few minutes. Can you hold down the fort?"

Jay nodded as he headed back to the coffee maker, again. Shasta looked up as Grae approached.

"You have got some explaining to do, girlfriend." Shasta smiled as she moved her book bag so that Grae could sit down. "Why do I have to hear from my lab partner that my best friend is back in school? Why haven't you called me?"

"What? Who is your lab partner?"

"Mark's sister."

"Mark, the guy I work with at Big Walker?"

"Yes, his sister is a nursing major. She texted me this morning and asked how you were and I told her that I hadn't seen you. Then she told me that she just passed you in the hall. Have you got your phone on dead or something?"

"Oh, I forgot to turn it back on this morning. I got kind of mad at it last night."

"You got mad at your phone?" Shasta gave her a strange look. "How is your head feeling?"

"Oh, no, it's not that, I got a message last night that sort of upset me, so I just turned it off." Grae looked behind her and saw that Jay was now standing at the main library desk, drinking coffee. "I just needed some space."

"What's going on, Grae?"

"Well, I guess with everything that has happened with me, I didn't get a chance to tell you. Gav and I broke up."

"Oh no, Grae, I'm so sorry. What happened?" Shasta closed her book and looked intently at her friend.

"I don't know. We've been having some differences."

Grae couldn't tell Shasta the whole story. She hadn't had the courage to tell her friend about her travels. She longed to, but Shasta had enough of her own problems to worry about.

"He left a message yesterday on my phone asking how Perry was. It was really short and formal; like he was talking to someone he didn't know." Grae paused and thought about her own words. Perhaps that was how Gav felt, like he didn't know her.

"Wow! This is why I don't date. If two people as together as you two can't make a relationship work, there is no hope for dysfunctional me." Shasta was obviously trying to cheer her up. "I'm here, if you want to talk about it." Shasta started filling her book bag with her heavy books that were strewn out on the table.

"You need one of those rolling bags for all of this stuff. You are going to get a hernia lugging all this stuff around."

"But, at least I will know some of the symptoms for that diagnosis. I really hope that you get accepted into the program. I need someone else in these trenches with me." Shasta stood up. "I've got one more class today, and then it's off to work. So how are you feeling physically and when do you go to the doctor?"

"I am feeling pretty good now. I go to the neurologist tomorrow. The hard thing is that I can't drive until the doctor releases me."

"So, are you coming in with your mom?"

"Yes, it makes for a long day here. I'm not going to go back to work, I guess, until next week. If the doctor says it's okay."

"Well, I hope so." Grae stood up and Shasta hugged her. "Keep me in the loop." Shasta pointed her finger at Grae. "I know where you live. I've even made friends with your brother."

"Yes, Rocky Balboa."

"What?" Shasta did a double take.

"Yeah, my brother got in a fight at school yesterday defending Carrie's honor."

"Really? That's a little surprising."

"Try a lot surprising. He's got two shiners. He was more scared of Mom's reaction." Grae laughed as Shasta started to walk away.

"I thought my house has a lot of crazy stuff going on, but I think yours tops it."

"Oh, Shasta, you don't know the half of it. The Mansion has a life of its own."

When Grae walked back over to the genealogy library, she found that Alice was on the phone. She picked up her stack of research and returned to the long table where she preferred to work. Jay was sitting there pouring over a box of what appeared to be old letters. The paper was thin and yellowed and the smell was musty.

"I have found a gold mine." He did not look up. "This whole box of letters was labeled Civil War Correspondence. There are all sorts of letters between soldiers and from soldiers to their family or friends. It's a wealth of information about those who fought in the war and were from this area." The blank stare on Grae's face must have told him something. "There are letters in this box from David Graham."

"Squire David wasn't in the Civil War! He was too old..."

"Not that David Graham, his son, the one we now know as Major David Graham. He wasn't a major then, but he did outrank most of his contemporaries."

"That's great and all, Jay, but why does this excite you so?"

"Because from what I have read so far, there are several letters in here that he wrote to his mother, his father, and his sisters, and they are all from the period of 1862-65. They call him Davy. And, that's not all--there is another box of correspondence that appears to be letters he wrote back to his family and friends during part of that time."

Grae sat down across from him and began working again on her assignment. "Well, that's great. It will keep you busy for a while."

"Just me? Grae, this could give you a wealth of information about Martha and what actually was happening to her during that time. Letters to her only son would be very revealing, I would think. I imagine that the letters written by the Graham sisters would not withhold details from their brother, especially if their mother was ill."

"I understand, Jay, but what am I supposed to do with this information if I find it? This whole quest to learn about the Graham family is playing havoc with my life. My mother is furious about my trips and forbids me to take anymore. Each time I come back, I feel strange, and now there might be something serious physically happening to me as a result of them. And, my boyfriend thinks I am cheating on him with a 1700's doppelganger version of him. You can see why the prospect of more letters with more twists and turns to the Graham history doesn't exactly make my heart jump with glee. You know what will happen if I read them."

"You will find another mystery that you will want to solve."

"Or a twist in the current one. What if these letters give more proof to your theory that Martha was murdered? Are you going to pull out your pocket watch and travel back to 1863?" Grae's head hurt again.

"Grae, I understand your apprehension. I understand how scary these medical problems are for you. I appreciate why Kat doesn't want you to make any more journeys. I do not understand why your boyfriend has this paranoia over Patrick McGavock." Jay smirked and laughed softly. "Patrick was not jealous of Gav. He was envious. He knew that Gav had your heart."

"What? How would you know what Patrick thought?"

"Have you forgotten already who told me of your existence? I sat across from a man who was well up in his eighties. His hands were drawn with arthritis. His legs would no longer hold him erect. His hair was snow white. But, his mind, it was sharp, and full of stories. He told stories of a girl who took his heart when he was eighteen and took it to another time. In his eyes, I saw her, this young woman who was as alive seventy years later as she was that fateful day in 1786. Gav could learn a thing or two from this man. It's easy to love someone who stands before you every day." Jay paused and took a deep breath. "I have debated telling you this, but I think that you deserve to know it. This knowledge may make your heart heavy with guilt, but you have an obligation to bear some of this burden that Patrick carried.

He would challenge that it was not such, but, indeed, it was a load he had no choice but to carry."

"I don't know that I want to hear this, Jay." Grae stood up and began to walk away. But, Jay's next words stopped her dead in her tracks.

"After he told me his story about this girl from another time, I asked him how he got over such a sudden loss. He said, 'I have never gotten over it.' I asked if he still loved her. He said, 'Yes, I still do.' So, you see, I find it unacceptable that this young man who has been so emotionally and physically close to you cannot have at least a semblance of the same devotion. Why, it should be in his genetic makeup, if nothing else. Loving you is in his genes."

"I...I wish you hadn't told me that." Grae turned back to face him. Tears flowed down her cheeks like rainfall. A floodgate of emotion opened. She tried not to sob, but it was no use. Hiccups were certain to follow.

"Oh, now, you're crying. I didn't mean to make you cry."

"People always say that after they have...hic...told you something heart wrenching. Did you expect me to...hic...laugh after what you just said?"

Jay started laughing.

"What's so...hic...funny?"

"You hiccup when you cry. That's so cute."

"Cute? My eyes will be...hic...swollen shut soon and you think this is cute. I've got to go find some sugar." Grae got up and headed to the back.

"Sugar? There's some back there with the coffeemaker."

"Really? Einstein...hic...I never would have thought of that." Grae was still crying and the hiccups were getting worse.

"Why do you want sugar?" Jay asked as he followed her.

"It...hic...cures the...hic...hiccups."

"Who says?"

"Joseph Baker." Grae was about to ingest a large spoonful. She held her nose.

Jay started laughing again. "I'm not so sure I would believe a remedy that a dead man told me."

"He wasn't dead at the time...See, I got through that whole sentence without a hiccup. That one, too."

"And you've stopped crying!"

Grae shook her head. She got herself a bottle of water, a couple of tissues, and headed back to her work area. Jay poured more coffee and followed her.

"Okay, I've had enough of talking about Patrick and Gav. If you are going to torture me, let's at least learn something. Give me one of those boxes of letters."

Jay eagerly handed it over to her.

"If you are going to do this, you should do it right."

Grae quickly retrieved two sets of gloves from Alice's desk. Jay nodded and put a pair of gloves on before touching the documents again. As Grae removed the lid from the box, she immediately smelled the musty odor of decades of neglect. After carefully lifting the first few pieces, she noticed that some of them were still in their original envelopes.

"This is just amazing to find them in such good condition. All of these postmarks appear to be in the 1860s. Think about that. It's hard to tell where these letters have been in the years since and what natural elements they have had to fight against in order to survive until today. I'm really surprised they haven't been placed into protective covers."

"Oh, I forgot to tell you. Alice said that these two boxes just came in. Someone donated them during Thanksgiving week. She said that she was going to ask you to work on preserving them. She asked me if I would make a log of what is in them. I think she just wanted me to leave her alone. I kept asking her where they came from when I saw her labelling the boxes earlier."

"She must trust you; that's for sure. She normally supervises our patrons when they want to look at original documents. Keep it up and Alice just might put you on the payroll."

They both began to carefully look at the documents. Some of the writing was smeared with age and damage. Other passages were easily readable.

"Grae, I'm sorry. I shouldn't have told you about what Patrick said, not in that way. I shouldn't be offering my opinion of Gav." Jay didn't raise his eyes to meet hers.

"It's okay. I realized it to an extent. Remember, I saw him again in 1830. It's very flattering. Humbling. But, it's also worrisome. To think that someone who only knew you for a short period, in actual time, formed such a strong attachment. It's almost like they reached inside you and saw the best of you, and then focused on that indefinitely."

"Hmm, that's an interesting way of looking at it. Knowing Patrick, the short time that I did, and hearing the way he talked about those few isolated days he spent with you in 1786 and 1830, it makes me wonder if there really is such a thing as one love for some people. I've got to admit, I haven't thought a lot about love in my life." Grae listened as Jay's tone grew serious and reflective. "There have been a few girls, women, who I cared about. There have been others that I just casually knew and dated for a time. I've always been so focused on other things, like this research. I'm not sure that I have kept my senses sharp to realize love when it came my way." Jay paused for a moment, but Grae remained silent. "Patrick allowed himself to have relationships through the years. He spoke of a couple. He cared for the women. But, he had one true love and he knew her as Arabella. She had other names on later journeys. She had a real identity several generations after his own, but she was the one person who fully captured his heart. Paraphrased, that's what he told me. I hope I haven't missed my own."

They were both silent as they returned to their work. Grae let her mind travel back to imagine the lives of those who had penned the writings before her. Whoever donated the documents took the time to put them into chronological order.

"This portion that you have given me appears to have been written by David Graham, Davy as Martha and Squire called him, during the years he served in the Civil War. What are those that you have?"

Grae looked up to see that Jay literally had the whole table covered in documents. There were the letters that were part of the new collection as well as other files, journals, maps, and documents that he had retrieved. He appeared to be making comparisons and long lists of notes. He noticed that she was staring at the piles around him shaking her head.

"Hey, don't knock my system. I am a trained researcher. This is an organized mess that will get worse before it gets better. I have my own system." Jay waved his hand across each pile. "There are letters in this box addressed to Captain, and later Major, David Graham from many members of his family as well as friends, comrades, and families of the men who served under him. I've also been digging out some of the journals, diaries and other documents that are on file here related to that time period and the people who corresponded with him. There is a very interesting puzzle to piece together when you read what all of these people have to say about the time period and what was occurring. There are some very interesting tidbits about Martha and what was going on at the Graham Mansion during the Civil War. Much of the activity within that household was anything but civil during that timeframe."

"That does not surprise me. Remember, I lived in that house. Squire set a tone that affected everyone who walked through the door."

"We read accounts in history books. We see movies depicting the era. But, it is amazing to read firsthand perceptions of how the war was unfolding. Let me read to you a passage from Bettie Graham's journal about the beginning of the Civil War."

"That Bettie was a feisty one as I've heard. I've read some of her published journal." Grae smiled thinking about the young woman, as Jay began to read.

"This first entry is from April 19, 1861—'I hear this morning that Virginia has seceded, and that all slaves are rising in rebellion and that all the men have to stay at home and keep them down. Oh! How terrible, too terrible to think of. I wish almost that I could never hear of these horrid affairs, but so it must be...' Then on April 22, she continues—'Oh! I feel as I might never see home again. If I could only be there once more. If they are doomed to death let me die with them, I pray.' Bettie had a flair for the dramatic."

"I've read her journal and remember thinking that she could have been a stand-in for Scarlett O'Hara." Grae laughed. "I can just see her in a huge, hoop skirt talking about 'them Yankees' coming to burn down the Mansion." Grae sorted through the piles of letters in front of her making a stack of those that she had already read.

"Well, perhaps, the character that Margaret Mitchell created was not too far removed from the affluent, young southern ladies of the time."

"Do you know when her brother formed his regiment?" Grae watched as Jay dug through his piles of documents. "This complicated system you have here…" He held up a finger for her to stop talking.

"David P. Graham of Graham's Forge mustered and organized the Wharton Grays, Company B, 51st Virginia Regiment, in late July of 1861. He was elected Captain. William Tate was made First Lieutenant, John Robinson became Second Lieutenant, and William Painter, Third Lieutenant."

"Didn't Bettie Graham marry a Robinson?"

"She did indeed. John Robinson would later become her husband. William Tate was the brother of Nannie Montgomery Tate, the future wife of Davy Graham."

"I just read a letter where he talks about these men. Let me find it and read it to you." Grae carefully looked through the pile of previously read letters. "It amazes me how many of these letters, the ones that Davy wrote to his father, are still in perfect condition. Like Squire just read them once and put them away. Here it is."

Captain D.P. Graham
Co. B 51ˢᵗ Va. Regiment, C.S.A.
Camp Joe Johnston
Bonsack's Depot, Va

Squire and Mrs. David Graham
Cedar Run Farm
Max Meadows, Va

August 25, 1861

Dearest Ma and Pa,

It is my hope that this letter finds you and my
lovely sisters well. My health is quite the same with
but a pesky cough to contend with. Ma, in my tent
late at night I think of you. In these wee hours I
am reminded of your strength and wit which gives
me a feeling of peace from the chaos at hand. For
it does occur to me that although we have been
gone from the "comforts" of home and Camp
Jackson but a few days, I do sense that all will be
forever changed when I lay eyes upon you both
again. I pray that I may show fortitude, like you,
when the fight begins and that you will know me
when I return to you. I pray that I will be diligent
and wise, like Pa, so that I may lead these fine
men and serve this noble Effort.

Pa, I realize that you know much about such
things...horrors that cause you to fear for my life
and well-being. I know that it is your wish that I

resign my duty with honor and return to Graham's Forge to make iron for the Confederacy. Please know that I fully respect and honor your wishes. I know in my heart that you love me and value our Cause. It is the love of my family and God that sustains me when I am weak, but alas I cannot abandon my men. I cannot. I will not leave the War. I have discussed your request with our friend and confidant John Robinson. John has tried his best to persuade me to leave; he has assured me of his ability to lead the men with Lt. Tate. But in the end, John has agreed to resign next month and return to Graham's Forge to assist you as you see fit. It is my strong opinion that if John was to remain with the 51st, he would soon be promoted to quartermaster, as his abilities and talents would become obvious to our superiors.

Now for some news about our circumstances. There exists a sharp contrast between Camp Joe Johnston and Camp Jackson, far beyond location and name. Upon our arrival here, an epidemic of measles broke out resulting in two deaths from Co. C. In addition, General Floyd, our former relaxed and colorful commander at Camp Jackson, is now pressing for the acceleration of our training and our immediate transfer to join his Brigade in the Kanawha Valley for it appears that Co. B. is one of the best drilled units in the Regiment. Although we were mustered at Graham's Forge only a month earlier, Lt. Tate and myself are looked upon as well-trained drillmasters due to our one-year tenure as V.M.I. students. We also enjoy undeserved privileges from our commander, Col. Wharton, and his adjunct, Peter Otey, as they are respected V.M.I. alumni. You see the Colonel, who was a civil engineer before the war, quietly approves of our adopted name, "The Wharton Grays". Much beloved and admired, the Colonel graduated second in his V.M.I. Class of 1847 and possesses organizational and leadership qualities, much admired here abouts. In addition to the Wharton Grays, the 51st is made up of ten companies including some familiar names from the Wythe Rifles, Floyd Gamecocks, Bland Tigers, Nelson Rifles, an eleven-piece band, a chaplain, and a surgeon.

I have recently taken the opportunity to speak with some of the other officers of the 51st. They tell of the hardships left to their families at home, tending their farms and bringing in the crops. Pa, my men and I wish to thank you for your keen wisdom and advice directing me to postpone the mustering of the men at Graham's Forge until after the wheat and corn crops had been harvested. The men and I are grateful to you Pa, for your hard core is tempered only by your prudent and just thought, which I shall try to emulate in the coming months.

Ma, I can see your half smile as you read this next story. You see, when we arrived at Bonsack's Depot, we simply set up our camp and made ready for our orders and training. Well, the Commissary Sgt. Samuel Wheeler promptly issued rations to our company. Unfortunately, Sgt. Wheeler neglected to inform us that the rations constituted a three-day supply. Thus the men consumed their provisions in but one day and went without for the next two! I must add a note here for you to pass on to Sister Bettie. Please tell her that Mr. Robinson's conservative and sound nature allowed him the wisdom to save half of his rations which he promptly shared with me! You may also tell Sister that her friend Nan Tate's brother, William, found a robust apple tree and a patch of watercress in the local creek here that successfully sustained us for a few days.

I am pleased to report that a young Swedish engineer, Ludwig Augustus Forsberg, has joined the 51st Regiment here. Forsberg and I have spent a few sleepless nights discussing the recent engagements and strategic value of the Kanahwa Valley and agree that we will soon see action there. As you know the bountiful valleys of southwest Virginia possess the South's sole salt production source, fertile valleys for crops, strategic railroads and telegraphs, and our very own lead mines which is the source of lead for a full third of the bullets used by the Confederacy. Indeed, with the unsettling second secessionist movement taking a firm hold in western Virginia, it will be difficult to tell friend from foe.

I want to tell you that I do believe we will soon be sent to the Kanahwa Valley near Charleston. I shall write to you as I am able so that you may also correspond with me and our families will know of their loved ones. Be assured that I love you both. May God bless our family and all that we hold sacred in this life.

Your devoted son,

Davy

"Jay, what do you know about Camp Jackson?"

"As you know, it was located in Wytheville, near the present-day South 20th Street area. At the time, the property was used as the fairgrounds. Alice was telling me earlier today that she has heard there is a recent effort to have the area historically marked and included in local Civil War tours. It started out being used as a regional induction and training center in May 1861. It is unclear as to how long it was used for that purpose. Anyway, during its time, it housed over twenty companies with as many as two thousand soldiers."

"Time. Oh, my, time! What time is it?"

"It's about ten after three."

"And today is Tuesday?"

"Yes. Is your head hurting you again?"

"No, but yours is going to be hurting if you don't stop distracting me. I've not finished this work and I've got to get to class." Grae gathered up the clipboard and files associated with the research she was doing for a customer and handed it to Jay. "So, I guess you will need to help me finish this." She gave him a big smile. "I've got a lab to get to, followed by a test!" Grae picked up her book bag. "Alice will be back in a little while. She's in a meeting. Please clean up this mess."

"Yes, ma'am."

FIVE

Kat and Grae rose early the following morning. Grae's appointment at the University of Virginia Medical Center was at ten. It would take three hours to drive to UVA. They would leave a little after six to make sure they allowed enough time.

"Dad, you and Perry are on your own for breakfast." Kat was filling two travel coffee mugs with the hot beverage as Grae entered the kitchen. "Hmmm, Grae, this Blue Christmas coffee smells delicious. You make sure you get a bag of this for Lucy. She will be thrilled that you have named one in honor of Elvis."

"I can't remember how Elvis took his coffee." Grandpa Mack poured himself his second cup.

Grae did a double take. "What? Grandpa, how would you know how Elvis drank his coffee?" Grae was amazed that her mother didn't have the same reaction.

"I knew Elvis." Grandpa said, nonchalantly. "I was in the Army with him."

"Really? Why haven't I ever heard this story before?"

"I don't know, little girl. I've told the story before. I knew him fairly well back then. We were in boot camp together in Fort Hood, Texas. He was just a regular guy. He pulled KP duty and guard duty like the rest of us."

"Does Lucy know this?"

"Why, certainly. In fact, when I moved in here I gave her some of the photos I had of me and Elvis and the guys from back then."

"I've got to hear more about this." Grae shook her head in disbelief.

"But not this morning, we've got to get on the road." Kat gave her father a hug. "Make sure Perry gets out of that bed in time to get to school."

"I think I am going to get him up right now and enlist his help with some chores. As a reward, I will take him to the diner with me for breakfast." Grandpa smiled as he headed toward the staircase. "You girls be careful. I know it's going to be a long day. I hope you come back with some answers from those Wahoo doctors."

"Now, Dad, let's not get into the college rivalry. UVA has an excellent medical center."

"I'm not arguing with that. I can appreciate any school in Virginia for something other than football."

Grae and Kat headed toward the back door. Thankfully, Grae could hear that the old Jeep was running and she hoped the heater was producing some heat.

"That remote starter comes in handy on these cold mornings." Kat and Grae quickly got in. "Grae, this trip is going to be a good thing. We are going to find out what is wrong and get it fixed."

"What if you are right and it has something to do with my...ah...travelling?" Grae said as she clicked her seatbelt.

"Well, I don't think that is really possible. I was just angry when I said it. I just don't want you to risk your life that way."

Grae decided that perhaps silence was best on the topic. As they travelled north on Interstate 81, Grae watched the sun as it slowly began to rise. The usually busy interstate was quiet during the early morning hours. Kat brought along an audiobook for the trip, *Big Stone Gap*, which was written by a Virginian, Adriana Trigiani. They listened in silence for quite a while, getting deep into the story.

"I think I heard that this story is going to be made into a movie." Grae stopped the CD as they pulled into a gas station on the outskirts of Charlottesville. The time had passed quickly.

"Oh, really. I didn't know that." Kat pulled up to the gas pump. "I'm going to go ahead and fill up so we will be ready to leave after the appointment."

Grae looked to her right as her mother was pumping gas and saw a royal blue SUV parked next to them. On the other side of the pump was a royal blue sedan. Grae looked straight ahead and watched as a small car pulled into a space in front of the convenience store. It was also royal blue. "Oh dear." Before each of Grae's previous journeys, a color had played a predominant role in her life for the weeks before she travelled. "What in the world could all of this blue mean?"

Grae took the last drink of coffee in her mug. "Ugh, cold Blue Christmas is a strange taste." She paused. "Blue Christmas. Great! I am even drinking blue."

"What did you say?" Kat was hopping back into the Jeep.

"Oh, just that Blue Christmas doesn't taste good cold." She needed to be more careful with what she said.

The good thing about going to a university medical hospital was that you got cutting edge treatment and were seen by a team of renowned doctors and medical students. The bad news was that you had to recount your entire medical history multiple times to multiple people. Grae was becoming sick of her own story. Her mother just looked frustrated. Even though Grae's medical records from her recent hospital stay were sent in advance, there were still numerous tests that were repeated and new ones added.

A nurse, who reminded Grae of Hot Lips Houlihan from the television series "M*A*S*H," began drawing blood after a resident, who reminded her of Michael J. Fox, gave her and her mother a rundown of how the morning and afternoon of tests would proceed. The receptionist gave them twenty forms to fill out. She reminded Grae of an actress, the woman who portrayed Edith Bunker. Grae felt that she needed to limit her sitcom viewing in the future.

She counted eight vials of blood when Hot Lips was done. "Is this a deposit for the local Vampire Bank?" Grae laughed as the nurse put a cotton ball and a piece of tape on her arm. Hot Lips didn't seem to be amused.

"If you will now follow me, I will take you to radiology."

Kat rolled her eyes at Grae as they filed behind the woman down a long medicinal-smelling hallway to where several of the next tests on Grae would be conducted. All of her tests seemed to be abbreviations. She had an M.R.I., an E.E.G., and an E.N.G. Kat had detailed conversations with each of the technicians that were performing the tests. Grae noticed her mother made precise notes in a small notebook that she brought with her, including listing everyone's name. With her mother paying that much attention, she decided she could relax a bit. The tests were tiring. It wasn't the first time that she had undergone an M.R.I., but it still felt to Grae as if she was going into a coffin tunnel and the noise was horrendous. At one point, she felt like she was about to have the tilted time-travel feeling, but she focused her view on the tiny television screen above her head. Gilligan was climbing a coconut tree with the exasperated Skipper looking on from below. Her life was indeed one big sitcom.

After the tests were over, they were advised that it would be two hours before they would be seeing the neurologist with the results. Since it was way past lunchtime at that point, Grae and Kat decided to go to the cafeteria while they waited. They found that it was quite an advanced meal facility with a variety of different menus. Grae and Kat ended up making different food selections and met back in the center of the dining area.

"It's good to see that you have a healthy appetite, despite all that you have been through today." Kat looked at Grae's full tray.

"Well, they took so much blood out of me, I thought I better start building it back." Grae inspected the contents of her hamburger before returning the bun to its top location and cutting the sandwich into two sections. She always cut her sandwiches that way.

"Looks like you have a great start there." Kat's own tray contained a grilled chicken salad, a bowl of split pea soup, and a rather large piece of chocolate cream pie.

"I didn't realize that chocolate was a food group in your normal lunch meal."

"This is not a normal lunch. I need this to counteract the stress of watching my daughter being tested. Besides, your selections don't seem to have the American Heart Association's stamp of approval."

"I am the patient, I am allowed." Grae smiled as she took a big bite out of her burger. Sweet potato fries and strawberry shortcake completed her selections. "I have fruit and veggies. I admit that they are not in their natural state, but they are there."

Grae looked around the area as she chewed. For mid-afternoon, the area was busy. Employees were seated in small groups of three or four. She wondered if many of the people there were like herself and her mother, to have tests or procedures.

"Is it me or did you think that just about everyone we encountered this morning looked like an actor off of a TV show?"

Grae almost spit water on her mother as she made the statement. "That is exactly what I was thinking. I was afraid that I had watched too much television growing up."

"Well, you probably have, but I guess I was right there with you. Hot Lips didn't have much bedside manner. Her real name is Loretta, by the way."

"Isn't that the first name of the actress?"

"Yep. I thought I would laugh in her face when I noticed it. I couldn't bear to look at you." Kat smiled as she took her last bite of pie. Grae marveled that her mother was actually eating her pie first. "Well, there's one good thing about coming here for your tests."

"What's that, the pie?"

"No, although it was good. At least we will not have to wait for weeks on the results. They do everything here and part of the learning process is for the residents to see the testing, the results, and how the doctors translate that into a diagnosis and treatment."

"One-stop shopping. Too bad they don't have a drive-thru."

"You are getting punchy, my dear. Good thing you didn't have to take a sarcasm test today." Kat stole a strawberry from Grae's cake.

"Oh, but I would have passed it with flying colors. I'm just glad we didn't bring Perry."

"Why is that?"

"Perry in a food court like this. You might have had to take out a loan."

Kat was suddenly caught up in an email on her phone.

"Is everything okay?"

"Yes, it's a message from a co-worker. Her daughter was having some medical tests today, too. She is only eight. They are afraid she might have leukemia." Kat let out a deep sigh. "I have so much to be thankful for. My children are almost grown and you have been healthy." Kat reached over and squeezed Grae's hand. "Whatever this is, it's going to be minor and fixable."

"Sure it is." Grae smiled and squeezed back. "This head is too hard and stubborn to have anything wrong with it."

Kat looked back at her phone.

"We better start making our way to the doctor's office. Perhaps we will get to meet Carol Brady."

"Oh, wouldn't it be delightful if my doctor was actually a lookalike for George Clooney's character on "ER?""

"Darling, if your doctor looks like George Clooney, he is way too old for you. Now, he would be just the right age for your youthful mother."

Their celebrity sightings were limited to the testing area. The receptionist at the neurology office didn't even remotely look like anyone famous. It turned out that the doctor, Linzy Price Megginson, was slightly younger than Kat. After answering some of the same questions over again, Doctor Megginson poured over the now-growing file of Grae's test results.

"So, Grae, you've been having these fainting spells for about a year now, is that correct?"

The doctor had a pleasant, but direct, tone. Three interns stood behind her. She was seated on a rotating stool. A laptop was positioned on a shelf that came out of the wall in front of her. The three students, two male and one female, were all in somber attention and each took notes.

"As you know, we are a learning institution. You will hear me convey the diagnosis to these interns, and then I will translate any terminology that I need to for your understanding."

Grae thought that the comment almost sounded condescending.

"I would much prefer to give it to you directly in patient-friendly terms, but these future doctors have to have their daily quota of doctor lingo." Doctor Megginson smiled then, as did Grae. Perhaps they did speak the same language.

"Unless you tell me that I have some sort of incurable condition, I think I am going to like you." Grae caught the eye of one of the male residents as she completed her comment. He looked familiar. Glancing at his nametag, she saw "Baker" and about choked on her own saliva.

"You, okay?" Kat asked, as all eyes turned in her direction.

"Ah, yeah, I thought I was getting the hiccups. Must be mistaken." Grae flashed them a smile. It was reciprocated by the intern named Baker. She was sure that future nurses would call him Doctor Handsome.

"You will see that these test results indicate that the M.R.I., E.E.G. and E.N.G. are all within normal limits." The doctor paused and gave the students time to read the results on the screen. "Based on Grae's medical history and personal reports, recent hospitalization findings, and the testing here today, I believe we can confirm with relative certainty that the patient is negative for a brain tumor, Multiple Sclerosis, Meniere's Disease, stroke, epilepsy, or some sort of chemical imbalance. In addition, there is no evidence to indicate any present or recent illicit drug use. The only residual drugs noted here correspond with her last hospital stay."

Grae glanced at her mother who appeared to be wishing she knew shorthand. She was writing like crazy. When she realized the doctor had stopped talking, she looked up.

"That all sounds good," Kat said.

"Yes, for the present, we have ruled out the most worrisome options." Looking up from the laptop, Doctor Megginson paused as she stared into the questioning eyes of the future M.Ds. "In the absence of vertigo, disequilibrium, syncope, or other neurological diseases and disorders, this cluster of symptoms is consistent with Hyperventilation Syndrome. Please note that this relatively rare disorder always presents itself with a physical or emotional trigger, which precipitates one or more of the following problems: dizziness, tingling in the lips, hands and feet, headache, weakness, and fainting. An example of a physical trigger might be reduced air pressure at higher altitudes." Doctor Megginson paused and looked at Grae. "I do not believe we asked you if you were a frequent traveler."

Kat dropped everything she was holding—notebook, pen, and purse. Doctor Handsome quickly bent down and retrieved the items for her.

"You mean by plane?" Despite the seriousness of the conversation, Grae almost laughed out loud at her mother's reaction.

"Yes, air travel. Are you a frequent flyer for some reason?"

"No."

"Well, then, let us examine the possible emotional triggers as these include pain, stress, fear, and anxiety. Both the patient and mother confirm the presence of these precursors just prior to each event as well as the symptoms noted above."

"You think this is all in my mind." Grae felt anger growing inside her. It was like a diagnosis that Squire David might appreciate.

"No, Grae, I do not. But, I do think that this might be influenced by your emotional reaction to some situations in your life. The answers on your questionnaire indicated that there has been turmoil in your family's recent history. Separation from a parent can cause extreme anxiety. You and your family relocated to another area for reasons of financial necessity. You changed schools and were exposed to new environments and new people. These things individually could be detrimental to your emotional health. Combined, they could result in some severe physical and emotional reactions."

"What do you suggest that we do to help prevent her from having more of these episodes?" Kat's tone was very serious.

"My recommendation is for Grae to have a regimen of cognitive behavioral therapy with a licensed psychologist. I would also recommend that the psychologist include biofeedback in the treatment. A low dosage trial of benzodiazepine has also been found to be effective in these cases."

"What is benzodiaz...whatever?" Grae asked.

"It's Valium." Kat replied putting all of the items she was holding back into her purse. Grae gasped.

"It would be a very low dosage." Doctor Megginson closed the laptop. The three students began moving toward the door. "I also recommend a follow-up visit with us in about six months. In the meantime, I will be in communication with your psychologist and your general practitioner. Do you have any questions?" There was complete silence in the room. "Well, then, it was a pleasure to meet you. One of our young interns here will lead you to the nurse's station where we will have your prescription and some other information waiting for you." Doctor Megginson nodded and left the room. She was quickly followed by the two male students. The female student led Grae and Kat from the room.

Neither one of them said a word until they got to the Jeep and Kat spoke. "Do you think these episodes are being triggered by psychological issues?"

"No." Grae didn't know whether she should scream or cry. Her frustration level was high.

"Neither do I. What the doctor recommended I am sure is the type of treatment that some people need. I had a period or two in my life when Valium got me on the other side of a situation." Kat held up her hand as she saw that Grae was about to speak. "That is a discussion for another day. But, I do not think that is what you need. Now that I know with almost certainty that there is not something physically going on, like a tumor, then I am more convinced that perhaps it is your journeys. We really don't know what our bodies go through during time travel. There isn't exactly any research on it."

Grae thought about the data that Jay had collected from all of the journals of former time travelers. She dare not mention it to her mother. It would take Jay off the approved friends' list.

"Mom, I just can't imagine that this travel has really harmed me. It just doesn't make sense."

"I know, Grae. I realize that you only see the good in your travels. I know that you have done good things during your journeys. I remember." Her last journey had teamed Grae with her mother as her seamstress assistant. It was a rare opportunity for Grae to get to know a younger version of her mother.

"What do you remember?"

"The other night I dreamed about my time as a seamstress for Margaret McGavock. I had almost forgotten about that time. I really never wanted to remember it again. But, suddenly, the next day, I remembered this wonderful young woman who was so good to me. I had no idea, at the time, that she would one day be my daughter."

"Oh, Mom, that time with you, with Loretta, it was so special to me." Grae began to cry.

"That was a good time. But, you must understand, that was my last journey, and it was the most difficult one I ever made. Something happened on that journey that changed my entire life. You are so lighthearted about this. You have surely seen enough to realize what dangers there can be."

"Mom, yes, for the millionth time. I know that time travel is dangerous, dire and disastrous. I have seen people born. I have seen people die. I have almost been killed. There's some horrendous stuff back there. But, guess what? We have no shortage of it here. My father is in prison. He's dying of cancer. We lost everything. My best friend's mother can't control her emotions. Their family is splitting up. My brother has two black eyes because someone likes his girlfriend. My boyfriend dumped me because he is jealous of someone who is dead. I have something going on in my head that even the doctors don't understand. Life sucks!"

Kat remained silent after Grae's rant. Grae sat and looked out the window. She was exhausted.

"Grandpa is making chicken and dumplings for dinner."

Grae broke out in laughter at her mother's U-turn in the conversation. "You might just have a future in comedy."

"My dear, it's nice to have a future in something."

They made good time on their return trip home. The aroma of Grandpa Mack's specialty greeted them before they opened the front door.

"Oh, Dad, that smells wonderful. I forgot what a good cook you are."

Grae watched as Kat hugged her father from behind. He was standing at the stove stirring a large pot of his creation.

"It's been a long time. Those dumplings look delicious."

"Too long. It's been too long. It was time for them to be made."

"What made you remember?" Kat took off her coat and shoes and was rolling up her sleeves to begin washing the dirty dishes in the sink. Grae pushed her away and started the washing herself.

"Well, actually, it was our conversation about Elvis that made me think of this recipe. One of my jobs in our unit was cooking, and that boy sure did like it when I made these."

Grae smiled thinking about the long ago celebrity eating her grandfather's cooking.

"Grandpa, what do you think Elvis would be doing if he was still with us? Would he have some big theater in Las Vegas?"

"You know, darling, I have thought about that many times. I think he would still be singing in some way, it was a part of who he was. But, I think in his soul, he might have been a preacher. He seemed to have this spiritual side to him that was really even bigger than his entertaining. All that celebrity, I think overshadowed who he really was. It was an image he was constantly trying to live up to. It may have been what ended Elvis Presley, more than anything. All that ambition was really just a deception. He was searching for salvation."

Grae stopped what she was doing and thought about her grandfather's words. She wondered if they applied to the man who built the house she was standing in; another man with great wealth and power whose life went terribly wrong.

As Grae prepared to go to bed, Shasta called. She sounded very tired.

"How did it go at the doctor? I meant to text you earlier in the afternoon, but things have been kind of crazy.

"It was okay. We think the diagnosis wasn't quite right." Grae paused. She could hear her friend yawning. "Shas, you really sound tired. Are you okay?"

"Lack of sleep catches up with you eventually. One of the boys has been sick and the other had a big science project due today. Being a mother is hard." Shasta laughed, but Grae could tell it was a weak attempt at humor. With the hours that her father worked and her mother still taking treatment for her mental health issues, Shasta was a single mother of sorts to her two younger brothers. "If I can just get through the next two weeks..."

"Next semester will be even harder, right?"

"Probably, but if you get accepted into the program, you can endure the torture right beside me." Shasta gave Grae another weak laugh. "Seriously, Dad said the other night that his sister has offered to take the boys in. She has two boys of her own, but they are both away at college. She wants to help. I think that if things don't improve with Mom, Dad will about have to agree to it. She just lives over the border in Carroll County and said she would be willing to drive the boys each day so they don't have to change schools."

"Well, that would be good. It would help with their adjustment to living somewhere else."

"Yeah, I hate to see our family breakup, even if it is temporary." Shasta yawned again. "I've got to go. There are clothes in the dryer calling my name. I hope you will tell me about the doctor's visit tomorrow."

"Okay. I hope you get some rest later."

"Hey, I'm just training for those long nursing shifts I will be working one day."

"You mean doctor shifts, right?"

"Yeah, well, we will see about that. I've got to run."

As Grae hung up the phone, she thought about Martha Graham's children. She wondered if they ever felt as Shasta did, torn within their own family. Grae was sure that Shasta's father had tried to make the process easier than Squire David ever would have done.

SIX

The doctor had recommended that Grae wait until the following week to begin driving again. It was about the only thing that Kat agreed with in the diagnosis. So, on Thursday, Grae rode with her mother to school and planned to spend the time before her class in the genealogy library.

"We are going to try to go visit your father on Saturday." Kat broke the morning drive silence. "I thought that since you are feeling better and are not going to be working, it would be a good time. I am sure that Mister Abbey will keep you busy once you get back to work until Christmas." Kat shook her head and laughed. "And when I told your father about Perry's fight, he begged me to bring you both. I think he is dying to see Perry's black eyes." Kat paused. "I'm sorry, that was a poor choice of words."

"Rarely do those words have such a double meaning, but I am sure in this case you are right. He would love to see Perry with his wounds of war. I think it is a good idea for us to go. How does he sound?"

"Well, you know, the phone calls are short. He wanted to know how you were doing. He sounds tired, weak. I also called the doctor. He said that he is doing very well with the treatments. He said he would prefer to discuss his progress with me in person. That could be good or bad, I suppose. I asked him how your father's appetite was. The doctor said that one thing about this treatment is it doesn't seem to make patients nauseous. So, I asked if we could bring your father some food. He said he would try to arrange that."

"Are you thinking orange gingerbread?" Grae smiled, remembering all of the mornings in her childhood that she awoke to that smell. It was her mother's special recipe. There were mandarin oranges in the batter as well as in the sweet glaze that went on top.

"Yes. That and some good strong coffee should put a smile on his face."

Grae paused for a moment and glanced at her mother's profile. "Do you still love Dad?"

"Grae, loving your father was never the problem in our marriage. He always gave me a level of understanding that few people could convey. But, your father liked power. That can be a driving force in someone's life. It can be positive. It can make people work hard and endeavor to succeed. But, it can also take them over. When power becomes more important than the people around you, it's a sign of trouble. I was so caught up in keeping our little family life flowing that I ignored the signs. I pretended that the affluent life he was building wasn't also making us a poor family emotionally. I don't think that he ever intended for all of that to happen. I think power and ambition can be addictions. Sometimes a person has to hit rock bottom before they can begin to climb back out."

"He took us to the bottom with him." Grae looked out the window as they turned into the college drive.

"He did. Thankfully, we had Grandpa and this community to take us in and help us on our road back." Kat smiled, as they slowly made it up the road to the college. "Do you think Shasta might want to come with us to North Carolina?" Kat parked the Jeep. As they were leaving the Mansion, Grae had told her mother about the possibility of Shasta's family having to separate for a while. "I was thinking it might get her away for a day. Get her mind off her family as she experienced the drama of ours." Kat laughed as she slammed the door. "I would also like someone along to help drive. Grandpa is going to be guiding some hunters this weekend. And, before you say anything, we are going to honor what the doctor said and not let you drive until next week."

"Okay, Mom. I will ask her. Not sure what her work schedule is like, but she mainly works in the evenings during the week."

"If you want me to bring you anything back for lunch, text me. I plan to go out and do a little grocery shopping."

As Grae and her mother parted, she saw Jay walking briskly toward her mother with a tray holding four Starbucks cups.

"Oh, I hope those are Peppermint Mochas." Grae said to herself.

A male student walking past her turned in her direction. Grae smiled. She watched as Jay handed one to her mother whose smile showed her gratitude. Kat briefly turned back and smiled at Grae as Jay walked on in her direction.

"Trying to make brownie points with my mom so she will invite you back to dinner?"

"I will do whatever I need to in order to be able to eat more of Kat White's delicious cuisine. But, this morning, I thought I would get an early start on the letters we were reading. Those bearing hot beverages on a cold morning are always looked upon kindly."

Jay made a little bow that reminded Grae of how the gentlemen acted at the wedding party on that fateful night in 1786. It gave her a mixed feeling to think back about that night, which was so joyful and tragic at the same time.

They entered the library and found that only Alice was there. Normally the first one to arrive, she was walking toward the back.

"If you are heading to the coffee pot, I would stop if I was you. Mister Stone has brought us a special hot beverage."

Alice turned around to find Jay presenting her with a hot cup.

"Oh, my! What is the occasion?"

"Well, I hope that we have something to celebrate."

"Oh, what's that?" Grae asked as she took a little sip from the steaming brew. She thought that she saw a bag with the same logo as her cup peeking out of Jay's backpack.

"I hoped that you might have some good news from your visit to the doctor."

"Well, I almost forgot about that. I guess it is good news. I had a whole team of doctors, nurses, technicians, and interns at my disposal." Grae grinned at Alice and Jay. They both continued to have serious looks. "They did lots of tests and asked lots of questions. They think I need therapy and drugs. That these episodes are caused by emotional triggers because of stress in my life. Mom and I aren't buying it."

"So, what will you do?" The look on Alice's face showed concern.

"We will continue to monitor my condition and watch for signs. I think it was just something isolated. I mean, who knows, it could even have been related to a virus or something that didn't show up on any of the ER tests."

"Well, I guess that is true. It could be. You really haven't seemed ill in any other way. But you've got to be careful and you don't need to ignore what your body tells you. It will tell you the truth." Alice placed her coffee on her desk.

"We will hope that freshly brewed coffee will be just what the doctor ordered today." Jay was obviously trying to lighten the mood.

"Legal stimulants were probably not in her diagnosis." Grae smiled at her friend. "But, it sure does sound good to me."

"You've got to read this letter from John Robinson to Squire David. It is quite a page turner and it's only two pages." Jay had dug directly into the letters as soon as they got settled for the morning. "He really gives a concise account of the Gauley River Bridge engagement and the Battle at Carnifex Ferry."

"So now I am supposed to magically become a Civil War expert too?" Grae rolled her eyes and pointed to the bag in his backpack. "Is that celebratory food?"

"Oh, yeah, I forgot. I got a couple of different kinds of pastries. I should have offered your mother one."

"She's on a diet. I will eat hers." Grae smiled as she opened the bag Jay handed her. "I guess it would be rude not to offer one to Alice."

"Eventually she will write a report about your volunteer service and could probably serve as a nice reference for you." Jay gave Grae a big grin.

"Darn! I hope she doesn't like chocolate, because I am seeing something wonderful in here that is encased in chocolate."

Grae returned from offering Alice a selection and found Jay staring straight ahead with one of the letters held up ready to read.

"Did she take the chocolate one?"

"No, I shall let her live. She selected something that looked suspiciously healthy. It contained raisins."

"Oh, I hope that healthiness didn't rub off onto the others." Jay laughed as he watched Grae carefully take out the chocolate pastry. "Take a seat and prepare to listen, this is a great letter."

2nd Lt. John W. Robinson
Co. B, 51st Va. Regiment, C.S.A.
Sewell Mountain Camp
Nicolas County, Va

Squire David Graham
Cedar Run Farm
Max Meadows, Va

September 20, 1861

Dear Sir,

First and foremost I wish to tell you that Davy is
safe and well, the dangers of the present
notwithstanding. Our efforts of late have been
such that writing has been an impossibility and
now, with a brief break for myself, Davy asks that I
send you this message along with his love. Davy
realizes that you must be more than worried
about him, thus the purpose of my authorship, as
he is presently committed to the breastwork
fortifications currently under construction.

Forgive me as I write to you beyond Davy's simple
request, for his humility will prevent him from
telling you of his valor on the field and his
perpetual encouragement to the men. It is my fear
that you and your dear family may not learn of
his courage, thus my purpose as I record my
observations for you.

On August 29th Col. Wharton received orders from
Gen. Floyd to move the 51st to Camp Gauley in the

Kanahwa Valley, even though Wharton reported his 400 troops lacked sufficient training and guns. We were quickly marched through Alleghany, Green Briar, Fayette, and Nicolas counties, passing through Lewisburg on September 2nd to Floyd's camp at the Gauley Bridge. We had a skirmish with the enemy at Locust Lane just before our arrival at camp which seemed to bring General Rosecrans' army of twenty thousand down upon us in force on September 10th. Our fortifications on the north side of the Kanahwa and Gauley Rivers near Carnifex Ferry were strong and Floyd's Brigade held the line until dark with many Federals wounded and little damage to our boys. Co. B. had command of the rear guard with Davy as our commander. Taking stock of our precarious position before the battle, Davy and W.R. Stone decided to make a temporary foot bridge just in case escape was required. Col. Forsberg, W.R. Stone, and Davy quickly surveyed the land, designed a serviceable bridge, and instructed our talented men from the mines to fell trees and construct the bridge. As if by magic, the foot bridge was in place when General Floyd surprised his officers with an order to withdraw his Brigade and cross the river. Sir, for the life of me I do not understand our retreat near Carnifex Ferry for we had sufficient artillery and troops in position to repel the enemy, no matter their large numbers. I can tell you this for certain thousands of boys hurried to cross that foot bridge that day, thanks to the industry and forethought of your son.

After the battle we marched towards Big Sewell Mountain for days on end, pummeled by torrential rains and swallowed up whole by the relentless muddy roads. It was during this time that General Robert E. Lee joined us for a few days. His appearance alone gave us great diversion from our long suffering for over half of the men are ill with pneumonia, fever, measles, and dysentery. Tremendous hardship is evidenced on every face here, Sir, thus our small victories become like a warm embrace upon our very souls.

I confess to you, Sir, that it is not my wish to leave this War or this company of men who are my friends and comrades. However, I will do as I have promised, for certain realities must give us presence of mind during trying times. And if my travels home should run afoul in these next few weeks I shall take pleasure in knowing that I have told you of the honor displayed by your son during this chaotic time.

God's blessings be with us all this day.

Yours truly,

John Robinson

P.S.....Please give my regards to Mrs. Graham and Miss Bettie Ann.

"Well, Mister Robinson had an air of drama to his writing, didn't he?" Grae had finished her first pastry and was digging in the bag for another.

"I'm not sure if I would characterize it that way. You must remember that this was the Civil War. There wasn't anything pretty about it. There were a lot of dramatic moments in just about every situation."

"Yes, I understand that. I just thought that it sounded rather formal and dramatic for a soldier. He certainly was impressed with Davy Graham." Grae consumed the last bite of her second pastry and pushed the bag away.

"John Robinson would later marry Bettie Graham. He had probably spent a good amount of time with the Graham family. Besides, Davy Graham was a Captain, at the time. He was known to be a leader and was beloved by his men. Unlike what we know of his father, Davy had great concern for those who served with him. There are countless documented occasions where it would have been easy for him to step away from the war, but he chose to stay with his men."

"I bet that Squire David didn't like that. I imagine that he wanted him back at Cedar Run."

"You would be correct. While I was at the Mansion with Doctor Minson, I witnessed a dialogue between Squire and Martha about that very thing. He did not want to lose his only living son in the Civil War. He wanted to insure that he continued to have a male heir. It was a tense dinner conversation."

"Ah, but we know that he had another male heir. It's a shame that Ama's son never got to know his half siblings in Virginia."

Grae left Jay to continue dissecting the letters as she began to work on some of the research that was assigned by Alice. It took her back to the section of the library that was closer to Alice's desk. She found her deep into studying what appeared to be some budgetary documents. Alice was dressed in a beautiful deep royal blue sweater. It looked wonderful on her. Grae found herself drawn to the color.

A flash of an image appeared before her eyes. It was the image of a beautiful fountain pen. It had a pointed silver nib and a stunning royal blue shell with an unusual swirled design. It was being held by a man. Grae could only see his back. He was sitting at a desk writing a letter by lamplight. Grae staggered toward the wall as the vision left her view.

"Grae, Grae, are you okay?" Alice jumped up from her desk and ran toward Grae.

"I'm okay. Really, I'm okay. I just got a little dizzy. I've probably had too much sugar." Grae tried to laugh it off but doubted the expression on her face was convincing.

"You sit down a minute. Should I call your mother?"

"No, no. I think it was the sugar."

Grae hated lying to Alice, but she couldn't exactly tell her that she had a vision of a man from the past. She had to look away from her as the blue of her sweater was making her dizzy. Grae knew in her heart that this wasn't related to anything wrong in her brain. Alice went to the break room to get Grae some water as Jay came up behind her.

"What happened? Are you okay?"

"I just had a vision." Grae whispered.

"Like of the future?"

"No, one that is no doubt courtesy of Back in Time Airways."

"What?" Jay looked confused.

"I saw something from the past."

"How could you tell?"

"Did you wake up with a new brain today? It looked like the past. A man was sitting at a table writing a letter by lamplight. Shhh, Alice is coming back. Act natural." Grae cringed at her last statement. She was afraid to imagine what might be natural for Jay in this situation.

"Drink this." Alice's phone rang as she passed the bottle of water to Grae. "Kegley Library." Her always cheerful greeting was the only acceptable way to answer the phone. Grae began to drink the water as she and Jay listened to her side of the conversation. "Yes, that is correct. We are located within the WCC main library that is located in Smyth Hall…Yes, Smyth is the newest building…Your grandson attended here in the 80s. How delightful…No, you do not have to make an appointment unless you would like us to help you find something specific as that may take a little time…You are very welcome…Thank you. Bye-bye." Alice hung up the phone and looked at both of them.

"Researcher?" Grae asked as she drank more water. Alice was pointing at the bottle.

"Yes, her husband was a distant relative of the McGavock family." Grae choked on her water causing Alice and Jay to look alarmed.

"Drank too fast." Grae said with a choked up stutter.

"Drink slower, but drink up. If you have had too much sugar, drinking water will help. You need to drink that other bottle I brought up, too."

"The one that Jay is drinking?"

Alice rolled her eyes and pointed to the break room. Without a word or hesitation, Jay headed in that direction.

"Bring two." Alice yelled after him.

"Really, Alice, I'm okay." Grae stopped drinking and started to get up.

"Sit down and drink." Grae complied. She wasn't sure where she would put the second bottle that Jay handed her. "I'm going to call Kat."

"Please, don't. She's been so worried. You can watch me like a hawk the rest of the day, but let's give Mom a break. If I have any more strange symptoms, I will call her myself. I blame Jay for all this."

"Hey, what did I do?"

"You brought excessive amounts of caffeine and sugar and forced me to consume them." Grae's serious tone quickly turned into a grin.

"You know, I could suspend him from using the library."

Grae marveled at how happier Alice seemed since she began dating the professor. She wondered what happened with the young man those many years ago that made her shy away from relationships. Grae had a little bit of a broken heart, but even if Gav was permanently out of her life, she knew that she wouldn't give up on love.

"I think I am going back to my work while I still can." Jay left them and Alice pointed at the water bottle again.

"Alice, can I ask you a question?"

"Certainly." Alice sat back down at her desk and returned to her budget work.

"Who was the guy that you were in love with in high school?" Alice looked surprised. She sighed and shook her head.

"Oh, Grae, that was a lifetime ago. I really don't want to talk about it."

"Sometimes, it helps to talk about things that bother us. Especially when you can talk to a good listener who doesn't know the story." Grae finished off the first bottle. She smiled. "I still have another whole bottle to drink."

"You are a convincing girl." Alice closed the file in front of her and looked at the long row of glass windows that separated the genealogy section from the rest of the library. "His name was Edward, Eddie. He was the younger brother of my best friend." Alice paused and looked deeply into Grae's eyes. "Are you sure you want to hear this?"

"Oh, yes, I love stories, especially love stories." Grae pulled her feet up into the chair and wrapped her arms around her legs. It was her "safe ball" position, as Perry teased her.

"Eddie was a year younger than me. Most of our growing up years, I just thought of him as a pest. He would try to play tricks on me when I would come for sleepovers at their house." Alice smiled at the memory. "I spent the summer before I turned eighteen with my grandparents in New England. I was gone for almost three months. When I returned, it was like Eddie had all of a sudden grown up. He was literally several inches taller. He had spent the summer working out and training for the football team. He wasn't the scrawny pest. He was a gorgeous hunk. I was smitten."

"Oh, that sounds wonderful. Was he head over heels for you?"

"Well, as a matter of fact, he was. It turned out that he had a crush on me for several years. His sister knew about it all along and hadn't told me." Alice paused and took a drink of her water. She motioned for Grae to do the same. "So, pretty quickly, we became inseparable. We were *the* couple in school. It was like magic. I couldn't believe how lucky I was. We dated all throughout my junior year and on into my senior year, until…"

"Until?"

A tear fell down Alice's cheek.

"It's just amazing. It's been over thirty years and it still hurts." Alice looked straight at Grae. "I think you've heard enough. It didn't work out. The end." Alice abruptly rose and picked up the budget file. She wiped her cheeks. "You seem fine now. You have plenty of work to do. I have to take this paperwork over to the business office."

Without another word, Alice walked out, leaving Grae to wonder what horrible thing happened to Alice's true love.

"There are so many more interesting letters." Jay broke the silence.

Grae had almost finished her assignment. Jay had not disturbed her since Alice left. She looked at the clock and was surprised to see that almost an hour had passed. Grae hoped that Alice was okay.

"Have you been reading Davy's letters or those written to him?" Grae was making the copies needed for the client's research.

"A little of both. It's interesting how perspectives can change in how history is told. Let me read you this one from Martha to her son."

Mrs. David Graham
Cedar Run Farm
Max Meadows, Va

Captain D. P. Graham
Co. B., 51ˢᵗ Va. Regiment, C.S.A.
Newbern, Va

December 10, 1861

Dear Son,

A mother's letter to her only son during a time of war is a sacred thing. The only gift more priceless is your love and well-being this day. I am thus relieved that you will find respite from enemy hostilities and perhaps enjoy a hot meal so near to home. Oh how I long to see you!

Your father and sisters are well and my health continues to be sufficient for the needs of the family. Son, it clarifies my thoughts to put them down to you! It eases my mind to express them on paper rather than to have the worry clogged up in my head like the rocks impeding the natural flow of the clear and cleansing spring waters within Cedar Run Creek. There are days when the creek waters are a murky grey blur and for the life of me, I cannot see the bottom, or the beauty of the life within its shore. But then you know this about me and you hold me close when I am weakened.

Now. You will be pleased to know that your father and John Robinson are successfully managing the mines, furnaces, the forge, and the store in spite of the loss of their best workmen. They send much-needed iron to Tregadar in Richmond for artillery production and supply lead directly to the shot tower to build our ammunition stores.

Thus far, the Yankees have not seen fit to attack our operations here, yet I do fear these critical enterprises along with the nearby railway and telegraph lines will not elude their military sensibilities as time goes on.

I continue to enjoy serving as Mary Bell's and Bettie's tutor with calm ruthlessness and unimagined pleasure. Presently I have them both reading Charlotte Bronte, Jane Austen, Charles Dickens, and, your favorite, Nathaniel Hawthorne. It restores my faith to observe your clever sisters engage your father with discussions of literature and politics at the dinner table! Preferring to rollick in the great outdoors, Emily has escaped my teacher's grasp and is attending a fine girls' school in Wytheville. The talented Mrs. Ephraim McGavock is owner and head mistress and hails from New York City. I quietly appreciate her views on women and education as they are aligned with my own inclinations. This is my promise before God, that my children will know the beauty and power of knowledge and self-sufficiency.

Davy, you must be curious to know how I came to discover your camp's location for this correspondence. Your precocious sister Bettie and Nan Tate have become friends of late, the later bringing sheets of piano music here for Bettie's practice and their mutual entertainment. As you know, Nan's father, Captain Charles Campbell Tate, is leader to the Home Guard and will be present for your upcoming Grand Review in Newbern. Nannie tells us there will be five Regiments of infantry there, including our friends in the 45th "Mt. Airy Rough and Ready", the 22nd, 36th, 50th, 5th, and the 20th Mississippi, 13th Georgia, the 8th Virginia Cavalry, and three artillery batteries. Mercy! How can one remember all these numbers?

We have welcomed quite a few guests here since my last letters. Reverend Painter continues to serve the Anchor and Hope Presbyterian Church where your grandfather, Robert Graham, is recognized as a founding elder. I am grateful for the Reverend's visits here as his kind spiritual reflections lift my moods substantially. Did you know that Nannie's brother and your able-bodied Lieutenant, William Tate, was a teacher at the Anchor and Hope Institute after you boys left V.M.I.?

Sister Betsy Chaffin surprised us two days past with a huge apple cobbler and an ancient jug of Pa's peach brandy. She is quite the sly one, always pestering your father to release his firm hold on my "delicate condition" while imbibing him with a glass of his favorite drink.

Margaret McGavock also visits regularly as we have the good fortune to share many of the passions that exceed the simple bonds connecting most sisters-in-law. Now in her seventh decade of life, Margaret is a kindred spirit beyond blood to me. She has survived the loss of daughters Mary, Sally, and most recently, Nancy, and husband Joseph, yet she celebrates life with daughter Cynthia and her grandchildren Hugh and Sally, and with a new baby expected at any time! Did you know that her husband, the spry Mr. Randal McGavock, is very close in age to your own father? Why we recently attended a dinner with Margaret, Cynthia, and Randal at the magnificent Ft. Chiswell home of Randal's nephews, Cloyd and Stephen McGavock. As you are well aware, this mansion is a masterpiece of Georgian architecture and exudes an exquisite mix of European and American design. I was not alone in noticing that your father was having some difficulty hiding his jealous admiration of the structure. After a lovely dinner, our handsome hosts entertained us with a rather unique story, which I must share with you. It appears that their father, James McGavock II, was a close friend to President Andrew Jackson. As you know the McGavocks are powerful land owners here in Ft. Chiswell and in Nashville, Tennessee. According to Cloyd, when General Jackson's entourage traveled from Nashville to Washington D.C., they always stopped at their father's nearby tavern for refreshment and "a gentleman's conversation". On one such occasion, your father was present, having just purchased Cedar Run Farm and was newly absorbed in the world of iron making. Never one to shy away from an opinion, "Old Hickory" spoke of his ambitions to become our next president. He then voiced his ardent support for slavery and his resolute intent to remove the Indians from our realm, indeed to force their "civilized relocation" to the distant central plains of our country. And son, much to my surprise, Cloyd reported to us your father's fervent response to General Jackson's diatribe! It appears that your father then approached the General and politely announced his disdain of the General's opinion regarding the Indians, fiercely describing Jackson's plan as both dishonorable and appalling. And with that pronouncement, according to Cloyd, your father took his leave from our future president and the namesake for Wytheville's Camp Jackson. Your father spoke not a word as Cloyd told this story, instead engaging in a faraway gaze as if propelled back to another time. And I could not help but drift away as well, all this time thinking myself alone with the knowledge of one of your father's long ago, concealed passions.

But I digress from the present. Your Uncle Joe Graham visits often and sends his prayers for your safe return. He is up in years now and complains of bouts with dyspepsia and rheumatism and reports that he has found substantial relief from the healing waters of Grayson Sulfur Springs. Perhaps I should visit with him there soon.

As I reluctantly close, I hear Bettie playing Christmas songs with sweet Nan attempting to sing harmony. How lovely, the music of life is to us all. Oh Davy, I do miss you so! You must promise to write to us soon. I hear fine accolades of your leadership from the families of your men. I am so proud of you, my son. God has truly blessed us and I am grateful to Him who is all-knowing.

Your Loving Mother

P.S...Reverend Painter and I often read this passage from Joshua 10:25 and I wish for you to read it now.

"Joshua said unto them, 'Fear not, nor be dismayed, be strong and of good courage: For thus shall the LORD do to all your enemies against whom ye fight.'"

Alas son, some of our enemies are not visible to us yet they walk with us every day. We must trust God to show us the way.

"Martha certainly had a lovely way with words. I can just see her sitting at the desk in the music room." Grae paused, as she reflected on Martha's letter. She didn't realize that they were not alone.

"You, my dear, have a wonderful imagination." Alice had quietly returned. "I have read many of these documents in this library. Actually, I suppose I have read almost all of them. But, I can't say that I have often imagined the writers sitting in their homes writing them."

Grae was fearful that she had said too much. She darted her eyes to Jay who seemed to be suddenly preoccupied with straightening things.

"I've finished that assignment. It's all ready to mail." Grae handed the large manila envelope to Alice.

"Wonderful! The other two that I gave you are quite small in comparison. You should have time to do some of your studies before you go to class this afternoon." Alice smiled and gave Grae a little hug. "The color has returned to your face. I bet you did have too much sugar." She gave Jay a scowl. "It was kind of you to bring us some treats, but next time aim for a smaller selection. We ladies need to watch our figures." Alice gave Grae a wink. "I am going to lunch now. Can I bring either of you anything?"

"No, that's okay. Jay is going to go get us a sandwich later."

Jay gave her a surprised look. "Ah, yes. We are going to have a sandwich." His voice sounded robotic.

Grae glared at him. They watched as Alice walked out into the outer library. Professor Dreamy, as Grae had begun to call him, was standing at the door waiting for her. Even though Grae could only see her back, she knew that Alice was smiling.

"Earlier you said you saw something."

Grae had been surprised that Jay hadn't brought up the subject sooner. She was learning that he seemed to let things simmer in his mind before he spoke of them.

"Yes, I did. I think it was Squire David writing a letter."

"Why Squire? We are reading the letters of his son."

"There's not a whole lot of logic associated with anything regarding this...this experience for me, here or there. I don't know why it would be Squire, except that he seems to be in my head."

"Maybe it's like a side effect of some medication that you have recently taken. Who knows what they gave you in the hospital?"

"Jay, you and I both know that isn't what caused this. It's a side effect of time travel and it probably means something. I've been thinking about some of the things you said a few weeks ago. Mainly about the research that you said you did regarding the people you found who had been time travelers."

"You mean the journals that I went around the country finding. Yes, it was a quite tedious, but an eye-opening process."

"Well, did any of them talk about having any medical problems in the present?"

"You know, that's a good question. I remember a few of them talked about physical things that occurred after their travels. I will have to go back and study my notes. I do remember one journal that had a bizarre occurrence, or it seemed that way to me."

"What was that?" While Jay was talking, Grae gathered the documents she needed to complete the two other research assignments.

"Well, this one woman, her name was Renee Winston. In the late 1940's, she was a young woman in Iowa. She worked in a hospital. She was a nurse, a surgical nurse. Her portal was actually the operating room. Anyway, Renee travelled only once, but her diary said that she visited California around the turn of the century, early 1900's. She was there for almost a year. She fell in love and married a man there and conceived a child. She actually had planned to just stay in that time. Then one day, quite unexpectedly, she found herself back in that operating room."

"Wow! That must have been quite traumatic. She must have been heartbroken. It reminds me of Mary."

"She was devastated and shocked to learn that she was still pregnant. It was a different time and she lost her job at the small hospital. Her superiors thought it was disgraceful to be a nurse who was pregnant out of wedlock. So Renee was not able to go back into the operating room and see if she could somehow be transported back in time to her husband."

"Oh, that is horrible. How very sad for her."

"The child was born, a son, very healthy. Renee was understandably relieved, as she did not know what time travel might due to a fetus. She confided her experience later to one of the other nurses who was a dear friend. That woman arranged for Renee to go back to the operating room. But, at the last minute, Renee backed out. She was too afraid that she would not be able to travel with her baby. She could not leave her child behind." Jay paused and drank some water. It gave Grae a moment to ponder how serious and tragic the story was. It was indeed as The General had told her, dire and disastrous. "Her friend convinced Renee to go to California and try to find her husband in the present time. Renee did that. She asked around and learned that he never remarried. He had continued to hope that one day he would find his bride and their child."

"Oh." There were tears in Grae's eyes.

"It would remind you of Patrick's story. Renee went to visit him. He was over seventy. He recognized her immediately, but thought that time was playing tricks on him. How could she still be so young? How could their child be a toddler? Almost fifty years had passed. She tried to explain. He tried to understand. But, it was too much for him. He died of a heart attack several days later."

"Oh my. That is unbelievable. Did you ever get to meet Renee?"

"No, but I did meet her son. He seemed very hesitant to talk to a stranger about his family history. But, he did confirm that the journal had been written by his mother."

"Wow! It really makes you wonder about all of the other stories out there. I have got to get back to Alice's assignments." Grae looked down at the short list Alice had given her. "These will not take long at all. If you help me, we can get them done quickly." Grae started to walk to the back section of the library.

"Oh, I'm sorry, I have to go get your lunch, remember?"

Grae turned to see Jay putting on his jacket. He was smirking.

"Okay, wise guy, that actually sounds wonderful. I'll have a turkey and ham sub with everything."

"What's everything?"

"Never mind, I will text Crystal; she knows."

"Crystal, isn't that your friend that does Madison's nails?"

"Yes."

"How will texting her help me know what to get on your sub?"

"She works at the sub place on Thursday afternoon. She will have it ready before you get there."

While Jay was off getting lunch, Grae worked to complete her two additional assignments. One was searching for an obituary of a prominent Wythevillian from the early 1900's and the other was locating several documents from the Crockett family file. Since she gathered most of the files earlier, both tasks took little time. She was back with the letters when Jay arrived with the sandwiches.

"Crystal's cool." Jay put down the bag of subs and a large bag of Kettle chips. Two bottles of soda and two cups of ice were in a carrier that he set down in the middle of the table.

"No, Crystal is awesome. If I wasn't a poor college student, she would be doing my nails all the time."

"Madison comes home with some really interesting color combinations and designs on her nails. But, most importantly, she comes home relaxed and happy. That's not easy with her husband being overseas."

"It must be rough. Does she hear from him often?"

"As often as he can. Mostly via Skype and email. They have been a couple since they were thirteen."

"Really? That's hard to imagine."

"Yeah, we all thought the same thing, but I don't think that either one of them ever went on a date with anyone else. It really bothered my mother for a while, but then she just finally accepted it. They've always been happy. Very few disagreements in all those years. Keith is a good guy. I sure hope nothing prevents him from returning home." Jay slid a sandwich down to Grae and knocked over a cup of ice in the process. "Sorry."

"Perhaps we should keep the food and beverages down on that end and the letters on this end." Grae knew that Alice did not like food of any sort to be in the library, especially the liquid kind.

Jay went back to the break room and came out with a roll of paper towels. He carefully laid out huge sheets of them over the table, and then placed their food on it. "It looks like we are having a picnic."

She smiled and began to dig into her sandwich. "Jay, I have a question about something you said the other day. When you said that Patrick had relationships, you didn't mention whether or not he had children. Did he?"

"He had one son."

"I wonder why Margaret McGavock didn't tell me any of this when she talked about Patrick's life?" Grae took a big bite of her sub.

"Well, perhaps, it was a family secret, or maybe Patrick kept his life private."

"What do you know about the son? What was his name?"

"You will find this quite interesting. I am not sure what the reasoning was behind it. Did you ever tell him what your real name was?"

Grae stopped chewing and thought about the question. "Well, I...I don't think so. I don't remember telling him. Why?"

"He named his son Graham, Graham Patrick McGavock." Jay paused and watched Grae for a moment. "In age, he was between Squire's sons, Robbie and Davy. He was serving in the Civil War at the time I met Patrick."

"He must have come late in his life."

"Yes, I believe he told me that he was in his sixties when his son was born. It wasn't that unusual in that time. Men had multiple families. He said that he never imagined that he would live long enough to see him grown."

"Do you know when Patrick died?"

"No, I don't. But I would be glad to research that if you like."

"I think I would like to go visit his grave if it could be found."

"I will work on researching Patrick's life. He lived most of it in North Carolina. I think he was quite a successful businessman, but I also think his manner of doing business was far different from Squire's."

"Thank you. I appreciate your help with this. It would be interesting to know more about what his life was like. I want to know that he had happiness and contentment." Grae took the last bites of her sandwich and balled up the wrapper. "Let's get back to those letters. I found these while you were gone. They are Christmas greetings from Davy's sisters in December of 1861. They are quite comical. It is interesting to read the differences in their phrasing and what is important to them."

Miss Mary Bell Graham
Cedar Run Farm
Max Meadows, Va

Captain D.P. Graham
Co. B, 51st Va. Regiment, C.S.A.
Fort Donelson
Tennessee

December 20, 1861

Dearest Brother,

I write to you today wishing you good health and
all the best that this world may provide as
Christmas approaches. I find myself terribly
conflicted with our family's warm pleasantries
and festivities, while you and your men suffer from
God knows what afflictions! I worry and miss you
so dear Brother.

But I forget my orders. Brigadier General Ma
Graham has issued her official decree, signed,
and delivered to your adoring sisters. Hear Ye!
Hear Ye! As of this moment, our regiment of three,
timid sisters is directed to write ONLY joyous
tidings to our favorite (and only) brother as
Christmas is upon us. I do confess to you that I
continue to fear the wrath of Ma, even as a proper
young lady of eighteen years of age, thus I shall
obey our Commander. Let no blood be spilt on my
account.

As I write to you, alone here in the Parlor, I am pleased to report that Bettie has put aside tormenting me with her newest interest, a borrowed banjo. Instead, Bettie, always the fierce competitor, is winning at cards with Bunt and Nan. And, no, they are NOT making any wagers, as you have so discretely taught her. Ma is nearby, sewing a lovely lace collar on my new Christmas gown while humming "Rock of Ages". The ever-present Gracie is serving us delicious fruit cakes and hot tea. As you see, life here is as it has always been except you are not here with us. And the storms outside! Storms of both weather and battles! We cannot help but think of you marching through these merciless tirades of rain and snow fearing the enemy will take your very last breath at any minute.

Oh dear! I shall be quartered and hanged if I do not resume my glad tidings at once. Uh-hum. Where was I? Ah yes, music and cards and fruit cakes. You have certainly surmised by now that Pa is indeed away on business, Richmond I believe. The war, it appears, is good for the iron business if nothing else.

I hope to have an appreciative audience for my new Christmas gown this week. I have received several letters from our mutual friend, Private Harold Matthews, of the 4th VA, now serving admirably within "Stonewall's Brigade". Private Matthews states that he may be blessed with a brief furlough for the holidays along with Colonel William Terry and Nan's brother, James Tate. I will attempt to not break rank and entreat the Cedar Run Brigadier General to relax her pickets and prepare several days of fine rations in hopes of a visit from Private Matthews.

I will close now, lest I revert back to the unspoken truths of our circumstances dear Brother. If you could only appear before me for just a single moment as if by magic, I would hug your neck, kiss your cheek, and tell you full force how much you are loved and adored by this Sister. Return to us Davy! God bless you and your men and protect you with all His might. Amen.

Your loving sister,
Mary Bell

Miss Bettie Ann Graham
Cedar Run Farm
Max Meadows, Va

Captain D.P. Graham
Co. B, 51ˢᵗ Va. Regiment, C.S.A.
Fort Donelson
Tennessee

December 20, 1861

Dear Brother,

I miss you more than I can ever say. There is no other person here equal to you in Ten Pins much less Charades. And it is only you who joins me in the barn for the pleasure of a fine cigar. It is simply too quiet and sedate here without my charming and witty older brother.

I would be remiss, however, if I did not send my regards to you for your support of Mr. Robinson's return from the hostilities in the field for the daily battles waged here under the supreme command of Pa. While the accommodations here far exceed yours, I must say Mr. R has distinguished himself with bravery beyond the call of duty under the scrutiny of Pa's eye. Mr. R's other attributes have not escaped my gaze as well, including the fact that he is not unpleasant to look upon nor converse with. Enough about that subject.

And what of home? Ma has your devout sisters devoid of spare time and idle hands. We sew. We cook. And we study. My performance in the kitchen notwithstanding, I do exceedingly well with mathematics and literature. Last week I finished reading Charles Dickens' <u>Great Expectations</u>. I dare say that I share a few of Estella's eccentricities and Pip's love of life. I am now struggling to read <u>Jane Eyre</u>, finding its characters far too familiar to me! Charlotte Bronte has created a fictional world (or is it?) at Thornfield Hall with an insane wife locked away in the attic, living estranged from Mr. Rochester, her wealthy, impenetrable or should I say impenitent husband. I am fond of Jane, who eventually marries Mr. Rochester as "her equal", after his crazed wife kills herself by setting fire to Thornfiled Hall. You will appreciate this edict from Jane, "Laws and principles are not for times when there is no temptation, they are for such moments as this." Well done Jane. Would that I could speak so eloquently.

I continue to put my thoughts down in my journal, although I lack the discipline of devotion to it. I much prefer to observe Pa's business endeavors, play at the piano, and visit friends. YOU MUST RETURN SOON SO THAT WE CAN RESUME WHERE WE LEFT OFF DEAR BROTHER! I miss you so.

In closing I have a riddle for you. What other fine and familiar female will miss you as I do, for she shares our same blood but not our parentage?

You may give me your answer when your return home to me. I can reassure you, it is not the likes of Miss Havisham, no matter the depth of affection.

With love from your most affectionate and favorite sister,

Bettie

> Miss Emily Graham
> Cedar Run Farm
> Max Meadows, Va

Captain D.P. Graham
Co. B, 51st Va. Regiment, C.S.A.
Fort Donelson
Tennessee

December 19, 1861

Dear Brother Davy,

Do you remember our last hunting expedition when I expertly killed the fat, grey rabbit? And we skinned and cooked it covertly over a fire on a sharpened wooden spit and devoured it? Remember? It is this memory and a hundred others that I bring back to life and relive when I get to missing you. Now, you have my official permission to try this bit of magic yourself, although it will only work with memories of you and me. Ha! Remember when Pa caught me shooting woodcocks with you in the hay field? Why he promptly berated us, forbidding my use of guns of any kind, for "it gives the appearance of impropriety for a young girl of high social standing to do such a thing." Hogwash. I like hunting. Come home soon so we may continue to be outlaws and vagabonds together.

Speaking of becoming a proper young lady of good lineage, I am receiving some much-needed instruction in that arena. In fact, I MAY display such a brilliant polish that, upon your return, you will not recognize me. I now attend Mrs. Ephraim McGavock's private girls' school in Wytheville. Her name is Abigail Williamson McGavock and she reigns from New York City. I find her manner of instruction profoundly interesting and her strict discipline both ingenious and sinister. Madam McGavock addresses me as Miss Emily Marie with absolutely no tolerance for "Bunt", the perfect name you gave me so long ago. Last week I did confess to Madam that I was terribly sorry to have "bunt" the cookies that I had made. She simply pretended I was invisible. She is talented that way.

My best friend at school is Cousin Sally McGavock. Her father, Mr. Randal McGavock, is close in age to Pa but far apart in natural temperament. Perhaps Mr. McGavock's secret is marrying a proper young lady with a good lineage. You do recall that Mr. Randal and Mrs. Cynthia ARE cousins. Indeed. Sally's granny, Mrs. Margaret McGavock, visits Ma and Pa often with Sally, much to my eternal happiness.

Brother, I have a secret for you to guard. I am reading _The House of Seven Gables_, perhaps one of the few Hawthorne books that you have not read. Well let me tell you about it, for it is filled with witchcraft and the supernatural! Did you know that Hawthorn's ancestors actually played a part in the Salem Witch Trials? And these same ancestors lived in a large gabled home in Salem, Massachusetts some 200 years ago? There are days when I fancy myself living then! Yes, as I gaze upon our own ornate and imposing home I can see myself transforming into the cheerful and lovely Phoebe Pyncheon or the vexed and beautiful ghost of Alice Pyncheon, who forever haunts their home. My secret is this. There are times when I feel the spirits of the dead walk among us in OUR home. I am certain of it. And what is more astounding, I am not afraid of them! Do not speak of this to anyone. It is our secret.

What is NOT a secret just now is how unfavorable the quality of the singing voices I am hearing from the living room. These voices are not wicked, mind you, only somewhat tainted for young ladies of good lineage. Ah, Bettie has now changed to my *favorite Christmas song, "Jingle Bells", and I am compelled to go and join her and Mary Bell at the piano.*

My dear Davy, I am intent on seeing you soon! Please be prepared, for as soon as I see you I will run to you, hug you, and dance for joy, perhaps giving the appearance of impropriety for a young lady of such high social standing.

You loving Sister,

Bunt

"Oh my, that was something. I met those girls. What little I saw of them gave me the impression that they were each very different." Jay was cleaning up all of the remnants from lunch as Alice returned.

"Ah, I see that you did get some lunch. That's good. Are you feeling better now, Grae?"

"Oh, yes. I am fine now." Grae stood up and retrieved her work. "Here are those two assignments. Do you have any more that you need done?"

"No, not for today. It looks like you two have been deep into those Graham family letters. You better be quick about going through them. I got a call the other day from a lady who is interested in writing a book about the Grahams and their life in the Mansion. She said that she was going to try to come after the first of the year and do some extensive research."

"I wonder if the owner of the Mansion knows about that."

"I think he does. She said that she was a friend of J.C.'s. I think she said she was from North Carolina."

"Hmmm, interesting. I'll have to ask Grandpa if he has heard anything."

"Well, you two continue with whatever you are doing. I will be in the office for the rest of the day. I have a ton of research of my own to do for a grant application." Alice returned to her desk near the front.

"I have an hour before my class. How many more letters are there?" Grae rolled her eyes as Jay picked up an envelope box that was sitting on a chair next to him. "You haven't looked at any of those yet?"

"Not in detail. It appears that unlike the other two boxes, these are a mixture. They seem to be to and from a variety of members of the Graham family."

"Still in that same time period?"

"Yes, those years during the Civil War."

"Well, you keep working on the ones you were organizing and I will start on that box. I think I am going to ask Alice if she would like for us to go ahead and place these letters in acid-free folders with the same type of paper between them."

"I'm impressed that you know all the terminology."

"Alice is exacting and I've paid attention. If a researcher is going to be here soon, I am sure Alice will want the letters catalogued and protected."

Grae found Alice was on the phone. She made a motion with her hand indicating that the person on the other end was very talkative. Grae decided to write her question in a quick note. Alice began to smile and nod her head affirmatively and quickly wrote a reply telling Grae where she could find the materials she needed. As Grae came out of the back room, she saw that Shasta was standing outside the door looking in.

"Hey, are you looking for me?" Grae noticed that her friend looked a little perkier.

"Yeah, I saw your mom when she was returning from lunch. She asked me if I would go with you on Saturday and help her drive. Are you okay with that?"

"Sure. It sounds like a great idea to me. But, be forewarned, I don't think it will be a very happy trip."

"Oh, I understand. I'm just glad to be able to help you guys for a change. Your mother has been super nice to me. You know about what she did for my father and my brothers, don't you?"

"I don't think I do."

"She arranged for your grandfather to take my Dad and the boys hunting while we are in North Carolina. Sunday is the day that the boys will be moving in with Aunt Jolene. So it will be a nice day that they can have together before everything changes."

"How did she know? I just told her today."

"Apparently, your mom went to school with my Dad and Aunt. She said that she and Jolene have kept in touch all of these years."

"Well, I had no idea. But I've learned a lot about my mother since we have lived here."

"I think I can work things out with work to be able to go. That's where I am heading now. I will let you know tomorrow." Shasta gave Grae a quick hug and dashed out of the library.

Alice was still on the phone when Grae passed her desk. She was now holding her head.

"Get lost?" Jay said as Grae returned carrying a box of acid-free folders.

"No, Shasta stopped by. She's going to go with Mom, Perry, and I to North Carolina on Saturday."

"Oh, are you going to see your father?"

"Yes. We aren't sure exactly how he is doing with his treatments. But, Mom thought it would cheer him up to see Perry with black eyes."

"What?" Jay made room for Grae to put the box in the center of the table. She also had two sets of white gloves for them to use.

"Didn't I tell you? Perry got in a fight at school. He has a couple real shiners."

"What was the fight about?"

"Carrie. The other guy was flirting with her. Perry told him to back off. I had kids from the school texting me about it."

Grae put on the gloves and began to carefully place a letter inside a folder. Jay followed her lead. The gloves seemed to bring out an awkwardness in him that she hadn't seen before. He looked like he was afraid to touch anything. It made Grae laugh.

"Why don't you let me put the letters in the folders and you can make a log of them for Alice on your laptop?"

"That's a great idea." Jay smiled as he quickly took the gloves off. "Those things make me feel..."

"Girly?" Grae giggled at how quickly he could get them off.

"Awkward." Jay gave her a big cheesy grin as he neatly put the gloves back on her end of the table. "Did Perry get in trouble with your mother?"

"Grandpa was the one who went and picked up Perry at school. Apparently, there were a couple of teachers that saw what happened and he didn't face any trouble there. I think he would have been in deep with Mom had it not been for the fact that he was defending Carrie. Mom has never condoned fighting. But, she taught us to stand up for our friends, if the need arose."

"Good philosophy...why aren't you handing me any of those letters that you have already protected?"

"Because I want to put them in chronological order, and then read them."

"I can put them in order. You just keep protecting them. Then, we can read them together."

"It's amazing that someone went to the trouble of keeping these letters safe all these years."

"You're right. I wonder why they weren't at the Graham Mansion."

"Well, it's really been a long time since a Graham lived there. I guess almost a hundred years, now. So, I suppose that most of these letters that came to the house didn't stay there too long thereafter. I don't think that Alice mentioned who brought them in."

"Alice didn't mention what?" Neither one of them saw Alice approaching. She had the ability to sneak up behind them, like a cat. They both jumped.

"Ah, we were wondering who donated all of these letters to the library. It is really an amazing collection." Jay turned his laptop toward Alice so that she could see how he was logging the entries. "Alice, will this be helpful for you to use? I was going to ask you specifically what types of information you needed to have in the log, but that phone call seemed to be monopolizing your time."

"That phone call. What a talker!" Alice shook her head. "It was a gentleman from Great Britain, of all places. He is doing research for a book about time travel." Grae and Jay shot each other quick looks. "He was looking for journals that people who have time travelled have written."

"Do we have any of those?" Grae asked the question so quietly, she wondered if Alice heard her.

"No, we do not. And I don't want any here." Alice turned to leave them but stopped. "It was an elderly woman who made the donation. She is a distant relative of someone in the Graham family."

"What was her name?" Jay asked.

"It was actually her caregiver that brought the boxes in. That woman's last name was Casper. I remember because it made me laugh. It's an unusual last name. The woman who made the donation was Mary Baker, I believe."

"Mary Baker? Is that what you said?" Grae couldn't believe her ears.

"Yes, she had some connection to the Graham family, a niece or something."

"Where does this woman live?" Jay could see the shock crossing Grae's face. He knew that her mind was racing too fast to form any further questions.

"Somewhere nearby. I asked the Casper lady where I could send a letter of thanks for the collection, and she gave me an address. I sent the letter right away and filed all the information. Why do you want to know?"

"Well, I was just thinking that if she was close enough to the Graham family to have this collection, she might have some very interesting stories that have been handed down to her as well. If she still has the mind to remember them."

"Oh, the lady said that Missus Baker is very sharp. She said it was her idea completely to make the donation." Alice turned again to leave. "What exactly is it that you are researching, Mister Stone? I don't believe that I ever quite heard what your main topic was." The look that Alice gave Jay was one of suspicion.

"I'm ah...doing a thesis about mental illness in the nineteenth century. Ah, and I am focusing on how women were treated, medically and by society. Martha Graham is a good subject for that, don't you think?"

Grae hoped that her eyes weren't revealing her amazement at Jay's answer.

"Perhaps, but who else are you including?"

Grae intently watched the banter between Alice and Jay. It was becoming a tennis volley.

"Ah, well Mary Todd Lincoln, for one."

Grae saw that Jay's eyes were darting back and forth. It was the universal sign of someone searching their memory for something that probably wasn't there.

"That's part of the research, but I need to find historical women with mental disorders."

"But Martha Graham wasn't a historical figure." Alice was just not giving up.

"That's going to be part of my contrast. I will include lessor known subjects. They will all have lived fairly affluent lives."

"Okay. I will make a copy of the contact information for you before you leave today." As Alice left the room, Jay let out a sigh that could almost have been heard at her desk.

"Good grief! What did I get myself into there?"

"You handled it very well. Did you notice her reaction to time travel though? It was swift and definite. I wonder why."

"That's what you got out of that conversation? I felt like I was on a witness stand. I didn't realize that I hadn't offered any explanation about my research. I've got to make sure that Madison has her story straight. As inquisitive as Alice was, she might bring up the subject to her."

"I guess you just weren't as direct as you were with me." Grae rolled her eyes and went back to putting the letters into the acid-free sleeves.

"What?"

"I'm investigating the murder of Martha Graham. Could you have been any blunter?"

"Well, I knew who you were and where you had been." Jay resumed logging information about the letters. "Are you thinking what I'm thinking about Mary Baker?"

"Jay, that just isn't possible. It must be a descendant."

"Not possible, huh. Well, that's what a whole lot of people would say about time travel. Actually, probably about ninety-five percent of the population would say it was absolutely, without a doubt, impossible."

"Yeah, but, she would have to be...gosh, I don't even know how old."

"Around two hundred years, depending on when you actually counted from, I think." Jay paused and wrote down some numbers. "Mary McGavock was turning eighteen in 1830, right?"

"Yes, but she was also about that same age in 1786 when she was Mary Baker."

"So, anyway you look at it, it's very old."

"What makes you think that she could live that long?"

"Because she messed with time. It doesn't seem to be the forgiving sort. It likes to play by its own rules."

"How in the world would she have kept that information hidden? People would suspect after a while."

"Perhaps, but you also know how it is with older people. They are easily forgotten. Didn't you tell me something about she only had one child who lived?"

"Yes, it was a very sad story."

"So, she might not have had too many descendants and could have outlived them all. Then, once she began outliving her neighbors, she might have just become known as an old woman in the area."

"But, for that long? Surely someone would have done the math."

"Well, if she had the financial means to keep herself going, probably no one paid too much attention." Jay paused and began making stacks of documents across the table. "Think about the neighborhood where you lived in Charlotte. Was there an older woman who lived there?"

"Yes, Missus Hudson, she lived about a block away. She made wonderful cookies." Grae smiled, thinking about how all of the children would find their way to her house just by the smell of the cookies. "She would leave her kitchen window open as the cookies would cool. All the kids in the neighborhood would gravitate to her house."

"Sounds a little like Hansel and Gretel to me."

"No, Missus Hudson was delightful. In the summer, she would have little individual size jugs of milk in a big cooler of ice in her kitchen. She always made us come inside and sit in the kitchen. She said that we needed to cool off."

"Did any kids ever become missing in the neighborhood?"

"Stop it! Everyone loved Missus Hudson."

"Okay. How old was she?"

"Oh, she was ancient. She looked really good though."

"How long had she lived there?"

"For as long as anyone could remember. She just never seemed to change."

"I rest my case."

"But, really, I don't think Missus Hudson was a time traveler."

"That's not the point I was trying to make, but how would you know? Most people don't think that you are a time traveler, either. The point I am trying to make is that there could be someone who lived right in your midst that you have no idea how old they are or how long they have been there. Mary Baker might have lived in the same house for two hundred years and the generations that grew up around her could have just taken her existence for granted. Families move in and out, neighbors change. Or, maybe, she herself moved around."

"Okay, Sherlock, I guess you are just going to have to investigate that. Get the address from Alice and go visit her."

"I intend to and you will go with me."

"Me, why me?"

"Because you know her."

Grae got a very sick feeling. "I knew a young woman named Mary Baker. I wouldn't recognize her."

"Oh, but, you, my dear, have not changed. She will remember you."

For the first time, Grae began to feel afraid.

Grae walked in a daze to her classroom after the conversation about Mary Baker. She didn't know why the thought of possibly seeing Mary again caused such a feeling of apprehension for her. She loved Mary. It just scared her to think that she could be face-to-face with someone from her travels in her present time.

"Are you going to go into the classroom, Miss White, or do you plan to take in the lecture from the hallway?" Grae's finance professor, Mister Bybee, always had a sarcastic comment for her. It was one of the reasons she liked him. She was sorry that their time together would soon be ending as she transferred to another curriculum.

"I think I will go on inside," Grae said with a smile.

"Wunderbar." It was one of his favorite words. It was a German expression used in English, meaning 'wonderful.' Somehow, it made her feel that way.

SEVEN

"Mister Abbey called while you were in the shower. He is desperately in need of coffee."

Grae was surprised to hear this out of her mother's mouth on Friday morning, even before a greeting.

"Good morning, Mom."

"Good morning, Grae. He sounded desperate."

"You mean things aren't wonderful and marvelous on the mountain this morning?"

"I don't believe they are. I think he felt bad to call. The first thing he asked was how you were doing. When I told him that all was good, but you couldn't drive until Monday, he asked if you could work if he came to get you." Kat chuckled as she handed Grae a plate of food. "Sounds like business is booming. He said that he had all sorts of mail orders for coffee and people coming in every day to make purchases. He said they have tried to duplicate your brews, but no one does it like you.”

“Ah, sounds like job security to me.” Grandpa Mack peaked out from his newspaper and held his cup out in Grae’s direction. She filled it up with coffee, and then filled her own. She was anxious to sit down and dive into the plate of food.

“Mom, this smells awesome. What’s in it?” Grae could tell from the outside that it was one of her mother’s famous omelets, but it was always a mystery about what might be inside. Kat was creative.

“I call it ‘That’s Italian.’ I think you will love it. Perry ate two.”

Grae slid her fork into the fluffy creation and immediately smelled the aromas of an Italian restaurant. She could see Roma tomatoes, onions, mushrooms, and Ricotta and mozzarella cheeses. As she took her first bite, she tasted fresh basil and oregano and a hint of parmesan. Her ever-ingenious mother had served it with garlic toast.

“Oh, Mom, it’s delicious.”

“Thank you, dear. Make sure you go back upstairs to brush your teeth and gargle before we go. Perhaps, I should make this as a weekend breakfast in the future, but I felt like it was a good way to start this Friday morning.” Kat loaded the accumulated dishes into the dishwasher, leaving the rest for Grae to load. “I’m going to finish my hair. We need to leave in about fifteen minutes. Don’t forget to call Mister Abbey.”

“Mmm, hmmm.” Grae answered between bites.

“You better be getting back up that mountain, Belle girl. It’s about to be Christmas and your boss needs to make that cash register jingle as much as possible.” Grandpa Mack drank the last of his coffee and set the mug down in the sink. He gave Grae a kiss on the top of her head and headed toward the back door.

She finished her food in a couple of bites and loaded up the rest of the dishes. As she pushed the button to start the dishwasher, she looked out the kitchen window. Her grandfather was walking on the well-trodden path to the barn. And there, a black cat with white paws walked by his side.

"Grae! Hurry up!"

The sound of her mother's voice broke Grae's gaze. She left the kitchen and ran up the steps. After a quick, but thorough, brushing of her teeth and gargling, she got her stuff from her room, and flew back down the steps. Her mother was already in the Jeep waiting.

"Hello, Mister Abbey, this is Grae." Grae began her conversation as she got into the Jeep. "...Yes, thank you...Yes, Friday, that's right...No classes on Friday...I am riding into town with Mom right now...okay. If you could park in front of Smyth Hall, I will be in the library. I will watch for you from there...You're welcome...Thanks...Bye."

"Had you intended to go with me today? I assumed so when I heard you taking a shower." The Jeep was almost down the driveway by the time Grae finished her phone call.

"Yes, I want to put some more hours in at the library. But, I will be glad to work for Mr. Abbey, too. He's going to pick me up about ten, so that will give me two hours at the library."

"What has Alice had you doing with all this extra time this week?"

"Well, I have been getting her caught up on a lot of requests that people have sent in for information. It's amazing how many people from all over the country are researching their family history and it leads them to Wythe County." Kat slowed down and stopped behind a school bus that was loading. "Mom, can I ask you something about Alice?"

"Sure, but I don't know much about her life since we got out of school."

"Well, she told me a little about a boy that she was in love with in school." Kat's knuckles grew white as she gripped the steering wheel. She remained silent. "I just wondered if you remembered what happened. She must have been really in love with this guy. I guess he broke up with her."

"Is that what she said?" Kat's voice was monotone.

"No, actually, she didn't say what happened. She started to cry and stopped talking about it."

"How did you come to have this conversation with her?"

"We were talking about Professor Dreamy." Kat looked in Grae's direction. "I mean Professor Gibbs. She has been so happy since she started seeing him. Anyway, she said that she hadn't had any serious relationships since the one she had in high school. I couldn't resist; I had to ask her about it."

"Old hurts can be as hard to talk about as new ones."

"Yeah, I didn't mean to upset her. I just wanted to get to know her a little better."

"I'm sure she realized that. I wouldn't worry." Kat looked over her shoulder as she merged onto the interstate. "Did she say anything else about this boy from high school?"

"No, just that he was younger than her and was the brother of one of her friends. I thought you might have known them since you two were in school together."

"Yes, I remember her dating someone. It's been a long time ago."

"Well, the important thing is that she is happy now." As Grae said the words, she looked down at her cell phone. Her text message icon showed four messages waiting, but none of them was from Gav.

When Jay rolled into the library after nine that morning, he found that Grae had finished putting the letters from all three boxes into the protective folders and was beginning to organize them by year.

"I thought we were going to keep them organized by the writer of the letter."

"Have you had your coffee yet? You are such a grump." Grae looked up from the piles in front of her. "Alice said she would like to have them organized by date, but we can also cross reference them in the electronic files by writer and receiver."

"Well, okay, then. No, I haven't had my coffee. Madison forgot to buy any yesterday."

"I know where you can buy some." Grae gave him a big smile. "That is…after I go into work later this morning and make some."

"I thought you weren't going back until next week." Jay headed to the break room. Grae decided to get herself a cup, too, and followed him.

"Mister Abbey called this morning and sounded desperate. Apparently, he is getting many orders online for coffee to be mailed, and they've had a lot of customers at Big

Walker, too. So, he is going to come by and pick me up in about an hour. He said that he had a meeting at three. I need to work longer than that in order to get a large amount of the beans going, so I guess Mom will have to pick me up after she gets off work."

"I could come get you, if you want. I've never been up there."

"Really? Well, you should do that. It is a totally cool store and the views are gorgeous. Didn't you tell me at some point that you like to hike?"

"I used to spend about every weekend of my life hiking. But, that was before I was bitten by the time travel bug." Jay rolled his eyes and drank more coffee. They returned to looking at the letters. "Okay, since you have put them in order by date. I guess you are going to make me read them that way?"

"It would seem to be the logical thing." Grae picked up a stack. "There are just a few in the 1861 pile. I suppose that it was not as eventful as later years." Grae began looking at the 1862 stack. "Here's one about a battle in Tennessee. It is from Davy to his mother." Grae began to read.

Captain D.P. Graham
Co. B, 51ˢᵗ Regiment, C.S.A.
Camp near Abingdon, Va.

Mrs. David Graham
Cedar Run Farm
Max Meadows, Va.

March 12, 1862

Dear Ma,

It is my fervent hope this letter finds you, Pa, and my sisters well. I confess myself to be both weakened by the horrors of war and strengthened by the knowledge of your safety and well-being. I take great comfort knowing my family is thus sheltered from the pain and suffering I have witnessed, for it is indelibly etched forever into my memory.

First, allow me to put your mind at ease. Although I am indeed exhausted from battle, travel, and relentless foul weather, I am well. Second, I announce with great joy my upcoming furlough home. I shall see you soon. What a blessed sight you will all be for these weary eyes.

As you may know, Floyd's Brigade received orders to abandon winter quarters just after our Grand Review in December. We were to proceed full force to aid General Albert S. Johnston in Bowling Green, Kentucky, which is perhaps several hundred miles north of Nashville, Tenn. After bidding a hasty farewell to our half-finished winter huts, we marched off to Dublin Depot. While my family celebrated the birth of our Lord, my men and I were transported across western lands that I have never seen before. We traveled from Dublin to Bristol then Knoxville to Chattanooga. From Chattanooga we went to Nashville and then on to Bowling Green, arriving there on January 2nd. We then moved on to camp at Russellville, all the while snow and rain serving as our unwelcome and constant companions.

On February 6, the Federal Navy attacked and quickly defeated our newly constructed garrison at Ft. Henry, strategically built on the east Tennessee River so as to guard the supply routes into eastern Tennessee and to prevent Union gunship passage. We in Floyd's Brigade were immediately sent by steamboats to Clarksburg and finally Ft. Donelson, the latter located on the Cumberland River and less than 20 miles directly east of Ft. Henry.

Ma, I thank God every day for your steadfast commitment to my Geography lessons so long ago; truly, for this knowledge of terrain has been an advantage to me time and time again. As I thought about the Union's western Tennessee advance by water and land, I came to some conclusions. First, if Ft. Donelson were to fall into Union hands, Kentucky would remain a Union state, the Tennessee River would become a Federal

river, and eastern Tennessee and Nashville would
be unprotected from the advancing Yankees. As
you are well aware, the waters of the Tennessee
River flow from the Ohio and extend well into
Alabama; a fearsome consideration for the
Confederacy. Second, to further add to my worry,
our superiors told us that we would grow from
7,000 to 17,000 strong at Ft. Donelson, yet there is
little optimism that our force either exceeded the
Federals in numbers or artillery. In fact, our
Generals quietly stated that it is a foregone
conclusion that we will not be able to hold the
fort. So, we fight to be defeated and choose the
most favorable escape? And so I ask myself, THAT
IS OUR STRATEGY?

General Floyd was chosen as commander of Ft.
Donelson upon our arrival, with General Pillow
second in command and General Buckner third
in command. Col. Wharton was promoted to
commander of the First Brigade under General
Pillow while Lt. Col. Massie became commander of
the 51st Va. And, yes Ma, this is the same Mr. Massie
who was my arithmetic instructor at V.M.I.

Do forgive me, Ma, but I have need to tell you
about the events of the day for they make no sense
to me. For four days my men worked day and
night in the chilling rain, sleet, and snow to
finish the breastworks and rifle pits. With snipers
and gunboats frequently firing upon us, we slept
in our trenches without benefit of fires. Our

Brigade served under General Pillow and beside General Nathan Bedford Forrest's cavalry. On Feb. 15, we rose before dawn and were the first to fire. We took the Yankees at such a surprise their coffee was still warm in their cups. We attacked the Federal line along the right flank and swiftly took the field. We moved our force some two miles behind enemy lines and successfully took the main road, thus opening up a potential escape route if the need presented itself. It was then, as if struck by lightning, that all logic and reasoning were burned beyond recognition, and confusion and poor decisions reigned supreme.

We may never know the truth but I know what I know. At noon General Pillow issued his order to General Forrest and Col. Wharton to withdraw the cavalry and First Brigade back to our original lines. Lt. Col. Massie, also present for the order, requested a confirmation from General Floyd, which he did not receive. And so, we followed orders, all the while knowing that since dawn, the 51st had at least 9 men killed and 40 wounded or missing. I actually overheard Gen. Forrest exclaim from his horse to Major Kelly, a Methodist minister, "Parson, for God's sake, pray! Nothing but God Almighty can save that fort!"

Once safely removed from the fighting, I could see the action from a hilltop. General Buckner covered the left flank with heavy casualties. I witnessed the 2nd Ky. firing their buck-and-ball flintlocks from the nearby battery, these guns are very deadly at close range but of no use far away. Indeed there was massive smoke and noise from the eight Union ironclads' artillery fire, but the boats shot high or plowed up a bit of earth, rarely inflicting any real damage. Our boys though, they sent those "invulnerable" Yankee gunboats back down river. Yes, our guns! Our men! Repulsed the Union Navy with seven, 32-pound guns, a 10 inch Columbaid, a 6.5 inch rifle, and shear will that day.

The smoke from the ironclads did hit its mark with our Generals, I'm afraid, for at the end of that valiantly-fought day, Generals Floyd, Pillow, and Buckner decided the fort would surrender to Buckner's former classmate, General Ulysses S. Grant. To add to my profound disbelief, General Floyd and General Pillow RESIGNED from the Cause so that they and their men could escape capture. Yes, Ma, I should have become a prisoner of war on September 16th along with some 12,000 other Confederate soldiers at Ft. Donelson.

Just before daybreak on the 16th, the 51st was the first to board the GENERAL ANDERSON steamship with the 20th Mississippi Regiment guarding us. Ma, I could not look upon those men as I walked past. I could not.

Our Brigade went on to Nashville and successfully defended the supply stores there, enjoying its own bag of black gold. Real coffee!! On Feb. 22 we arrived at Murfreesboro by rail and then traveled on to Chattanooga to assist with the defenses there. It was our own Swedish engineer, Lt. Forsberg, who showed us how to destroy the many bridges there, thus slowing down the Federal advance towards Nashville. This trip back to Virginia was a final one for Brigadier General Floyd, as President Davis chose to relieve him of his command, blaming Floyd for the great loss of Ft. Donelson.

My men and I arrived in Abingdon only a few days past, our hearts heavy and our bodies either ill or consumed with fatigue. Presently I suffer from mild Dropsy and Biliousness, but they are nothing compared to the hospitalized sick and dying at Emory and Henry College. Oh, it will be Heaven to return home, Ma.

I end with a rather odd observation. It seems I have acquired an unwelcome companion from Ft. Donelson, a ghost of the living. The phantom appears as the vague image and loud voice of the brash Union general, Ulysses S. Grant. Yes, he is the brilliant general who so expertly excised the Confederate army from its western Tennessee strong-holds. I cannot seem to shake his demonic intensity, Ma, nor forget his calm ruthlessness as he responded to General Buckner's request to negotiate the Ft. Donelson terms of surrender...

"No terms except unconditional and immediate surrender can be accepted."

I am a soldier, Ma. I follow orders. And yet, you and Pa have taught me all my life to think for myself and to use what God has given me. I fear that the failings of Ft. Donelson may be but a harbinger of events yet to come. I pray to God that I am wrong and the Confederacy will rise victorious and we may return to our homes, our families, and our lives once more. We must all pray for the Salvation that surely awaits us all.

Your loving son,

Davy

"What in the world is dropsy and biliousness?" Grae made a face at the sound of the words.

"I know that they were common ailments of the soldiers at that time. Let me do a search and find out." Jay clicked away on his keyboard as Grae returned the letter to its folder. "Biliousness is defined as including nausea, abdominal pains, headache, and constipation. Dropsy was a swelling caused by accumulation of abnormally large amounts of fluid caused by kidney disease or congestive heart failure."

"That sounds rather serious. Perhaps that is one of the reasons for his furlough."

"I'm thinking that Bettie's journal mentioned her brother coming home on furlough." Jay started going through his own collection of papers and found the copy of Bettie's journal.

"I bet that Squire tried to convince him to leave the army and come home to Cedar Run. He would be more concerned about insuring that he had a male heir and growing the iron business than the cause of the war." Grae continued to skim over the letters in the stack. "All of this curly writing is making my eyes hurt."

"That curly writing, as you call it, is becoming a dying art. By the time we have children they probably will hardly ever sign their names on anything. It will all be digital."

"How many children did you plan on us having?" Grae's tone was sarcastic, but Jay's face still turned red.

"I…oh, I didn't mean you and me. I was just…I meant that when we were older and had our own families."

Grae started laughing. "You are such an easy target. I knew what you meant." Grae returned to the letters. "Have you seen any that were from Squire?"

"No, I haven't yet. Do you think he was much of a letter writer?"

"Well, most gentlemen of the time were. But, I am almost positive that he is the man I saw writing a letter. I don't think these are visions that I have as much as they are snippets from time travel." Jay furrowed his brow as he thought about what Grae said.

"Do you ever remember seeing him writing a letter?"

"No, but…well, I don't know. I guess I wonder if maybe I could be having little blips back in time or something. I still wonder what powers might have transferred into me when I tangled with Eve before she died. Taking that broach off her, I can't describe it. I felt something happen. These spells have intensified since then." Grae paused to gather her thoughts. "I've not told the doctors this because I can't really explain it without telling them about time travel. And I certainly do not want to tell Mom. But, it kind of feels like an electric current is passing through me without pain. You know, like you accidentally shock yourself a little and you feel a small jolt. It's like that, but it doesn't hurt. It's just uncomfortable or unnerving."

"If it is any consolation, if it is caused by time travel, there probably isn't anything that any doctor could do to help you, anyway. I'm going to go back over my research from the time travel journals and do a search on medical conditions. I recorded a lot of data about physical things that happened to travelers after they returned, but I didn't retain too much of it. Honestly, I was more concerned about the psychological effects. At the time, I was scared that I was losing my mind." Jay looked away from Grae.

"Wow, I didn't realize that."

"I guess I didn't want to scare you too much when we first met. I was so glad to find you, finally. There may be thousands of living time travelers around the world, but trying to find one is impossible. There's no group on Facebook." Jay laughed softly. "They don't hold conventions or support groups. Hi, my name is Jay and I travel through time. It can be very lonely and very frightening. Even though your mother doesn't approve of your travels, at least you were able to talk to her about it. You had a family history of people who lived through it. That is more important than you realize."

"I never thought about it that way. I guess you are right."

"Even while I was still back in time, I seemed to grasp that if I ever got to return to the present, I would have trouble coping. That's why I practically interrogated Patrick about you. I don't think he knew exactly from what time you were from, but he realized that it was quite a ways in the future. It gave me hope."

"I am certainly glad it did. I am glad we have each other."

"Ah, Grae, I don't want to alarm you, but I think that Santa is waving at you."

Grae turned and looked through the glass that separated the genealogy section from the regular library. Standing there looking in was Mister Abbey with a big coat on and a big smile. His white beard and hair certainly did make him look like Old Saint Nick.

"Oh, gosh, I forgot about the time. I've got to go." Grae waved back and hurriedly began to gather her stuff. "So, you will pick me up this evening?"

Jay smiled and waved at the man as well. "Certainly, I can't wait to drive to the North Pole and pick up one of Santa's elves."

Grae shook her head. "Do you know how to get there?"

"Oh, I'm sure that someone can give me directions. It's been there for a long time, right?"

"Yep, over sixty-five years, and if Big Walker Brews keep going strong, it will certainly be longer. Okay, I will text you later, but you should plan to come up by five or so. You want to have time to look around before we close."

Grae was delighted to return to the top of Big Walker Mountain. She got out of Mister Abbey's car and breathed in the clear, crisp air.

"Hello Seven Sisters! I've missed you!" Grae ran to the overlook and gazed out on the horizon. Snow covered the tops of seven smaller mountains that could be seen in the panoramic view. They were called the Seven Sisters.

Mister Abbey was unusually quiet on the drive up the mountain. They had only exchanged a few questions and answers. Grae thought she saw a look of concern on his face.

"Mister Abbey, is everything okay?"

"No, it's not, Grae. I've been very concerned about your health, and I'm afraid that I may have let my business side rush you back to work." He shook his head as he opened the front door of the store for her. As they walked in, Grae could smell the delicious aroma of some of Mary Lee's baking. It smelled like cinnamon rolls.

"Oh, Mister Abbey, don't feel that way. I am fine. Actually, I have missed work and feel very bad that I have let you down during such a busy time of year." Grae took off her coat and hung it up in the back room.

"Good gracious, Grae! You are single-handedly responsible for a huge amount of new business. Not only are we getting all these online orders from individuals and stores, but also there have been new customers coming in who have never even been here before. All because they heard about your wonderful and marvelous coffee!"

"Well, it sounds like I better get to work then…right after I have a cinnamon roll."

"They are pecan, sweetheart." Mary Lee appeared from the kitchen with a large tray of pecan rolls. "But they do have cinnamon in them. We had to have nuts today. It's a nutty day." Grae smiled. Mary Lee had a quirky sense of humor.

Grae dove into the work of roasting beans. It wasn't a fast process, but some of the new machinery that Mister Abbey recently purchased did make it easier to do large quantities. Grae looked at the list of orders that were waiting. She then inventoried the small quantity of bags that were left. They were mostly a few of the fall flavors, such as Candy Corn, and the general year-round flavors that she created. She was going to need to make twenty small bags of each of the six holiday flavors and about thirty bags of three of the general ones. This would fill the online orders and maybe enough to sell in the store until the following weekend.

"Hey, Grae, great to see you!" Mark, her co-worker, usually arrived at the store by mid-day. "I've been worried about you."

"Oh, Mark, I appreciate it. Thanks for all your help on the day that I was ill."

"Well, did they find out what was wrong with you? I heard that you went to see a doctor at UVA." Mark began scanning in some of the new products that Mister Abbey was unpacking.

"I'm not sure that they really gave us an exact diagnosis. At least, not one that seemed to make sense to my Mom and me. But, they did rule out many serious conditions, like a stroke or tumor. We are just going to see how it goes. I feel great and am glad to be back to work."

"Well, you've got a lot of job security on that clipboard there." Mark delivered most of his comments in a monotone voice, but it still got a loud chuckle out of Mister Abbey.

"She's really brewing up some business." Mister Abbey laughed at his own joke. Mark and Grae shook their heads.

The day flew by. Grae didn't realize that it was after five o'clock until she heard Mark talking in the front of the store to someone who sounded familiar.

"Is it too late for me to climb the tower?"

Grae laughed as she came around the corner and saw Jay dressed like he was going hiking in Iceland.

"Well, it's starting to get dark."

"I've got a flashlight."

Grae and Mark began to laugh. The sound made Jay turn in Grae's direction. "Did you bring your Eskimo dogs, too?"

Jay literally had ski garb, and then some, covering every inch of his body. She glanced at the indoor/outdoor digital thermometer that hung near the door. It read thirty-seven degrees outside.

"Hello, I want to climb the tower."

"Is that why you are dressed that way?" Grae shook her head. "You do realize that there isn't a ski slope on top?"

"You are so funny. I don't know how I managed to function all day without your wit. The air at the top of the tower is probably colder than it is here on the ground."

"That would be correct." Grae just laughed and put a big yellow sticker on his parka. It was his ticket to go up the tall tower. Jay just stood there. "Do you want me to go with you?"

"Well, I thought there might be a tour or something?"

Grae walked to the back to retrieve her coat.

"Grae, do you think that is a good idea?" Mark gave her a very concerned look. "I mean with all that has happened to you. I will go up with him." He started to go get his coat.

"No, I will be fine. I've been up the tower tons of times. Heights don't bother me." Grae smiled at him as she followed Jay outside.

"Wow! That's a lot of steps." Jay looked straight up as they began to climb.

"Two hundred to be exact, from base to top. Here's a good thing to remember. Don't look down until you get to the top."

Jay nodded and began climbing. They were both silent as they made the rising journey.

"Wow. I mean, wow!" Jay exclaimed as he reached the top and took in the view. Grae was a few steps behind him. "This is incredible. It's like you can see forever. Like being at the top of the Empire State Building and seeing something green on the horizon." Jay laughed at his joke and turned to look at Grae. She was standing to his left, gazing down. "It looks like there is a storm coming. If I have my bearings correct, I think it is coming from Bland County. We might should get back down and get on the road. Can you see it?" Grae did not respond. Jay moved closer to her and grabbed hold of her arm. Her head stayed down. "Grae, are you okay?" Jay physically turned her around. Her eyes were bugged out like she had just seen something horrible. "Say something." He shook her again.

"I've got to go back. Someone is down in the well. They are dying."

Jay put his hands on Grae's face and made her look into his eyes. "What are you saying? Who's in the well?" Her face began to relax. Her eyes began to return to normal. It was as if the trance she was in was broken.

"I looked down…and it was like it was a big hole there. I could see water in it. There's a man at the bottom. He's been injured. He's dying. No one will help him."

"Where, Grae?" Jay looked over the railing to where Grae was looking down.

"Not here, at the Mansion. That old well that is on the side of the house with the stones in a circle. It is a holding pond for fresh fish."

"It's filled up now, isn't it?" Jay took hold of Grae's shoulders. She appeared to be swaying.

"What I saw isn't from the present, it was the past. I saw soldiers there. Maybe he was a soldier." Grae broke free of Jay's grasp and turned back to the railing. She looked back down below.

"I think it's time we got down from here. You are scaring me and I know that a storm is heading this way. We need to get down this tower and down this mountain."

Grae let Jay take hold of her hand and pull her down the steps. The wind was becoming fierce and had done so all of a sudden. As they reached the bottom, they found Mark waiting for them. He had Grae's things in his hand.

"We've got to get out of here. My father called and said there is a horrible storm heading this way. Three inches of snow fell in about ninety minutes in Bland. The wind is taking down tree limbs. I'm hoping my Jeep has got the power to get me home. You all need to get ahead of it, if you can."

Grae took her stuff from Mark, and he turned around and locked the front door. Jay was already in his vehicle starting the engine. After everyone was in their vehicles, they pulled out and went separate ways.

"Are you okay to drive in this?"

"Grae, I grew up in Massachusetts. Snow is commonplace from November to April. We will be fine." No sooner had the words left his mouth then they drove into what looked like a blizzard.

"Wow! I have never seen the weather change so fast." The road in front of them had spots of snow, but the wind was twisting and turning it. The pattern looked like snakes made of powder shimming through water. It was almost spellbinding.

Jay slowed the vehicle and slid it into four-wheel drive. The sun was setting. It would be a slow drive down the mountain. Jay didn't know the road or the turns of the byway. Visibility was low.

"Okay, there's a turn coming up. There are several in the row." Grae tried to imagine that she was herself driving so that her memory could help tell Jay where the curves were coming. The drive that should have taken fifteen minutes took twice as long, and then some. Grae heard her phone beeping. She had missed three calls from her mother and one from Mister Abbey.

"We're fine, Mom...Jay's a great driver...Are you still in town?...Okay, we will meet you there." Grae clicked off the phone. "She's waiting at the college." Grae began to dial Mister Abbey's number, but stopped. "Thank you."

"What? It's driving, Grae. In a storm like this, it could go either way." Jay chuckled, but his voice still sounded stressed.

"No, for up on the tower...I don't know what happened there. But, I'm not telling my Mom. It's visions or flashbacks or something. I don't know. It's not anything physically wrong. No doctor will be able to fix it. I just need to go back and find out what it all means." The bright red of a stoplight shined in front of them through the blowing snow. Grae watched as the stoplight swayed back and forth in the wind.

"You know, Grae. I'm getting a bad feeling about you going back in time, again. Maybe we should just stop all this research. Maybe we should just let the Graham family rest in peace.

"That snow storm was over as quick as it started." Grandpa Mack had almost finished reading the Saturday paper by the time Grae got downstairs. "I appreciate that Old Man Wind blew the snow right off the roads. Saves me from having to put the blade back on the truck."

Grae found her mother flipping eggs and stirring gravy. A large pan of biscuits was already waiting on the sideboard. She'd heard the shower running as she finished dressing and assumed that it was Perry getting ready for their trip to see their father.

"Looks like I can get my pick of breakfast for a change. Perry is still getting ready." Grae began building a plate of food.

"Are you feeling okay?" Kat looked at the large plate of food Grae made for herself.

"For some reason, I am extra hungry. Maybe it's the weather." Grae began taking a few bites of eggs as she put some strawberry jam on a hot biscuit. "I got a text from Shasta. She is on her way. She said you had invited her to eat with us."

"I thought that since we were getting a little later start because of last night's weather, we could all have a good breakfast together before we head out. Perhaps that will hold us until we can stop for dinner on the way home." A knock at

166

the back door interrupted the conversation. Grandpa got up and opened it.

"Morning, little girl, get yourself on in here." Shasta was dressed in layers with her jacket hood over her head. As she took her coat off, they could hear the crackle.

"I don't think anyone's going to want to hug you immediately." Grae smiled as her friend walked toward her.

"Yeah, that was a pretty loud crackle. It's this crazy hair of mine. It goes everywhere."

"Good morning, Shasta. I hope you are hungry."

"Good morning and I am. I don't often see a breakfast like this unless I try to make one." Shasta sat down next to Grae.

"Well, hurry up and fill your plate. Perry will be downstairs any minute, and then all bets are off." Grae grinned as her mother handed Shasta a plate with scrambled eggs on it.

"I heard that." Perry appeared at the doorway into the kitchen. "You act like I can't be trusted around food." Perry walked around the table toward his mother at the stove. As he walked behind Grae, he grabbed a piece of bacon off her plate.

"See! I rest my case."

"Alright, you two. Sit down and eat. We've got to get on the road soon."

The drive to the prison was rather uneventful. Traffic had been moderate. Shasta had driven the first two hours, and then Kat took over. After going through all the checkpoints, they left Shasta in a waiting area. She had brought some of her homework, anticipating that the visit would take a couple of hours.

Tom White was in the hospital portion of the prison. Security was just as tight, but it still looked and felt like a medical center. Kat had arranged the visit in advance, so she expected to be able to talk to the doctor who was handling Tom's care. She didn't expect to also find Tom's lawyer there, as well.

Dannon Lange was the top defense attorney in North Carolina. He'd spent the first ten years of his career in Los Angeles as a gopher for some of the attorneys to the stars. He learned all the tricks and angles, and then a tragedy brought him back to his home state. His only brother, four years his junior, developed a rare form of cancer. He left a bright future in Hollywood to help his brother and family. That was a decade earlier, when the Tar Heel state called him home, and he decided to stay. He built a reputation as a ruthless attorney who won million dollar cases and set the innocent and guilty free. That was until the case of Tom White came along. It was the only blemish on his record of victory.

Grae did not remember hearing much about the lawyer. So, she assumed that his contact with her mother had been minimal. Kat's body language told Grae that her mother was surprised to find him standing before her in the waiting area.

"Good morning, Kat." The weekend meant little to change his attire. Every time Grae had seen him on television, he was always attired in bespoke woven suits made from exclusive Savile Row fabrics. These were the same type of suits that David Letterman wore each night on television. Kat had made the comparison one night while she and Grae were watching their nighttime favorite. A Google search had confirmed their suspicions. Dannon Lange liked to dress to impress. The suit of the day was charcoal in color with tiny pinstripes. He was handsome in all of the traditional ways.

"Mister Lange. What are you doing here?" Kat's use of his formal name in contrast to his personal greeting meant volumes for the tone she was setting.

"Tom told me that you and your children would be coming to visit today. I need to talk to you."

"We came so that the children could have a holiday visit with their father, and I could consult with his doctor regarding his care. I don't think that it is the appropriate time to be discussing any suit you may be considering. I am not involved in that."

Grae couldn't help but smile to herself as she heard the word 'suit' used by her mother. No doubt, Kat was recalling their conversation about the attorney's fashion sense.

"I understand that, but I really think you are going to want to hear what I have to tell you. It will affect your entire family. We need to talk before you see Tom's doctor. I've arranged for an office where we can speak in private." Kat glared at Dannon.

"Very well. Kids, you sit tight here until I'm finished with Mister Lange. I will not be long."

Grae and Perry saw a look that was usually reserved for serious punishment cross their mother's face. They nodded and sat as Kat followed Dannon down a hallway.

"I wonder what that's all about." Perry reached for his phone before he realized that he hadn't brought it inside. Cell phones weren't allowed in federal prisons.

"Whatever it is, Mom doesn't look happy. Why in the world wouldn't this lawyer guy call Mom and make an appointment?" Grae got up and started pacing. Apparently, her movement made the security guard nervous. He gave her a look that made her want to sit back down.

"Maybe he wanted to tell her whatever it is face-to-face." Perry scooted over on the couch, so Grae could sit beside him. Only a few more minutes passed before Kat and Dannon returned to the waiting area. Kat could not hide the look of shock on her face.

"I'll be in touch soon." Dannon nodded to the rest of them. "I hope you have a pleasant visit with Tom." Dannon left and all eyes went to Kat.

"Let's go see your father." Kat put on a smile.

"Mom, what did he want?" Grae took a hold of her mother's arm.

Kat turned around. "We will talk about it later, at home." The sound of Kat's voice was understanding, yet firm.

Grae and Perry followed their mother to another locked door. She wondered how many locked doors they had to go through to get to their father. Kat spoke to the person behind the glass, another guard. He told their mother that Doctor Happel wanted to speak to her before she left.

"You're very popular today, Mom." Perry's attempt at humor got a stern look from Kat.

After each of them had been searched again, the guard then searched the bag that Kat had brought for Tom. They had each only brought identification in with them; no money or other valuables. The keys to the Jeep were left with Shasta.

"The bottom box is food I brought for my...for Tom." Kat's slip had not escaped the ears of her children. "The top bag is for you and your staff." Kat gave the guard a weak smile.

"For us, ma'am?" The guard looked confused.

"I make prize-winning brownies. Tom says that you are very kind to him. Being kind to a very sick prisoner is not in your job description, I'm sure. But, his children and I appreciate it."

Grae and Perry exchanged glances. There was something, almost forgiving, in Kat's tone.

"Well, thank you, the guys and I will enjoy them with a good cup of coffee."

"Oh, that bag of coffee is for you, too. My daughter roasts those beans herself. It's like a little business of hers." A look of pride passed over Kat's face. It filled Grae's heart. Her emotions would be hard to keep in check once she saw her father.

"Again, we thank you. Now, this is going to be a little different environment than when you last came to see Tom. You may not remember, but I was one of his guards at the other hospital. All of the doors to the rooms are locked, from the outside. So once you go in, a guard will be with you, and you will be locked in the room. You will be allowed two hours. The doctor will probably come during the latter part of that time."

"Okay, we understand." She looked at Grae and Perry. They nodded.

The guard handed the bag back to Kat, and then he led them through two more sets of locked doors. These were even more serious locks than the previous. The loud noise as they opened and closed, the clicking sound, it all reminded Grae of something, but she couldn't imagine what it was.

The elevator they entered would not move without the guard turning a key. As the elevator began to travel upward, Grae became very nervous. It was a strange feeling.

She had looked forward to seeing her father, but, now that they were there, she was apprehensive. The doors opened and they stepped onto the third floor. In most respects, it looked very much like a regular hospital. There were nurses and doctors moving around, and technicians taking equipment up and down the four hallways that were viewable from the center nurses station. What did seem out of place were the many armed guards that could be seen. The guard who accompanied them motioned to another one, who was talking to a nurse.

"This is Tom White's family." The guard nodded and asked to see each of the visitor badges that were issued to them. "Ma'am, this is Officer Wallace. He will be staying with you for the duration of your visit and will return with you when it is over."

As their original guard turned to leave, Kat stopped him. "Excuse me, what is your name?"

"Oh, I'm sorry, ma'am. I failed to introduce myself. I am Officer Trey Edwards. I hope you have a pleasant visit with Tom."

"Thank you, Officer Edwards."

Kat turned and followed Officer Wallace down the hallway. Grae and Perry followed. Halfway down the hall on the right, they stopped in front of a door and waited as the guard unlocked it.

"Dad's in the Pi room." Perry's voice had a little chuckle to it.

Kat turned around and looked at him strangely. "What?"

"He's in Room 314. You know, Pi."

Kat still gave him a strange look.

"It's the ratio of a circle's circumference to its diameter, ma'am." Officer Wallace spoke up, smiling slightly. "It's a mathematical term."

"Oh, yes. Funny, Perry." Kat walked through the open door.

The room was larger than Grae expected, but as she looked around, she realized that it was probably made to hold more than one patient. A curtain was pulled between the two sides of the room. Kat walked ahead and stopped suddenly in front of Tom's bed.

"You're here."

Grae and Perry heard their father's voice before they saw him. It sounded different. It sounded...

"Hey, Dad!" Perry walked past Grae and into Tom's view.

"Hey, there yourself, son. Let's see those shiners."

Grae came up behind Perry and saw that her father looked incredibly different. He almost looked like a new man.

"Dad! You look great!" Perry looked at his mother and Grae.

"Ah, Tom, you look so much better. I didn't know...the treatments are working?"

Tom gave everyone a big smile. Perry was leaning down to hug him on one side of the bed. Grae walked around to the other side, but Tom's left hand was handcuffed to the bed.

"Guess I am well enough to be considered an escape threat." Tom gave them a half smile.

As he took turns hugging his children, Kat watched. Grae turned toward her mother and saw a faraway look in her eyes, which were filled with tears. Kat bent down and away from Grae on the pretense of reaching for the bag of goodies, she had brought, but Grae saw that her mother was wiping her tears away. Something had changed in the room.

"We brought you some treats, Tom." Kat regained her composure and took the box of baked goods over to his bed. Tom's eyes grew wide as Kat opened the lid. A smile crept over his face.

"Oh, I never expected to taste your delicious sweets again." Tom broke his stare on his ex-wife and looked into the box. "Grae, can you get me one of those hand cleaner things over there?"

Grae looked at the nightstand next to her father's bed and saw a container of hand wipes. She opened the container so that her father could take one out. He leaned over and used both hands to clean them with the cloth. After dropping the cloth onto the bed, he took the napkin that Kat handed him and chose a treat from the box.

"Is this what I think it is?"

"Orange gingerbread." Kat closed the box and set it down on the edge of the bed next to the railing. Tom slowly bit into the cake.

"Oh…oh…it is wonderful. I haven't been able to taste anything for months and the food here is well, what you would expect, not award-winning like yours."

Tom smiled as he took another bite. Grae filled up a cup of water from the pitcher on the nightstand and tried to hand it to her father. He couldn't take it from her though because of his left hand being restrained, so Grae held it as she put the straw in his mouth for him to take a drink.

"Thank you, dear. Oh, I feel like I've died and gone to heaven."

"Tom, those are strange words from someone who is battling cancer." Kat gave him a disapproving look.

"Battling cancer and maybe winning."

Perry and Grae looked at their mother after their father's statement.

"I'm anxious to meet this Doctor Happel and find out about the status of your treatment. What happened to your previous doctor?" Kat sat down in a chair next to the window. There were bars on it giving the light a blocked entrance look into the room.

"He was at the other hospital. He still consults with Doctor Happel." Tom pointed to the box. "Can I have another?" Perry picked up the box and opened it as his father peered inside. "Mint chocolate brownies?" Kat nodded a reply.

"So, Dad, how long have you been feeling better?" Grae sat down in a chair that was next to the bed.

"Well, they stopped the chemotherapy about a month ago. Actually, it was probably close to the last time you all visited. Then, they started this new stuff, this experimental cocktail. It didn't make me sick. I could eat and keep the food down. They gave me intravenous vitamins of some sort, too. It is amazing. I just started feeling better." Tom took another large bite of the brownie. Grae watched as her father savored it, smiling as he swallowed. "I think the doctors are as surprised as anyone." Tom took the last bite and motioned for Grae to give him the cup of water. "Did Dannon meet you when you arrived?"

"Yes, he did. Quite frankly, Tom, I didn't appreciate the intrusion. He could have called me to discuss his news."

"He thought it would be better to deliver in person."

"You and I will not be discussing this today."

"What's going on, Mom? Why can't you tell us what Mister Lange said?" Grae looked back and forth between her parents.

"Grae, we are not going to discuss this now. Just drop it and visit with your father." Kat got up and walked toward the guard. "Can you please let me out so that I can find the doctor?"

"Ma'am, let me call the nurses station and see what his status is. Doctor Happel, correct?"

"Yes." Kat stood quietly next to the guard as he conversed with someone at the nurses' station.

"Okay, ma'am. They say that the doctor is nearby, so let me take you out there." He turned and spoke to Grae and Perry. "I will be locking you inside." Kat followed the guard out. A click was heard from the other side.

"Locks. It's the only constant in my life these days." Tom shook his head. "So what have you two been up to? Defending your girlfriend's honor, huh? What did her parents have to say about that?"

"They brought me a huge Italian dinner. It was awesome." Perry beamed.

"Now those sound like good people. You are dating their son, right?" Tom turned to Grae. The smile left her face. "Uh oh. Did I say something wrong?"

"Grae and Gav are sort of on a break, Dad."

"I'm sorry, honey. I didn't know. That's the worst thing about being in this old place, I don't know much about my kids anymore." The light left Tom's face. Grae could see the sickness return. His incarceration and illness had aged their father.

"It's okay, Dad. We are just seeing things differently right now."

"He's a good guy. He will be back." Perry gave his sister a big smile. "He asks about you all the time."

Grae gave him a look of surprise. "When do you talk to him?"

"Every few days or so. Sometimes it's about sports stuff. But, lately he's been asking me about you."

"Why didn't you tell me?" Grae suddenly felt very nervous and anxious. She hadn't expected to hear that Gav was actually checking up on her.

"Well, I figured that he didn't want you to know. I thought that it was a good sign that he was asking about you, and I didn't want that to change." Grae was amazed at how mature Perry had become.

"That's good, son. You did the right thing. Just like it was the right thing to take up for your girl. Now, I am not condoning fighting, but there are times that you need to take up for yourself, your family, or your friends. Violence is not the answer, but sometimes you don't get to ask the question."

The three of them continued to chat about a variety of things. Their father asked them about school and how the weather had been. He asked how their grandfather was and if he could still work circles around anyone. They were so caught up in their conversations that they didn't realize that Officer Wallace had re-entered the room until they heard a knock at the door. He let their mother back inside, closed the door, locking it. Grae thought that Kat looked strange.

"Have you had a good visit?" No one answered Kat. "Did you lose the ability of speech while I was gone?"

"We've had a fine visit, Kat. I appreciate you bringing them here. I appreciate everything."

Grae sensed that there was more behind the words than their face value.

"Well, I think our time is about up." Kat looked at the guard, who nodded. "We're going to leave the rest of these sweets with you. Perhaps you can con a nurse into helping you with them." Grae and Perry shook their heads. "Okay, that was a poor choice of words."

"No, it's alright. I deserved whatever Kat had to say. I should never have…I should never have let myself get into this mess." Tom paused and looked at all of them individually. "Thank you for coming." Grae and Perry hugged their father as Kat walked toward the door. "Kat, can we talk about what Dannon told you?"

"Not now, Tom, I can't talk about it now. I will be in touch."

Grae and Perry waved at their father as they headed to the door.

"Stay out of trouble, slugger." Tom gave his son a thumbs up. "Everything will be okay, sweetheart. Gav will be back." He blew Grae a kiss.

Kat walked straight ahead, not saying a word. Officer Wallace escorted them to the elevator and all the way down to the area where they had met Officer Edwards. He was waiting to escort them through to the less secure part of the locked institution. Shasta saw them coming and was ready to follow them out.

"Thank you, Trey." It was all Kat said before they walked away.

"We are not going to talk about it now." Less than thirty minutes had passed before Perry began asking his mother about her meetings with Dannon Lange and Doctor Happel. "We are going to stop at that barbecue place that you like and have a nice dinner and then we are going home."

No one said another word until they reached the restaurant. Kat parked the Jeep. Perry was in the front passenger seat. Grae was in the seat behind him with Shasta behind her mom. Kat turned to speak before they got out.

"Listen, I know that you are curious about what's going on with your father. I understand that, but both the doctor and attorney told me some serious things and I need to process them first before I talk to you about them."

"Missus White, would you like me to leave you all alone?" Shasta looked a little uncomfortable.

"No, Shasta, it's fine. I know that you are Grae's best friend and that she entrusts you with her secrets. I think you understand family trauma well enough to know to use your discretion with what you hear from us."

Grae thought about what her mother said. She didn't share everything with Shasta.

Kat turned back to her children. "I will tell you this much so that you do not worry. Your father is responding to the treatment in a positive way. He may just make it through this."

Perry looked back at Grae. His eyes were filled with tears. Grae's emotion came out in a sob.

"Shasta, why don't you and I go on in and get a table and give these two a few moments to themselves?" Kat smiled at her children as she and Shasta got out of the vehicle.

"I wonder what will happen now." Perry verbalized what Grae was thinking. It was obvious that something was about to change.

EIGHT

"So, your father is better. That's amazing. From the way you described his condition, I would have thought that he wouldn't be getting better." Grae and Jay were back in the library the following Monday.

"We really didn't expect this. No one told us how the treatments were going. Whatever this experimental stuff is, it has worked a miracle."

Grae smiled as she opened up the box of filed letters. They were all organized by date and protected from all the fingers that would later try to examine them. It made her feel good.

"Grae, I've been thinking about what happened on the tower. I really think that maybe we should stop this research into what happened to Martha." Jay's look of concern gave Grae a feeling of contentment.

"I appreciate your concern. I have a feeling that whether we do this research or not, I am going to have these visions. There's something that happened back there that I brought back with me. I think that the only way I am going to be rid of it is if I do find the truth. Sal told me that the truth would set me free."

"Who was Sal again?"

Jay put down the papers he was reviewing and gave Grae his full attention. It reminded Grae of the little boy down the street in Charlotte she used to babysit. When it was time to read a story, Martin was all ears. He would gaze at her as if she was about to reveal the most important story in the world. She wondered what that little boy was doing now.

"Sal is one of the wisest women I have met. She taught me things about life that I had never fully grasped before. She was strong, loyal, and devoutly courageous. She was the wife of Big Bob. He and his nephew were hung for the murder of Joseph Baker."

"So, Sal told you that you should seek the truth?"

"Actually, no. She told me that the truth would set me free. I think that she meant that no matter what any of us are enduring, it is the truth that really matters. Maybe there is not a perfect answer, but eventually, the truth of a matter is revealed and the knowledge of that is freedom."

"Deep, Grae. Have you always been this wise?"

"Nope, not hardly. I think I've gained a few years on these journeys, at least in some things." Grae looked down at the stack of papers.

"Maybe you will make wiser decisions in the future."

Grae wasn't for certain what Jay was referring to, but she imagined that he was talking about Gav.

"I think we need to continue with this research. We need to find out as much as we can about Martha and her condition and what was going on with her family during that time."

"But, Grae, your mother is right. It is very dangerous."

"I'm tired of hearing that. Lots of things in life are dangerous. But, you can't just live in fear. You know that I've got to go back. I've got to know what the truth is. I've got to know why I've been led back to the lives that occupied Graham Mansion."

"Okay, okay. Let's get back into these letters and see what we can find out. I've made some notes about some that I think we should especially take note of."

"When did you do that?"

"Well, Grae, you must remember, I don't have a life. Madison went to visit an old college friend over the weekend. I spent most of my weekend here."

"How did you get in here? This part of the library isn't open on the weekend."

"Alice is in a very good mood these days. She seems to have a newfound trust of those of us who are of the male persuasion." Jay winked. Grae remained silent. She wasn't buying it. "Okay, Alice was working some over the weekend on that budget stuff she told us about. She let me hang around. I was not allowed to eat doughnuts."

"That, I believe."

"Now, you remember the last letter I read talked about Davy coming home on furlough? Well, I found a later letter from Bettie that refers to her brother's visit and the things that occurred during that visit. You just have to read it. It is hilarious and sad all at the same time. Bettie must have been smitten with that Captain Forsberg, because she talks about the gift she made him. But the interactions between Squire and his son speak volumes to the dynamics between them. It almost makes you wonder if Davy didn't know some of his father's secrets."

Miss Bettie Ann Graham
Cedar Run Farm
Max Meadows, Va.

Captain D.P. Graham
Co. B, 51ˢᵗ Regiment, C.S.A.
Camp Narrows
Giles County, Va.

June 25, 1862

Dearest Brother,

Can it be that you have been gone from us but five weeks? I find that I can no longer trust the clock nor can I depend on the calendar. It seems like an eternity since you were here. Is it the same with you?

Our family remains as you left us. We are well with the beauty of the Virginia hills blooming all around us. Why just yesterday Bunt helped me pick a bushel basket of early sour green apples. We will soon make Ma's exquisite apple butter. Those who are not appreciative of our industrious labors will be summarily drawn and quartered.

Mary Bell, Nan, and I talk often of your delightful, three-month furlough with us. It is grand knowing the men who serve with you. You must tell Col. Wharton that I chuckle aloud as I retell his funny anecdote about Mr. Robinson. And Brother, please do not be angry with me for not obeying your direct order! Why, Captain Forsberg has told me that he likes the needle case that I made for him. Your Swedish friend has also told me that my piano playing is very fine and wishes to visit again soon. You may give him my regards.

Do not worry my Brother. I do know who I am and what I am doing. Although my name is Elizabeth, I am not Jane Austen's Elizabeth Bennett, kindly awaiting her Mr. Darcy in _Pride and Prejudice._ I will live my life and I fully expect you to do likewise. (When you return I will show you some writings from Susan B. Anthony. While I denounce her abolitionist views, her thoughts about women are quite persuasive and have merit.)

For the purposes of this letter, let us turn our attention to you, for I have a confession. Do you recall your last day here in May? Pa and you were talking in the barn, away from everyone, well, almost everyone. I was there, hidden in an empty stall, quite by coincidence. I heard it all. I must tell you that I am so very proud of you Brother! Pa demanded that you honorably resign and return home to make iron for the Cause. He pressed you. He threatened you. And yet you were steadfast in your beliefs, unyielding to his relentless frontal assault, all the while reminding him of your love and devotion to him and Ma. Tears run down my face as I relive those moments now. Perhaps Thomas Paine did have it right when he said, "These are the times that try men's souls." And women's, I might add

It was not my intent to intrude or be disrespectful. I love and respect you and Pa beyond words. I am also certain of your love for one another and our family. But, I must say this to you and only you. Our father is consumed with power and profit, whether they come from this War or from a marriage to a woman he does not love.

Truth is sometimes our most difficult adversary. I do not assume to know the answers but I am blessed to have you to speak so openly about such things. There are times when I hear Ma's voice coming from my lips, and, in this case, from my hand. This is one of those times.

I have two requests of you. First, you must promise me to burn this letter after you read it. Share it with no one.

Second, you must one day soon tell me what you meant when you said this to Pa, there in the barn.

You said simply, "I know", as you stared directly into his eyes. "I know."

In closing I wish to profess my supreme faith in your wisdom Brother. Trust in yourself! Trust in God! He will deliver you safe and whole from the madness that surrounds you. You honor our family and the Confederacy with your service. Listen to God. He will lead you.

RETURN TO ME as I am your most affectionate, verbose, and favorite sister,

Bettie

"Well, I guess we should be glad that he didn't listen to her and burn the letter!" Grae laughed as she returned it to the folder.

"So, are you ready to go meet Mary Baker?"

Jay's question made Grae do a double take as she prepared to leave to go to her last class.

"Are you serious?"

"Yes, I have called and asked if a friend and I can visit Missus Baker. Her companion said that could be arranged."

"And just what have you told them the reason for your visit would be?"

"I'm doing research on the Baker family. It's true."

"I...I don't know if I want to do this."

"You've got to be curious. I mean, it is a longshot, but this woman, at the least, could be a descendant of your

Mary Baker. You might learn something about what happened to her."

"I guess you are right. I hope so."

"When do you want to go?"

"Let me find out what my schedule is on the mountain. I've got a lot of catching up to do there. I'm headed there now. I'll tell you tomorrow."

Grae collapsed into bed that night. Going to class, working at the library, and working at Big Walker all made for a very long day. She didn't realize how quickly she had become accustomed to the slower life she experienced the previous few weeks. As she lay in bed reading one of her books for a test the next day, she saw two blue balls roll across the floor.

"Hi, Clara, I guess I have been neglecting you."

Grae got out of bed and rolled the balls back in the direction they came. She waited for them to roll back, but nothing happened. "I'm sorry, Clara. I will play with you." Grae waited a few minutes, but nothing happened. "Hey, where did you go?"

The hairs on the back of Grae's neck began to stand up. Her back was facing the window on the door side of the room. She could feel the presence of someone behind her. "Okay, Perry, are you scaring Clara?" There was no answer. Grae turned around. She did not see anyone. But as her gaze travelled up to the window, she saw why Clara had not responded. On the glass it looked like someone had breathed on the window, and then wrote the words – *Don't Come Back.* Grae turned round and round in the room. "Clara, don't be afraid. He's just a big, dead bully!" Grae wished she could see the little girl who was probably cowering in a corner. "David Graham! You don't scare me! I know your secrets, remember? I know who you are!"

"Yes, the words were right on the glass." Grae described to Jay what happened the night before. "You know how, as a kid, you would breathe on a window pane, and then write something? That's what it was like."

"Can dead people breathe?"

Grae rolled her eyes as she took off her coat. She had worked on the mountain until mid-day and came directly to the library afterward so she could talk to Jay before her late afternoon class.

"How am I supposed to know?" Grae sat down and opened up the salad she picked up on her way there. "Isn't anything going to go right today? There's no fork in the bag."

"Calm down. I'll go get you one from the break room."

While she was waiting for him to return, she took a deep breath and tried to relax.

"There you go." Jay laid a fork down beside her plate. "Now, what are you so tense about?"

"I'm sorry, I'm just stressed. Too much is going on in my life at one time with school, being sick, getting back to work, and catching up on all of those coffee orders. The store is a crazy place. Mister Abbey got an order today from a shop in Asheville that has started carrying our coffee. They want fifty bags by the week before Christmas. Then, there is all that is going on with my father. Squire David is messing with me. My life is such a mess right now."

"Well, you need to forget about all that and eat your salad. I will read a couple of letters to you to help get your mind off of things." Grae smiled as she began to devour her salad. "The date on this first one is smudged, but I think it was written sometime in mid-1862, after one of the battles that Davy Graham was in."

Capt. D.P. Graham
Co. B, 51st Va. Regiment, C.S.A.
Camp Narrows
Giles County, Va.

Squire and Mrs. David Graham
Cedar Run Farm
Max Meadows, Va.

July 17, 1862

Dear Ma and Pa,

It is my devout hope that this letter finds you and my dear sisters well. Although I left you but two months ago, it feels as if years have passed. Time, like so much of life here, cannot be measured by standard rules. There is no gauge sufficiently adequate to judge the depth, length, weight, or breadth of this war.

As you know, Col. Wharton reorganized the Brigade, including the 51st Va., just prior to our departure from Wytheville. General Lee removed General Floyd and replaced him with General Henry Heth, a stern figure of a man, wielding a forceful authority over this command, the likes of which have not been witnessed until now. I pray that this new leadership continues to serve our brave men admirably, for during my limited presence in this war, I have seen too many woeful, misguided chieftains lead us afoul.

Was it Napoleon who said, "Soldiers win battles but the generals take credit for them"? Permit me to explain further. On May 16ᵗʰ, our soldiers and General won the day when our regiment, consisting of 800 men was ordered to support Gen. Marshall in Princeton. Noting our serious circumstances, General Wharton wisely positioned our unit on the crest of Pigeon Roost Hill and placed Adj. Peter Otey in command of our smaller unit. We soon discovered that we were not only surrounded by Col. Blessing's eleven companies of Federals, but there was also a battalion of reinforcements sent from Gen. Cox in Charleston advancing on our rear. Adj. Otey and our men valiantly repulsed the enemy, losing only our medical wagon in the fray. The Federals released back to us our surgeon, J.M. Estill and his assistants, however, the enemy summarily drank the captured barrel of Confederate whiskey.

The spoils of war, or should I say spirits of war, soon tilted the balance in our favor, for the inebriated Federals were easily routed as the 51ˢᵗ stormed their dozing pickets. While we were vastly outnumbered, we were in no manner outmatched, for the Federals suffered almost 80 casualties at our hands that day. Indeed, within a few days, our command forced the Federals to evacuate Princeton. While the men celebrated this welcome victory, we did become quite sullen as we finally entered Princeton. You see, only 10 out of the 100 original homes escaped the devastating Federal torch, and it was the bleakness seen in the eyes of the homeless women and children that tore at our hearts.

As we welcome new conscripts to our depleted ranks, I confess that I am selfishly reassured that the ones whom I love are safe from these horrors. It is my full intention to preserve our way of life, dearest Ma and Pa, and to honor our heritage.

As I must close for now, please permit me to tell you of a most remarkable new conscript in the 51st. He is Private Andrew Ratliff and he is a full-blooded Cherokee Indian, adopted and raised by the Ratliff family near Draper. Private Ratliff often quotes this Cherokee proverb as we pray over our dead and wounded.

"A man's highest calling is to protect a woman - so she is free to walk the earth unharmed. Man's lowest calling is to ambush and force his way into the life of a woman."

We fight for our women and children, so that they may be free to walk the earth unharmed. I am proud to serve with this fine young man and hope that you might meet him one day.

Please give my love to Mary Bell as she will soon be 19. And do tell all of my dear sisters to remain hopeful for I will see them again soon.

Your loving son,

Davy

"Davy just seems to be the epitome of a Southern gentleman and such a stark contrast to his father." Grae picked up the next letter and began to read aloud.

Capt. D.P. Graham
Co. B, 51ˢᵗ Va. Regiment, C.S.A.
George W. Summers' farm
near Charleston, W.Va.

Miss Bettie Ann Graham
Cedar Run Farm
Max Meadows, Va.

September 20, 1862

Sister,

I write this letter quickly to you, hoping that it finds you and our family well. I fear that the war has had a noticeable effect upon my health such that I am more hindrance than help to my men now.

On September 10th, the 51st as part of the Third Brigade under Gen. Loring's command, marched through the mountains for thirteen miles towards Fayetteville. Immediately upon arrival, our men, exhausted, without water, and running low on ammunition repulsed the Federals for three hours, inflicting severe losses on the enemy. Capturing the town and its vast supplies was a monumental victory for our Brigade and a few days later, we forced the Federals to retreat from Cotton Hill and across the Gauley Bridge. Finally, as we marched along the New River in the heavy downpour towards Charleston, I realized that my health was becoming perilously fragile, and that I would soon require medical attention. In fact, Lt. Tate thought me deathly ill, insisting that I ride the rest of the way in the medical wagon.

So it is with a bleakness of heart that I must tell you of my intention to resign from active service very soon and assume the post of Commander at Yellow Sulphur Springs. PLEASE DO NOT SHARE ANY OF THIS MESSAGE WITH ANYONE! NOT EVEN MA AND PA, FOR NOW. I know that I can trust your discretion dearest sister.

Now, I must quickly convey to you this difficult message, in the event that I do not survive. It does help me to know that you are the stronger of the two of us. I confess to you now my fear, for it is my belief that I have inherited some of Ma's mental difficulties. You see, every night since our stint at

Harper's Ferry, I suffer from a recurring dream. In this dream I am being chased through endless, foggy open fields and dense forests by another Confederate soldier. He calls my name, but I do not stop because I am certain he will kill me! Last night, I dreamed that I had fallen during the chase and the soldier stood over my heaving, terrified body. It was then that I saw his face. It was my own, except he was a bit older than me and his skin was darker. For just a moment I stared into his eyes and I saw Pa's eyes. And then I awoke.

Destroy this letter Sister! I wish no one to know of my own craziness or this apparition. Help me dear Sister. What does it mean? What in Heaven's name does it mean? Please pray for God's divine guidance Sister, for only He can show us the way now. Amen.

Your loving brother,

Davy

"I knew it!" Grae exclaimed as she finished the letter. "I knew that Squire couldn't hide a secret as big as a son forever. Martha finding out about this was one thing. But, he shouldn't have expected to conceal a sibling from his later children. Oh, I hope we find some additional letters about this."

"That certainly got your adrenaline going. You'd think from your reaction that Robbie was your missing relative."

The week passed quickly for Grae. She worked as many hours as she could spare trying to fill the growing number of coffee orders. Mister Abbey was pleased with the popularity, but he also seemed to have a look of worry when Grae would arrive thirty minutes early or stay an hour later. She knew that he was concerned for her health.

She was also consumed with two end-of-semester research projects that were due as well as the exams, which were coming up the following week. Perry had brought up the subject of their father a couple of times to her, but Grae advised him to remain quiet about it in their mother's presence. She knew that their mother would tell them when she was ready, and not before.

Grae walked through the back door of the Mansion on Friday night. She found her mother and Perry sitting at the kitchen table drinking coffee.

"Hey, what are you two doing?" Grae could smell the aroma of something that was just baked. Her stomach began to growl. She ate a small hamburger in route to the store that afternoon, but that was six hours earlier.

"Are you hungry, Grae?" Kat rose from her chair and walked toward the counter where Grae could see a crockpot sitting. "We had white bean chicken chili for dinner. I've kept some warming for you." Grae's stomach heard her mother's words and began to sound like a caged animal.

"I'm starving." She shrugged out of her jacket and kicked off her shoes as her mother filled a bowl with one of Grae's favorite soups. She knew her mother's version of the recipe had a slight kick. Grae sat down as her mother set a steaming bowl in front of her. She was thrilled to see corn fritters appear after the microwave dinged. "How many bowls did you eat?" Grae said to her brother as she let the first bite cool on the spoon.

"Four." Perry laughed as Kat put a small plate of corn fritters in front of him.

"We were waiting for you to come home, Grae." Kat sat back down at the table. Grae darted her eyes to her brother. "I'm ready to talk to you about your father."

Grae nodded and continued eating, the delicious tastes, overpowered by the thought of the words she would soon have to digest.

Kat took a deep breath. "As you could see, your father has responded well to the experimental treatment. He is not completely cured, but he has shown no further spread of the cancer, and a significant reduction in the size of the existing tumors. It has become apparent that we were not completely informed about the extent of your father's cancer. A fact that I find baffling since you two are his next of kin and by my connection to you and your father's legal wishes, I am still his legal next of kin. But, I suppose that his incarceration changed the rules. Anyway, his health is improving. The university from which these experimental drugs came from wishes to study him and his response more closely."

"Do they want to move him to another hospital?" Perry seemed very anxious to speed up the telling of the story.

"Let me continue, I am getting to that." Kat took a long sip of her coffee. "At the same time, Mister Lange has been working on your father's appeal. Do you two remember Terrence Cornwell?"

"Wasn't he one of the men that owned Dad's firm originally?" Grae remembered a very tall slender man with red hair.

"Yes, well, Terrence left the country right before your father was arrested. As you know, while your father admitted that he had some responsibility in these crimes, he has maintained that it wasn't his idea. The evidence seemed to point otherwise." Kat stopped and looked down into her coffee cup. "I really didn't believe him, but it now appears that a disgruntled woman who was involved with Terrence has turned over recordings of conversations between Terrence and another business associate. The conversations basically say that Terrence planned to turn the firm's most wealthy clients over to your father. It would appear like a promotion and a vote of confidence, but the plan was to gradually swindle them and to create a paper trail that led right back to your father."

"So, Dad didn't really commit those crimes! I knew it!" Perry jumped up from his chair.

"Your father is not completely faultless. He learned what was going on after some time passed. But, as it turns out, he was not the mastermind behind it." Kat looked at both of her children. "I'm sorry that I didn't believe your father, but you must understand that there were other things that contributed to my distrusting him."

Grae watched her mother closely. She knew about the controlling ways and borderline verbal abuse that her mother had endured. She wondered if there was more to that story than had been apparent to her and Perry.

"Terrence, along with another man, is being extradited back to the US. Apparently, he has been living a luxurious life in Costa Rica."

"And Dad has been dying in prison!" Perry's neck grew red.

"Hold on there. Your father is not completely innocent. He had a role in this crime. He didn't stop it. And, as far as his illness is concerned, it is possible that he may have received better and quicker care than if he were free."

"How can you say that?" Perry questioned his mother.

"Because, I know your father. He would have ignored his symptoms, even hidden them. He would have pretended that they would go away on their own. A sharp doctor in the prison system saw a change in his health, so he got treatment sooner. I'm not condoning experimental treatment on inmates by any means. But, the fact remains that your dad was able to try a treatment that he wouldn't have been offered by the general medical community. Your father was in stage four cancer. They rolled the dice, and he is now winning the game."

Kat motioned for Perry to sit back down. Grae had finished her chili and watched the dynamics between the two of them.

"His original doctor was very frank with me. He did not expect the treatment to work. He said that if your father was a regular patient of his, he would have told him to get his affairs in order. Perry, you can be mad all you want to about your father being in prison, but I think he would have already passed away if he hadn't been there."

"Some things happen for a reason that is bigger than we can see." Grae spoke for the first time in the conversation.

Kat turned to her and smiled. "Yes, that is very true and very wise." She took hold of Grae's hand and squeezed it. "So, Mister Lange has been told by the prosecutor that the process will soon begin to lower the charges against your father and overturn his sentence. He feels that it may be settled with time already served. That process may take a while though, as the extradition of Terrence and others will take time. But the prosecutor told Lange that he would be willing to grant permission for your father to be moved to a lower security facility in the meantime. He would be moved to a facility that is close to the Duke Medical Center where your father's treatment came from."

"That's great! Right?" Perry looked from his mother to his sister, smiling.

"Yes, it is."

"So, they might let Dad go free soon." Grae watched her mother's face closely.

"Yes, Lange thinks that this process will move as quickly as possible. There will be enough bad press from the fact that the prosecutor didn't try the correct people to begin with. Lange thinks the prosecutor will attempt to put a positive spin on all of this by using your father's health condition and the results."

"That's not right!" Perry's neck returned to its red color.

"Well, Perry, don't be so quick to judge. You must remember that your father's reputation is still tarnished by this. Even though he was not the instigator of this crime, he became a somewhat willing accomplice. It may not be a bad idea for the media now to portray your father as a sick victim. It may help him build back his career easier. I'm not saying that is right, but it is the way of the world. Lange will probably get your father an agent and put him on the talk show circuit."

"What?" Grae couldn't believe what she was hearing.

"I know, it sounds crazy, but he thinks the media will eat this story up. He sees headlines like 'Wrongly Convicted Man Receives Miracle Medical Treatment.' Lange has dollar signs in his eyes. I think your father is still not well enough to grasp what is happening. I don't really like the sound of all this, but, at the same time, I don't want your father to come out of this with the stigma of a criminal. That would not only affect his future, it would affect both of yours, too. It was the one thing that I have worried about, more than anything. How would his incarceration affect the two of you emotionally as well as how you would be treated in the future?"

Grae and Perry both remained silent. Grae realized she hadn't thought about the ramifications outside of her classmates learning that her father was in jail. She hadn't realized that her father's crimes might follow her, forever.

"So, you think Dad will really be completely released from jail?" Perry looked a little in shock.

"Yes, Perry, I think that is fairly certain. He will not have to serve anywhere near as long as he was sentenced. Best of all, it appears that this dreaded illness will not take him, at least not now."

"What does this all mean for us?" Grae knew that there was still something her mother wasn't telling them.

"Well, that's the other thing. Whenever your father is released from prison or the hospital, he asked if he could come here and stay for a while." Perry's face lit up, but then a look of concern crossed it. "I've talked to your grandfather and he is okay with it. Really, he will have nowhere else to go. Your Uncle Richard does not want to be involved. Tom has no assets left and no immediate income."

Grae looked at Perry. They exchanged some unspoken words.

"Mom, are you okay with this?"

Kat looked down at her coffee mug. It said World's Greatest Mom. She had several such mugs. She held the one that was her favorite. Grae and Perry had it made for her one Mother's Day. It had a baby photo of each of them at the age of one. Their faces and hands were covered in birthday cake.

"I'm happy that your father is getting well. It is nothing short of a miracle. I'm glad that those who truly conspired the bulk of this crime are now coming to justice. I still think that your father had an inexcusable role. He allowed greed to taint his judgment. But, I also know that having power is your father's biggest weakness." Kat stopped and looked at her children. "I want you to have your father back. I want him to have learned something from all of this. If you two are fine, I will be, too."

No more words were spoken. Grae and Perry each took a side and the three of them hugged each other for a long time.

NINE

"I'm sorry that I left you a message out of the blue, and then didn't return yours." Gav had left Grae a cryptic voicemail the night before. His voice played over and over in Grae's mind as she showered on Saturday morning. All his messages seemed to be in code.

The previous one had simply been four words—"We need to talk." She'd listened to it a dozen times and tried to figure out what those simple words meant. It was hopeless. His tone wasn't happy or sad. It wasn't formal or casual. With his latest response to her message, she knew that they were doomed to play phone tag. She thought about this, as she got dressed for work. The sun barely peeked over the mountain range as she sat down in the kitchen to drink coffee with Grandpa Mack.

"Your mother told you about your father?" Her grandfather drank from his steaming mug of coffee before he asked his question.

"Yes, Perry and I were quite shocked. Happy, relieved, but shocked."

"Too many changes, too quickly, jumbles your mind up."

The microwave dinged signaling that the sausage biscuits were ready. Kat had made plenty the previous day knowing that her family would be going in many directions during the weekend. Grae would be working long hours both days. Perry was going Christmas shopping with Carrie and her parents. Kat had a college conference to attend. Grae placed two biscuits in front of her grandfather where a large jar of apple butter stood waiting. He loved to slather the sweet goodness on about any kind of biscuit, but the combination with sausage was his favorite.

"The last two years have been a rollercoaster ride." Grae sat down across from him.

"We've got to keep an eye on your mother." Grandpa paused and took a bite. "This has been rough on her. It's not the first time that her world was turned upside down."

Grae waited for her grandfather to continue, but he was silent. "I'm not following you."

"There are a lot of secrets in this house. There are a lot of secrets in our family. You think that you know us, but maybe not."

Grandpa didn't speak again as he ate his breakfast. Grae knew better than to question him further.

The day flew by for Grae. The store was busy, but she spent most of her time roasting and flavoring coffee beans. Her day of work accomplished much because, by the time they closed, she had filled all the waiting mail orders and restocked the store's shelves.

"You have worked hard." Mary Lee came up behind Grae as she put the last of the bags in place. "You come from a family of hard workers." Mary Lee wiped down the bakery counter, and then put on her coat. "Take this home with you." She handed Grae a box of cinnamon rolls and brownies. "I bet Mack would like some with his coffee."

"I didn't realize that you knew my family." Grae turned out the lights and pulled the door closed behind Mary Lee. She shook the knob to make sure it was secure.

"I went on my very first date with your grandfather."

Grae turned around and gave Mary Lee a shocked look. "Really? Did my Granny know that?" Grae followed Mary Lee to her car. It was a long green Buick LeSabre.

"She sure did. She was there."

"What?"

"Your grandmother and I were very close friends back then. I dated your grandfather and she dated my brother. Mack and I had a brief love. I think it lasted all of a month. After that, it was all about his Belle from then on." Mary Lee got into her car. She paused, lost in thought. "Your grandmother was my maid of honor. I was her matron of honor. We shared our lives for a very long time."

Grae thought that Mary Lee looked sad. "What happened?" Grae realized that Mary Lee was studying her reaction very closely.

"Things change. Our lives take turns that we can't put in reverse. You need to remember that. Try never to do anything that you will live to regret. Yes, I know what I just said. Don't put yourself in a situation that ends with you having to live with the unthinkable. You can put on a happy face later, but it's never real." Mary Lee put on her seatbelt and reached for her door. "Get on in your car. We are going to go down this mountain together."

Grae followed Mary Lee down the mountain. The woman knew how to take the curves. Grae thought that Grandpa Mack might say that she straightened them out. She wondered about this woman's romance with her grandfather and long friendship with her grandmother. What could have possibly happened to separate them?

She was pleased to find that her grandfather was still up when she arrived home. Her mother was already in bed.

"Your mother had a long day at that conference of hers. She came home with a headache. She left some baked spaghetti in the oven for you."

"Where's Perry?"

"Oh, they were staying overnight wherever it was that they went. Going to see some sort of show or something. They're coming home tomorrow. It's just you and me, kid."

Grandpa's eyes stayed on the television, but he gave Grae a big old smile. Some black and white classic from the Wild West occupied his attention. She thought she had seen a glimpse of John Wayne when she first entered the room.

"Go on in there and warm up some food and come watch the movie with me. Bring me a bowl of ice cream when you come back."

Grae did as he suggested and returned to the living room to snuggle under a blanket and eat her very late dinner.

When a commercial interrupted the shootout, she decided to bring up the topic of Mary Lee.

"I learned today that you used to date Mary Lee, the lady that does all the baking on the mountain."

Grandpa almost choked on his bite of ice cream he had just taken.

"That reminds me; she sent you some goodies today. Hold that thought."

Grae jumped up from the couch and walked back into the kitchen. She slipped on her shoes and ran back to her car to get the box of baked goods. When she returned to the living room, she found that Grandpa's recliner was now in an upright position and the television was on mute. Before she could say anything, he started talking.

"What in the world got Mary Lee talking about me?"

Grae thought a minute. "Well, she was saying that I was a good worker and I come from a family of good workers. Then, she told me about dating you while Granny was dating her brother. She said it didn't work out, but that she stayed friends with Granny for a long time."

"That's true. Her husband and I used to spend every summer on the riverbank while the girls canned together like it was the end of the world." Grandpa smiled, reliving the memory.

"What happened? I don't ever remember hearing her mentioned or meeting her before I started working on the mountain."

Grae resumed eating her spaghetti as Grandpa opened the bakery box. He took out one of the cinnamon rolls from the bottom of the box.

"Oh, her cinnamon rolls are out of this world. I'm surprised there is any left as busy as the store was today."

Grandpa took a bite and savored the flavors before he continued talking. "Honey, things happen between people, and friendships get broken. Mary Lee said something that hurt your Granny's feelings. She didn't mean to hurt her. She was trying to be the friend that she had always been to your grandmother and make her see the truth." Grandpa set the rest of the roll down in his empty ice cream bowl. "You know, my Belle was stubborn. She knew that she should forgive the one friend who had always been by her side, but the hurt was bigger. It was bigger because it was the truth and she couldn't face the truth."

"What happened, Grandpa? I can't imagine what could be so big that it ended a lifelong friendship." Grae watched as he wiped his eyes.

"You can't imagine, because it is unimaginable. It left a hole in all of us who experienced it. The saddest part to me now is that no one talks about it. It's like it never happened."

"Grandpa, you're talking in riddles. I don't understand. Can't you tell me?"

"There's only one person who can tell you this story and I doubt she ever will." Grandpa picked up his bowl and leaned back into the recliner. He reached for the remote.

"My mother." Somehow, Grae just knew. "And, I'm willing to bet, it has something to do with time travel."

"You're a smart one. Remember that key you found in the closet, the one I told you not to show her?" Grae held her breath, waiting for him to continue. "If you really want to know, you show her that key. You see if that unlocks the truth she's been hiding in her soul."

Sunday was another early day for Grae. She would work until early afternoon, and then return home to hit the books. It was the week of exams. Her phone rang as she was blow drying her hair. She held her breath as she answered.

"Hello."

"Hey, Grae...I hope I didn't wake you." It was a very familiar and yet strange voice to her now.

"No, I was getting ready to go to work. I left you a message a couple of days ago."

"Yeah, I'm sorry about that. I've been busy. I should have told you in a message so you wouldn't have to keep trying to track me down."

Grae thought Gav's answer was a little strange.

"Um, well, here's the thing. Right after exams are over, there is going to be this big Christmas thing at Coach Beamer's house. He invites all his players. Well, you can bring a date, and well, all the guys are going to...so, I..."

"Gav, I'll make this easier for you. If there's someone you want to ask, just ask her. I don't want to stand in your way." There was a long pause.

"Okay, if that's how you feel, I will."

Grae could hardly hold back the tears. She wasn't sure that she could even say goodbye. She was about to just hang up when he started talking again.

"Grae, would you like to go with me to Coach Beamer's house?"

She dropped the phone. Looking down, she could hear him saying her name. She quickly grabbed it. "I'm here. You want me...hic...to go with you?"

"Yes, do you think that I am such a jerk that I would call you to tell you I was going to take someone else to something that you knew nothing about anyway?"

Grae wondered if she could count how many words he used in that long rambling sentence.

"Well, do you?"

"Oh, no, I just thought…well, I don't know…hic…what I thought."

"Go get some sugar and text me your answer later."

"What? Sugar?"

"Like that Baker guy told you about. Sugar cures the hiccups. You think I don't listen, but I do. I've got to go. Text me your answer."

"Okay."

"And, Grae, I really do want you to go. But only if you want to."

Grae stared at the phone after the call was over. She really didn't know how she felt. She didn't know if she wanted to go.

Shasta was waiting for Grae when she arrived home after work. Grae had invited her to come over on Sunday afternoon for her mother's food and a major study session. Even though their classes were different, they were both facing exams that week. Misery does love company.

"You look completely comfortable." Grae was glad to see that her friend felt comfortable enough at her home to come in a pair of lounge pants and an old sweatshirt.

"You have told me to make myself at home when I am here. Well, this makes me feel at home. This is not the day for glamour."

They decided to sprawl out in the front room. It wasn't one that Grae's family used often and it was a little mismatched in its furnishings. The best part was that there were two couches, which made for comfort and space.

"Mom is making her homemade deep dish pizza. You will love it."

"I think your mother could cook cardboard and it would be good." Shasta opened a thick spiral notebook with pages and pages of notes.

"I'm surprised that you still write so much by hand. Most of my classmates take notes on a tablet."

"Well, I really couldn't afford one. A laptop is too much to fool with carrying around. But, also, there is one of my nursing professors who told me that she thought taking notes by hand was still the best way to help yourself absorb what you are hearing. We will see how that works out for me next week."

Grae got up from her pile of books and started walking out of the room. "I really thought Mom would have brought us a snack by now."

As she got closer to the kitchen, she heard her mother and grandfather talking.

"You know you should tell Grae what happened." Her grandfather's voice sounded very serious. "It might help her to know."

"How in the world would that help her?" Kat's voice was tense.

"Maybe you could tell her things that would prevent her from making the same mistake."

"She will not make the same mistake. It is not possible. Besides, she is not going back." There was anger in her tone.

"Has it occurred to you that she might be able to find…"

"Don't you dare say it, Dad. Don't you say it! We both know that could never happen. It…it violates everything we know to be true."

"Everything we know to be true. That doesn't mean that there might not be truth that we do not know about."

"You are talking in circles, old man. Grae is my daughter and she is not going back in time again."

"How do you think you are going to stop her? How could I have stopped you?"

There was silence, a long silence. Grae thought that perhaps it was time to make her presence known, to interrupt the drama.

"Okay, Shasta, I'm going to get us some snacks." Grae was talking louder than usual, but she hoped that wasn't obvious to her mother. "Pizza sure does smell good."

"Ah, yes, thanks. It will still be a while before it is ready. I am making the first one for the McGavocks to pick up when they drop Perry off. What would you girls like to snack on?"

Kat didn't seem to have any intention of looking Grae in the eye. Grandpa Mack had made his way to the back door. As he put his boots on, he glanced back in Grae's direction and gave her a brief grin. It was an unspoken message that he knew that she heard their conversation.

"Have you made any of your party mix yet?"

It was an annual tradition for Kat literally to make gallons of the tasty treat. She included interesting ingredients, such as dried cranberries and chocolate Cheerios.

"Yes, I've made a savory batch. There's a pint bag that was left over from what I have packaged for gifts. It's in the spice cupboard. I was hiding it from Perry."

Grae laughed. Her brother's eating habits were forcing their mother to hide food from him.

"I never imagined that you would be hiding food from Perry."

"I never imagined that Perry would be eating so much."

Grae could see the smile on her mother's face. She grabbed a couple of diet sodas after retrieving the snack and left the room.

"That took you a long time."

Grae handed Shasta a soda and poured some of the party mix into a bowl for her.

"I had to snoop at the door and listen to Mom and Grandpa arguing." Grae didn't look up as she went back to her studying.

"What were they talking about?"

"Me."

"Well, then, of course you had to listen." Shasta laughed as she began to munch. "Oh my, this is so good. She made this from scratch, didn't she?"

"But, of course." Grae's accent was reflective of a well-known commercial. "Okay, there's something I need to talk to you about."

"Okay. I'm all ears. My eyes aren't leaving these pages, but my ears are all yours."

"Gav called this morning." Shasta's eyes immediately met Grae's. "He asked me to go to some special Christmas thing that Coach Beamer is having at his house for the team."

"And?"

"I don't know what to think of it. I thought at first that he was calling to tell me he was going to take someone else. He seemed offended that I thought that."

"Well, Grae, that would be a weird thing for him to do. You all broke up, but he doesn't have to ask your permission."

"I know, but you didn't hear how he did it. He didn't exactly sound friendly when the conversation started. I didn't expect him to ask me out." Grae looked out the window. She saw two deer passing across the yard. "I just don't know what to do. He sounded like he needs to go to this event and he needs to take a date. But, there was something about his voice that just sounded strange, distant."

"He's of the male species. I would say that it probably took a lot for him to call you. If it is just about going to some party at his coach's house, he could have asked anyone and not even mentioned it. He could have asked a friend. It must be important enough for him that he wants you there. So, I think that says something about how he still feels."

Grae pondered Shasta's words. Toto, the family dog, wandered into the room and sat down at her feet. "I have been so neglectful of you. It's a good thing you are so attached to Grandpa." Toto nuzzled Grae's hand as she got a good scratch behind the ears. "I guess you are right. I just didn't hear that in his voice."

Grae and Shasta studied until their eyes hurt. After Perry returned home and the McGavocks left with their pizza, Shasta and Grae took their slices and went back to their study room. Grandpa came in carrying the box that Grae found in the wall panel in her room. She had almost forgotten that it even existed.

"Your mother said that you found this upstairs in the wall. Girl, you are a champion at finding the unfindable. I bet that this box was placed in that wall by old Squire David himself."

Grandpa set the box down on a small table next to the couch where Grae was sitting. He sat down in a chair beside it. He took out his knife and began to work on the lock. Grae smiled as she realized that was the way she opened the box when she first discovered it. But, she used the small knife that Mary had hidden in the dress she had returned in from her journey to 1786.

It didn't take him too long before they heard a click. The hinges made a creaking noise as Grandpa opened the lid. Grae remembered the documents that were on top, but soon remembered she never dug deep into the box's contents. Grandpa seemed determined to do just that. One by one, he carefully took out the treasures that lay within.

"Oh, wow, this is exciting." Shasta knelt down in front of Grandpa as they all peered inside.

The top few items were the documents that Grae remembered seeing before. They looked old and official, like deeds. Grandpa lifted out a pocket watch. It immediately made Grae think of Jay and his time travel token.

"This ticker has seen better days. No doubt like the one who carried it."

Grandpa's way with words always made Grae smile. He was a poet of common speak. He opened the timepiece and found that the face had a small crack in it. But after he wound it a few turns, a slight tick could be heard.

"It might still keep a little time, but I wouldn't plan my day around its accuracy."

He next lifted out a piece of paper that was about the standard size of copier paper, but heavier with a slight texture to it. It was folded in two by the length. He opened it and a smile immediately came to his face.

"Now, she is a beauty. I bet Squire loved her." He handed the paper to Grae.

As soon as she touched it, she knew whose face she would see. Her eyes grew tearful and blurry as she saw a beautiful drawing of her dear friend, Ama.

Tears poured down her face as she gazed into Ama's beautiful dark eyes and soft smile. Grae gently touched the face on the paper and more tears left her eyes. Her mind was a whirlwind with all of the memories of her time with this woman in 1830. The happy moments somehow seemed to overshadow Ama's tragic end.

"Wow! She is beautiful." Shasta took the drawing out of Grae's hand. "There's something about her eyes. She looks like she has wisdom beyond her age. Like she was an old woman in the body of a young girl."

Grae was amazed at how accurately Shasta described her dear friend. She took the drawing back and could not break her gaze on the picture. She began to study it. The drawing was done in charcoals. Just enough different colors were used to add depth and meaning to the subject. The initials "DG" were scribbled at the bottom. This was drawn by the hand of David Graham. It was no wonder that it captured Ama so perfectly. Grae wondered if he had drawn this before she died or if it was done from memory, afterwards.

"I wonder who she was." Shasta returned to her books.

Grae thought for a moment about how she should answer that question. She glanced at her grandfather and he seemed to realize the truth of how she knew her.

"I bet that she was a love of old Squire's. Seems like I remember hearing some story your Granny dug up about her."

Grandpa Mack gave Grae a quick wink. His little lie would open up a way for her to tell the story. It was a long kept secret that few knew in its original time. But, as she looked into the questioning face of her friend, Grae could not think of any reason to withhold the information. It was a great love story and a clear glimpse into what made David Graham such a dark and ambitious soul. And, so, she began.

"Ama was Squire David's true love."

When the story was over, Shasta's face was red and puffy. She did not try to conceal how it had touched her. Grae wondered if the tears were cleansing to her friend's soul. Shasta had been through so much in her young life.

Grandpa Mack hadn't shied away from the emotion either. His old worn handkerchief had come out of his overall's pocket. He blew his nose loudly when Grae had finished.

"I always figured that love had turned that man cold. You lose your love, you lose your heart." Grae knew that his words were reflective of his own life. "I can't imagine it happening to him in his young days. At least I got to spend a lifetime with mine."

"What happened to the child?" Shasta's thoughts were on Robbie. It made sense; she was the caretaker of her own mixed up family. The child's welfare would be close to her heart.

"Robbie was sent to live with some friends of Squire's in North Carolina. The family name was Graham, a distant relative perhaps. So Robbie was raised a Graham, but not by his own father."

"Well, I'll be. Every generation has its own set of secrets" Her grandfather took the picture back and was studying it intently.

"It would appear so, and I bet that this one got more complicated as time passed."

Grae took the drawing back when Grandpa handed it to her as he got up and left the room. Grae laid it down and began looking back into the box. There were old coins as well as some money with Squire's photo on the bills.

"I guess you have really made it in this world when you have your picture on money." Shasta laughed as Grae passed the bills to her.

"Looks like Confederate money. It wasn't worth much after the war." Grae's gaze met something blue in the bottom of the box. Her fingers quickly found a very old fountain pen with a beautiful royal blue case. She was amazed at the good condition it was in. As she held it up to the light, a strange feeling passed over her. Grae saw the vision of the man sitting at a writing table. He stood and she could see this same pen was in his hand, but she couldn't see his face. For some reason though, she wasn't sure that the man she saw was Squire David Graham.

"Grae, Grae!" Shasta was snapping her fingers in front of Grae's face. "Are you okay? Where did you go just now?"

"I...I'm not really sure. Daydreaming, I guess." Grae clutched the pen in her hands. She knew she must keep it close. This was the object that would lead her on her next journey through time.

TEN

Both of them had two exams on Monday, so Grae and Shasta decided they would meet for a late lunch at one of their favorite spots, CJ's. Neither one knew what the initials stood for, but they loved the Stromboli and chef salads.

"I am so hungry!" Shasta said, as she took a large bite of her salad. "It's like I haven't eaten in weeks, and I devoured a bowl of cereal and a sausage biscuit this morning."

"It's probably nerves. The stress of these exams. I think I took a test in my sleep last night."

"No offense, Grae, but you just don't know the half of it yet. I'm sure your exams are hard, but these nursing classes are killers. My brain literally hurts." Her friend was eating at an alarming rate.

"Chewing is a good thing, Shas. You might want to try it."

"Oh, do I look like a cow chomping on grass? This is so good." Shasta took a drink of her iced tea. "I guess part of it is eating with someone else. It's been kind of lonely at the house. The boys are pretty settled with my aunt. Dad's still working a lot. I've been home alone most of the time." Her eating slowed and she began twirling her fork in her salad.

"How's your mother doing? You've not mentioned her recently."

"Well, we think she might be doing a little better. This new doctor has some wild ideas about her treatment, but some of them seem to be working. One thing that she has to do is write letters to Dad and me. We've learned a lot from those letters. She has captured feelings on paper that she could never seem to express verbally to us."

Grae thought about Martha's letters and journals. The documents were truly windows to her soul. Even though the rambling was, at times, hard to understand, they revealed glimpses of how complex the woman and her life truly had been.

"That's great. It's progress. And the boys are adjusting?"

"Yes, I'm sure they miss us, but their life is now more normal with my aunt and uncle. No more strange hours. They eat at normal times, go to school, do their homework, play, and then bedtime is enforced. They needed that structure. Dad and I just couldn't do it right now. Life got in the way." Shasta took another bite of her food. "Enough about me. What did you decide to do about Gav?"

"Well, so far, I am making him wait." Making the statement made Grae smile. "I thought I would text him tonight. It's funny. Carrie texted me while I was in my first class this morning and asked if my phone was working. I can only imagine what he was asking her. It will do him good to wait a little."

"You are going to tell him yes, aren't you?"

"Really, Shasta, am I that easy to read?"

Shasta laughed as Grae made a shocked face. "Yes. Don't decide on professional poker playing as a career. You don't have the face for it."

"Alright, yes, I am going to go with him. I don't know if it will change anything between us. We just, well, have too much to overcome."

"You know, you can talk to me about this."

"I know. But, it's complicated."

"Everything about both of our lives seems to be these days."

"Hi, Gav, I've thought about what you asked. I would like to go with you. Just text me the details or give me a call. Thanks for thinking of me." Grae pressed send and headed into her final exam on Tuesday morning.

"Miss White, I do not plan to give this exam via cell phone."

Grae gave Mister Bybee a quick smile and turned off her phone. As she slipped it in her backpack, she noticed that Jay was standing in the doorway.

"May I help you, young man?" Mister Bybee gave Jay a stern look.

"May I interrupt before you begin class and speak to Grae briefly?"

"You've already interrupted, so by all means, speak." Mister Bybee pointed at Grae, and then to the door. Grae quickly went out in the hallway with Jay.

"What is so important that you had to aggravate him before he gives our final exam?"

"I'm sorry, but I didn't think you would have your cell phone on because you are in class."

"Yes, I'm in class. You thought a physical appearance was less disruptive?" Grae shook her head and looked back into the classroom. Mister Bybee was getting ready to hand out the exams. "Never mind. What is it?"

"I just wondered what time you would be at the library." Jay looked nervously over Grae's shoulder.

"When this exam is over." Grae said, through her clinched teeth. Mister Bybee cleared his throat.

"And when will that be?"

"Whenever I am finished. Go away, Jay. I will be at the library when I can." Grae quickly went back to her seat as Mister Bybee laid the exam on her desk.

"We are so glad that you could fit this into your busy schedule." Mister Bybee gave her a slight grin as he passed by. Grae turned over the paper and gasped. It was an essay exam.

Two hours later, large Diet Dr. Pepper in hand, Grae entered the library. Alice was sitting at her desk typing. Grae could see two people huddled at a table looking at one of the large maps that the library had from different historical periods.

"Hi, Grae. How have your exams gone?" Alice looked up from her work and smiled at Grae.

"Well, the last one about killed me, but I am done for the semester. Woo hoo!"

Alice quickly shushed her and pointed to the two patrons. They didn't seem concerned with Grae's outburst.

"I have a mailing that I would like for you to work on. It will not take you long. Just a couple hundred pieces to fold and stuff. Jay's in the back. I've already put the mailing contents back there as well." Alice smiled as Grae nodded. "I really appreciate your help."

Grae walked by the people who were studying the map. From a glance, she could see that it was a historical map from the 1800's. Grae knew there were many family names on it that could still be found in the area. She also knew that she had met some of their ancestors, up close and personal.

"Oh, great, you made it. Ace the exam?" Jay looked cheerful, too cheerful.

"It was an essay exam."

"Oh, bummer. That could go a lot of different ways."

"Are you trying to make me have a bad day or what?" Grae looked at the cart beside the table. On the top shelf was a box filled with addressed envelopes. The bottom was filled with several boxes of copies. It appeared to be a fundraiser-type mailing.

"I think that Alice has me beat on that one."

"I wouldn't be so sure, Mister Stone."

"Uh, oh, we are back to formalities. I didn't mean to cause you any grief. I just wanted to find out when you would be here. I had to use Madison's counselling skills to even find out what exam you were having today."

"I believe the powers that be at this institution might call that an invasion of privacy."

"Cut it out. Can I just tell you about some of the interesting things I have found in all of these letters? I will even help you fold those mountains of papers."

Grae looked at the sample set of documents that Alice had left for her to see the order that the papers needed to be put in. It was three sheets of paper folded.

"Okay, but give me a few minutes to get settled." Grae began to place the stacks of paper on the table in front of Jay. She pulled out a bag of peanut M&Ms.

"Huge soda and bag of candy, this is a serious day." Jay chuckled as he began looking at his notes.

Grae smirked at him as she pulled her phone out of her bag and turned it on. She had no messages. "Okay, tell me what you have discovered."

"Well, it seems that by the fall of 1862, Davy Graham had developed poor health. I don't see anything that indicates the particular ailment he suffered from, but whatever it was forced him to resign from active duty in late September of that year."

"Wait a minute. I don't remember reading anything about him coming back to Cedar Run while the heat of the war was going on."

"That's right, he didn't. I said that he resigned from active duty. After that, he accepted the position of Post Commander at Yellow Sulfur Springs and remained there through 1864. This post was near Christiansburg, Virginia, only forty miles or so from his family home. The interesting thing about all of this is what also was happening simultaneously with another part of the Graham family." Before Grae could ask any questions, Jay held up his hand and continued. "One of the letters casually mentioned Jackey

Graham. I got to thinking. Could this be the man who raised Ama's son?"

"Robbie." Grae had stopped working with the papers and sat down in front of Jay. She had her drink and was eating her candy as if she was watching a movie unfold before her.

"So, I decided to do some research about this North Carolina family. Now, there is a connection to our Virginia Grahams as well. During the Revolutionary War, Squire's father, Robert, and his family, lived near Jackey's family in the Charlotte area. Robert fought in that war under Jackey's father, General Joseph Graham. The story goes that Robert saved Joseph's life during one of the Charlotte battles with Cornwallis. Both families were Irish immigrants, Presbyterians, and were in the iron-making business. It turns out that Jackey Graham had a much younger brother named William Alexander Graham, Sr., who was the former Governor of North Carolina and even had been a nominee for Vice President of the United States in 1852. This man had a son, William, Jr., they called him Willie. He was an officer for a North Carolina regiment in the Civil War and was wounded at Gettysburg. It appears that Willie and Robbie were close to the same age and served together."

"Robbie was in the war?" Grae was still mesmerized by the story Jay was telling.

"They were furloughed from duty so that Willie could recover from something. They travelled to the home of Willie's cousin, Mary Anna Morrison Jackson, in Lexington, Virginia, to rest and recover. Mary Anna was the wife of General Stonewall Jackson."

"That's interesting."

"It gets better. After they rested, Willie and Robbie travelled south to Yellow Sulfur Springs to access the healing waters there. They also came to see Willie's fiancée who lived nearby." Jay stopped and looked at Grae.

"Davy was at Yellow Sulfur Springs."

"Yes and the DNA thickens."

"Does he meet...?"

"Of course, he does. This wouldn't be an interesting story if he didn't. Don't you remember that we saw a letter a while back that talked about him meeting this man at Harper's Ferry? They joked that they could be brothers because of their same last name and resemblance." Jay laughed. "What is even better is the University of North Carolina has archived some of General Joseph Graham's family letters online. I am in the process of going through them. I have made some direct inquiries to some of the Graham descendants in North Carolina. I'm trying to find out if there is a connection between the Virginia and North Carolina Grahams. If these descendants have any good stories, perhaps we can learn if Davy ever discovered that Robbie was his half-brother."

"Oh, Jay, I don't know if that would have been a good or bad thing."

"Whatever it was, it either did happen or did not happen, and I am going to do my best to find out if it did. You see, I think that they did discover each other. I think that because of something that Martha told me when I was back in 1864. I think it was a hot topic in that house then. It also might have been part of the reason that her mental health treatment by Doctor Minson escalated. Squire, no doubt, didn't want to discuss this situation much."

Grae sat back down and stared at Jay again. Her head was starting to hurt. It had not bothered her for several days.

"What did she tell you?"

"One of the evenings that I was with her and Gracie in her quarters, she started talking about the importance of family. She seemed to have a grand vision of how her children's lives would be. She also seemed to have a prophetic understanding that she would not be there to experience it with them. She talked about how she wanted all of her children to embrace their strength and be individuals. I remember clearly that she said she hoped that they would be close to one another and welcome those extended family members beyond their Graham's Forge community, including her Peirce family as well as the Grahams. She was very resolute in her conviction that they honor their heritage. She wanted her children to know who they really were, and she saw the generational family connection as the way for them to learn that."

Jay paused and Grae could sense that he was travelling back in his mind. She remained silent.

"Then, Gracie said something to the effect that she doubted that Davy and Robbie would ever cross paths. Martha rose from her chair, in a dramatic fashion. It reminded me of a movie scene with Joan Crawford or Bettie Davis. She said, 'It is too late. It has happened. The course has been set. Davy knows.' When you told me the story of Robbie, it all started making a little sense. This information about Willie and Robbie being at Yellow Sulfur Springs just confirms it."

"I've got to say, Jay, you are quite the detective. I can't wait to learn what you find out."

Grae's mind raced with all the information that Jay had just revealed. It was like a novel that slowly released small crumbs of clues to some grand mystery. They began to speed up the process of their factory-like production system of stuffing the envelopes. When Alice entered the room a little while later, they were both hard at work in their quiet contemplation.

"You guys have got quite the system going here. I appreciate you helping, Jay."

"Ah, no problem. I should earn my keep somehow with all the research I have been doing here."

"I just know that your doctoral thesis will be outstanding when you are finished. I hope you will let me read it." Jay was relieved when Alice didn't give him time to answer and went on talking. "I didn't realize it, but those folks who were just here were from North Carolina. They are researching the Graham family. They are descendants of a man named Jackey Graham and his father, General Joseph Graham." Grae almost choked on her soda. "Grae, honey, you need to drink slower. That soda was full when you arrived here. All that carbonation isn't good for you. Anyway, somehow this Jackey Graham is related to Squire David Graham. You all keep up the good work." Alice left, and Grae and Jay just looked at each other.

"I don't just feel cold chills down my back. They are covering my whole body." Jay closed his eyes and shook all over. "I bet they have come because of my inquiries."

"Okay, that clinches it. Please continue with that research."

"I will. Do you have a busy work schedule the rest of the week?"

"Well, sort of. I told Mister Abbey that I would be glad to work extra hours since others had to cover for me while I was out."

"I called the lady who takes care of Missus Baker and she said that Thursday afternoon or evening would be a good time to come for a visit."

A sick feeling came over Grae as Jay said 'Missus Baker.' "Oh, I don't know. I am a little scared of this. What if seeing me upsets her?"

"You will never know if you don't try. She might be expecting you to find her."

Grae thought about that for a moment. It was a comforting thought and could be true. Mary would not have known the period of time that Grae came from, but she might have guessed it was a modern time. Grae looked at the calendar on her phone.

"Okay, let's make it late in the afternoon. That way if I go in early, I can just about work a full day on the mountain." Grae took a deep breath. "It would be so nice to see Mary again, but only if it brings good to her. I would never want to hurt her."

"I think it would be nice if you said grace, Dad."

Kat made the evening meal special by having the family gather in the dining room. It seemed that having a family dinner had become a rare occurrence, but on Tuesday evening, everyone was home at the same time, for once. A light snow was falling. Grandpa Mack had a roaring fire going in the dining room fireplace. While Grae had been deep in studying the night before, Kat began to add more decorations throughout the house. Rather than use some of the more modern looking decorations, Kat chose selections that were traditional. While she had used some tiny white lights to add twinkle, most of the décor were made of cranberries and magnolia leaves, stems from holly leaves and berries. There were wreaths that Kat handmade from English boxwood shrubs and garlands of pine and hemlock cuttings. It was beautiful. And, it harkened back to a time when the Mansion was first a home.

"Lord, I thank you for all the blessings that you have brought into this house. I'm thankful that you led my precious daughter and her children home to me. I needed them, Lord. You know that. They needed me." Grae looked up and exchanged glances with Perry. "I thank you that you have made our Grae Belle well again and that you have allowed Perry to learn many things from his battle." Grae smiled to herself. Grandpa's sense of humor was even apparent in prayer. There was a long pause. "I thank you that you have seen fit to open the eyes of those who had spread falsehoods and make us see clearly that these children's father was not totally the evil man I believed him to be. I am very thankful that you have laid your healing hands upon him and are restoring his health so that he may continue to be a father to these children. I ask you to give me the strength and restraint to allow me to forgive him for the hurt he has caused. Please give everyone in this home the strength to forgive themselves for past transgressions." Grandpa loudly cleared his throat. "Thank you for the delicious food we have before us and bless all in this home. Amen."

Grandpa did not make eye contact with anyone. His gaze and hands went straight to the platter of roast beef and vegetables that had been placed next to him. Grae looked at her mother who was watching him with a soft smile on her face. There was a look of sadness about her. It was a look that Grae realized she had seen many times through the years.

"That was nice, Grandpa." Perry spoke softly. An unusual occurrence, his plate was still empty. He had not reached for any helpings of food yet. "Mom, I know that there are a lot of things that Dad needs forgiving for. But, if by some miracle Dad has been released and is well enough, could he come here for Christmas? He could stay in my room. I could sleep on the couch."

Grae watched as her mother's look of sadness changed to joy. The smile that crossed her face was true and bright.

"Absolutely, son, we would love to have your father here with us. But, please do not get your hopes up. Your father's health is indeed better, but the judicial system can be slow." Kat handed Perry a bowl of food. "Now, get busy and start eating. The food is getting cold."

Grae watched as her family became animated in the activity of the table. She thought about her experiences sitting in the same room with another family. Hers was not so different in many respects; there was joy and happiness as well as sorrow and secrets. It was a shared legacy. But, just as the revealing of the truth about her father had brought a level of relief and closure to her family, she longed to learn of the truths behind the secrets that the Grahams had tried so hard to hide. She knew this was the root of her mission. There was a tiny fragment of this combined story that made her wonder if it was not somehow entwined—her family in the present and the Grahams of the past. Was there something that linked their stories and their secrets?

On Wednesday, Grae made her way up the mountain very early. It was just a few minutes past seven when she arrived. Mary Lee's old green Buick sat parked near the store. She knew that she would be greeted by some delightful aromas and was not disappointed when she opened the door. She found her older friend in a cloud of flour in the kitchen.

"I know you are behind me, dear, but my hands can't turn around to you."

Mary Lee was attacking a huge mound of dough in front of her vigorously. Grae could see that the oven was already hard at work. The smell of chocolate filled the air. A huge batch of Christmas brownies were reaching heated perfection.

"Good morning, Mary Lee. You must have gotten up before you went to bed."

The old woman cackled at Grae's comment. "Indeed, I did, my dear. I would welcome some of your good coffee. I'll trade you a cup for one of those blueberry muffins that I just took out of the oven."

Grae hadn't noticed the muffins that were already on the cooling rack. Her mouth salivated with the thought of the berry treats. "That's a deal! I will start a pot and get my roaster going."

As Grae put her coat and other belongings in the back room, she heard a ding on her phone. It was a text message from Gav.

"The dance is the Friday before Christmas. The invitation said for the guys to wear suits and the girls to wear cocktail dresses. I'm not sure that I know exactly what that is, but I'm sure you will figure it out. Thanks for saying yes. I am deep in exams."

Grae nodded at the phone before she turned it off. She was glad that she had agreed to go, but something about the whole thing really bothered her. She hoped that her mother had something she could wear. She wasn't thrilled with the prospect of having to shop for something at the last minute.

She thought about the beautiful purple dress that she had worn during her last journey. She was disappointed that she hadn't been able to have the portrait made for the Historical Society exhibit. When she had become ill, Missus Akers had retrieved the dress and said they would find another model and location for the portrait. It had taken her a hundred years in reverse and was now in someone else's possession. Life could be so strange.

A busy day had begun. Grae could almost say that she was sick of looking at coffee beans, but it was gratifying that the little idea born out of Grae's and her mother's creativity was now full-blown into a lucrative business venture. As the day passed, she moved from roasting new beans, to flavoring those she had done days earlier, to the final step of bagging. By early afternoon, she had over fifty small bags ready for orders or to go on the shelves.

"You have worked so hard, Grae. I appreciate your relentless pursuit of brew." Mister Abbey's smile was huge as he viewed all of the little bags in rows on the storage shelves. "You go and enjoy the afternoon. No coffee making for you tomorrow. You take the whole day off. We will see you on Friday."

Grae was thrilled to have a day off but wondered how the events of Thursday afternoon would affect her temperament when she returned.

"Can you just imagine what it was like for people in the South to learn about the Emancipation Proclamation?" Jay's sudden question caught Grae off guard.

"I'm sorry, Jay. What are you talking about?"

Grae was deep into the history of the Stuart family. A history major at Radford University had contacted Alice that morning desperate for some tidbits regarding the early Wythe County family. It was a family that Alice did not know much about, but she knew what documents and journals might offer the best information to pass along to the student. Grae had been reading for the solid hour since she had arrived from the mountain. Her eyes were heavy from rising early, working hard, and reading land deeds.

"I was just looking at some general history of the 1862-63 time periods and realized what a dramatic turn of events it must have been for President Lincoln to issue the Emancipation Proclamation on New Year's Day in 1863. No matter how a person felt about slavery, it was going to make a dramatic change in life as they knew it."

"Yes, Mom and I went to see Steven Spielberg's movie about President Lincoln and the real theme of the movie was how this whole saga played out in the legislature. It was quite dramatic with lots of congressional wheeling and dealing." Grae went to the copier to copy some of the documents she felt would be the most beneficial for the history student. The scanned documents would go straight to Alice's email as pdfs for her to send.

"It certainly changed the history of the South. I found this letter from Martha to someone in Pennsylvania. Perhaps it was a distant relative or old friend. Martha is very open about her opinions to this person and talks about how all of this change will affect her dear slave and companion, Gracie. It gives quite an interesting perspective."

Mrs. David Graham
Cedar Run Farm
Max Meadows, Va

Mrs. William Peirce
Cedar Avenue
Scranton, Pennsylvania

February 1, 1863

Dearest Emmy,

I am beside myself with worry and am compelled to write to you, my dearest friend and confidant. Although we are separated by this horrific War, we remain loving sisters by marriage, and dear friends from childhood. Oh, how I miss you.

First, I must reassure you that my family is well and our home is safe. It is my hope that you too are so blessed. I am pleased to report that Davy has resigned from duty and is now serving as a supply post Commander. Brother Alexander and his family live in Tennessee and Sister Betsy continues to visit me often, as she is as feisty as ever. I am certain she will outlive us all. I enjoy tutoring my lovely, bright daughters, but find myself less and less able to manage the demands of this large home. I spend a great deal of time attempting to harness my inner demons, pushing back the darkness that has haunted my life.

Alas, as I age in years, this darkness, too, has grown, almost appearing like a dense fog around me some days. There are times when only Gracie can reach me and pull me from its grip. And now, I am trying to understand Lincoln's Emancipation Proclamation. What will happen to our way of life without slavery? What will become of me if I were to lose Gracie?

I have read that Lincoln made a "covenant with God" to issue this Proclamation, yet, I find that it only addresses the slaves of the Confederacy. What of the slaves who still serve their masters in the Union states of Maryland? Kentucky? Do you know that many of our neighbors' slaves have simply left, moving into the Union-favored and protected western Virginia counties, which are moving towards their own statehood?

Emmy, you live in a large Union state and Brother William works for one of the North's largest iron furnaces. How is it there? What is it like to live amongst the Negro Freed Men and Women? And, how is it with your own sons fighting beside Union soldiers who were once runaway slaves? Is it truly civilized? Do you live a normal life in such a world? It is so foreign to my sensibilities. How did you adjust to such profound changes? I fear that I will lose everyone that I love! I fear that I will not be able to absorb and adapt to the changes that are all around us.

But do not fret. I will do what I must to hold my family together during these difficult times. Please tell my dear baby brother that I love him and miss him, although I have only generally forgiven him for moving you so far from me. I pray that we will see you all again and that our worlds will return to normalcy. I pray daily for the futures of our children and our country.

Thank you, dear Emmy, for your true and devoted friendship. There is no charm equal to the tenderness of your heart. I shall always cherish our childhood together, the memories forever embedded in my mind. I look forward to your letter, as I know you will help me to understand. Only through knowledge can we conquer our fear.

Your devoted Sister and Friend,

Martha

"It is good to see that Martha had, at least, a few friends who she could reach out to and discuss things with. She seemed so isolated when I met her." Jay returned the letter to its folder.

"Yes, her closest companion was Gracie. I'm sure that this would have been a delicate topic for them to discuss." Grae returned her attention to the documents before her. "While you were reading, I found a stack of envelopes in the bottom of the box where the letters came from. They were under some old manila folders. There are actually a few more letters here, but I think you might find that the envelopes are even more interesting than the contents."

Jay joined Grae at her end of the table. "Why do you say that?"

Grae handed Jay the stack. "They are all from Martha Graham to her children."

"Grae, they are all postmarked in either September or October, 1865. Martha died at the end of October. The stamps are beautiful. The colors are so well preserved." Jay continued to look through the envelopes. "Oh, two of them are stuck together." Jay put on the white gloves and carefully began to pry the two envelopes apart. He dropped the top envelope onto the floor.

"Be careful, Jay."

Grae reached down to pick up the envelope. As she rose, she saw that Jay was standing in front of her. His eyes were bugged out and his mouth was opened.

"You need to sit down."

"What is the matter with you?" Grae sat in the chair as Jay handed the envelope to her.

A deep shrill gasp escaped her throat as she read the front of the envelope. It was addressed to Bettie Ann Graham from her mother, Martha. A beautiful steel gray stamp was in the upper right hand corner and under the stamp was one word carefully written, "GRAE."

"Say something." Jay knelt down in front of her.

Grae's hands were shaking. "I've got to go back. I've got to return before she dies."

ELEVEN

"You know, history hasn't given enough credit to Toland's Raid."

Grae had met Jay at the library around noontime on Thursday. The shock of what they had found the previous day kept Grae awake most of the night. She just couldn't shake the haunting feeling of seeing her name on that envelope. They had remained quiet since arriving, partly because Alice was showing two patrons around who had just made a sizable donation.

"Toland's Raid?" Grae's voice was barely over a whisper. She was so tired. She felt like she had been up for days.

"The Battle of Toland's Raid occurred on July 18, 1863, on what is now Tazewell Street. It is a very interesting story and had a level of significance, but history books rarely note it at all. I mean, it appears that this Union General and his troops were overthrown by the old men, women, and children of Wytheville. That's quite a feat."

"Oh, yes, I've heard bits and pieces of the story."

Grae looked around and saw that Alice was now in the main library area with the couple. She nodded at Grae as they walked toward the main counter.

"There are Civil War Trail signs that mark the path the raid took from the top of Big Walker Mountain down. Mister Abbey tells visitors the story of Molly Tynes and that legend has it she was the young woman who may have warned Wytheville of the impending attack."

"It's quite an interesting piece of history. But, like many historical accounts of the time, it is riddled with some inconsistencies, versions, and legends." Jay took a folder from his computer bag and leafed through several pages. "It seems that earlier in July orders were issued at Camp Piatt, West Virginia, to strike Wytheville and the Mount Airy Railroad Depot, now Rural Retreat, telegraph lines, bridges, ammunition stores, as well as, the salt and lead mines nearby. That was quite an extensive order. A Union force of over eight hundred was sent led by Colonel John T. Toland with Lieutenant Colonel F. E. Franklin. Confederate Generals at the Saltville and Dublin Depots were alerted about the attack and sent Major Thomas Bowyer and two small companies of around one hundred and thirty men by passenger train to Wytheville with two pieces of artillery. When they arrived, they could not find horses or wagons to pull the artillery the three-quarters of a mile into town. So, they left it there and marched to the center of town to position themselves at the courthouse. Major Bowyer and some of his officers distributed arms to some of the citizens and organized them in defensive positions with the militia."

"Wow, Jay, I'm really surprised you have done this much research about this."

"Well, it kind of happened accidentally. As I was looking for information about the Graham family, I would find tidbits of history about things that were occurring in the area. Sometimes you just can't help yourself. You have to keep reading. The people part of all of these accounts interests me the most. It's fascinating how the local citizens reacted to threats during the war. Some of the historical accounts give a glimpse of that. One told that there were two residents, Lieutenant Colonel Abraham Umbarger and Major Joseph F. Kent, who helped mobilize the citizens and issue weapons to them. Many of the residents fled in anticipation of the attack, either to Camp Jackson or into the surrounding mountains. But about fifty to sixty old men, women, and children remained to aid Major Bowyer in the fight."

"Yes, I've heard that part of the story. Most of the young able men of the community were away fighting somewhere else, but that small group of locals stood bravely to defend their town."

"It seems that some of Toland's troops were sent to the Mount Airy Depot, but most proceeded on to Wytheville and followed the path that is now Tazewell Street."

"That's the street that the Visitors Center, the Boyd Museum, and the Rock House Museum are on."

"Was the Rock House Museum formerly the home of the Haller family? This account says that a bullet hole was left in one of the windows by this battle."

"Yes, the bullet hole remains today and is part of the tour."

"I think that there were several charges that Major Bowyer led, but it doesn't seem that all of them were very effective in stopping the Union troops as they advanced toward Main Street and in the direction of the courthouse. But it does appear that between the second and third charge, one of those bullets shot through Colonel Toland's heart while he was mounted on his horse, and then the third charge returned some murderous fire. The entire battle was over in about an hour. The wounded and casualty list was much higher on the Union side, but over eighty of the Wytheville residents engaged in the fight were taken prisoner including a gentleman whose last name you will recognize." Jay tilted his head in a questioning manner and waited for Grae to reply.

"Oh, don't tell me. I bet it was McGavock."

"Correct! Ephraim McGavock was taken prisoner. A slave of his by the name of George was killed trying to save him. His wife, Abigail, owned a private girls' school in the town. Ephraim was a direct descendant of James McGavock."

"Everything comes full circle in this saga, doesn't it?" Grae stretched and yawned. "That was a delightful summary of the battle, but I didn't hear anything in your account concerning the infamous Molly Tynes. Mister Abbey is just convinced that she was an important character in this story."

"I thought you might be interested in Molly, so I did copy some of that research as well." Grae leaned forward on the table and laid her head down on her arms.

"Am I putting you to sleep?"

"No, I just need some caffeine. You continue while I rest my eyes." Grae could hear a slight chuckle from her friend as he shuffled through more folders.

"Okay. Here it is."

Grae peeked open one eye as she heard Jay reading aloud and mumbling to himself as he skimmed the document.

"Mary Elizabeth 'Molly' Tynes was in her mid-twenties in 1863. She was a resident of Tazewell County north of Wytheville by some fifty plus odd miles. Legend has it that Toland and his troops camped near the Tynes' family farm on the night of July 17 and that some of them told Molly they planned to attack Wytheville the following day. Apparently, Molly had been attending Hollins College in Roanoke, Virginia, and had returned home that summer to visit. The legend continues that Molly rode on horseback all night over fifty miles of rough terrain to warn the people of Wytheville of their coming fate. History has dubbed her as 'Paul Revere in petticoats' and her home community still honors her today as a brave young woman who warned her neighbors that the 'Yankees are coming.' Look at the photo of her that I found. She looks more like a city girl than a mountain woman. She reminds me of a young Katharine Hepburn." Jay handed the copy of the photo to Grae as she raised her head from the table.

"Katharine Hepburn. I know the name, but…"

"She was in lots of old movies with Spencer Tracy who she was linked to romantically. You've said that you and your mother liked to watch classic movies together. I bet you have seen the one that she and Tracy did together in the 1960s. It also starred Sydney Poitier. It was called *Guess Who's Coming to Dinner*? It was quite controversial for its time."

"Okay, I remember now. You're right; Molly does sort of resemble her." Grae handed the copy back to him as she stood up and stretched. "I need to go get a soda. Do you want anything?" Grae reached into her bag and pulled out her wallet. Her cell phone fell out. She had forgotten to turn it on.

"No, I think I will stick with the java juice today. Did you get any sleep last night?"

"Not really, my mind just wouldn't turn off. I kept seeing that stamp and my name." Grae powered up her cell phone.

"I think it was wise that we took that envelope. I am not for stealing archives any more than you are, but there was no way that you could explain that to Alice."

"What did you do with it?"

Grae saw that she had a text from Gav. "Mom found a dress that she thought would look great on you. Carrie will bring it to you on Friday."

Gav had never been one to text long messages, but she realized that the ones of late were extremely direct and short. She wondered if this dance was such a good idea.

"I left it in my room at Madison's. I thought it would be best to not bring it back and forth here."

"I'm going to get that soda now. I may take a little walk to try and clear my head a little."

Grae took her phone and a little cash and walked out of the library. As she exited Smyth Hall, the December air greeted her with a cold breeze. That afternoon, she and Jay would go visit Mary Baker. In a week, she would go to the dance with Gav. A few days after that it would be Christmas.

As she looked around the campus, she realized how quiet it was without the buzz of students. The majority had finished their exams and was enjoying the break between semesters. Faculty and administrative staff were still around, but most of them were very busy making preparations to close out the year. Grae crossed the campus and entered

Fincastle Hall. In the snack bar area, she bought a soda. As she was about to leave, she saw that Madison was sitting by herself in the corner having a snack.

"Hi, Madison."

"Oh, hello, Grae. Won't you sit down?"

Jay's sister looked up from the magazine she was reading. Grae thought that Madison looked very tired. She actually looked the way Grae felt.

"Well, maybe for a minute. I just came in to get a soda."

"You're working with Jay today?"

"Yes." She wasn't sure how much Madison knew about the work that she and Jay were doing.

"I'm glad that he was able to find you. It's funny how life has a way of working out." Madison paused and fingered the magazine in front of her. "I worry about Jay." Grae remained silent. "Can we speak freely?" Grae nodded her head. "My family and I thought that something horrible had happened to Jay. We were worried for a while that he was losing his mind. My parents still think that. Our older brother refuses to think about it at all."

"What do you think?"

Madison smiled at Grae's question. "I think that my brother has a level of honesty that very few people possess. He is willing to risk what others may think of him to speak the truth in his heart. He was always that way, even when we were kids. If he did something wrong, he would go and find one of our parents and tell them. Rock and I would just stand back in amazement as he would go and tell on himself. He just couldn't stand not telling the truth." Madison paused and took a drink of her bottle of tea.

"It amazes me now how my family cannot believe him. He is saner than any of us. He's had no lapse in mental health, despite what he may even think about himself. He truly doubted his sanity until I moved here. He obviously knew this area existed. He'd been here, in some way. Right before I got this job, he was looking at sanitariums. He was going to admit himself." Madison looked Grae straight in the eyes. "Please, don't tell him I told you that. I applied for this job in this town for one reason—Jay. I knew that Keith was going to be deployed. I knew that if I got this job, Jay would come and visit me. Maybe being here could save my brother from himself. I didn't know that there was someone he could find here who could truly save him. I didn't know that he could find you." A tear rolled down Madison's face. Grae felt an identical one touch her own.

"Thank you." Grae didn't say anymore before she rose and left Madison. There were no more words that needed to be spoken.

"Are you nervous?" The ride to Baker's Island had been one of silence. Jay was closely following the GPS. Grae was watching the scenery pass by, remembering that the last time she had been anywhere near the area was when she travelled with Squire David as they took his son to North Carolina.

"No, I'm petrified." Grae looked at her friend and smiled. She would not reveal the conversation she had just exchanged with his sister, but she would hold its knowledge and meaning close to her heart. "All I can think about is what if it is her. What if she has lived all of this time and I scare her to death, literally."

"Well, if it is her, you can rest assured that she is made of a special type of resilience. I'm sure she doesn't scare easily. I have this feeling that she may know you are coming."

"How?"

"By virtue of the same magic that took her to 1786 to begin with. You've got to have a little special energy in you when you travel back in time."

"Then, you have that magic, too."

"I know I do. It led me right to you."

As Jay made his last statement, he made the final turn onto the road where they would find Mary Baker's house. Even from a distance, Grae recognized it. For some reason, it just looked like Mary. Although it was large, two stories, it was far from the mansions of the McGavock and Graham families. It was painted white, but longed for a fresh coat. The decline of the paint into a graying tone also made it fade into the background of the winter landscape. Its roof was pitched with an ornate turret on one side. The asymmetrical wraparound porch had obviously been added decades previously and retained the look of wear.

"I bet this house started out as a simple farmhouse." Jay put the car in park and stared up at the house. "It looks like there have been additions of that porch as well as the turret, gingerbread, and other moldings to make the house take on a more Victorian look. I bet that is the original iron hardware on those shutters. Long vertical windows were certainly popular once."

"It's about the door tax." Grae interrupted his comments. "You were charged taxes based on the number of exterior doors your house had."

Despite all of the intricate aspects of the house, it was an old rose garden on the side that drew Grae's eye. She stared at it, mesmerized. There was nothing beautiful about it on that December day; it haunted her like a graveyard to beauty.

The sound of Jay slamming his door broke Grae's gaze. She got out of the car and stood beside it, looking up at the house. A woman came out onto the screened porch. She was short in stature with blond curly hair. She gave them a friendly wave. As Grae and Jay walked up the walkway, Grae glanced up to a window on the second story. She saw a curtain move and wondered if Mary was watching them.

"Hello, Missus Casper, I'm Jay Stone and this is Grae White." As they walked up the steps, the woman opened the door of the screened-in porch. It creaked a greeting to them.

"Welcome. My name is Kitty and I expect you to call me that. Don't worry, I'm not a ghost, but I am pretty friendly." The woman laughed.

"I guess you get that joke a lot," Jay said as they stood on the porch waiting for her to take them in further.

"More often than I would care to admit in the thirty odd years since I married my husband. It must have been true love." Kitty kept her hand firmly on the doorknob. "Before we go in, I have a few things I need to tell you. First of all, Miss Mary is very happy to have you visit her. She doesn't get many guests and she agrees to see very few of them. Miss Mary is very old. She's so old that we don't really even know how old she is. Well, over a hundred, that's for certain. The Today Show people tried to send that guy who used to be Ronald McDonald here to interview her. But, she wouldn't have any part of it."

"Willard Scott?" Jay said, looking at Grae with his eyebrows raised.

"Yep, that was his name. One of their scouting people came, and my Henry had to show him his shotgun. They left rather quickly. Guess they had a more pressing story elsewhere." Kitty laughed and winked. "As I was saying, Miss Mary doesn't see too many visitors. All her family is gone. Her vision has some issues, as does her hearing, but Henry and I actually think both of those senses are better than she lets on. Her mind is sharp as a thumb tack. She was happy to donate those letters to the library, but I don't think she expected anyone would want to come and talk to her about them." Kitty gave them both a stern look. "I don't want you asking her any silly questions. I don't want you two upsetting her."

"Why do you think she agreed to see us?" Jay asked as Kitty turned the doorknob.

"She agreed to see this young lady right here. You just get to come with her."

Jay did not look at Grae, but he did reach back and squeeze her hand. Kitty opened the door. They entered the home of Mary Baker.

"I have worked for Miss Mary for about twenty years. My mother worked for her for at least thirty. The only things that she allows to be changed are things that wear completely out. I cannot imagine how old the furniture is in this house. She says that some of it belonged to her husband's parents. No one knows how long he's been dead."

"What was his name?" Jay asked, although Grae knew that he knew the answer.

"Charles." Grae whispered it to herself as Kitty said it out loud.

The foyer was very open and the ceiling rose up to the second story. Grae gazed up and could see that the staircase wound up to a loft that overlooked the foyer. She imagined that there were probably four rooms up there. That seemed to be the average for houses of its time. She assumed that it must date to the early 1800's.

"Do you know who built this house?" Grae's thoughts found a voice. Kitty seemed surprised to hear it.

"Yes, I do know that. It was Mary's husband. My mother always thought that Miss Mary was probably much younger than her husband. Perhaps she was his second wife. We don't know that for certain. But, it just doesn't seem logical that Miss Mary could have been married to the young Charles if this house is as old as we think it is. We think she must have inherited it after being a young widow of an old man."

Grae knew that was not the case. Charles was only a few years older than Mary in 1786. They both would have been in their mid-thirties if the house was built near the beginning of the nineteenth century.

"Those are some very tall windows."

Jay had turned back around and was facing the front door. The door was tall, but an average size for the one story. But, the windows on each side went all the way up. They weren't one glass either. Each pane was tall and slender and was separated with a rectangular pane of stained glass.

"Indeed. It gives this room some beautiful light, even with the porch screened in. Those stained glass pieces were done by Miss Mary herself. It was the work she did to support herself after her husband's passing. Her art is all over the world. She still dabbles in it a little when her poor hands allow."

Grae looked back at the staircase. There was a motorized contraption with a seat to take someone up the steps.

"If you will follow me, Miss Mary is waiting for you in the parlor." As they followed her, Grae pulled on the sleeve of Jay's jacket.

"Maybe I should go in alone," Grae whispered in Jay's ear as Kitty walked through the doorway ahead of them.

"Miss Mary, your visitors are here." Kitty's voice was loud. She turned and walked back into the hallway where Jay and Grae were standing. "What are you two waiting for?"

They looked at each other. Jay extended his hand for Grae to go first. Kitty walked back into the room and they both followed. The subject of their visit was sitting in a high back chair that faced a large curved picture window with a window seat. Kitty lead Grae over to the woman, and Jay stood to the side.

"Miss Mary, this is the young lady and gentleman who have come to visit."

Grae walked around to the front of the chair. Tall and slender, the woman was indeed of considerable age. Her hair was white as snow and stood high on her head in a loose bun. Her hands were withered and somewhat drawn. She was impeccably attired in a beautiful navy dress with long sleeves and a white crocheted collar. The woman had her head down. Grae watched as she slowly raised her head. The face matched the rest of her. The years of time grooved her features. But there was a strong light in her pale blue eyes. They met each other's gaze and the woman smiled. Instantly, Grae knew this was her friend from long ago. She extended her hand.

"I am very pleased to meet you," Grae said as she grasped the woman's hand. Her grip was strong and full of emotion. "My name is Grae White. This is my friend, Jay Stone." Jay walked into Mary's view, but her eyes never left Grae's.

"Kitty, please get us some tea." Mary's voice could be described as a strong whisper. "Perhaps this nice young man will help you."

"I can take care of that on my own." Kitty looked back and forth between the two of them. Grae could tell that she was suspecting something.

"I'd love to help you. Perhaps I could see a little more of this interesting old house." Jay gave her an enthusiastic smile.

Mary took her gaze from Grae long enough to nod at Kitty, but she did not release Grae's hand.

"Very well, follow me." Kitty and Jay turned and left the room.

Grae was about to kneel in front of her old friend, but as soon as the door closed Mary was on her feet and enveloping Grae in an embrace.

"Oh, I just knew that I would get to see you again one day."

Mary's voice, while not youthful, did not match her body. Neither did the energy and agility that she seemed to have as she jumped up to hug her friend.

"I...I don't know what to say. I can't believe it is you." Grae and Mary held each other at arm's length. They both shook their heads in amazement.

"You do not look a bit different. I would have recognized you anywhere. Oh, how I have longed to see you again." They both walked over and sat down on the window seat.

"Well, for me, not much time has passed since we met. It was less than a year ago actually."

"Time is a cruel thing. Since you left in 1786, time has sped up and slowed down so many times for me. After we left the farm, my life with Charles seemed to fly by. We raised one child, a son. This dreaded curse of time, I believe, killed the others that I carried." Mary looked down at her stomach briefly and held it as if a baby was inside. "But, I have long ago made my peace with that. I have made my peace with many things."

"Oh, Mary, there is so much that I would like to ask you." Grae looked toward the door. "But, I fear that we don't have much time."

"No, Kitty is quick and efficient, just like her mother, and her grandmother, and her great-grandmother, and her great-great-grandmother." Mary rolled her eyes and laughed. "I am ancient. I am a freak of nature. I am trapped by time."

"But you seem so comfortable with it. You seem so youthful, despite…"

"Despite the fact that, depending on when you count from, I am as much as two hundred years old?" Mary looked out the window and sighed. "I suppose that time does heal all wounds, even the ones you inflict on yourself. My Charles died in 1832. Our son passed in 1861. Most of my grandchildren were gone by the beginning of the last century. I have long since lost connection with any past great-grandchildren. They all think that I am long dead. It is safer that way."

"But, what about this house? How have you kept them from knowing you still live here?"

"You just learn to be creative and learn the power of money. My grandchildren moved away and had lives in other places. After my son died, I would receive a letter or a phone call occasionally. I had begun doing stained glass by that point and had gotten quite good at it. My main work was for large churches located in huge old cities. It was easier for me to set up a shop wherever the piece was needed and complete the work there. During one of those trips, Kitty's great-great grandmother simply told whoever inquired about me that I was gone. I think they assumed that it meant I was dead. When the person asked who would get the house, she said the church would, as she knew that I had exact instructions for the house and the land to be left in trust. None of my descendants have ever tried to contact me again. They are probably scattered around the world."

Grae watched Mary's face closely as she said these words. There was a sadness in her face, but there was a contentment as well. Grae thought about the descendant that she knew. Grae could hear Jay's voice being extra loud in the hallway. Mary quickly went back to her original seat and Grae stayed near the window.

"Why are you talking so loudly, young man? I am not deaf." Kitty seemed agitated as they returned. She had a large tray in her hand.

"These ceilings are so high. I just wanted to see what the acoustics were like. It is a lovely sound."

"Maybe to your ears, but not to mine." Kitty rolled her eyes as she set the tray down on a table close to Grae. "Is everything okay in here?" She looked back and forth between them. "You having a nice visit with this young lady, Miss Mary?" Kitty patted the woman on her shoulder and rubbed her hair. It was obvious that she cared deeply for her employer and would go to great lengths to protect her.

"This young lady is delightful. I just wish I could see and hear her better." Mary's whispered voice returned and she squinted in Grae's direction. Grae had to fake a cough to conceal a giggle.

"Well, I have brought you all some tea and some of the shortbread cookies you like. Do you need anything else?" Kitty picked up the afghan that had fallen to the floor and put it across Mary's lap.

"No, why don't you take that young fellow and let Henry show him the farm? He talks awfully loud; it makes me nervous."

Mary motioned in Jay's direction. He was already drinking tea and eating a cookie. He furrowed his brow and tilted his head. Grae motioned for him to go with Kitty when she turned toward him.

"Oh, the farm!" Jay said, with a mouthful of cookie. "I'd love to see the farm."

Grae was sure that this act could have qualified for Oscar status. Kitty shook her head and headed out of the room. Mary waved at Jay as he followed, grabbing another cookie and taking the glass of tea with him.

"You are quite the actress, Mary McGavock Baker."

"Oh, my full name, no one has ever said that before." For the first time in their conversation, Mary truly looked sad. "I had to put my McGavock past completely behind me. I had to virtually become a recluse when we moved here. I didn't dare take the chance that if I ventured back over near the McGavock properties that I would see myself."

"What?" Grae was having trouble processing the last thing that Mary said.

"When I travelled back in time, I landed in 1784. Shortly thereafter, I met Charles. We fell in love practically instantly. I really didn't fathom what had happened for quite a while. I thought that perhaps I was far away from my home. That maybe I had been kidnapped or something. I certainly had no idea how I got there or how I would return. I was so in love with Charles that I let those thoughts overshadow the fact that I had left my family behind. But, after a while, I started thinking about the whole of it. After you arrived, I realized that I had met you in 1830, just shy of my eighteenth birthday. We had a scary adventure with that crazy old woman, Evelyn. You had helped me escape sure death and given me that little knife. Something just told me that I needed to keep it with me. I can't explain it. It was like it was a good luck charm. What it was most surely was a ticket back in time." Mary paused and looked toward the table of refreshments. "All of this talking is making me thirsty. Would you get me a glass of tea, please?"

Grae got up and walked toward the table. Her head was pounding. She had experienced much of what Mary was telling her, with Mary herself. But, hearing it backwards filled her head with confusion.

"So...you..." Mary held up her hand as Grae began to speak.

"Don't even try, my dear. I have lived with this knowledge for three lifetimes and it still makes my head hurt."

Grae smiled as her old friend basically read her mind.

"When you arrived in 1786, the moment I saw you, I knew why you were there. I had remembered the story of Joseph Baker. My father had talked about it. He had been a boy when it occurred. His father had watched as Bob and

Sam were hung. I knew what was going to happen to Charles' father." Mary grew silent. "He was a good man. He loved his family very much. Somehow, I knew that I could not prevent it. I couldn't imagine that you would witness it. I didn't know why you had to be there when it happened." Mary stood up.

Grae could see that she did have some signs of aging. But, it seemed as if she had aged to a certain point physically and just stopped. Mentally, from what Grae had seen, she was far younger.

"I didn't know why I was there either. It was a very frightening experience. It was my first trip back in time."

Mary turned around from the window. "It was your first time! My goodness, you certainly handled yourself well. You fit in so well with the slaves. Sal loved you dearly. She mentioned you several times throughout the rest of her life."

Tears filled Grae's eyes at the mention of Sal. "Oh, I loved her so much. She was so good to me and wise. I just can't imagine what her life was like after Bob and Sam died."

"Sal was never quite the same, but the bond between her and Nannie continued. They died within days of each other. All those years, only once did I hear them talk about what happened. It was after we all moved to Baker Island. Nannie sat us all down, Sal included, and she told us what happened. She knew that Bob didn't have anything to do with it, but he was there. In those white men's eyes, Bob and Sam were guilty just for being there. Aggie wasn't hung, but she was sold off. It was another piece of grief that Sal had to bear. But, I don't think she could much stand the sight of her niece after that night anyway."

"What did they think happened to me?"

"Well, since I had seen you disappear once before, I thought that you might have escaped somehow. So, I helped with the story." Mary sat back down beside Grae in the window seat. "I made a story up. I said that I heard you had convinced one of the guards to let you out because you were sick and that you ran away. I told them that one of the slaves said you hid in the woods until the next wagon train came. I probably should have just kept my mouth shut and let them make up their own story."

"Why do you say that?"

"Because that story got back to Patrick McGavock and he hounded me for every detail as he was trying to find you."

Grae smiled, thinking about the lengths Patrick went to in order to try and find her.

"Mary, correct me if I am wrong, but Patrick was your uncle, right?"

"Yes, he was my father's brother."

"How did you explain that later?"

"Well, it's funny that you ask that because up until this point, he is the only person who has ever discussed time travel with me. I never even revealed what happened to Charles. After I was born and grew up in my original time, Patrick realized that I was the same girl whom he had known as Mary Baker. At first, he thought that I was my twin or something. I think there is some term for that."

"Doppelganger."

"Yes, a strange word it is." Mary paused, reflecting. "He didn't talk to me about it in my original time. I think he knew that would be dangerous. But, after I disappeared as Mary McGavock, he found out that the Baker family had relocated to their new homestead, and he came to find me there. As I mentioned before, I tried to stay in seclusion. It wasn't hard. I was in my sixties by then. I doubt that anyone would have recognized me, but I wasn't going to take any chances."

"By that point, he knew my story." Grae interrupted her friend. "I had revealed it to him on my second journey in 1830."

"Yes, I believe after seeing you for the second time and experiencing all of the evil that Evelyn caused, he understood that there were more possible things in this world than could be regularly viewed as normal." Mary looked out the window. "Kitty and your friend will be back soon. We do not have much time."

"Why do you think you have lived this long?"

Mary turned back to face Grae. "After I reached a century of life, the first time, I thought that I was just blessed with good health. It had felt like a curse at first because I outlived all of the people that I loved. But, it soon became a game to see if I could fool people into thinking I was just an average old woman, not a freak of nature in their neighborhood."

"Do you think that it happened because you stayed in the time that you travelled to?"

"Oh, most certainly, I defied time. So it has been showing me every day since who truly has the upper hand. Physically, I think my body stopped aging in my seventies. Mentally, I still feel much younger. Psychologically, well, that is where I feel the age the most. It is hard not to be bitter." Mary paused and took hold of Grae's hands. "I would not go back and change it, even if I could. I do not know why or how I travelled to another time. It is a mystery to me. But, I have had a wonderful life, several of them actually. My only regret is that I lost my family—my mother, my father, my siblings. I lost my life as a McGavock. I know that my mother, especially, suffered greatly. I thought many times about trying to go see her. But I was afraid."

"Afraid of what might happen?"

"Yes, I was afraid that if I stepped back into my time, I might undo the life I had built. I had lost so much already, I just couldn't risk it."

Mary and Grae sat in silence for a while. They watched through the window as Henry showed Jay around the farm.

"I must ask you. How did you get all of the letters that you donated to the library?"

"It is amazing how some objects will just gravitate to a home that will care for them. As I stated, I travelled the world quite extensively creating my stained glass projects. But, I would return to this house as often as I could. Many times I would find a small box or packet of these letters waiting for me."

"Where had they come from?"

"Someone had mailed them to me, I presume."

"Do you know who it was?"

"I didn't at first. But, later, I discovered the source. It all made sense." Mary paused and nodded to Grae's questioning look. "I would rather not reveal who gave them to me."

Grae looked deeply into Mary's eyes. They still held many secrets.

"I guess I better go when Kitty returns with Jay."

"Yes, that would probably be wise. She is already suspicious of you two." Mary took hold of Grae's hand. "But, you must promise me that you will visit me quite frequently. I need to hear all about your adventures, back there and here now. I have much to tell you, too."

ROSA LEE JUDE & MARY LIN BREWER

"I promise." Grae felt calm for the first time in days. Even though she had never been in the house before, Grae felt at home.

"That Kitty person definitely doesn't like me." Jay made the observation as he put his car into reverse. Kitty stood on the front porch with a scowl on her face as she waved to them.

Grae remained silent as the car slowly moved backwards. She gazed upon the house and shook her head.

"Just when I think that I can no longer be surprised about what will happen, something knocks me off my feet."

"So, you had a good visit?"

"Most definitely, it was so good to see Mary again. What an incredible life she has led! All of these years, she has been hiding in plain sight. In many regards, I am sure that it wasn't hard to conceal her identity and story. No one looks for you if they do not think you exist."

"Kind of makes you wonder who else is out there. There always have been rumors of famous people who disappeared or supposedly died who are seen every once in a while. Like perhaps, Amelia Earhart has lived out her life on an island somewhere or Elvis Presley has a farm in Texas. History may have portrayed lives to have ended a certain way, but it does not mean the story is true."

TWELVE

The semester had drawn to a close and the college would soon be shutting down for winter break. Grae and Jay had to make the most of the remaining time they had before the library was closed for a couple of weeks between semesters.

"Are you two almost finished with the preserving and logging of those letters? I am beginning to think that you are spending most of your time reading them."

Alice was cheerful on Friday morning. Like most of her colleagues, she would be enjoying a welcomed break. She was dressed casually on the final day before her winter vacation in skinny jeans and boots; her long-sleeved black t-shirt would soon be covered by a leather jacket. Grae bet that Professor Dreamy had a Harley.

"Do you have special plans for the holidays?" Grae wanted to divert her from the topic of the letters as much as possible. She and Jay had plans to copy some of them while she wasn't watching. Alice lit up at the question.

"I plan to spend some time with my family over Christmas, the regular traditional stuff with presents and a lovely dinner. But, over New Years, Murphy and I are going to go skiing with some of his friends. I've never been skiing before, so that should be a great adventure. I hope I don't break anything!"

Grae watched as Alice's excitement spilled over into a little look of fear.

"I'm sure you will do great. Stay on the bunny trails for a while and be sure to learn how to get up, fall down the right way, and how to snow plow. Perry and I spent a lot of winter holidays skiing in Boone. It was something that we did together as a family every winter."

"Oh, I almost forgot. Madison called first thing this morning and asked if you were working today. She wants to talk to you about your schedule." Alice turned to go back to her desk.

"I wonder if she has some news about my getting into the nursing program. I've been on a waiting list. Maybe someone dropped out." Grae began to put her coat back on. "I'm going to walk over there."

"I still have trouble imagining you as a nurse, all that blood and stuff."

Jay grimaced and shook his head. He was making a pile of letters from 1864 that he would copy while Alice was on her lunch break.

"Well, I doubt that will be my favorite part. But, my experience with Ama really changed my outlook on medicine.

I realized that her life could have been easily saved by modern medicine. I know that I can't go back and save lives, but maybe I went through that experience to help me decide what my life career should be. I may not end up as a nurse; who knows, but I would at least like to give it a shot. No matter where life takes me, I hope to be able to work in a field where I can really help people on an individual basis."

"Now, that I can see." Jay smiled. "Tell my sis that I think we should go to your house for dinner tonight."

"Oh, did we invite you?"

"Yes, thank you."

"Well, perhaps I will need to check in with Mom while I am over in that building." Grae stuck her cell phone in her pocket and headed out of the library. She passed Alice at the front desk. "I'm going to see Madison now."

Alice and the other staff waved. Grae made her way across campus and into Bland Hall. She stopped at her mother's office first.

"This is a nice surprise." Kat looked up from a huge pile of files when she heard a knock at her door. "I know, this looks like a lot of work. But, most of it is going into bankers boxes to file away. Out with the old; in with the new. What are you doing wandering around campus?"

"Madison left a message with Alice before I got in this morning that she needed to see me. I'm hoping that she will be telling me that a slot has opened up in the nursing program."

"Oh, I hope so, too, dear. I know it has been hard waiting to find out. You have not been able to register for classes yet, have you?"

Kat put several thick files into a cardboard box that was next to her desk. Grae looked around and saw that there were several such boxes sitting in the corner near the door.

"No, maybe I will get to do that today. It would be nice to know what I will be doing come January. What I really came by to ask is if we could maybe invite Madison and Jay over for dinner tonight? I'm only working a few hours on the mountain this afternoon. So, I could be home early to help you make dinner. I just thought that since they are going next week to spend some time with their parents, it might be nice to have them over."

"That's funny that you are suggesting this as I was just getting ready to call Lesley McGavock and see if they might want to come for dinner tonight, also. She has that dress for you anyway and it might be nice to visit with them before the holidays."

"Well, okay, a houseful then. What were you thinking about fixing?"

"I was thinking something that none of us would eat over the holidays, like maybe barbecue chicken."

"That's sounds wonderful."

"I'll think about the side dishes in a little while. I plan to take off early anyway. So, whenever you can get home, I will have a few tasks for you to do."

"Okay, see you later, Mom." Grae began to walk toward the door.

"Grae!"

"Yes." Grae turned back toward her mother. Like Alice, Kat was dressed very casually. It made her look so youthful.

"Good luck! Let me know what Madison says!" Kat gave her daughter a huge smile.

"Will do."

"Well, Grae, I could say that I have good news and bad news." Madison was the only one in the counseling department when Grae arrived. She wondered if everyone else had taken an extra day of vacation. "But, I just would be melodramatic. All I have for you today is good news."

"I got in?"

"You sure did. There were actually three slots that opened up and you got the first one. Based on the classes that you have already taken and all of the advanced sciences you came with, I don't think that you will have too much catching up to do. Here is what I propose your schedule to be for Spring semester. I've taken the liberty of enrolling you with Shasta in as many classes as possible."

"Oh, that is awesome!" Grae was sitting next to Madison and reached over to hug her. "I really appreciate that. I can't wait to get started."

"It will be a great new adventure for you, Grae. I know that you will do great. You seem to have the discipline to keep on task. You can't be a slacker in the nursing program."

"I know. I have already heard the stories from Shasta. I'm ready to work hard. I was just telling Jay that I want to do something with my life that helps people on an individual basis."

"It's a noble calling, that's for sure. I'm sure some of your experiences have led you to make this career choice." Madison handed Grae the sheet that listed her schedule and closed her folder. "I think that all of your financial aid is in order as well. You might want to check with the bookstore while you are over here and see if they have any of the textbooks. It will probably be helpful for you to go ahead and get those for the online classes you are taking so that you can catch up on the terminology."

"Thank you, Madison. I really appreciate all of your help. Mom and I were wondering if you and Jay might like to come have dinner with us." Grae stood up and laughed. "Well, actually, Jay invited himself over for dinner tonight, but Mom was already planning to have a group meal. We would love for you to come. I know that you guys are going to see your parents next week."

"Well, that would be very nice. What could we bring?"

"That would be a question for Mom. She's still in her office for a few more hours." Grae walked toward the door.

"Grae, I appreciated our talk yesterday."

"It was good. It helped me understand Jay better. When I first met him, I never thought I would be saying this. Jay is a very good friend."

"I know he feels the same."

Grae left the offices. She stopped at the glass window that looked into her mother's offices. As if she could instinctually detect her daughter's presence, Kat looked up to see Grae give her two thumbs up. Kat jumped up and did a little dance at her desk causing the whole office to follow her lead, all laughing and waving at Grae.

"That's fabulous, Grae!" Alice gave Grae a high-five when she returned to the library. "I am so glad I ordered this cake and balloons."

On the table in front of her desk was a small cake with CONGRATULATIONS in multicolored letters. Jay came around the corner with a noise maker.

"You knew, didn't you?" Grae punched Jay in the arm as he blew the noise maker right in her face.

"Madison did not tell me any confidential information. She just didn't correct me when I guessed."

"Let's dive into this cake before I have to go to work!"

As Alice went to the back to find some paper plates and utensils, Jay pulled Grae back to where they normally worked.

"I think I have found some evidence that Davy and Robbie knew about each other."

"What?"

"There are two letters from a R. D. Graham. They almost sound like they are in code. They are written in 1864. The first one has a stern, angry tone. The next one seems different. They are both in that folder in front of your seat. I am going to make copies of them later, but try to read them before you leave."

Grae, Jay, and Alice enjoyed the cake and chatted about their holiday plans. Grae looked at the clock and motioned for Jay to get Alice away from the area for a few minutes.

"Let's take a couple of pieces of cake to the guys at the desk." Jay sliced two pieces and had them on plates before Alice finished her last bite.

"Sure, great idea. You stop and give me a hug, Grae, before you leave." Alice smiled as she led the way toward the front. This gave Grae the time she needed to read the letters before she left.

> 1ˢᵗ Lt. R.D. Graham, C.S.A.
> Mrs. Thomas Jonathan Jackson
> Lexington, Va.

Maj. D.P. Graham, C.S.A.
Yellow Sulfur Springs
Montgomery County, Va.

July 20, 1863

Dear Major,

You may not remember me but I remember you. We met at Harper's Ferry at the conclusion of John Brown's Raid in 1859. Our men joked that you were my 'long lost brother' due to our similar physiques, facial features, and last name. We laughed and shared coffee by your fire that evening never expecting to cross paths again.

Now, these four long years later, I find myself traveling to your Post at Yellow Sulfur Springs with my wounded cousin and commander, Captain William Alexander Graham, Jr. It is our hope that the springs' healing waters ameliorate his wounds received at Gettysburg. Our men of Co. K, 2ⁿᵈ N.C. Cavalry Regiment sustained horrendous loss there as did many others.

To further confound our circumstances, I wish to share this true story with you. While visiting my Aunt Mary Anna Morrison Jackson, yes she is indeed Stonewall's widow, I received a letter for one of our fallen soldiers. As you know it is difficult to locate our units during war; I confess it took some effort to locate you sir. This letter was sent from the soldier's dead father and dated 1845. How can that be, you say?

My exact thoughts. The long-dead father had apparently instructed his younger brother, the uncle, to deliver this letter to the son after the father's death and when the son was "of age". As fate would have it this letter has arrived too late and the truth will never reach the son. Here is where I need your advice sir, as I have read this letter over and over again. Do I need to contact this boy's wife or surviving relatives? I am quite angry sir. Read on.

You see, this father tells his son that he is NOT his father! His mother is NOT his mother! His sisters and brothers are NOT his real family! This voice of death has no mercy for this poor young man. Indeed, the voice goes on to say that his last name IS lawful, but his true blood resides in Virginia, about 100 miles north of his now-illegitimate home place! The letter goes on to identify the father and mother of his birth, his birthplace, and his real family. Does this brother or these sisters know of their covert brother's existence?

Upon our arrival, it is my hope that you will assist me with this delicate matter. I am sure that you join me in appreciating the irony here within, my "brother." Capt. Graham and I look forward to

relaxing and recovering at the springs as the
waters will most assuredly have a cleansing effect
upon our long, long journey.

Respectfully
Your Obedient Servant.

R.D.

1st Lt. R.D. Graham, C.S.A.
Mrs. Thomas Jonathan Jackson
Lexington, Va.

Maj. D.P. Graham, C.S.A.
Yellow Sulfur Springs
Montgomery County, Va.

July 31, 1863

Dear Major,

I am in receipt of your letter dated July 27. I
thank you for your prompt reply as it is our plan to
depart for Christiansburg Depot by train tomorrow
morning. It would be most kind of you to send a
carriage for us upon our arrival on August 2nd,
barring any unforeseen events.

Sir, I appreciate your genuine advice regarding the issue at hand. I now understand that you, like me, are unaware of such a convoluted dilemma as this. It calms my nerves to know you share my grief. In my own case, my family and my faith have served as my salvation during times of great joy and great pain. Perhaps the solution is there my friend. That is my prayer.

Captain Graham and I look forward to our visit with you. I, too, share your faith in God.

> *"Trust in the LORD with all thine heart; and lean not unto thine own understanding."*

Respectfully your friend,
R.D.

Grae laid the letters down. Her hand was shaking. An image flashed before her eyes—the image of the man writing the letters. She felt as if she had read them before, or, by some strange twist of fate, she had written them herself.

"That's just silly. I couldn't have known this. I…" Grae looked around. She knew no one was there, but still the room felt strange. As she stood up to leave, she touched the letters again and felt a spark.

"Oh, Lesley, this dress is gorgeous! Grae, don't you just love it?"

Grae would not argue that the dress was beautiful, but it made her head hurt. The dress that Missus McGavock had found for her to wear to Gav's party was blue velvet, royal blue velvet.

"Why, this dress looks just like the drapes at Graceland!"

Kat had invited Lucy over for their Friday evening supper. She was festively attired in her 'Don't Get Your Tinsel in a Tangle' sweatshirt. She had Elvis' Christmas hits loudly playing on a CD player. Ironically, Blue Christmas was serenading them.

"I'm sorry, Lucy. What did you say?"

"I SAID THAT THIS DRESS LOOKS LIKE THE DRAPES AT GRACELAND. DO I NEED TO TURN THE STEREO DOWN?"

Perry quickly came to the rescue and turned the volume to a more acceptable tone.

"We've never been to Graceland," Lesley McGavock said as she removed her hands from her ears. "But, I understand that they have never redecorated it. It still looks like the seventies. Surely, with all the money they make from tours, they could afford to redecorate by now."

Grae had to turn away to keep from laughing in the poor woman's face. She knew that any minute now Lucy was going to blow a gasket.

"They are keeping it that way because that is the way it was when Elvis left. May he rest in peace."

"Lesley, let's go upstairs with Grae while she tries the dress on." Kat commented as she saw Grae try to keep a giggle in. "Carrie, why don't you and Lucy check on the chicken? I bet it is ready to come out of the oven. You can take it out and put the rolls in. Dinner will be ready in about fifteen minutes."

Grae shook her head as she walked up the stairs ahead of her mother and Lesley. It was going to be a long night.

After dinner, the group divided into two basic directions. The men went to the living room to watch an old James Bond movie that Grandpa Mack liked. The women stayed in the dining room and discussed the latest new little shops that were being developed in the downtown area, among other things. Grae managed to keep Jay from joining the movie and lead him into the front parlor.

"Did you manage to get copies made of the remaining letters we still need to read?"

"I sure did." Jay retrieved a box from the front foyer. "I brought them all with me. I read them as I copied them. There are some interesting things in these letters. There are a few more from Robbie to Davy, including one that alludes to a confrontation between the two half-brothers and their father."

"You don't say. I would like to see that."

"I am almost certain that it happened, and that Martha and Bettie witnessed it. This letter all but tells the whole story. It is as if Bettie hears enough to know something is going on, but not enough to know exactly what happened. However, she does see a dramatic change in her parents."

Miss Bettie Ann Graham
Cedar Run Farm
Max Meadows, Va.

Major David Graham, C.S.A.
Yellow Sulfur Springs
Montgomery County, Va

August 25, 1863

Dearest Brother,

I hereby dispense with all formalities and
greetings, dear Brother, in fervent hopes that you
can calm my worry, for it churns my stomach and
darkens my every waking hour. Ma, Pa, and I
have been gone from our visit with you but for a
few days, however, it is as if we now reside in
another world! Brother! THEY ARE SO DIFFERENT!
What happened? What could produce such an
effect upon our stalwart yet stoic parents?

Brother, please do not think for an instant that I
am not capable of absorbing the truth. Do not feel
like you must protect me from our family; it is
falsehood that I cannot abide, but you of all
people KNOW THAT about me.

This is what I do know. Ma and Pa visited your
cottage after we all retired from supper. I was put
off that they did not include me in their visit to
you, so I followed them to your cottage and
overheard your conversations. The windows are
open this time of year. I know Ma and Pa

interrupted a conversation you were having with another soldier. I could only see the back of his uniform, but I could tell you were both upset, yet you shook hands and you both greeted one another as if you were brothers.

I saw Ma first. She gasped, her face turning pale as if the blood had drained from it. After a long moment of everyone staring at each other, frozen stiff with surprise, Ma pushed her shoulders back, walked forward towards the soldier, smiled, shook his hand, and introduced herself. Then she said the strangest thing. She calmly said, 'I have seen you in my dreams. I hear your mother's song to you as a baby. I leave you now with your family.' Then, Ma left the cottage. What did she mean?

Then I saw Pa step forward out of the shadows. I would not have known him except I saw him enter from that very door. Pa was ---he was---sobbing. I have never seen Pa cry. I have never seen his shoulders slump and shake. I have never witnessed his hands and voice trembling, but there it was. His deep, penetrating gaze upon this soldier never let up, and all I could think of was he was looking at a living ghost. His face said what could not be said, for this was a ghost he loved with all his heart.

I overheard some of your conversation, especially the words 'ama', 'so long ago', 'baby', 'my father and General Graham', 'Jackey', 'pride', and 'my *love for her was forever'. I did not linger further, as I was worried for Ma. When I found her back in our hotel room, she was humming "Amazing Grace" and would not speak of her encounter further. Ma was peaceful, Davy. She was peaceful.*

But I am NOT at peace! You must tell me what I already fear. Can it be that the man who is our father, has a hidden past, a secret that can no longer be silenced? You must answer me Brother! I must know the truth.

Your Devoted Sister,

Bettie

"Okay, I wasn't expecting that. I'm glad that you managed to get some of those before the break. I have a feeling that Alice may have them all put away by the time we return."

"You may be right. The letters from late 1863 into 1864 were not as interesting as the previous ones. It may be because Davy served a large portion of this time at Yellow Sulfur Springs and did not see any battle. He briefly mentions the Battle of the Cove that occurred near Wytheville. In a couple of letters, he speaks extensively about the deaths of Jimmy and William Tate. These are the brothers of Nannie Tate. They die in separate locations, two years apart. But, overall, the letters mainly include questions he asks about life at home. I haven't gotten to the ones from 1865 yet, so he may have more interesting things to say as the war draws to a close."

"What are you two in here talking about? You can't always be working on your research."

Kat entered the room with Madison behind her. From behind Kat's back, Grae could see that Madison was giving them a concerned look.

"You caught us, Missus White. I've been boring Grae again with my research. I'm sure she will be glad to be rid of me for a few weeks. Perhaps I will be able to begin writing my thesis."

"You haven't started writing yet? You've been doing a lot of research to not have even begun." Kat picked up the plates from the dessert that Grae and Jay had brought with them. "Don't you think you should put some of that on paper? You don't want to forget it."

"Oh, I don't think it will be possible for me to forget what I've learned."

It was Saturday morning. In a little over a week, it would be Christmas, and Perry wanted to go shopping.

"I've got to find something for Carrie. I have no clue."

Perry's dramatic urgency amused Grae. Kat was officially off for three weeks and seemed open to taking her son shopping.

"How did you get so much time off?"

"Well, I've been saving my time in case I needed it for an emergency, and you know that we didn't go on vacation. So, I am in the use or lose category. I had four days that I could not carry over. I thought a long holiday break would be enjoyable. I could do all that I needed to do for Christmas and still have some time to spare."

The three of them were in the kitchen. Grae was eating a little breakfast before she began a long day on the mountain. Perry was looking through a stack of sales papers that their mother had saved from the previous Sunday newspaper.

"Have you heard any more about Dad?" Grae meant to ask that question before, but with all of the company the previous evening, she hadn't gotten the opportunity.

"No, I haven't and I really thought I would have heard from someone this week. I'm not sure it would do any good to try to call today. I doubt that I could reach his doctor or lawyer." Kat sat down at the table between her two children with a cup of coffee. "Do you want to try and go visit him one more time before Christmas? I guess that we would mostly need to plan around each of your work schedules."

"Yeah, that would be good." Perry looked up from the jewelry store flyer he was studying. "After today, I think I am scheduled to work every day until Christmas, but maybe I could get someone to take one of my shifts."

"That's a lot of working there, young man."

"Having a girlfriend is expensive!" Perry smiled and showed his mother something out of the flyer. "Do you think that Carrie would like a watch?"

"Have you ever seen her wear one?"

"No, she just usually looks at her phone."

"Well, maybe, we should consider something else then. You should have mentioned this to me yesterday. We could have asked her mother last night. What do you think, Grae?"

"I think you might want to answer the back door."

"Why?" Kat turned around and looked at the closed door.

"Because Dad just waved at me through the window."

"It was just amazing! I looked up and there he was."

Grae's day had begun in a shocking way, but duty called and she was busy helping in the store.

"Your father, the one who has been near death and in prison, was at your back door unannounced?" Mark, Grae's co-worker, was helping Mary Lee fill the bakery display case.

Grae had just made three pots of coffee. The store wasn't full, but there were at least a dozen people milling around. Even for the Christmas buying season, it was looking to be a busy day.

"I guess I haven't told you the most recent parts of our family saga. Our conversations have been too filled with my health."

Grae poured Mary Lee a cup of Snow Cream coffee and took it to her in the kitchen. The woman had an unusual amount of brownie batter on the front of her apron.

"Thank you, dear. I don't seem to be functioning on all pistons today. My fingers have a mind of their own and feel like dropping things today."

Grae returned to the front with a tray of oatmeal raisin cookies for the display case.

"The experimental treatment they were doing on Dad had some extremely positive results." Grae resumed her conversation with Mark as he arranged the cookies in the case. "I guess he is basically cured."

"That's wonderful, Grae. But, they usually don't let people out of prison because their medical problems are gone."

"Oh yeah, around the same time, they discovered that it was really Dad's boss that stole most of the money. Dad was somewhat involved, but only after the bulk of the embezzlement had occurred." Grae paused as she put the empty tray on the counter. "He told us he wasn't responsible all along, but there was so much evidence telling a different story, we didn't believe him. I feel rather ashamed now. I didn't believe my own father."

"Well, I can't say what I would do in the same situation. But, I do know that we are taught to believe in authority and sometimes they get it wrong."

"It made sense at the time. It all happened so fast. We were living this affluent life and a court order came and took it away. We had to believe that it was true. I think my mother just wanted to get us as far away from it as she could. She didn't take the time to think about another possibility."

"So, back to today's story. How did he get to your back door?"

Mark lifted the stack of trays that had held all of the bake goods and carried them back to the kitchen. Mary Lee was sliding a huge sheet pan full of brownies into the oven. Grae followed to help.

"Well, it seems that Mom had turned her cell phone off on Thursday because it was almost out of charge. Since she came home early yesterday and started her vacation, she forgot to turn it back on. Dad's lawyer had been trying to reach her because he knew that Dad was being released from prison. His doctors also felt like he could travel and spend Christmas with his family. He didn't know any other phone numbers to reach Mom. The phone at the Mansion is in J.C.'s name and Dad couldn't remember his name. So, the lawyer drove Dad here this morning."

"That's really an incredible story. I bet you were sorry to have to come into work."

"Well, not really. There was a lot of drama going on when I left. Mom is not big on surprises. And, she doesn't like this lawyer guy. Perry was thrilled. Grandpa was grumpy. Dad looked tired."

"What an interesting Christmas you will have, Grae. What an interesting Christmas indeed."

After her ten hours on the mountain, a light snow began to fall as Grae drove home. "This weather is nuts," she said to herself as she entered the town limits. "Yesterday it was almost sixty degrees and today it's snowing."

Grae stopped to get gas on I-81 at Exit 84 near the Mansion. As she was standing there pumping, she was surprised to see Gav come out of the convenience store. She looked around and didn't see his car. He had almost gotten into his parents old Suburban when he noticed her. He closed the door and walked toward her. She felt a twinge of excitement and apprehension as he approached.

"Hey, I didn't expect to see you. Perry said you were working."

Gav looked different somehow. It had been less than a month since Grae had seen him, but so much had happened since then.

"Yeah, I just got off a little while ago. I was heading home."

"The Mansion is kind of a strange place today, stranger than normal." Gav chuckled at his own joke. Grae didn't join him.

"You've been to the house?" Grae heard her tone and realized it wasn't very friendly.

"Yeah, I was just there. I...ah...met your Dad."

Grae rolled her eyes and returned the gas nozzle to the pump.

"He was very nice. I wasn't expecting him to be there."

"Neither were the rest of us. So, was there something in particular that you stopped by for?"

"Yeah, I wanted to talk to you about next Friday. I've got a lot going on that day. I was wondering if it would be okay if I got my Dad or someone to drive you to Blacksburg? Then, I could bring you home after the party." For some reason, this question just rubbed Grae the wrong way.

"Why don't I just drive myself? Then, you won't have to bother with me at all. Maybe you could have me seated next to someone else at dinner." Grae put the gas cap back on and slammed the cap cover closed.

"It's a party, not a dinner. Why are you getting so mad? All I was trying to do was avoid being late. I have an exam that morning and some other things to do. I can't get up here and back to Tech without making us late."

"Maybe you should move some of your 'other things' or maybe they are more important than picking up your date."

"You don't understand."

"Then, why don't you explain it to me." Grae had one hand on the top of her doorframe and the other on the door. She was ready to get into her car.

"I can't tell you."

"You used to be able to tell me anything." Grae dropped her head. She knew her tone was harsh. But, not only was the conversation making her head hurt, her heart hurt as well.

"Things used to be different. A lot has changed in the last few months. Things aren't the way that they seemed."

"Look, Gav, I'm sorry that I am grumpy…"

"No, it's fine. Just go along with this, Grae. Let me send someone to pick you up. Trust me; you don't want to know about what I have to do that day. I've got to go. I'll let you know the details later."

Gav turned and walked back to his car. Grae felt bad. She didn't want their conversation to end that way.

"Wait, Gav." He didn't turn around. Grae watched as he got into his car and quickly put it in reverse. He just raised his hand to her as he pulled away.

"There is the prettiest barrister I have ever seen."

Tom White pulled his daughter into a hug as soon as she walked into the living room. He quickly sat back down in the recliner that was next to Grandpa's. He looked exhausted.

"I'm not a barrister, Dad. I roast coffee beans and flavor them with oils."

"I'm sorry. I think I knew that. My memory has been affected by all of these treatments and meds."

Grae would have previously described her father as tall and athletic. But, now, he had a frail look. His once year round tan was replaced by the pallor of illness and indoor confinement. The man who once worked out at least four times a week and played basketball with his co-workers now looked soft. It was her father's eyes that showed the most change. Once full of sparkle and light, they now had a hollowness to them. He looked like he had lost a part of himself. Perhaps that was true. A year had certainly made a huge difference in his life.

"Well, I guess it has been hard knowing what our lives have been like when you just hear bits and pieces." Grae wasn't sure if that was the right thing to say to her father. It was certainly the truth. "We haven't known much about you either, except that you have been sick."

"I am so happy that it is all behind us. We can go back to being a family again."

Grae was silent as she pondered her father's comment.

"Can't we?"

Grae knelt in front of him. "Dad, we never stopped being a family. We are just a different type of one than we used to be."

"Grae, I don't want to put you on the spot by asking this. I don't expect you to betray any confidences or anything. But, I don't have anyone else to ask. I know it would make Perry very uncomfortable."

"This must be a doozy of a question. I don't think there is much that you couldn't talk to Perry about."

"It's about your mother." Tom breathed in a deep sigh. He leaned his head back on the headrest of the chair and closed his eyes. "I almost don't want to know the answer." Grae took hold of her father's hand. He opened his eyes and smiled at her. "You are such the young woman now. It amazes me." Tom stared deep into his daughter's eyes. "Has your mother been seeing anyone?" He looked at her nervously. She almost felt sorry for him.

"Not that I am aware of. I don't think so. She works and is here. She hasn't made a lot of time for herself in the last year."

Grae thought about her own words. She had been so caught up in her own life that she hadn't thought much about what her mother was doing, or not doing.

"That's a relief. But, it surprises me."

Grae stood up and put some distance between her father and herself. She thought she heard a little of the old Tom White emerging.

"Why? Did you think that Mom was just going to get divorced and run into the arms of another man? This has been a rough, rough time for her. She's uprooted us. We lost about everything we owned. She had to face the embarrassment of having been married to a convicted criminal. She had to find a job."

"No, no, no. Grae, you have misunderstood me." Tom tried to stand up, but his legs just would not hold him up. Grae was shocked to see how weak her father was. "I meant that your mother is wonderful. She is everything good and right and beautiful in the world. She's the only wise choice I have ever made. I knew that she was the better part of our marriage. I just never realized that she was the better part of everything in my life. You kids and Kat, you're...well...you are the only things that I had that were worth losing. You all are the only things that I am afraid of not getting back." Tom paused and wiped his eyes. "I have imagined all of these months that there has been some really smart man out there that found her. I know I couldn't compete, not after the mess I made with our lives. Not after the way I did not appreciate or care for my family. I took everyone for granted, most of all, your mom. She deserved better."

"I'm not going to argue with you or contradict you. Pretty much everything you said is true. Things will work out with Perry and me. You are our father and we love you no matter what. We will soon be adults, so the playing field will change. We hope that the game will be played more fairly." Tom smiled and nodded his head. "We want you in our lives. But, I can't speak for Mom. She is really the one who lost the most. I don't know if her heart can forgive you for tearing her life apart. But, I do know one thing for certain. She's every bit of the person that I always knew she was and even more. You or any other man will not get control of her life again. It's a new game with Mom. I don't know if she will let you try or not."

Grae turned and left the room. As she walked through the doorway into the foyer, she almost collided with her mother. Kat put her finger up to her mouth to tell Grae to be quiet. Then, she put her arms around her daughter and gave her a long, strong hug.

"Thank you." Kat whispered the words into Grae's ear. She could hear the emotion in her mother's voice. "I am so thankful you are my daughter."

THIRTEEN

The following days flew by as everyone seemed to have many directions to go in. Grae worked long days on the mountain. Perry's shifts seemed opposite to hers. Their mother was busy with Christmas preparations. It appeared to them that she would never stop baking.

"I realize that you all must think I have opened a bakery."

Kat began the conversation during a rare lunch time when her entire family was home. It was Wednesday. Grae was off and Perry had worked an early shift helping to unload a tractor trailer full of extra holiday food for the grocery store.

"It's just that several people asked me to make some special desserts. I really hated to turn them down."

"So, it appears that your mother is making a different type of cake or cookie every day this week. I think it is wonderful!"

Tom sat at the table heartily eating the chicken pot pie that Kat had placed in front of him. Perry had almost devoured his first one. Grandpa was in third place with Grae and Kat watching the view from the sidelines.

"You think it is wonderful because you have gotten to taste some portion of them."

"I like to do my part."

Kat smiled at him. Grae shifted her eyes back and forth to watch the exchange. Her mother's attitude toward her father had softened somewhat since she overheard his confession. Regardless of how it all turned out, she knew that her mother was going to do her best to help him recover his strength. Lots of rest and Kat's nutritious cooking were already beginning to bring back some of the color to Tom White's complexion. It was amazing to her how quickly love and care could change a person's health.

"I think this is the first time I have really seen you in several days, Perry. Did you find a gift for Carrie?" Grae leaned against the countertop as she ate her pot pie. Her mother's cooking skills continued to amaze her. "Oh, my gosh, Mom. This is delicious."

"Thank you, dear. I put a little twist on an old recipe."

"Well, yes and no." Perry came up for air from his second serving long enough to answer Grae's question. "I got her an iTunes gift card."

"How romantic." Grae rolled her eyes and shook her head.

"The girl likes her music. But, I know that isn't enough. I'm just not good at this."

"I'm sorry, Perry. I have let you down." Kat sat down between Tom and Perry and began to eat her pot pie. "The surprise of your father arriving changed our shopping plans on Saturday. He seems settled now. Maybe we could go shopping tomorrow."

"You need to give her something pretty, something that she will want to keep forever, like a locket." It was the first words that had been uttered by Grandpa Mack since their meal had begun.

"A locket, Dad? That's a little 1950's."

"What difference does that make? He needs to show his sweetie that he is a sentimental fool. Every girl likes a fool. You sure did."

"Oh, Mack, you've still got that sharp humor. I had almost forgotten about it." Tom raised his eyebrows as he exchanged glances with Grae. "I have missed it so much."

"Tom, I was just trying to give your son a relevant example of what it takes to make his lady happy. You must have had some success at that, once upon a time, to have landed my wonderful daughter. Maybe you should take your son shopping."

"Dad, I really don't think that Tom is up to going shopping."

"No, no, Kat, the old man is right. This is Perry's first girlfriend, and I should be helping him with this important purchase."

Perry beamed at his father as he looked at his mother cautiously. "Is that okay with you, Mom?"

Kat seemed to be in her own little world. "Yes, certainly, that's fine." Kat forced a smile. "He seems a little stronger. I wouldn't plan for it to be too long of an excursion."

"Well, I've got to go back into work again this evening and most of tomorrow. I guess it will be Friday evening before we could go."

"That's perfect." Grae rejoined the conversation and everyone turned in her direction. "Well, Gav was looking for someone to drive me to Tech. You two can take me there, and then go shopping."

Tom started to speak, but Kat gave him a look.

"Sure, honey, I guess we can trust Perry's driving in Blacksburg."

Tom chuckled and looked nervously at Grandpa Mack.

"Well, I suppose I could drive you all down there." Grandpa seemed less jovial with the direction the conversation was going.

"No, Dad, that won't be necessary. I will go with them. I would love to be able to take some photos of Grae and Gav as they depart for this dance."

"It's not a dance, Mom. It's a party at Coach Beamer's house."

"Oh." Kat paused as she began to pick up some of the dishes. "Do we need to stay in Blacksburg until it is over?"

"No, Gav will bring me home." Grae turned away from them and began to load the dishwasher.

"Well, I've just got to ask. Forgive me. Why can't this young man come and pick you up?" Tom asked, anger creeping into his voice.

"He says that he has something to do." Grae continued to work on the dishes.

"More important than picking up his date?"

"Tom, you don't know Gav. He is a very nice young man. He has a wonderful family. Perry's girlfriend, Carrie, is his younger sister."

"Kat, I don't care if he is a Kennedy. I don't understand why he can't drive here and pick up our daughter for an event at his school that he wants her to go to."

"Now, that right there sounds a lot like the old Tom White." Grae laughed as she turned around.

"Young lady, don't take that tone with me."

"You know absolutely zero about my life, Dad. I realize that you have been all vindicated and healed and everything. But that doesn't fix the fact that you have missed over a year of our lives. We've had a few things happen since then. I don't like it that Gav isn't picking me up. It's a real drag to have to be driven to a college party by your parents. But, Gav says that he has something important to do, and I guess I need to believe him." As Grae said the words, she realized their meaning was true. There was silence for several moments.

"I'm sure that Gav has a good reason, Tom." Kat picked up her plate and walked to the sink.

"Very well, then. We will escort you to your date." Tom smiled and turned his attention back to Perry. "And then, we will take this fellow to find something awesome for his girl."

The tension in the room lifted. But, the look exchanged between her and Grandpa said everything.

"Grae, can I come by and show you something?" It was Friday morning. Grae was straightening up her room when she got the call from Jay.

"Sure, what's up?" There was a silence on the other end. "Did you drop the phone?"

"No, I...ah...I just really don't want to tell you this over the phone."

"Gosh, Jay, you sound mighty serious." Grae looked at the clock. It was almost noon. "I've got to leave at five to go to Blacksburg."

"Oh, yeah, I forgot; Gav's party. Well, I can come over in the next hour or so. Will that work?"

"Yeah, sure. I'll see you in a little while."

Grae sat down at her desk. There was something very wrong in Jay's voice. She absentmindedly picked up the blue foundation pen that she had found in the old box. A scene flashed before her eyes. The man was once again sitting at a table writing, but, this time, he turned and she saw his face. It was the face of a stranger. Yet, it was somehow familiar. She had no doubt that it wasn't Squire David. The room began to swirl. She dropped the pen. The movement stopped.

"GRAE!" She heard her mother yelling from the bottom of the stairs. Slowly, Grae rose and walked out of the room and to the top of stairs.

"YES!" Grae could hear Kat walking up the first flight of stairs.

"Grae, Lucy called and said she would be glad to do your..." Kat stopped talking as she saw Grae. "What's wrong? You don't look so good. Are you having another episode? What's happening?"

Grae walked toward her mother and put her arms around her. Kat embraced her.

"Tell me what's wrong."

"You've got to talk to me, Mom. You've got to tell me what happened to you." Grae whispered these words in her mother's ear. At first, she felt her mother's body stiffen, then she relaxed. "I'm going to go back, Mom. I have to. But, you've got to tell me before I go. You've got to help me."

Kat began to sob.

Kat and Grae sat curled up on Kat's bed. Propped up by several large down pillows and covered in one of Granny Belle's beautiful quilts, they snuggled as they once had when Grae was young and home sick from school. It was a comforting feeling for Grae.

"I didn't know much about time travel. But, I was curious. It wasn't a taboo subject in the family, but few brought it up at Christmas dinner either. I was in my senior year of high school. I should have been more concerned about who was going to take me to the prom than who I would meet a century ago." Kat laughed briefly. "But, I guess you know a little about that yourself. During my first trip, I travelled to 1920 and spent some time with Nannie Graham, the Major's wife. She was very old by then and I was her companion for about a month. Once I got over the fear of never being able to go home, I actually enjoyed the experience."

"I never thought about what the different periods you travelled to might have been. I haven't read much about her. I bet she was an interesting lady."

"She was. She had been a widow for a very long time. Her love for her husband was strong and it lived on with her in this house." Kat sighed and pulled the quilt up around her. "My second trip was a few months later and I went back to 1785 when the Baker family first settled on this property. I got to be the niece of someone who knew the Bakers on that trip. I met another Nannie that I liked very much."

"Why didn't you tell me that when I told you about my first journey?" Grae crawled out of the covers and faced her mother.

"I considered it. But, I didn't want to give you any more reason to go back again. I thought maybe when we were both older; we would compare trips to keep your daughter from travelling."

"That's not funny."

"I'm not laughing." Kat reclined back on the pillows. "My third and last trip was the one where you met Loretta, a seamstress apprentice."

"Okay, so what happened to you on these trips that were so horrible? You seemed to enjoy those first two trips. I was there for your third. Nothing bad seemed to happen to you."

"You have no idea what happened to me on that trip. You only saw a portion of my journey." Kat's face took on a stern look, a look of fear.

"Then, why don't you tell me."

"I need you to promise me three things first. You must never tell anyone what I am about to tell you. You must never try to do it yourself. You must forgive me." Kat did not wait for Grae to reply. "I was somewhat of a handful in my teenage years. I liked to date guys I shouldn't have dated. Go to places I had no business being. By the time I took my last journey, I was a little bored with the process. I thought I could shake it up a little bit."

"Wait! I'm sorry. Are you talking about the sweet little Loretta I met in 1859?"

"Yes. Haven't I ever told you about how great I was at acting?"

Grae just shook her head.

"So, I did something very foolish. I took someone with me."

"You can't do that. Can you?" It had not really occurred to her that taking someone on a journey was really possible.

"It is possible. But, it is disastrous." Kat burst into tears. "And you must promise me. You must swear to me that you will never do that yourself!"

"Okay, okay. What happened?"

"I was young and I was stupid. I thought it would be fun to take someone with me. I didn't know what the consequences would be. I didn't know that my time was up, and I couldn't go back again."

"Your year was up."

Kat gave Grae a very shocked look. "How do you know that?"

"Ah…well, I can't remember. Maybe I read it somewhere."

"I don't think there is a *Time Travel for Dummies* out. You couldn't have read that anywhere." Kat gave Grae a stern look. "Come on, tell me."

"I really don't think that I should. It would betray a confidence." Grae hoped that this would keep her mother from pressing further.

"That's not going to work this time. If someone in the present told you this, I want to know who they are. If someone in the past told you, they must have suspected what you were doing. Either way, it sounds dangerous. I want to know who."

Grae took a deep breath and gave it some quick thought. "Okay, but you have to promise that it will not change your opinion of this person."

"Grae, I don't see how I can do that. My opinion will naturally change because this will reveal much about this person. It doesn't mean that I will feel negatively though."

Grae didn't like the evasiveness of her mother's answer. She studied her mother's expression. "You are being very evasive about telling me what happened to you on that last journey." Perhaps Grae could get her mother off the question and back to her story.

"Evasiveness must run in this family, like our predisposition to sarcasm."

"And our ability to take it on trips."

"Grae, I am not going to continue telling my story until you reveal this part of yours." Kat folded her arms and leaned back on the pillows. Grae caught a glimpse of what she remembered of Perry's defiance as a toddler.

"Okay, but don't think that you can influence my friendships just because I reveal secrets of my friends."

Kat nodded.

"It was Jay who told me about the year limit."

"Jay? How in the world would he know that? Is it part of his research?"

"Well, you might say that." A questioning look crossed her mother's face. "Jay has time travelled."

"What! How?"

"I guess the same way we did."

"From here?"

"Oh, no. He was in Massachusetts when he travelled, but his trip brought him to the Mansion during the mid-1800s."

"You have got to be kidding me."

"Nope, I am not. I was pretty surprised when he told me. It's the whole reason that he and Madison are here."

"Has she travelled, too?"

"No, but she applied for the job at the college so that it would give Jay a logical reason to come here. He was having some real problems dealing with his experience and he wanted to learn more."

"More about what?"

"More about someone who he had learned about while he was back in time."

"And who was that?"

"Me."

"You met him back in time. This is getting very weird."

"No, I didn't. I haven't travelled to the same time that he was in. He met someone who knew me from my journeys." Grae choked back the emotion that always seemed to come when she began to speak of him. "He met Patrick."

"The young man who was so much like Gav?"

"Yes, I knew him as a young man and as an older man. He was an even older man when Jay met him. Patrick knew that I had travelled from the far distant future. Jay was amazed to learn that it was his own time as well."

"Grae, that is just incredible. It gives me cold chills." Kat motioned for her daughter to get under the covers with her. They snuggled from a cold that was not present in the room.

"Please, don't tell anyone."

"Darling, telling someone is the last thing I will do." Kat paused and pulled Grae closer to her. "It explains why you two developed such a quick and strong friendship. I had wondered if something else was going on."

"No, Mom. But, yes, we have become very close friends. We have had no choice really."

"I understand."

"Now, you've got to tell me who you took back in time…"

"HELLO! ANYBODY HOME?" The sound of Jay's voice echoed up the stairs.

"Well, speak of the devil." Kat jumped up off the bed. Her movement was so fast that she almost sent Grae tumbling off the other side. "WE'LL BE RIGHT DOWN." Kat yelled from the doorway as she straightened her clothes. "Don't worry; I will not say anything to him, right now."

"Mom!"

Kat gave her daughter a quick smile, and then left the room.

Grae found Jay a few minutes later in the front room of the house drinking a large mug of her mother's Russian tea. A plate of sugar cookies was untouched on the table beside him.

"So, you sounded very anxious on the phone. What's up?"

Jay stood up as Grae entered the room. It was a chivalrous habit that Grae, for the first time, realized that Jay always did.

"Your mother left you some tea. It is very delicious."

Grae saw a steaming mug of the brew next to the plate of cookies. It was her mother's special recipe. She always kept plenty of the mixture ready during the holidays. Grae sat down in the chair opposite of Jay at the small table.

"Okay, I am sitting down and drinking my tea. You can talk to me now." Grae glanced at the old clock that chimed on the mantle. She would need to leave in two hours. She hoped this wouldn't take too long.

"I told you that I would try to find out more about Patrick. The truth is that I had already started researching him long before I came to Virginia. I gathered a lot of information online. Recently, I was able to contact a historian by the name of Mister Lattimore in North Carolina who lives just one county over from Catawba Springs in Lincoln County near Patrick's estate. He was a great help and sent me a huge packet of documents. I've been reading them on and off for about a week. I've also done some other research about his family line."

"You mean his ancestors? They would have been the first McGavocks who came to the area."

"No, his family life after him, his descendants."

Grae gave him a confused look.

"I told you that he had a child, right?"

"I'm sure that Margaret McGavock told me that Patrick never married or had children."

"Well, like many things in the Graham and McGavock families that story isn't entirely true. He had a son. I am not sure who the mother was, or if she and Patrick were married. But, Patrick told me himself that the mother of his child died in childbirth."

"Just like Ama."

"Patrick raised his son alone."

For some reason, this information hit Grae hard. Tears began flowing down her cheeks. Jay just nodded and kept talking.

"I've traced the family line to the present day. It's really kind of amazing. Each son since then had only one son. There were some daughters in later generations, but only one son in each family. All the way down until today."

"Well, that is unusual. But, Jay, I'm not sure why you are telling me all this. What does it matter?" Grae watched as Jay took a really deep breath. Something was wrong.

"The last three male descendants of Patrick don't live very far from here. The family sold their estate in North Carolina and moved to Virginia about fifty years ago."

"Okay, well, that's not too unusual. North Carolina and Virginia are adjoining states. I don't understand why this is so interesting to you."

"The gentleman who moved his family to Virginia is named Taylor McGavock. Apparently, Taylor was a family name on his mother's side."

Grae nodded and glanced at the clock. "Jay, I really don't have a lot of time. I've got to get ready to go to Gav's party."

"Taylor lives in a nursing home in Christiansburg. He has one son, Jason." Jay was silent for a moment. "Jason has one son. His name is James. James McGavock, I think you know him as…"

"Gav." Everything began to tilt. The pain in her head grew strong and then, nothing.

"Grae! Grae! Speak to me!"

Grae could hear Jay's voice. It was loud and soft at the same time.

"Open your eyes!"

Slowly, she did as the voice commanded. She saw Jay's face right in hers. He looked pale.

"What happened?"

Grae found herself on the floor in the front room. Jay helped her up into a chair. A mug was on its side on the floor with a puddle of liquid around it. Grae glanced around to find something to soak up the spill. Finding nothing, she just pointed at it.

"I'll get it. You sit there. Are you okay?" Jay took several napkins that were lying on the table and cleaned up the spill on the wooden floor.

"Yeah. What happened?" Grae looked around and tried to remember what had been happening. Jay was here to tell her something.

"You passed out after I told you about..."

"Gav." It was all coming back to her. Jay had told her that Patrick and Gav...

"He is descended from Patrick. He is a direct descendant. If my calculations are correct, Patrick is Gav's great-great-great-great-grandfather."

Grae sat there and shook her head as Kat entered the room.

"I came to see if you all enjoyed...what's going on here?" Kat watched as Jay stood up from cleaning the spill.

"I spilled my tea, Mom. I'm just clumsy I guess." Grae smiled as Jay put the wet napkins into Grae's empty mug.

"It was delicious! The cookies have something extra in them besides regular sugar cookie ingredients, don't they?" Jay was talking, but Kat's eyes were focused on Grae.

"Lavender." Kat said in a monotone.

"Jay was just getting ready to leave now. I've got to be rude and push him out the door. Time's a wasting! I've got a party to go to." Grae hoped that her upbeat tone would throw her mother off track.

"Yes, I've got to go. Thanks so much for the tea and cookies." Jay started to walk out of the room with Grae following behind him. Kat followed.

"Jay, I have a tin of cookies and some of the Russian tea mix for you to take home and share with Madison."

"Oh, that's very kind of you. We are going to be leaving in the morning to go see our folks. We can make a thermos of that tea and snack on those cookies on the way." Jay opened the front door. "Merry Christmas to all the Grahams and Whites!" Jay gave Kat and Grae brief hugs. "Oh, I almost forgot something. Madi will kill me. I'll be right back." Jay ran down the front steps and to the left of the house where his car was parked.

"What did he come to tell you?" Kat turned around and faced Grae. They were both standing in the doorway.

"Oh, he just completed a big portion of his research and he wanted…"

"Tell me the truth. When I entered the room, you looked like you did in the hospital. If you don't want me to prevent you from going to Gav's party, you will tell me the truth."

Grae could tell that her mother's threat was a serious one. "Okay, wait till he leaves. He's worried enough probably as it is."

Jay came back up the steps. Kat and Grae both walked out onto the porch with big fake smiles.

"It's an assorted box of some specialty foods from Massachusetts. Our mother sent this for your family." Jay handed a very large box to Kat.

"Oh my. That is very kind of her. Please give her our thanks. You will have to give me her address so I can send a proper note of thanks."

"Sure, I'll email the address to Grae." Jay paused and looked back and forth between the two women. "Well, I guess I better go. Thanks again! I hope you have fun at the party. Merry Christmas!" Jay turned and left.

"Safe travels to you and Madison." Kat yelled to Jay as he got into his car. She and Grae went back inside. Kat put the large box down on the floor. "What did he say?" A look of concern replaced the smile she had just given Jay.

"Gav is a direct descendant of Patrick." Grae paused as she watched her mother absorb what she had just said.

"What?"

"Patrick McGavock was Gav's great-great-great-great-grandfather. The resemblance between young Patrick and Gav isn't just coincidental or a distant family trait. Gav is a direct grandson of Patrick."

"How does that make you feel?" Her mother's question was a good one. Grae hadn't exactly let her mind go there.

"It's comforting and strange all at the same time. I'd like to think that might make a difference to Gav. That it might make him feel good about my connection to his grandfather." Grae shook her head and started up the stairs. "But, with Gav, it's really hard to say."

"Grae! It's time to go!"

Grae could hear her father's voice coming from downstairs. It was an odd sound to her. She couldn't remember the last time she heard him call for her. But, it was certainly something she had experienced countless times growing up. She took one last look in the mirror.

"What do you think, Clara?" Grae looked at her reflection in the long, old mirror. She could see the reflection of two small yellow balls rolling behind her. They were Perry's latest purchases for their young invisible friend. "I'll take that as a sign that you like it. I'm not sure if I think this dress is old or modern looking." The dress that Gav's mother had brought her to wear was cocktail length in the front and longer in the back. It was primarily made of royal blue and black velvet. It also had some satiny accents, primarily in the sleeves. As she turned to look at her profile, there was a distinct glittering quality about it. "That little shimmer that happens when I turn must be why she thought it would be a good dress for a holiday party."

"I imagine so." Kat came up behind Grae, causing her to jump. "You look very pretty." Kat began fussing with the back of Grae's hair. She had declined Lucy's offer to give her some royal blue streaks of color to match the dress. But, her crazy friend had given her a very beautiful jeweled butterfly barrette to hold her hair up. Grae had made soft curls around her face and down her neck to complete the look.

"Oh, Mom, I am just dreading this night. I wish that I could just cancel out the last few months and go back to when I first met Gav. He used to look at me like I hung the moon."

Kat laughed at her daughter's choice of expression. "You have an old soul, my dear."

"GRAE!" This time it was Perry's voice echoing up the staircase.

"I think they are in a hurry." Grae picked up a small black purse with a long strap. Her mother had loaned it to her for the evening. She slipped her cell phone into the bag.

"Don't fret about this evening. Just go and have a good time. Act as if nothing has happened between you two. Men love to ignore problems. It's us women who tend to do all the remembering. Just have fun and turn a few heads. Make him glad you're his date or make him jealous with the attention you may get. Maybe tonight will make things better. If not, at least you will know."

Grae put on a long black coat, another loan from her mother. "I sure am glad that we are close to the same size." Grae began to button the coat as her mother walked out of the room ahead of her.

"That makes two of us."

Gav met them at the street when they arrived. He didn't seem too keen on them going into his dorm. Grae could only imagine what went on within those walls. Actually, she really didn't want to know.

"Gav, is it?" Tom White got out of the Jeep and extended his hand to Gav. He shook it immediately.

"Yes, sir. Thank you for bringing Grae here."

"I sure do hope it was something important that kept you from picking up my little girl. In my day, parents weren't usually involved much with dating transportation."

"It was important, sir. I couldn't get out of it."

Grae wondered if Gav would tell her what he had to do.

"Very well, then. I believe that Kat wants to get a couple of photos."

Perry was leaning against the Jeep rolling his eyes at Gav. The photography was soon over and Grae's family had left. Gav motioned for her to walk ahead of him down a long sidewalk to the parking lot of the dorm.

"You look very pretty, Grae." Gav opened the passenger door of his Jeep and Grae got in.

"Thank you."

She felt like she was on a first date. They made idle conversation on the way to the party; mostly talking about their classes and other safe topics. After Gav stopped the car at the house, Grae started to let herself out but Gav stopped her.

"Listen, Grae, I know that I have been a jerk for the last couple of months. Everything's been really weird. Moving down here and starting college. Trying to keep up with classes and practice. All that crazy Eve stuff. I've probably jumped to conclusions about what goes on while you are on your trips. I guess I'm just jealous. That Patrick guy seems to have your heart."

Gav became quiet and looked straight ahead through the windshield toward the house. Grae watched his profile as car lights shined through. He looked so much like Patrick.

"You're right." Gav immediately turned in her direction. "He does. From the moment, I met him in the cafeteria."

"What?"

"James Patrick McGavock, weren't you ever curious where your middle name came from?" Gav gave her a very strange look.

"My grandfather chose it. He said it was a family name."

"Family name, huh? See any similarities there?"

"Oh, Grae, that guy was what two hundred years ago. I'm probably not even from the same McGavock family."

"Yes, you are. You are a direct descendant of Patrick McGavock. Every generation of your family has had one son, and only one son."

"How do you know that? Have you been talking to my father about this?"

"No, Jay did this research for me. He traced Patrick's family tree all the way down to you. So, you see, yes, I do love

Patrick because, while I am back in time, he is you." Grae opened the door. "Can we go now?"

Gav just nodded his head and got out of the car. He sprinted around it to help her out. After he closed the door, he put his arms around her and drew her close to him.

"Is this for real?"

Grae knew what he was asking, but decided to answer a different version of the question.

"I sure hope so. I've invested time in you in for three centuries."

Gav leaned down and gave Grae a long kiss. She felt a tear leave her eye. A feeling of relief washed over her.

"Let's go have a good time!"

The night was over too soon. The house was beautiful. The food was delicious. And, there was a band, so they danced and danced. Grae liked everyone that she met. The girls who were dating Gav's friends were all friendly and talkative. It may have been the week before Christmas, but Gav and Grae were very hot when they left the party and opted to stop and get ice cream at a car hop location nearby.

"We didn't dance that much at the prom." Gav ordered a double banana split. Grae opted for strawberry shortcake.

"Yeah, it felt good. I couldn't believe what a great dancer Dante was."

"Oh, yeah, he and his brothers were background dancers at some place in Vegas last summer. They come from a show biz family. I thought I was never going to get you back once you started dancing with him."

"You don't think that his girlfriend got mad, do you?"

Gav stole a strawberry off her cake and Grae took a bite of his split.

"Are you kidding? The poor girl was exhausted. She's an accounting major. She told me that you could dance with him all night for all she cared." They both laughed. "I really am glad you came. I wasn't sure when I first asked if you would agree to it."

"Well, I was a little afraid that I would feel out of place since I really hadn't met too many of your friends here."

"Yeah, that's my fault. I was afraid for you to be down here when Eve was lurking around. But, I didn't make much effort once she was gone." They sat in silence for a few moments and ate their desserts. "Grae, are you going to take any more...trips?"

Grae looked up at him. He had a very serious look. "I guess it would make you feel better if my answer was no. I am afraid that would be a lie. I know I will probably go again."

"What keeps making you want to return? What are you trying to find?"

Grae thought about the question. It was a fair one.

"It's very hard to answer. Partly because I really don't know myself. I just have this feeling that there is an underlying truth that I need to be finding. That there is a wrong that I need to make right. Each time I learn more about the Graham history and all of the intricate mysteries that are part of their family. I can't help but think that there is something bigger than all that. Something that hasn't been revealed yet."

"It scares me, Grae." Gav stared intently at his dessert. "I've had dreams about you not coming back. Like no one believes you ever existed. You just disappear."

Grae thought about his words. A feeling of revelation came over her.

"That must be it." Grae stopped eating. She turned to Gav. "I've got to go home."

FOURTEEN

"Did you have a good time?"

Upon returning home, Grae found her mother in the dining room. Bags and packages were strewn out on the floor. Kat had turned the dining room table into a wrapping area. Grae fingered rolls of ribbon and glittering tags. Kat liked to make her own bows and add special little touches to the wrapping.

"The gift starts when you first see it."

Grae remembered her mother saying that when she was a child. Her little hands would hold ribbon or sprinkle glitter. It was a happy time.

"Yes, I do like to decorate the boxes." Kat smiled as she worked the shimmering blue ribbon back and forth through her fingers. "Was the party fun?"

"It was. Everything was decorated beautifully and they had a great band. One of Gav's teammates used to be a professional dancer with his brothers. I danced and danced with him."

Grae watched as her mother finished the large bow and carefully secured it. There was a stack of unopened Christmas cards on the end of the table. Next to it, Grae could see one of her mother's detailed lists. She appeared to have many tasks ahead of her.

"Mom, we didn't exactly finish our conversation."

"No."

"I know that you don't want to talk about it. But I am going to anyway." Kat didn't look up. "You took someone back in time with you and you left the person there, didn't you?"

"Not by choice."

"You had to leave quickly and go back to your time?"

"No. The person who came with me...he wandered off. He went on his own adventure." Kat laid the ribbon down. Grae could see that her hands were shaking. Suddenly, she got up from the table. "I can't talk about this. We can't ever talk about this. It's over and done." Kat walked toward the kitchen. "Don't mention this to Grandpa. Don't you dare bring this up with him." Her tone was harsh. It changed instantly. "I'm glad you had a good time. I'm going to bed now. Turn off the lights when you come to bed. Good night."

Grae stood in shock and silence as her mother left the room. She could hear her turn out the light in the kitchen, and then walk through the foyer and up the stairs. Grae didn't seem to be able to move. It was almost as if two different people had just left the room. It wasn't a side of her mother she wanted to see. But, Grae knew the nagging of the truth, the solving of the mystery was going to be relentless. This was the reason that she was making these journeys. This was the truth that would set her family free.

The beep of her cell phone brought her back to the evening's events. It was Gav. "I hope everything is okay." Grae read the text. "You seemed so determined to get home that I was afraid to ask."

"Everything is okay." Grae's reply wasn't entirely true. "I'll tell you about it later. I work tomorrow afternoon. Goodnight."

Grae turned out the lights and walked into the foyer. She fingered the key on the chain around her neck as she passed the closet.

When Grae got upstairs, she was met by darkness and silence. It was cold in her room. She changed out of her dress and carefully took down her hair. She made sure to put the butterfly barrette in a safe spot. The girls at the party had been impressed with the jeweled accessory. She must remember to ask Lucy about it when she returned it to her.

She decided to change into a granny gown, as Perry called it. It was long and flannel and the palest shade of blue with tiny flowers. As she pulled on a sweatshirt jacket over the gown, she smiled as she caught a glimpse of her reflection. What a quick transformation she had made. She looked at her bed. It would be warm with all of the layers of blankets and quilts. But, she still felt a little restless, hyped up from the evening's events.

On her desk, she saw one of the textbooks she had picked up at the college bookstore. It was an introductory volume to anatomy—a topic that she could not learn enough about. She decided to take the book and a notebook and go downstairs for some cocoa. She could snuggle by the smoldering fire in the living room and read for a while. As she picked up an ink pen and a highlighter to use, her eyes glanced at the blue fountain pen she had found in the wall box. Grae wondered if this had penned some of the letters she and Jay had read from Squire or other members of the family. Did an object have a memory, an imprint of what it had been exposed to? If so, there was little doubt that this pen knew some Graham family secrets. She stuck it and the other writing instruments in her pocket and headed downstairs. Toto had left whatever bedroom she had been visiting and decided to join her as she made her way to the living room. Grae set down her books on the couch and put another log on the fire.

"You want some cocoa, Toto?" The small dog wagged her tail. "Chocolate is not the best choice for you, but you can have some warm milk."

The silence in the house made the click-click of the dog's paws seem loud as they walked toward the rear of the house. Grae thought she saw a light on in the closet as she walked by. She opened the door to turn it off, but only found darkness.

The door knob was cold in her hand. Ice cold. Frigid. Painful. Everything began to tilt, and Grae could feel the speed of a piercing cold wind begin to suck her into the closet. She heard someone yelling, an echo from far away. She smelled the stench of death. She heard the wails of a man screaming in pain. A splash of blue satin flashed before her eyes. The smell of candles being blown out. A little girl gasping for breath. A mist encircled her. It smelled like fire. She began to fall as swirls of light flashed before her. A sharp pain seemed to burst inside her head. She heard Toto barking, and then everything went black.

ANOTHER TIME

FIFTEEN

"You appear to be lost, ma'am."

Grae turned around and found a soldier sitting atop a beautiful horse. He tipped his hat as she looked up at him. There was something about his face that was familiar.

"I...I think I may be."

"May I ask why you are on the road, in the cold, by yourself?" The man gave her a curious look.

Grae searched her mind for a valid excuse. She also quickly looked down to see what she was wearing. She cringed. Her attire wasn't much different than when she left the present. She had on a long nightshirt with a short coat over top.

"Ah..." Grae's mind raced trying to think of a reason why she would be on a dirt road in a nightgown.

"I am travelling to my home and I passed a wagon train several miles back. Did they leave you behind?" The man had just written her a great story and he didn't even know it.

"Yes...Yes, they stopped to water the horses and I got out to use the..." Grae stopped herself just in time. "I got out to relieve myself." She bowed her head in embarrassment. "I was also a little sick on my stomach from the ride and I took longer than I expected. When I returned to where I had left them, the wagon train was gone."

"Was there not anyone accompanying you on this journey?"

"Well, there were others in my wagon, but I do not really know them. They were asleep when we stopped. It was still dark." Grae looked to the east and saw that the sun was rising.

"That is certainly unfortunate, ma'am."

The man got off of his horse. Grae noticed from his expression that the process of dismounting seemed to bring him some pain. Standing before her, Grae realized that the man was an officer. He looked like he had stepped right out of a history book or a fine old oil painting. His appearance was very gray. His jacket was gray wool with sky-blue cuffs and collar facings. There was a single gold star on the far left corner of the collar bar. Grae wondered what rank that indicated. The double-breasted jacket had two rows of brass buttons that caught a glimmer of the morning sun as he dismounted. Gray trousers matched the jacket with a light blue stripe down each side that was about a quarter of an inch wide.

"May I introduce myself? I am Major David Graham."

Grae felt a gasp rising out of her throat. She reached her hand up to her mouth to stop it.

"Oh, are you becoming ill again?"

"No, oh, no." Grae quickly put her hand down by her side. "I am just overcome at my good fortune that I have been found by a member of our fine military and not by some scoundrel who might wish to harm me." Even as she heard the word 'scoundrel' come out of her mouth, she knew that she had been a little over dramatic.

"Well, thank you, ma'am. I am on my way to my family farm. I would be glad to escort you there. Are you familiar with our part of this great land?"

Grae pondered the question. Just about any way she answered it might mean problems for her later. "Well, I am not sure. I have been in Virginia before. I am in Virginia, am I not?"

"Most certainly. You are in the County of Wythe. My family owns property called Cedar Run Farm. I am sure that my mother would be delighted to welcome you into our home. Would you like to ride?"

"Do we have far to walk?" Grae knew the answer to the question. She always came back to the Graham Mansion property. It could only be so far.

"No, not at all. But you have not been feeling well."

"I believe part of my ailment might have been the rough riding while lying down. I think that walking in the fresh, albeit cold, air will do me some good." They began to walk down the road. He led the horse behind them. "You are going to visit your family, Major Graham?"

"Yes, I am part of a conspiracy. Please call me Davy."

"A conspiracy?"

"My sisters are conspiring to surprise my parents with an anniversary party in a few days."

"How lovely!" Grae knew that such an event would probably not be lovely for the wedded couple.

"So, Miss...I do not believe you mentioned your name."

Grae's mind began racing again. A name was a key part of her new identity. There was no sense in trying to fool those whom she had met before. Martha and Squire would know her immediately. There were probably slaves as well who would recognize her from her last visit in 1859. Grae wondered what year she had landed in.

"My name is Sarah...Sarah Leedy."

"Well, Miss Leedy, where were you headed with this wagon train that left you on our humble farm?"

"It is Sarah. I was headed west."

"Yes. That would be a common direction. But, I must say that travelling through the South during this time of war is probably not the wisest of decisions."

"I was travelling to help care for my grandmother in Tennessee."

"No greater work than caring for family." Davy smiled and nodded as the Mansion came into view. "Our home is ahead. I expected to return to find snow covered hills for the holidays." He had just given Grae a strong clue to the timeframe.

"Oh, my, it is impressive. It is hard to believe that we have reached this time of year again. I have been on the road for so many days. Could you tell me what the date is?"

"I thoroughly understand your quandary. A soldier experiences the same things as the long days of battle run together. Today is Monday, December 12, 1864."

Grae was amazed at her good fortune. Davy even gave her the year.

"It is a full two weeks before Christmas. Somehow, I doubt that another wagon train will be through during this time. What are my other transportation alternatives?"

"I am afraid they are limited during this time of turmoil. The war has made transportation precarious, at best. The train would be your best alternative, but schedules are not as timely as they once were. I am sure that the Graham family will more than welcome you into their home during your stay. We can arrange for a messenger to take a telegraph to the depot that will let your family know what has happened to you."

Grae nodded at his suggestion, but she knew that it would be a message that would never reach a true destination.

"It looks like your home is bustling with activity."

Grae saw people, mostly slaves, moving in every direction. Animals were being tended. The sound of wood chopping filled the air. Large white sheets were flying like sails in the winter wind. She shuddered to think of how cold they would feel on a bed, but how wonderfully clean they would smell.

"Cedar Run is a work of efficiency. My father does not leave much room for laziness. A lazy slave will end up a sold one, or worse." Grae could only imagine what the worse might be with Squire David. She didn't doubt that he would not spare punishment. "But there are some dark men and women on this farm who have managed to please him for many years. I do not know what shall happen to them if we lose this war and President Lincoln is successful with his emancipation plans."

"And, your mother, does she run her household in the same manner?"

Grae thought it best to not comment on the political matters of the day. If she were to seek refuge once again on the property, she had better mind her tongue.

"My mother likes the house to be run in a certain way. She has high standards. But her manner is much gentler, when she is herself." Davy paused and stopped on the hill above the house. Grae realized that it was the very location where the house that Lucy lived in now stood. "Perhaps I should share some knowledge with you before you meet the family. At times, my mother is not well and confines herself to her rooms."

Grae would like to have been able to react to his comments. He obviously had some of his father's traits. The desire to shield the family from negative opinions had been passed from father to son. Grae merely nodded and followed him.

"Massa Davy, yous come home from da war."

A large black man walked toward them. By his dress and manner, Grae assumed that he was one of the head slaves. She had noticed as they walked toward him that he appeared to be supervising some of the other slaves.

"I am home, Obadiah. I am home. How are you?"

"Well, it wouldn't do me no good to complains. Massa Graham, he justs woulds sends me away."

Obadiah smiled at Davy. His teeth were a little stained from the same tobacco that he had just spit on the ground. He finally noticed that someone was with Davy. Obadiah darted his eyes back and forth at Grae, but didn't look straight at her. She imagined what he must of thought about how she was clothed.

"Let's go on to the house. I think I see one of my mischievous sisters peeking at us through the window."

Grae followed Davy across the side lawn, but found herself being drawn to the round rock fishing well. She stopped and looked down into it. Immediately, she saw a man, a soldier, just as she had seen from the tower at Big Walker. An ice-cold feeling came over her. This time, he appeared to be reaching toward her, but she still could not see his face.

"Sarah! Sarah!"

Grae could hear Davy's voice loudly next to her. "I'm sorry. This well…it brought back a painful memory for me."

Grae began to walk away from it. Davy followed close behind. As they approached the steps to the porch, Grae saw a young woman walk outside.

"It is you! Our Davy is home. He's really here."

The young woman was in her older teens. Grae thought that the first sight of her conjured the idea of money. Her dark green dress was simple in style, but it shimmered in rich color. She was tall and slender with dark brown hair, long and thick, and olive skin. Her eyes were the color of dark chocolate and they smiled with mischief. Grae wondered if this might be…

"My most wicked sister, darling Bettie, why are you surprised to see me?" Bettie leaned down from the top step and her brother embraced her. "You are the one who summoned me." He whispered in her ear.

Bettie's smile turned to a look of disdainful curiosity as she saw the young, oddly dressed woman behind him. "Darling brother, I did not realize that you would be bringing a guest with you." Bettie gave her brother a wink.

"Neither did I. I found this poor young woman on the side of the road. It appears that the wagon train left her behind."

"That would be a strange story. Were you not aware of its departure?"

Grae could tell that Bettie was not buying the story.

"The wagons stopped to water the horses. I believe that many of us who were riding under cover were still asleep. The other women who were in my wagon were snoring." Grae smiled at the two of them. Neither returned the sentiment. "I was feeling sick. So, I got out of the wagon and went into the woods to relieve myself. My stomach was not well and I vomited my dinner. I sat down for a few minutes to settle myself. When I returned, the wagons were gone."

"What of those who you were travelling with? Would they not have missed you?" Bettie was relentless with her questions.

"As I said, they were asleep when I left the wagon. I did not know any of them previously. I was travelling alone to Tennessee to visit my grandmother."

"What part of Tennessee?"

"Memphis." That would be the first Tennessee city that would come to Grae's mind. Lucy would be pleased. Grae was amazed that Bettie seemed to be satisfied.

"Dear sister, are you finished with your questioning? Young Sarah was a wandering stranger, and I showed my Christian spirit by leading her to our home."

"Our mother will be pleased. Our father, well…" The two siblings exchanged glances. Lack of words spoken did not cease them from communicating. "Our father shall question you more than I have."

Two young women hastily walked through the doorway and into Davy's arms.

"Where are all the little girls who once lived here? They have been replaced by young women."

They smiled in delight at the sight of their handsome brother and the attention he showered upon him.

Grae imagined that during Davy's years of military service, there no doubt had been dramatic changes in his three sisters. It appeared that Mary Bell, the oldest, was around twenty-one; Bettie just a few years behind, and the youngest, Emily, was in her mid-teens. They all shared features and coloring similar to Bettie. Grae took a very deep breath as she saw the form of Martha draw close to the doorway with Gracie behind her.

"My son! Safely returned to his home. Praise our Almighty Father for his mercy."

Davy slipped out of his sisters' embrace and walked into the arms of his mother. Grae watched as this woman, whom she had grown to know, closed her eyes tightly as her son embraced her. A look of relief and joy crossed her face as tears trickled from both of her eyes. She appeared to have not noticed Grae. Her entire attention was focused on her son. That was not the case with Gracie. She could almost feel the holes upon her body that the slave woman was staring through her.

"You are looking well, Mother."

Davy paused and stepped aside to bring Grae more into view. Martha glanced in her direction. She looked back at her son before she realized what she had just seen. Her eyes came back to Grae and a shocked look replaced the happy one.

ROSA LEE JUDE & MARY LIN BREWER

"Mother, this is Miss Sarah Leedy. I found her on the side of the road." Martha did not appear to be breathing. "The wagon train that she was travelling with left her while she was stricken with nausea in the woods. That is why she is still in her sleeping attire. I knew that you would insist that I bring her here for shelter."

Grae wasn't sure that Martha really heard a word her son had said. But Grae was grateful that he had told her story. She really didn't want to lie to Martha.

"Mister Davy, you just hand this child over to Gracie, and I will see dat she has what she needs." Gracie held out her hand to Grae. She wasn't sure if Gracie had bought the story or not, but the woman seemed to want to do something about the situation. "Come on now, Miss."

Grae walked past Martha as she followed Gracie. Her old friend could not take her eyes off Grae. She noticed that this had drawn the attention of her son.

"Thank you, Major Graham." Grae nodded at Davy and the others as she followed Gracie.

"Certainly. Gracie will make sure you are comfortable."

Grae followed Gracie into the house. She could feel everyone watching her. The buzz of conversation that would follow her departure would set the tone for how the visit to 1864 might proceed. Gracie led Grae up the very familiar stairs to the rooms on the second floor. She was not surprised to find that Gracie took her to the same room that Maria and Loretta had shared in 1859. People were creatures of habit. Guest rooms tended to stay the same.

"You can sleep here. I will finds you some clothes." Grae sat down on one of the beds. The stress of the journey was catching up with her. The night's sleep she had missed

SALVATION

was crying for satisfaction. "You never does come with clothes." Gracie muttered the last comment under her breath, but Grae heard it clearly.

"What did you say?" Grae asked the comment lightheartedly, but looked Gracie straight in the eyes.

"Nothing, miss. I will finds some of the girls' clothes that will fits you."

Grae took a long look at Gracie. Another five years had made a difference in the woman. Her hair was whiter. Her posture was bent. Grae wondered how much of it was the toiling of slavery or the stress of the family that she served.

"Thank you."

"My name is Gracie. In case you don't know." Another carefully chosen comment. Gracie closed the door behind her as Grae smiled.

"This is going to be an interesting visit."

"You have basically just walked off a cliff."

Grae jumped off the bed and halfway across the room as the voice of The General spoke to her from under the bed.

"How in the world...?" Grae bent down and looked as her friend came out from under the piece of furniture. He was limping and had a scabbed place on one side of his face. "What happened to you?"

"It's part of the persona." The General stretched and jumped up on the bed, snuggling into the covers. "Cats fight. Sometimes we win. Sometimes we lose. Everyone gets roughed up a little."

Grae sat down on the bed and gently stroked his back. "I am very glad to see you. How did you get in here?"

329

"I am not so glad to see you in this century." The General broke free from Grae's grasp and lay down on the opposite end of the bed. "I slipped in the back while everyone was on the front porch welcoming Davy home. I figured that they would put you in this room. You have opened yourself up to extreme risk by coming back here so soon."

"Now listen, first off, you act as if I have some choice in the time period that I come back to. I can't go online and make a reservation."

Grae stood up and walked toward the window. She could see Davy walking around the property.

"What's this 'online' you speak of?"

Grae turned and gave The General a questioning look. "You know, the Internet, the World Wide Web."

"Don't know anything about that." The General rolled over on his back, flipped again, and began licking his paws.

"Just exactly what time period did you come from?"

"We're not going to discuss that."

"I know that you are somehow connected to my mother. I'm guessing when she was around my age." The General was still silent. He had progressed to cleaning his coat. "Had Arnold Schwarzenegger become President yet?"

"WHAT? The Terminator?"

"Ah, so you are from the Twentieth Century!" Grae grinned.

The General sat up and opened his mouth. But, just as fast, he jumped off the bed and hid underneath. There was a knock on the door.

"Yes, come in." Grae sat back down.

"I brungs you some clothes and some food."

Gracie's arms were full of clothing. There appeared to be two dresses, some undergarments, and a nightgown. A small female black slave was behind Gracie. She kept her head down as she put a tray of food and drink on a small table.

"Thank you very much. I didn't expect any food." Grae felt her stomach growl at the aroma of the breakfast food on the plate.

"Well, your belly tells me otherwise." Gracie let out a hearty laugh. Grae had forgotten how joyful this woman's laugh sounded. It was good to see her again. "What be your name child?" One eyebrow went up as she asked the question.

"I am Sarah Leedy." The words didn't flow out of her mouth very well.

"Mmm, hmmm. Is that so? Well, I knews a girl named Maria who looked a mighty bit like you. You has a sister?"

"No, ma'am."

"You know, I don't take too kindly to people hiding the truth. Me and Miss Patsy, we loved Miss Maria. We would be glad for her to come back to visit."

Grae knew that Gracie was baiting a trap. "Who is Miss Patsy?"

"Hmmm, that be my personal name for Miss Martha." Gracie stared hard at her. "Alright then, you eats that food."

The same young slave came back in and filled the basin with water. She laid a couple of linen clothes beside it.

"You get cleaned up and gets some rest. We will sends someone for you when lunch is ready."

Grae smiled at them as they left.

"Is it sausage or ham?" The General was out from under the bed in a flash.

"Sausage." Grae picked up a piece and broke off some for him. Then, she put the rest of it between one of the hot biscuits. "Oh my." She mumbled as she chewed. "I forgot how good everything tastes here."

She took her fork and stabbed the fried eggs and potatoes. She felt The General rub against her leg, so she handed him the rest of the biscuit and sausage that was in her hand. There was plenty more on the plate awaiting her. After her stomach was full, she washed her face and surveyed the clothes.

"I think I will see if I can slip outside for a while." The General sat at the door. "Could I have some help here?"

Grae turned around and opened the door. "Stay out of trouble."

"I would say the same to you. But, in your case, it is too late."

"It is most fortunate that our darling brother came along when he did."

Bettie had begun the lunchtime chatter as soon as everyone was seated. It appeared that a grand feast was prepared to welcome the soldier son home. The only seat at the table that wasn't taken was the one on the far end, Squire David's seat.

"Yes, I am most grateful. I do not know what I would have done otherwise. All my belongings were on the wagon."

Grae was surprised to find some money tucked inside the pocket of the coat she wore. That and the fountain pen were the only items she found. It continued to amaze her how things could just appear on her person while in transit.

"I am sure that we can assist you with funds to pay for your passage." Davy spoke up as he handed one of his sisters a plate of fried chicken.

"Oh, I do have some money. I kept that on my person as I travelled. I would like to pay for my room and board while I am here."

"That will not be necessary, Miss…Leedy, is it?" It was the first comment that Martha had directed to her.

Grae was certain that her conversation with Gracie had been shared with the mistress of the house. But, she could still see that Martha was sizing her up.

"We have inquired about the stagecoach and train schedules." Davy turned the conversation to a more straightforward topic. "I am afraid that the only stagecoach that is due through here before Christmas is heading north. Passenger trains are in short supply as well because so many of the rails have been blocked or damaged by Union troops. If the Union intended to disrupt our transportation, it succeeded in that mission."

"You will just have to stay with us through the holidays, Miss Leedy."

The youngest Graham daughter, Emily, who was nicknamed Bunt, seemed enthralled with having a new person in the house. The precocious young woman was sent to retrieve her to lead Grae to the dining room. She chatted constantly with a whirlwind of questions.

"Yes, I think that will be the most appropriate solution. We cannot have you wandering about looking for lodging so close to holiday time. It is atrocious that you will not be with your loved ones. You shall have to make due with our family festivities."

"Oh, that is so kind. But, I really don't want to impose."

Grae looked around the table. The family seemed happy. They were eating heartily, laughing, and chatting. Even Martha seemed relaxed and animated. Then Grae remembered who wasn't at the table, and it all made sense.

"Sarah, my mother will be insulted if you do not accept our offer. Isn't that right, Mother?"

Bettie gave her brother a strange look. "Davy, shall we go and visit Nannie this afternoon?" Bettie said as Grae surmised what she was trying to do.

"Will I be able to send a couple of telegrams soon?" Grae interrupted the conversation. "I would like my family in Memphis to know that I will not be arriving as scheduled. I would also like to contact my fiancé. He studied the law at the University of Virginia and is now an assistant quartermaster in Richmond. He works closely with Tredegar Ironworks on the James River. I do not want him to be worried."

Bettie's eyebrows went up and a smile crossed her face. Message received. Grae was glad she had read all of those lengthy Civil War documents as she had copied them for patrons of the library. She hoped that she had her facts straight enough for believability.

"Most certainly!" Bettie replied. "Sarah could accompany us when we go to visit Nannie. You can compose messages before we leave, and we will send someone to the telegraph at the depot in Max Meadows."

"That would be delightful! What is our fair Nannie Tate up to these days?"

Davy's expression changed as he spoke her name. Grae wondered if the romance between them had already begun or if this young man's heart was yet to be turned.

"Oh, just pining away for some handsome soldier to return and snatch her from the sentence of spinsterhood." Bettie laughed loudly.

Martha shook her head. "You must excuse this girl, Miss Leedy. She tends to say whatever little thing comes into her head."

"Oh, I quite enjoy that, as I tend to be that way myself."

A big smile crossed Bettie's face as Grae replied to Martha. A chuckle was heard around the table.

Grae spent a half an hour composing telegrams to her imaginary family, the Presleys, in Memphis, and her equally non-existent fiancé, John Wayne. She laughed under her breath at how delighted Lucy and Grandpa Mack would be that she had included their favorites in her adventure.

Then, it was off to the home of Nannie Tate. While the landmarks were somewhat different, Grae found that it was easy to follow the lay of the land. The Tates lived near the present day Fort Chiswell Mansion. She thought she heard Davy call it the McGavock Mansion. That made sense since they were the original owners.

During the short ride in what Grae thought was a fancy carriage, brother and sister discussed a variety of topics. After Bettie had caught Davy up on the latest news regarding several of their friends, the subject of their parents and the imminent anniversary party began.

"There are so many things that we cannot get because of this dreadful war, Davy. It makes having a party with any semblance of affluence almost impossible."

"And, why, my dear sister, must this party be such?"

"Why, Davy Graham, have you forgotten everything that our father has taught us? We must always appear to be prosperous and without reproach, no matter what is actually transpiring within our walls."

"Ah, my sister, your sharp tongue speaks the truth. I fear that Sarah shall want to take up residence at the Tates if we continue this conversation much further."

Davy glanced in Grae's direction. She understood why his men were so devoted to him. His manner was such that you were drawn to him. He had a caring heart.

"I am delighted to hear this family banter. I must confess that I grew up with only one brother. It was not the large family that you are accustomed."

Grae knew in order for her stay to be a successful one, she needed to form a friendship with Bettie and Davy.

"Well, that would make for a quieter setting. I have decided that I shall be amply prepared for when I take a wife, as I have been surrounded by those of the fairer sex for most of my time on this Earth."

"And, on that note, my dear brother, you have arrived at the home of a young lady who I feel is the strongest candidate for this wife-taking as you call it." Bettie gave Grae a nudge with her elbow. "I am so glad that you will get to meet Nannie so early in your visit with us. She is my best friend, aside from this hairy fellow here. I do so long for her to be a sister of the family as she is already a sister of my heart."

"Bettie, stop this talk. Nannie's mother is already standing at the door. She shall hear you."

Grae took in the view ahead of her. She saw a vast expanse of land that would rival the Graham property. It appeared to be a working plantation with barns, slave quarters, and a spring house surrounding the large two-story home. Grae could see fields where, in kinder weather, acres of crops would be in production. Horses and cattle were also in view.

"Bettie Graham, how delightful for you to come to visit. Oh, my, and it appears you have brought that handsome brother of yours. Were we expecting him home from the war so soon?"

"Good afternoon, Missus Tate, I am home for but a short leave, from now through the holidays. Then, it is back to my assignment." Davy bowed to the woman as he greeted her.

Behind Missus Tate, a young woman appeared. From the look in the girl's eyes as she caught sight of Davy, Grae could only assume that she was Nannie. The young woman was petite in size, but not stature. Her skin was a creamy ivory color and it complimented her strawberry blond hair. Her features could be described as elegant. Her face showed kindness. As Grae watched Nannie approach her future husband, she thought about how this woman would live many years past his death in the Mansion. It was good that this young heart did not know what she would later face.

"When I am back in my time, I work part-time in a genealogy library."

Grae was very tired when they returned from the Tate farm. She had retired to her room to rest before dinner. Grae waited for The General to respond. He must have snuck back into the house while she was gone, as he looked very comfortable on the bed opposite hers upon her return.

"Is there a point to you telling me that tidbit of information?"

"Besides the work I do there, I often have time to learn more about the Graham family. I have been reading many letters that are from this very time that we are now in. It's kind of amazing to actually meet the people who wrote them."

"Kind of amazing?"

"Okay, it is amazing. Like today. I met Nannie Tate. She will marry Davy Graham and become the last true mistress of this house. She will live here long after Davy dies. I think they were really in love."

"I think that reading all of those letters is what gives you the idea about travelling. You need to stop it."

"You sound just like my mother."

"Well, you should listen to her." The General curled up in a ball with his back to Grae.

"How did you become a cat?"

"I've told you before. I broke one of the rules of time travel. Well, actually, I broke several."

"But, it doesn't really tell me how you became a cat? It also doesn't tell me who you really were."

"Neither of those things matter anymore. All that matters is that you get back to your time and stay there."

"What about you getting back to your own time?" Grae got on the bed with The General and moved him until he was facing her. He hissed.

"You see me on the Mansion property in your time."

"Let me rephrase that. What about you getting back to your own time in human form?"

"That's impossible." The General jumped off the bed.

"Most people would say that it is impossible for a human to be turned into a cat."

"Most people don't believe in magic. It takes magic to do this. It takes magic to undo it." The General turned and left the room.

"Well, perhaps, I will need to learn a little magic."

A knock awakened Grae. She had quickly fallen fast asleep after The General left. She expected it to be one of the slaves with water for the basin. As she sat up, she noticed that the basin was already filled and another dress was waiting for her. It was blue. The door creaked open and Bettie stuck her head in.

"Have I disturbed you?" She was already in the room with the door closed before Grae had a chance to answer. "I have just got to tell you something before we go down to dinner."

"Sure." Grae watched as Bettie walked toward the blue dress that was hanging from a hook on the wall.

"I must admit that when Gracie first chose you some of my clothes, she only took ones that I had discarded. I felt badly about it once I got to know you a little. This dress is a much better one. Gracie's daughter, Violet, makes all of our dresses. We are so fortunate. She learned from a very talented designer and a seamstress who worked for our Aunt Margaret several years ago."

Grae smiled. She knew those women. She hoped she would perhaps have the opportunity to see Margaret McGavock.

"I am grateful to have any clothing you are willing to share with me."

"Violet will start on a dress for you tomorrow."

"Oh, that isn't necessary."

"But, you must have one for the party. It is just a few days away. Violet is very fast. I already talked to her about a couple of possible designs. We will pick out some fabric from father's store tomorrow." Bettie grabbed her head. "Father! That is whom I came to talk to you about. My father has returned from his business trip. He will be at dinner tonight. I must prepare you."

"Will he be upset that I am here?"

Inside her mind, Grae was rolling her eyes. She could write a book on Squire David Graham.

"Yes. No. Well, I'm not sure. Father likes company when he has someone to impress. I am not sure that he will want to impress you. I wish that we had a better story to tell than that Davy found you on the side of the road. But, we will tell him that your fiancé is studying law and serves the Confederacy with distinction. That will impress him."

Grae thought about how much she did not care to impress him. She would love to tell his family a story about how he abandoned his own son because of his shame and guilt. Grae had a feeling that at least one member of the family already knew that story.

"I hope my presence doesn't displease him." Grae had a bad taste in her mouth from saying those words.

"I will be entertaining at dinner. Father is always tired after these trips. He does enjoy my stories. I know that he will be pleased to have Davy home. This visit is a complete surprise to my parents. They did not think that he would be home for the holidays. We will certainly surprise them with the anniversary party." Bettie paused and took hold of Grae's hand. "My mother's health is very delicate. She has bouts of melancholy and strange ailments. We are concerned about her. Father has no patience. It is an embarrassment to him. I love him dearly, but there are times that I do not like him very much."

"I am sorry to hear that your mother is ill. Is she under a doctor's care?" Grae wasn't sure if that was a proper term for the time. But, she was anxious to know if Doctor Minson was still in the picture.

"Mother has had many doctors. Father is the only one who they discuss her care with." Bettie paused. She seemed to be considering her next statement. "Father has taken her to doctors in other places. There is one doctor that he seems to trust above others. His name is Minson. He is here now. The first time he stayed with us was last year. He had the most interesting assistant with him. I was actually staying most of that week with Aunt Margaret. She was ill and I helped nurse her. I forget the young man's name. But I think that I might have been most taken with him, if I had more time to get to know him." Bettie giggled and fanned herself. Grae knew that young man's name.

"I hope that your mother's condition will improve. She seems like a fine person."

"Oh, my mother is. She is strong and smart in many respects. But it is almost as if there is a little knob inside her that gets turned the wrong way. I do fear that it is not something physical, but only a mental incapacity. I do fear that we all may have it. My father is the one who turns the knob. I am sure of it." Bettie whispered, as if her father might be listening at the door. "I am his pride and his thorn. I defy him every chance I get." Her giggle returned. "That is another reason I wanted to speak with you. You must be an accomplice to my latest badness. But, it is goodness really. Can you keep a secret?"

"I have been known to keep large ones." Grae joined her new friend in a giggle. It felt good.

"I knew you would be. My sisters and I have a secret that we are hiding in my room."

Grae furrowed her brow. "I don't understand."

"The secret is a little girl. Her name is Clara. We just love her. She is the sweetest thing." Bettie began to whisper. "Her father used to work for us. He did deliveries for the store. A while ago, his wife got sick. It was so sad. Their two older children, a boy and a girl, died. They all had the fever. Father told him to stay away, not to bring his illness to the store. But, I know that he sent food and other supplies to their home. The wife died shortly after. Mother was very concerned about them. She knew they had a younger girl. She sent Gracie over there. When she returned, she told us that the father was about gone. The little girl seemed fine, but she wouldn't talk to Gracie."

"How very sad. She was watching her whole family die." Grae thought about the sweet little girl who shared her room.

"Yes, it was. That little girl weighed on Gracie's heart. She told Mother about how she had found her. Mother told her to go get the girl and take her to one of the old slave cabins in the woods. So, Gracie and a couple of the other slaves did just that. They mixed up a strong bath and scrubbed the child with lye soap. Then, they fed her all sorts of roots and herbs. The slaves have their ways of healing people. It is a lot like the medicine of the Indians."

Grae's thoughts escaped to Ama and her father, the medicine man. "All of this helped her?" Grae was anxious to hear the rest of the story. She knew that this little girl eventually found her way into the Mansion. Grae wondered if a real live Clara was now just across the hall.

"It did. She started eating and talking a little. In the meantime, her father passed as well. No one seemed to miss the little one. One of the slaves would stay with her at night. No one else got sick. My sisters and I plotted with Mother to bring her here. Father would be furious. But, he is gone a lot. Everyone in this house knows she is here, but him. It is great fun. She has a little pallet in my room. We are teaching her to read. She has developed a little cough of late. But, we think that was from a rambunctious day that we all spent in the snow a few weeks ago." Bettie rose to leave. "I just wanted to let you know about our little secret."

"I cannot wait to meet her."

"I will leave you to dress for dinner. It will be time soon. Do not be late. Father deplores tardiness." Bettie smiled as she closed the door.

Grae sighed. It would be wonderful to meet Clara. But, it was sad to know how that story would end. She recalled The General's warnings about not changing anything. It would be very hard.

Grae turned around and looked at the blue dress that was waiting. The sight of it made her reach for the key that still hung around her neck. It had become so much a part of her that she barely noticed it. She had learned that wearing it every day was not a necessity. It proved to be a wise choice on her part. Her recent visits to doctors and hospitals made for opportunities that her mother could have found it. She was glad that the key was not around her neck on the day she collapsed at Big Walker. Still, it was never far from her. Sometimes the key was in her pocket or purse. She seemed to need it with her to feel whole. Another knock came to the door. Grae walked over and opened it.

"Miss, I be Violet. I sews." The young girl who Grae had last seen in 1859 was now a young woman. Violet was strikingly beautiful. Her clear caramel skin had a glow to it. Her dark coffee eyes sparkled. Grae looked down and saw the reason. Violet was expecting. If she recognized Grae, she did not show it on her face. Grae thought that Gracie had probably prepared her for the meeting.

"Yes, I have heard of you. Come in."

It was evident that the young woman had developed her new trade in the years since they last met. A long measuring tape hung around her neck. A pencil was tucked securely behind her ear. She had a large oversized notebook and some paper as well as a few swatches of fabric.

As Violet laid the notebook down, Grae took a closer look at it. "May I?" Grae gestured to the large leather book. Violet nodded and stood waiting. Grae opened it and gasped. She and Loretta had used the same one during those few time travel years previous. She thought of the hours that her mother poured over the drawings working with Violet so that every seam was perfect. Every delicate detail was beautiful.

"Is something wrong, Miss?"

Violet's voice brought Grae quickly back to the present. She must undo her slip.

"Oh, they are just so beautiful. Are these your designs?"

"Well, these here are not. I does have some of mine in da back. That blue dress there on the wall, that be my design. I keep it simple in the shape, but you see there are many little delicate touches. I learn that from my teacher. She show me that you can take sumthin' simple and make it special with a little extra handiwork."

"Do you still work with your teacher?"

"Oh, no, she be gone. Miss Loretta, she justs disappeared one night. I be afraid sumthin' frightful happen to her. But, my mammy, she says that she just go back where she come from."

Violet fingered the large sheets of paper in the notebook. Grae could see that there were some of the sheets that belonged to the real owner of the portfolio. A few of Grae's sketches were still there. Grae could tell that it was the small drawings and notes of Loretta that truly held a special place in Violet's heart. Grae hoped she could share this information with her mother one day.

"Let me see some of yours."

"Oh, ma'am, are you sure? They tell me that you are probably from sum big ole city. You probably have sum fine clothes."

"You don't think your designs are fine? I say they would stand up on their own anywhere. Your work is beautiful." Violet bowed her head, embarrassed with the praise from Grae. "What are you going to make for me?" Grae stood up and twirled around. "What do you think would look good on this stick of a body?"

Violet stared at Grae. She got up and walked around her. Then, she returned to the notebook and pulled out a sheet from the back. Grae was amazed. The design was beautiful. It was not a fancy dress, but it had formalness to it.

"My favorite part of it is da buttons that I puts on the front. I thinks it looks like a soldier's uniform." Violet's smile was large. She patted her stomach. Grae wondered if her child's emotions were following her mother's and causing some commotion to go on within her.

"Will this be your first child?"

"Yes."

"Is the father here with you?"

"No." Violet's expression had changed.

Grae chose not to ask further. While a house slave's life was better than those in the fields were, a slave was a slave. Their lives were not in their control. "I am sorry, Violet." This woman suddenly looked old and young to Grae at the same time. She could almost see her whole life flash before her. It was filled with toil and sadness. Hardship. Her work would be her shining star. The toil of escape for her enslaved soul.

"No one hurt me. No one took me. That always be my mammy's fear. I love dis man, dis baby's father. He be a slave on Miss McGavock's land. She be good to him. Miss Martha she gonna talk to her when da baby come. She gonna see if I can go be there. Mammy not like that much. But Massa Graham not know. She thinks it better he not know. Miss McGavock she like pretty things. He have soft spot for his sister. She can make it so."

Grae knew the words were true. Margaret could make about anything happen, when it came to her brother. She imagined that the woman's age was no doubt catching up with her.

"I hope that works out for you."

"I needs to take your numbers." Violet took the measuring tape from around her neck. "I will be working day and night to get this one dun in times for da party." Violet began to measure Grae's arms and back.

"Oh, I can pick something simple if this is going to be too much work."

"Miss Martha and Miss Bettie say you gonna have a new dress for da party. So, it gots to be so. I can make it so. The work it come easy to me. It passes the time."

Grae could tell that Violet would have trouble measuring the length, so she hopped up on a chair so the young woman would not have to squat down.

"You smart and kind. This baby dun make it hard to get near da ground." It only took her a few more minutes to get the measurements she needed. She handed Grae the stack of fabrics. Grae returned them to her without looking at them.

"It is up to you. I trust your judgment."

Violet's eyes filled with surprise and tears. She simply nodded, gathered her things, and left the room.

"Your mother changed her life, you know." Grae jumped as The General's voice startled her from under the bed.

"I didn't know you were here."

"Squire David would have sold Violet to some other slave owner as spite against Gracie. He would have done it during one of Martha's weak spells. The girl would have been long gone before Martha could have done anything. But, this talent that you and your mother saw in her young mind and heart, it is what has saved her. Good seamstresses are a rare thing in the rural parts of this young country. Most women can sew. Few can make beautiful garments. Squire wouldn't take that talent away from his family. It is part of their appearances. This girl makes all of Squire's shirts. She makes them perfect. She keeps his suits in fine repair. She makes Easter dresses for his daughters and fine gowns for his sister.

This baby is a minor thing. He will let her go to Margaret's without any argument. It is part of his posterity. You and your mother gave her a life."

Grae's heart swelled as tears filled her own eyes. Her mother's talent guided Violet's hands. But, Grae knew it was her own personal journey to 1859 that made the connection possible. Perhaps there were smaller reasons for her journeys. Small imprints that she had left which would not change the time, but would make it slightly better.

"Father, we have told you about the young lady that is visiting us." Grae thought that Davy's tone was quite formal to address his father. "She has been stranded in our rural community. Miss Sarah Leedy, I present to you our father, Squire David Graham."

Grae held her breath as Squire looked up from drinking his coffee at the end of table. She was the last one to be seated. All eyes were on him awaiting his reaction. His eyes were the only ones that were watching Grae. He choked on the coffee that he had just supped. His eyes grew wide as he coughed. She could feel the glow of hatred penetrate the room. She was standing on one side of the table. His seat was to her right. A quick glance told Grae that Martha was enjoying her husband's shock. She was surprised to see Martha look in her direction and nod.

"What did you say this woman's name was?" Squire was wiping coffee off the front of his vest with a napkin.

Grae saw that Davy looked addled by his father's reaction. "Sarah Leedy, Pa. Are you all right? Have you choked?" Davy walked toward him. Squire shooed him away.

"I am fine. I drank too fast. The coffee is cold. Get me a fresh hot pot!"

Slaves scurried to the winter kitchen at his command. Squire remained standing as Davy led Grae to her seat at the table. She kept her eyes on him. She must make sure that her reaction to him did not seem familiar. It was hard. Their shared experiences left a lasting impression on her feelings.

"Well, Miss Leedy, welcome to our home." He did not look her in the eyes as he spoke his words.

Grae sat in the chair that Davy pulled out for her. She sat between Mary Bell and Emily. Bettie sat to the right of her father. Davy sat to the left of his mother. An older gentleman sat between them.

"I thank you, sir, for the hospitality I have been shown here." Grae glanced at Squire. He was staring straight ahead at Martha. A glance in her direction revealed that Martha's eyes seemed to be twinkling.

"Yes, I am certain that my family has been hospitable. They are known to invite anyone into our home without permission."

"Father. Really. Miss Leedy is from a respectable Memphis family and her fiancé has studied law at the fine Mister Jefferson's school in Charlottesville." Grae noticed that Bettie touched her father's sleeve as she spoke to him.

"Is that so?" Squire's eyes shifted in Grae's direction. "What sort of business does your father do in Memphis?"

"He does not. My mother's family hails from there. The family name is Presley. Their business is rock." No one at the table understood her joke, of course. "They have rock quarries."

"Ah, that is a fine business for growth. The Earth's bounty will sustain that for quite some time." It didn't surprise Grae that Squire's comment would be about business.

"Doctor Minson, will you pray for us this evening?" Grae's eyes bugged out as Martha asked for the doctor's assistance. Martha took hold of Davy's hand and everyone's heads bowed as the doctor began.

"Lord, we thank you for the abundance of food that you have provided us this day. We pray for the continued well-being of all those at this table. Amen."

"Mister Graham, does Miss Leedy remind you of anyone?" Martha's question made Grae's blood chill. She didn't have to fake the questioning look she gave Martha. She noticed that Davy whispered something to his mother.

"Not that I can recall." Squire David took servings of food as the items were passed to him. He did not look up.

"Oh, I think that she resembles Miss Rapson, the young dress designer who was employed by Margaret a few years ago. Why, they could be sisters, twins. Bunt, don't you remember Miss Rapson?"

"No, Mother, I do not remember her." The youngest of the Graham daughters kept her head down.

"Well, I suppose that everyone just thinks that I am imagining things. I suppose that is what you think, Doctor Minson."

The look on Martha's face was one of growing agitation. As Grae cut her eyes toward Squire, she saw a smirk growing. He seemed to detect her gaze and looked her straight in the eyes as he chewed a mouthful of venison. The way he had looked at Martha made Grae sick to her stomach.

"You've hardly touched your food." Bettie's comment interrupted the exchange between Grae and Squire. "Are you not accustomed to venison, Sarah?"

"Oh...ah...actually, I am not. It is not so commonly found where I am from as it probably is in this country setting."

"So, you are from Memphis then, Miss Leedy?" Grae chose not to verbally answer Squire. She simply nodded and put a piece of biscuit into her mouth. "Where have you been living then? Where were you travelling from?"

Grae's mind raced. It needed to be a location that was far enough away that she could not easily go back there. "Richmond."

"And who is in Richmond?"

"My fiancé and his family. They live in Richmond."

"Why were you not travelling by train?"

"Train schedules seem to be temperamental at this time, the wagon train was more available. It seemed an interesting adventure, and that it was. The road is long and bumpy no matter how you travel it. A wagon train was leaving Richmond and they had some extra space."

"And, what will become of your belongings now that you are not there to keep up with them?" Squire was relentless in his questioning.

"Pa, Sarah sent a telegram to her intended in Richmond and to her family in Memphis. I am sure her belongings will be retrieved when the wagon train reaches Memphis."

Grae merely nodded and smiled at Davy. He gave her a look of apology.

"We went to visit the Tates today, Pa." Bettie took the conversation in another direction. "Nannie was so surprised to see that our Davy had returned for the holidays. She was so happy to see him."

"I am sure that was the case. We were all surprised, but nonetheless happy. It would make my heart glad if he would resign his post and come home to start a life with young Miss Tate. I'm sure that your mother would like to see some grandchildren before..."

"Before what? Before you permanently put me away. Or are you planning something more final?"

"Mother. We have guests." Bettie looked mortified by her mother's comments.

"If Sarah is going to be staying here for any length of time, she might as well know that sometimes I disappear for days at a time." Martha looked at Grae. "Not by my choosing mind you. The good doctor here and my husband have a special type of therapy for me. It involves strange concoctions and keys." The word 'keys' struck Grae. Her mind began to race. Could all of her journeys have such a simple theme?

"I said, what do you think of that, Miss Leedy?" Squire's voice brought her back to the table conversation.

"Pardon me, what did you say?"

"You seem to be in your own world. Is that where you would prefer to be, in your own world?" Squire's piercing eyes, each a different color, stared at her.

"Pa, I am going to respectfully ask for you to not keep badgering Sarah. I have asked her to be a guest in our home. It is still my home, is it not?" Davy's tone was strong and direct. Grae could feel the tension begin to lessen.

"Yes, son, it certainly is. We will honor your desire to be hospitable. I apologize, Miss Leedy. I have allowed my temper to get the best of me. I should not be embarrassing my children with my ramblings." Squire rose from the table, throwing his napkin on his plate. "I will leave you all to enjoy your dessert. Prissy, bring mine with some more coffee to my study. Good evening." Squire did not make eye contact with anyone else at the table as he left.

"Prissy, I think you can take the plates and begin serving the cobbler now. Miss Leedy, I hope you like apple cobbler. It is made with our own fall apples. My Davy loves cobbler." Martha's tone had changed completely. She patted her son's arm and looked lovingly around the table. Doctor Minson looked like he was asleep.

"What did you bring me?" The General was pacing near the corner of the room when Grae returned from dinner.

"Dinner was fine. Thanks for asking. Squire cross-examined me as if I was on trial. Martha accused Squire of wanting to have her committed or possibly killed. The doctor, who Jay thinks murdered Martha, basically fell asleep at the table. Bettie talks too much. I hate venison, but the cobbler was delicious." Grae collapsed on the bed.

"Did you say venison?"

The General jumped up on the bed and began to sniff Grae's pockets. She reached into one and pulled out her napkin. It was filled with small pieces of the meat. As The General was eating, Grae washed up and changed into her nightgown. She realized that her day had actually begun the day before in her time. Jet lag was no comparison to time travel lag. Every part of her body hurt, even her teeth.

"I miss my toothbrush."

"Don't even get me started. I miss having fingers." Grae held back a laugh. The General looked up from chewing. "Go ahead, laugh. It's all you can do at this point."

"Why don't you want to tell me what really happened to you? Who are you? I think I have put a few pieces of your mystery together by things my mother has told me. But, there are these big huge gaps and nothing makes sense."

"Grae, I realize that you are curious and I understand that. But, if you know my whole story, it will only be a burden for you."

"A burden? Why do you say that? You are my friend; I want to help you."

"That would be the burden. You cannot help me. What's done is done. My human life is over and the responsibility for that solely rests with me. I broke the rules, so I must pay the consequences. Dire and disastrous, as they are. You are a loving and caring person. That is evident in everything you do. My story would weigh heavy on your heart. There is already one person who I am sure carries guilt with her every day."

"My mother?"

"Yes, your mother. She was the best friend I ever had...until I met you." The General moved over and nuzzled Grae's hand. She stroked his soft fur.

"I miss you a lot when I am back in the present. I see you occasionally, and I want to talk to you so badly."

"Grae, you are always welcome to talk to me. I will be glad to listen to you."

"But, you can't respond to me, can you?"

"No, I cannot. That is part of my punishment."

"Punishment for what? This is infuriating. Mom won't tell me, and neither will you; but you certainly both have opinions about how I should travel."

Grae stood up and walked toward the window. The edge of moonlight shone down on the ground. She could see

Davy and Bettie walking. They were no doubt discussing the dinner conversation.

"Grae, it's really for the best."

"If you will not tell me what happened, answer a few questions of possibility."

"Oh, I don't like the sound of this. But, go ahead." The General stretched out on the bed and looked at Grae intently.

"Was it a spell of some sort that turned you into a cat?"

"As I have said, it was my punishment."

"Could it be reversed?"

"That would be doubtful."

"Why?"

"You just are not going to let up, are you?"

Grae gave him a big grin as she sat back down on the bed.

"I was punished for breaking the rules of time travel. In the first place, I was not supposed to travel. I did not personally have the power to do so. I came with someone else."

"My mother."

"Yes, your mother rather unwillingly brought me on her last trip. She had confided to me about her travels. As, I said, we were very close. I was so intrigued by everything she told me I wanted to experience it myself. It wasn't hard for me to accomplish. Your mother and I spent a lot of time on the Mansion property while your grandfather was working here. Many of our friends explored the far corners of the property with us. It was always an adventure." The General sighed and bowed his head. "But, that wasn't enough for me. I was curious."

"Curiosity killed the cat." Grae shook her head as she realized how ironic her comment was.

"Curiosity killed the boy and made him into a cat."

"But, you didn't die literally, did you?"

"No, but there is more than one way you can die. It doesn't always have to be a literal, physical death. You can be dead when you no longer exist in your own time. Remember, Mary McGavock. She didn't physically die, but she was just as dead to her own family. Her original life was gone."

"Well, I don't guess you know that Mary is really still living. I went to see her in my own time."

"I am aware of that, Grae. I'm sorry to hear that you visited her."

"Why? What was wrong with me going to see an old friend?"

"Mary McGavock Baker didn't just travel back in time. She stayed there, and then over lived her own life. It was as if she passed herself in the layers of time. I do not know what her outcome will be or when, but her punishment is long because of the multiple ways she broke the rules. She may have to live with it for eternity."

"You mean she might have gained immortality?"

"Don't make it sound so inviting. I considerably doubt that she sees that as a blessing. She was cursed because she dared to imagine that the life she was given could be better lived completely in another time. I share a similar fate."

"There must be some way to fix all this. Some way to right the wrongs and bring harmony back to time."

"It would take magic, my dear. You've seen what magic can do. You should not tamper with it. Elizabeth Peirce did, to escape her situation, and spent the rest of her life with the branding of a witch. Evelyn tried to use it to change the heart of another. She had a life of misery and revenge. You were there for the ending. Certainly not a pleasant one by any stretch of the imagination."

"No, you are correct. Is their magic linked to your situation?"

The General stood up after hearing Grae's question and jumped down to the floor.

"Grae, it doesn't matter."

"You said you went with Mom on her last trip. That was in 1859. How would you have known Elizabeth and Evelyn? You travelled back there on my trips. But, did you also travel there on your own?"

"Grae, stop! I've told you, I broke many rules. It started by hitching a ride with your mother that was far from the end of my reckless behavior. You do not need to pursue this line of thought any further. You need to concentrate on not doing anything that interferes with your returning to your own time." The General walked to the door. "Open it, please."

Grae did as he asked. She quietly followed him down the steps and opened the front door. As he slipped through the doorway and off the porch, she saw Davy and Bettie walking back toward the house. She quickly turned and found that she was face-to-face with Gracie.

"What you doing roaming round in your nightgown? Yous got a chamber pot up in your room."

"I...I was thirsty."

"You not gonna find nothin' to drink on the front porch." Gracie laughed under her breath. "Come on. You lucky you not run into Massa David. He justs went out to the barn. There be a colt comin' in the night."

Grae followed as the woman led her to the kitchen downstairs. Gracie pointed to a chair as she headed to the cold closet and retrieved a pitcher of milk. Grae had only drunk water at dinner and her mouth salivated thinking about the delicious taste of fresh milk that she remembered.

"Thank you. I was so thirsty." Grae took her first sip. "I suppose it is where I have been travelling for so many days."

"You been travellin', I be sure of that. But ole Gracie and Miss Patsy, we think you been travellin' for years."

Grae choked on the mouthful of milk that she was about to swallow. "What...what do you mean?"

"I mean that Miss Patsy and I know about trips people sometimes take. Miss Patsy, she had a sister-in-law who took a special kind of trip that she done never come back from. We think you do the same. You are the spitting image of the glorious girl who done helped my sweet Violet learn to sew. Miss Patsy knows it. I knows it. Massa David knows it. You been in this house before and your name was not Sarah Leedy."

Grae was afraid to look Gracie in the eyes. She couldn't lie to someone she liked so much.

"You go on and take your milk now. You think about what ole Gracie done said." Grae rose and began walking toward the doorway as Gracie continued talking. "You know what the truth is. Sometimes it be somethin' that is hidden in this here house. Massa David not like the way things truly be sometimes. He want to hide things. But, the truth...the truth it sets you free. The Lawd done told us that."

Grae kept walking as the image of Sal crossed her mind. That woman was with her every time she returned to another time. Sal always seemed to travel along.

It was late that night when The General returned. Grae heard a scratching at her door. He slipped in quickly and onto the bed that was opposite hers. He looked tired.

"How did you get inside?"

"I slip in and out with the slaves. I am not the only cat around. They pay me no mind. Getting upstairs is a harder maneuver."

"Gracie knows." Grae got back into her own bed and under the covers. Despite the warmth from the fireplace, the room had a December cold. "She says that Martha and Squire know as well."

"It's hard to hide your identity when it has only been a few years since your last visit."

"I don't think I have too much to worry about. Martha and Gracie loved the last me. Squire hates me no matter when I come."

"He didn't always hate you."

"Yes, but the sight of me reminds him of the worst part of his life. I understand that. I even sympathize with him. Losing Ama was horrendous on everyone who knew her. What he doesn't like is that I know his secret."

"That secret is all grown up now."

"Oh, I just don't want to know anymore. I know too much about this family already."

"Precisely why your mother and I think you should stop the exploration. You don't want to know what you don't know."

"Enough of that debate. What should I do about Gracie? Should I come clean with her?"

"Gracie is a powerful force in this house. She could make your time here hard. Having her as an ally could be very important. There's something brewing in this house. I'm not quite sure what it is. I think you should tell her that she is right. It should be a secret that is shared between you, Gracie, and Martha. I would not admit to anything in David's presence. He has power, mega power for his time. He could very easily have you disappear again permanently." An ice-cold chill passed over her. She knew the words were true. "Now, go to sleep. Tomorrow is your first full day in 1864. You better have all your senses intact."

"Good night."

It wasn't long before she heard The General's even breathing. He had quickly fallen asleep. She knew that he was her guardian in this time, and, probably, her own time. As much as she wanted to know who he was, she truly longed to be able to help him. She wanted him to return to his human state. To be the man he was meant to be before one foolish mistake turned his whole world around. Her thoughts drifted to her father. He was another foolish man who now had been given two second chances, perhaps three. He had regained his freedom, his health, and a chance to rebuild his family. Grae wanted the same for The General. He had been a dear friend to her mother. She was sure that her mother's life would be better today if her friend could return to her life. Perhaps Gracie and Martha knew some of the secrets of the magic The General had mentioned. Perhaps, Martha knew some of Elizabeth's secrets. The magic seemed to trace back to her.

SIXTEEN

"Rise and shine, sleepyhead." Grae sat straight up in the bed as Bettie's voice awakened her. "It's way past sunrise. You will sleep the day away."

Grae squinted as Bettie drew back the curtains and let the morning sunshine in. "What time is it? I must have really been sleeping hard." She knew that it had been probably close to midnight before her mind had let her rest.

"It's after eight o'clock. You already missed breakfast. But, have no fears. Gracie had them save two big plates of everything for you. You do not want to miss this breakfast. Mother always instructs the slaves to make all of Davy's favorites when he returns on furlough. You will gain weight from just one meal in this house."

Bettie's hearty laugh was infectious. Grae thought for a certainty that had they lived in the same time, they would have been fast friends. No sooner had Bettie stopped talking than Gracie came into the room with Violet close behind her. They each had a tray that seemed to be heaping with food.

"I sees Miss Bettie done woke up the dead in here." Gracie laughed. Behind her, Violet seemed to have the beginnings of a dress draped over her arm. She smiled shyly at Grae as she set the tray down. "You lucky that ole Gracie saved some breakfast for you in the kitchen. Massa Davy, he be one hungry man this mornin'. He likes his home cookin'. Violet done gots the bodice and skirt of your new dress cuts out and pinned up. She will wait until after you eats all this good food before she try it on you. You will be bigger by then."

Everyone laughed except Grae. Her eyes were transfixed on the dress that Violet had laid on the other bed. The color of the fabric was mesmerizing. It seemed to almost shine, yet not at the same time. It looked like metal, and the only word that could adequately describe it was gray. Gray, just like her name.

"Okay, Sarah, we will leave you to eat. Then Violet can come back and do her measuring and fitting. After that, I need your help. Davy has agreed to get Mother and Father out of the house to go and have lunch and a visit with Aunt Margaret. This will give us some time to work on the party preparations. So eat up. There's a big day ahead."

"Yes, Miss Sa-rah." Gracie said the name slowly and gave Grae a wink. "You get out of that bed and eat this food. Time's a wastin'."

Grae did as she was told. After splashing some of the cold water on her face that Violet had poured into the basin,

Grae turned back to the three who were standing watching her.

"I need some privacy please." Grae pointed to the chamber pot.

"Oh, yes, certainly." Bettie actually looked embarrassed, which surprised her. Gracie just chuckled. The three left the room.

"You want me to leave, too." Grae didn't realize that The General was under the bed.

"Well, I...ah..."

"It's okay. I was just kidding. I need to visit the outdoors myself. Open that door for me, but be sure to save me some of your breakfast. A nice little pile of pork under the bed would be a welcome mat for me when I return. Crack the door a little when you leave." The General headed to the door. Suddenly, he turned back around. "I am sorry that I was so hard on you last night. It really is better if you do not know the entire story...oh, and leave me a saucer of milk, if you can."

"I will." Grae wanted to say more, but silence might better suit the situation at the time.

She returned to her most pressing need. People in her modern time just didn't know how fortunate they were. Toilets were everywhere. The whole chamber pot experience was way more like camping than she liked.

She washed her hands and dug into the plates of food. There were fried eggs with big orange yolks, fresh sausage patties, potato cakes, stewed apples, and biscuits. A large glass of milk would wash it all down. Everything tasted delicious.

Grae's eyes kept finding their way back to the dress. The color was beautiful. It was demur in many respects, but striking in other ways. She couldn't help linger on the idea of how the color mimicked not only her name, but also on how she often felt about all the things she had learned on her journeys. These trips were full of adventure, but they were also very gray, somber, depressing in many respects. She could be a participating member of the audience, but she couldn't change the outcome of the show.

"Now, I have to get into all of these layers of clothes before I can even put it on." She had finished eating when there was a knock at her door. It was Violet.

"You ready for me to helps you?"

"I guess I will need help."

Grae began by putting on the bloomers and cotton slip. Violet lent a hand with lacing up the corset. She would never get used to that misery. Then, she stepped into the petticoats. Grae would not complain about modern day undergarments again. Even wearing pantyhose was nothing compared to the brutal layers that women of the nineteenth century had to endure. She studied the young woman as Violet helped her into the carefully pinned dress.

"What do you want this child to be, a boy, or a girl?"

Violet did not look at Grae. She continued carefully to put more pins into certain areas.

"I am amazed at how closely you made it to my size." Grae broke the long silence. "Even after that breakfast, it fits almost perfectly." Grae laughed, trying to ease the tension. She hadn't imagined that asking such a question would be wrong.

When Violet was finished, she helped Grae to remove it, taking out just enough pins so that the others were not lost in the process. She folded it over her shoulder and picked up her things. Grae completed dressing in a rust-colored dress that had been left for her.

"If this baby be a boy, he will face a life of hard work and beatings. If he be smart, he will have to hold that inside hisself. If he runs from this life, he will surely die. If it be a girl, her life be about the same. Only...only she gots to worry about some man taking her and making another one of these or worse. White or Negro, there be some man who will try to possess her. Take from her and never give back." Violet looked Grae straight in the eyes. "I want this child to live. I want this child to be free."

Grae felt a sadness grow inside of her. She knew that freedom was just around the corner for the slaves. She also knew that it would only be a word on a piece of paper for a very long time.

The door of Bettie's room was wide open as Grae walked down the hallway to the stairs. She had gone down a few before she heard giggling. As she turned around and went back up, the giggles changed to full-fledge laughter. It was a welcoming sound.

"Violet is almost finished with your dress. It is a bright red color. It will be beautiful for the party and our Christmas festivities!" Bettie's voice was loud and forceful.

"Now, sister, you know that we cannot parade our dear girl out at the party. Pa will have a fit or worse." Mary Bell's voice was equally forceful, but also tinged with worry.

"You have forgotten that our dear Davy is home. I am sure that he will figure out a way for Pa to see what a good idea it is to have our dear little Clara here with us."

Grae's ears perked up at Bettie's last comment. She had almost forgotten what Bettie had told her, the previous day.

"Can I come in?"

Grae stuck her head around the door and almost gasped at the sight of the room. It was not the bright blue she was accustomed to. The walls held pale green color wallpaper with tiny little flowers. The ceiling was a pearl white paper with interesting swirls throughout. The beautiful wood chair molding was the same as well as the wall of windows on each side, but the color that Bettie lived with was certainly more soothing.

"Sisters, make room on the bed for our new friend, Sarah."

Mary Bell and Emily made a place for Grae to sit between them. Bettie sat in a straight back chair next to the fireplace. Standing next to her was a very tiny girl. Her skin was so pale it was almost translucent. She turned her face shyly away from Grae and buried her head on Bettie's shoulder.

"Oh, Clara, do not be afraid of our new friend. Sarah has come from a faraway land and has ended up becoming our new friend quite by accident." Bettie pulled Clara away from her and looked her straight in the eyes. "It is just like magic brought her here to us. I think she came just to see you." Bettie pulled the girl into a hug. She winked at Grae over Clara's shoulders. Grae heard giggles in stereo on both sides of her.

"That's right, Clara. I have come here just to see you. I heard that there was a beautiful little girl here in this big old house."

Clara slowly turned and faced Grae. She nervously had her hands up near her mouth.

"I heard that this little girl was very sad." Clara turned back to Bettie and buried her head again. This time she crawled up into Bettie's lap. "So, I came to make her happy. I see that has already begun. How beautiful you will look in your pretty new dress."

Clara slowly looked back at her again. There was a very stern look on her face.

"Mister Gray does not like me." It was not quite a whisper, but it lacked the volume to be considered anything else. Grae looked at Bettie.

"She is speaking of our father. She calls him Mister Gray. She can't seem to remember our full name. It does fit his disposition."

Grae's hand rose to her mouth to stifle a laugh, but Bettie beat her to it with a loud cackle. She turned back to the little girl.

"We must practice this. Good evening, Mister Graham." Clara's eyes were big as saucers as she watched Bettie. "Say it with me. Good evening, Mister Graham."

"Good evening, Mister Gray ham."

"No dear. It is not Gray ham…it is Graham. Say it all together fast."

"Gray ham…Grayham…Graham."

"Very good!"

Clara beamed as Bettie complimented her. Grae watched as Bettie had the little girl say the phrase repeatedly. Eventually, she added Missus Graham to the mix. Grae was in awe to see this sweet, living breathing being who was now trapped in this room for eternity. She silently vowed to buy her more toys and play with her more often.

"We must talk about the party."

The youngest Graham sister, Emily, was a very animated young girl. Grae hoped to learn the true origin of her nickname. 'Bunt' did not seem like a socially acceptable reference for young ladies, such as the Grahams.

"Gracie has helped us plan a wonderful menu." Mary Bell took a list out of her pocket. Grae imagined that Mary Bell would run a strict house one day. She seemed very precise in lists and instructions.

"Sarah, we have invited the most distinguished members of our community. You will get to meet the best families in our area." Bettie seemed sure that this would impress Sarah. Grae obliged by seeming very happy with her news. "We were very surprised to learn that Doctor Minson is quite an accomplished pianist. So, we have asked him to play some of our Mother's favorite pieces. I have heard him practicing and his musical skill is quite enchanting."

Grae thought Bettie's description of the doctor's skills was quite unusual. She must remember to ask Jay if he knew of Doctor Minson's musical talents.

"Aunt Margaret is having her best cook make the most scrumptious cakes." Mary Bell continued with her list. "There will be red velvet. That is Pa's favorite. There will be an apple cake. Our mother loves pound cake. We will serve it with lemon curd."

"I like chocolate." Bunt made her declaration known.

"What do you like, Clara?"

Grae left her spot on the bed, sat down on the floor with Clara, and noticed that Bettie gave Mary Bell a raised eyebrow look at her seating choice. Clara looked up from the doll she was holding. She had the biggest blue eyes Grae thought she had ever seen.

"You can tell me."

"My mam she made gingerbread. It was the bestest, especially with milk."

The small voice said her words very carefully as tears ran down her face. Grae would use her mother's recipe and make this sweet girl a big pan of gingerbread.

"I think we need to have some gingerbread."

Grae looked at the three sisters. They all nodded in agreement.

Grae believed that if she had calculated all the paper hearts she had cut out in her life up to that point, it would not have equaled to the number she cut out in that one day with the Graham sisters. The scissors were primitive to her standards. They were using old newspapers, which made her fingers black. Mary Bell had a plan that hearts would be hanging by red ribbons from every available spot in the house. They would need to get Mister and Missus Graham out of their home twenty-four hours in advance to have the time to hang all of the tokens of love. It was a shame that the depth of love shared by the children was not mirrored between their parents.

"Gracie says we are overdoing it, but I think it will be enchanting." Mary Bell had a dreamy look on her face as she carefully slipped ribbons through the holes that were created by Bunt in each heart.

"Have you planned your dream wedding?" The question was already out of Grae's mouth before she thought about the implications of it. She forgot that copies of *Modern Bride* magazine weren't found at every newsstand in 1864.

"Oh my goodness, yes! She has this horrid album in her room with all sorts of catalog pictures and swatches of fabric." Bettie answered the question for her sister. "She even has names for her children. She corresponds with Mister Harold Matthews. He is in the Stonewall Brigade. But, he has not asked for her hand, as of yet." Bettie rolled her eyes.

"My gown shall be pearl white with tiny embroidered flowers. Violet and I have been working on a design." Mary Bell seemed to have tuned out her sister's taunting. "I shall have four attendants, unless my intended has more sisters than I do. The attendants shall wear flowing gowns of lavender and shall carry the colors of spring in their bouquets. Father shall wear a coat and tails with a top hat like our Mister Lincoln."

"Mister Lincoln indeed. You shall have no one to make all those lovely dresses if he has his way. All of our slaves will be roaming free."

Bettie was cutting out hearts as well. They were working in the dining room. A young slave that she heard Mary Bell call Ruth had brought them some sassafras tea. Grae found the taste to be strong. She asked for more sugar.

"Sister, I thought you were the progressive one in the family. You used to want Pa to free the slaves when we were away at school."

"I had forgotten how much they are needed for our day-to-day existence here. We could not function without them."

While Grae knew that it wasn't a line from Margaret Mitchell's classic tale, she could still hear Scarlett's fiddle-dee-dee in Bettie's tone.

"As I was saying, my wedding shall be beautiful. It shall be in early May before the heat of summer causes discomfort. The church shall be draped in lavender ribbons and Lily of the Valley. The service shall be simple, but I will have music." Mary Bell looked up at Grae and nodded her head. "My wedding cake shall be a delicious fruit cake with white icing. The dinner shall be ham glazed with brown sugar and all sorts of delectable vegetable dishes. Gracie's hot buttered bread fresh from the oven shall be my one indulgence after the ceremony is complete. I shall be a married one then, my figure can suffer." Mary Bell's head rolled back as she cackled with laughter. Her two sisters joined her. It was a rather scary sound to Grae.

"Davy is concerned about how Pa will react to this surprise." Bettie spoke in hushed tones and looked around to see if anyone was lurking nearby. "He is also frightfully inquisitive about Doctor Minson's treatment of Ma. He thinks that the Doctor is listening too much to Pa."

"Well, our brother is not wrong in his concern. You and I discussed at length if we should chance an outburst from Pa. But, we agreed that he will not make a scene in front of all our distinguished guests. It will be a grand opportunity for them to see Ma. She will be having a good day. The endless questions we receive at church or at socials about Ma's health have to be put to rest. You may not have fears with John Robinson in your sights. But, I must be ever watchful of how the families of my potential suitors view our status. The questionable health of my mother could ruin my chance of marrying well."

"Oh, Mary, Mary, quite contrary, John Robinson is but one of many I have in my sights. We must make sure that none of our suitors only smell the Graham money. We do not want to end up unloved and confined to a marriage of convenience and profit." Bettie rose from the table. "I think we have played with hearts long enough. Our lunch was a scant meal. Let us hide our progress and go for a brisk walk. A piece of Gracie's apple pie will be our reward upon return."

All four of them gathered up the vast number of hearts that were created. As she scanned the supplies, it appeared that their work was completed. Bettie's timing made it appear otherwise. The twinkle in her eye showed Grae that everything Bettie Graham said and did was carefully calculated.

"My sister is fine. There is no need to waste our time with such a fuss. We shall honor her with a simple family dinner. She does not like parties."

Squire David interrupted the lively dinner conversation to speak his opinion regarding Margaret's coming birthday. Davy's day out with his parents had been productive from his sisters' point of view, but he looked exhausted.

"Mister Graham, our dear Margaret shall turn eighty years of age before the New Year comes. It is our duty to celebrate this momentous occasion." Martha's words were clear and direct. Grae remembered the forcefulness from her last visit to Martha's home.

"It's all nonsense. Let Cynthia host such an affair. It is her duty. She is married to a wealthy McGavock cousin; she has plenty of resources at her disposal."

"Have you not forgotten that Cynthia is the only child of Margaret's left? I have spoken with her and she will be assisting, but the party shall be here. Margaret has doted on you from infancy. She has hailed your achievements and hidden your indiscretions."

Grae watched Squire's face as Martha made her last statement. She was surprised that steam didn't come out of his ears.

"Margaret is too old for a birthday party. We shall not discuss this further." Squire returned his attention to his plate, spearing a potato with his fork.

"But, Pa, Aunt Margaret loves parties. She has given so many for us in the past." Bettie interrupted her father's eating. He did not look amused.

"Yes, when Bettie and I returned from boarding school, she had a wonderful social for us. It was delightful to see our friends and neighbors after such a long time away." Mary Bell offered her opinion, too. Martha's smile grew with each comment.

"They are right, Father. Aunt Margaret has always been so caring to us. Did you know that she sends socks, paper, pencils, and stamps for me to distribute to my men? These are luxuries for our soldiers." Davy's comment was the last straw. Squire laid down his knife and fork and looked around the table. His gaze rested on Grae.

"Miss Leedy, I believe that is what you call yourself. You must have an opinion about this matter. Everyone else does. Should we host a party for Margaret?" Grae looked Squire in the eye. She knew he was using the topic as an excuse to try to make her slip up about knowing Margaret.

"Well, sir. I do not believe I have met this lady since I arrived. But, she sounds like a delightful person. If for no further reason, the honor of her reaching the milestone of eighty years would seem to make it an appropriate time for a celebration." Grae tried to hide her smugness.

"Well, then, I suppose my opinion means nothing. Why should it in my own house? Go forth. Throw her a grand affair. I shall fight no longer. I do not think that she shall enjoy the attention being focused on her. As you have said, she honors others with her words and deeds. It is not her preference to be the guest of honor. We shall see." Squire David pushed himself away from the table and stood up. "Arabella, has my family made you comfortable?"

Grae froze. The sound of the name she had used during her first and second journeys turned her blood as it came from his lips. His thoughts were surely on Ama at that moment—the death of his Native American beauty, the mother of his abandoned child. He had walked behind her. She could feel his eyes piercing through the back of her head.

"Father, Miss Leedy's first name is Sarah." Davy looked apologetically at Grae.

"Ah, she bears such a resemblance to a girl I once knew."

Grae watched as a look of concerned understanding crossed Martha's face.

"One of my teachers mentioned in one of his lectures that we all have a twin somewhere." Bettie broke the tension. "It would be a rare occurrence to actually meet that person face to face. But, I think it would be delightful!"

Squire did not acknowledge his daughter's comment. He merely left the room. Grae knew that it was only a matter of time before she and Squire would have a confrontation. She must consult The General on how she should prepare.

SEVENTEEN

"It frightens me to say what I am thinking."

The General was pacing the floor in front of the bed where Grae relaxed after the stressful dinner. She had told him about Squire David's use of the name, Arabella.

"I don't understand."

Grae was still so incredibly tired. Every joint of her body hurt. She knew that she shouldn't physically hurt as much as she did. She was too young to feel so old. The feeling of time travel lag was certainly not a new one for her. But, this time was different. Sleep, food, and fresh air weren't enough to offset the feeling. It was as if her bones hurt from the inside out.

"You asked me how you should handle Squire. How much should you reveal? My thoughts, my inclinations, on this topic are frightening me. Because I think that you should tell him the truth."

"The truth! What? That I boarded Time Travel Airlines for a journey to another century for the fourth time. Where's The General? What did you do with him? You must be an imposter."

Grae stood up and began pacing between the two beds. The General was still pacing at the foot of the beds. It looked like they were making a moving 'T'.

"For all of Squire David Graham's faults, for all of his indiscretions, shortcomings, horrid behaviors—we cannot forget one very important trait of his. He was a man ahead of his time. He was brilliant in many respects. He was well read. His mind was open to many things. It is one of the reasons why he was so successful."

"Okay, he was smart and a great businessman. I get that. You think he's going to understand time travel and not want to have me burned at the stake?"

"Yes, I do." The General stopped and jumped up on Grae's bed. "He will believe. He will understand because of Ama."

Grae almost fell down. "What?"

"Native Americans have strong beliefs. They are deep rooted in the spirit world. Their concepts of time are different from other cultures. Squire David spent a lot of time with Ama and her father. He was taught many things. Just because he left that life, or maybe I should say that life left him, it doesn't mean that it didn't influence him. Just as we know, his love for Ama is still in his heart somewhere. We also know that those teachings, most likely, are still within his mind."

"Well, let's assume, for a moment, that you're right. That still doesn't mean that it will make him believe me. He hates me. This version of me and every other version I have been." Grae put her hands over her eyes and began to rock back and forth. The headache was returning.

"Perhaps, but he really doesn't know you. He doesn't know who you are or where you came from."

"But...what difference does that make? Why should he believe me?" Grae couldn't understand what The General was trying to tell her.

"He knows that Arabella made a connection to Ama. Grae, there is no doubt that he and Margaret tricked you into going to North Carolina with the baby. He intended to leave you there to raise his son, to be the child's mother. You only looked at the dangerous place he put you in. You were right to do so. You had to get out of there, but think about it another way, now. He trusted you with his child. He chose you to be the one. It wasn't some long friendship or familial relationship. You were a stranger. I can't help but believe that it was a request of Ama's. She was an incredible woman. She could see inside your soul."

Grae took a deep breath. Her head began to feel better as she thought about the beautiful woman who had befriended her so easily.

The General continued his reasoning. "I believe she may have chosen you to be a mother to her son. That could be one of the sources of Squire's anger. You leaving meant that he couldn't fulfill one of her last and strongest wishes."

"This is hard for me to grasp."

"Grae, you are eternally connected to Squire David Graham. The anger you have seen from his spirit in your time has a direct correlation to the real things you experienced together in his time." The General's words smacked Grae in the face with a force so strong that she fell back on the bed. It was overwhelming.

"How could that be? How could that be?" Grae's mind raced.

"Grae. This is why I think you should talk to him and tell him the truth. Tell him your bizarre, complicated, multi-century story. Tell him who you are, who your mother is, how you live all those hundreds of years later in his home. Your connection to him is stronger than both of you realize. But, it's like Sal told you—the truth shall set you free." The General left the room when he finished speaking.

Grae sat in the darkness, crying and praying for the strength to do what he told her. In her heart, she knew what The General said was true. Her connection to Squire David might have been what originally started her entire journey. Yet, the confrontation with him in his time, in his house, was going to be something that Grae would never forget.

The next couple of days passed quickly in the Graham household. It was becoming a world of distractions. The anniversary party preparations were well underway with whispered messages passing between siblings and the slaves who helped them carry out their plans. The most influential accessory to their crime of merriment was their aunt, Margaret McGavock. Even on the edge of her octogenarian status, she was a willing and able accomplice to her nephew and nieces' plans. Her, not-so-secret, upcoming birthday affair was proving to be a nice little distraction for Martha. Margaret decided that she could best help the Graham children by taking away their biggest obstacle, their father.

"Margaret insists that I take her to see Cousin Fiona today." Squire David announced on Friday morning. "I do not understand why it is so urgent."

"Well, Pa, I would imagine when you are almost eighty years old, time is of the essence."

Davy smiled at the others around the breakfast table that morning. Grae was cautiously guarded during meals since Squire's questioning, but he had hardly acknowledged her existence since then.

"I suppose. Margaret knows that I will lose enough valuable business time with all the upcoming holiday nonsense. Why she has chosen this precise day as a time of travel is beyond me."

"Pa, it is probably for that very reason." Bettie decided to help her brother with his line of reasoning with their father. "With her advanced age, she probably thinks this could be her last holiday season. She wishes to engage in as much family time as she can."

"Well, it would appear that my children have this all figured out."

Grae thought she almost detected a smile of amusement quickly crossing Squire's face.

"I have never denied my sister anything that she has asked of me. I shall not start now."

"I am certainly glad to hear that, Mister Graham." Martha said as she entered the dining room. Grae thought that perhaps she was not feeling well when she was not with the family for their morning meal. "I will spare no expense then in the grand celebration of her birth."

The smile quickly left Squire David's face and he exited the room shouting for one of the slaves to get his coat.

"Sometimes I think that you live for the moments when you can rile Pa." Davy's statement was rather brass, but not far from the truth from Grae's observations.

"Davy! You should not speak to our mother that way." Mary Bell was horrified at her brother's words.

"No, daughter, he speaks the truth. You should not be chastised for speaking the truth in this house." Martha nodded as a small older slave woman poured coffee into her cup. Another young one placed a plate of food in front of her. "When your father and I were first married, before any of you existed, there was a time when banter such as that was a joyful sound in this house. We seemed to have a better understanding of who we were in this relationship. It was an exciting, hopeful time."

"What happened, Mother?" Bettie's voice was soft and childlike. Her eyes were full of wonder at the thought of such an idyllic household.

"I learned the truth. My illusion was finally broken." Martha looked around the table at her children. Grae felt awkward. She knew that Martha was speaking privately to her offspring. "Promise me that none of you will marry for convenience or monetary gain. I do not want my daughters to take husbands for wealth and security. I do not want my son to take a bride who has a bounty attached to her. If material things are involved in the family, so be it. But, only if love, trust, and, most of all, respect, is at the core of your union. Nothing else matters. Nothing else is real."

Martha's words were finished. She began to eat her breakfast as her children sat in silence around her.

"I would like for you to tell me who you really are."

Grae had been sent into the parlor to retrieve a hidden box of ribbons and found Martha there sipping tea and reading. "I beg your pardon." She was afraid to look her old friend in the eye.

"I do not believe that you are Sarah Leedy as you have been introduced. In fact, I do not believe that your name has been any of those by which I have met you, now or previously. Sit down, please."

Grae sank down on the parlor couch that was behind her. She wished that The General were nearby to advise her with a swish of his tail.

"Some say that my mental state is not as it should be. I know that I have spent way too much of my life in a darkness that seems overwhelming at times. I have endured much sadness and grief. My children who have lived to grow and dream are the true sources of light in my heart. However, there is one thing that I feel most confident about; I know exactly whom the people are who have passed through my life. I know those that I have called friend. I have seen into their souls. I met a young woman a few years ago. She was under the employment of my sister-in-law, Margaret. Our souls became intertwined. It was not our first meeting. She had sat at my father's table in 1830 surrounded by an entourage lead by my now husband. I was too enamored that night to know she was even there. Words may never have passed between us. Yet, my heart knew that it would encounter her again. She sits before me today." Grae kept her head down. "She has no reason to fear me, in this life or the next. I know her heart is pure. I know she comes here not so much by choice as by duty."

Grae's head slowly rose and she met Martha's eyes. It was time. "You speak the truth."

"The truth is all we need." Martha smiled. "I welcome her again into my home. I warn you though. He knows as well. His senses are keen. I can accept what I do not understand. I do not know if that is possible with him. He harbors anger that has fermented for decades. There is a stench of wrath in his heart. He did not give love its place of honor in his life. So, now, he hardly knows how to use it or feel it. It is all folly and waste."

"Will he seek to harm me? Will he brand me as Elizabeth was branded?"

Grae's questions seemed to startle and surprise Martha. She drank more tea and stared into space for a time.

"He usually tries to conquer that which he fears. I gather that you are a part of his anger, his loss. Another wife might even be envious of you. Indeed, you know the first and only woman he has ever loved. You are a link to her. That is apparent when he looks at you. I have long since relegated envy a box to dwell in. It is of no purpose in my life. I do not admire or resent the woman that holds his heart. I pity that she is not here to keep it. My life would have been better if she had lived."

As Grae pondered Martha's words, a feeling of courage came over her.

"My name is Grae. It's short for Graham, Graham White. My life is in the twenty-first century, about two hundred and fifty years from now. I live in this house with my mother, brother, and grandfather. And, I almost forgot, my father lives there now as well. Your house is still a home."

A smile crossed Martha's face. "That is a lot to grasp. Over two hundred years, it is unimaginable. Are you my descendant?"

Martha's question was a logical one, but one that Grae had not thought much about. It struck her as strange at that moment. She had spent so much time studying the Graham family, she had not thought about how it might connect to her own. Grandpa had said that they were from another set of Grahams.

"My mother was a Graham, but I do not think that we descended from your family."

"Since our last meeting, I have wondered if you have some connection. You have a resemblance, faint, but there." Martha paused and studied Grae's face. "Are you a witch? Please do not misunderstand my question. I hold no threat to my words. My dear Elizabeth possessed vast powers. I loved her dearly and wish she would return to me."

"No, I am not a witch. I really do not possess any powers."

"Then, how is it that you can travel between times?"

It was another question Grae had thought little about. It seemed futile to speculate as to how she did it. She was more concerned with the why of the matter.

"I really don't know. I inherited this ability. Remember Loretta who taught Violet how to sew?" Martha thought a moment, and then nodded. "Loretta is my mother. Well, she wasn't my mother when she was Loretta. She became my mother when she grew up." Martha's face showed no signs of understanding. "I know; it is hard to grasp. Let me just leave it that my family seems to have this ability. This seems to be my token of passage." Grae pulled out the key that was hidden beneath her dress.

Martha stood up, dropped the book from her lap onto the floor. She walked over to Grae and reached out to touch it, but hesitated.

"The last time I saw this, I touched it, and you disappeared before my very eyes."

Grae hadn't thought about that aspect of her last departure. That must have indeed been shocking and frightening for Martha.

"I am sorry about that. I did not know that would happen. You see, I was also giving you back Elizabeth's broach."

Martha nodded and lowered her hand. She did not seem to want to touch the key again. Grae returned it to its home beneath her clothing. "I believe that some of Elizabeth's power is contained within the broach. I think it caused me to be sent back to my time, at that moment."

Martha sat down on the couch next to Grae. Her words seemed to have weighed Martha down.

"Elizabeth." Martha exhaled and years of weight seemed to leave her shoulders. "She was a sister of my soul. My dreadful brother never even tried to understand her. She was just one in a succession of poor women who married the same wrong man."

Grae was surprised to hear Martha speak that way about her brother. History did tell the same story. Alexander had many wives, many dead wives.

"I do not understand how she came to have that gift. Many people used her to help them execute evil deeds. In the end, as I understand, she was killed by someone she was trying to help."

"Who? When?"

"I am not sure when it occurred exactly, but it had to have been in the late 1700's. The person who did it was Evelyn Newton."

"That name. How do I know that name?"

"She was a woman who was in love with Patrick McGavock."

"Oh, yes. I have heard Margaret speak of her. Eve, I believe she called her. She said Eve had a vengeful heart. She was killed in a fire at..." Martha's memory seemed to catch up with her speech.

"At the cabin that once stood here. Yes, first it was the Baker's home."

"Then, Mister Graham lived here. His son was born here." Martha stood up and walked toward the window. There was a long pause. Grae waited for more revelations.

"Yes."

"You were present for that, weren't you?"

"Yes."

"Is that why he hates you so?"

"I am not sure. Perhaps, I remind him of that time." Grae was careful with her words. She did not want to reveal any more details than necessary.

"You may speak freely. Patrick has told me all about that time. Unfortunately, he did not tell me before I was married."

The admission rather startled Grae. She forgot to control her inquisitiveness.

"Would it have made a difference?" Grae covered her mouth quickly. "I am sorry. I should not have asked that."

"No, it is fine. It is a fair question. Even knowing all that I do, I am not sure that I would have acted differently. If I had, I would not have my wonderful children. They might have been those of another man, if they existed at all. They would not be the same individuals that I now so love in my life."

Martha sat back down in her original seat. "But I can say for a certainty, I would not have allowed Mister Graham to handle me as he does his business deals. I would have made it clear from the beginning that the deal he made with my father did not involve the treating of me like a piece of property. He may have had no intentions of love being part of this…this deal. But kindness and respect are commodities that he could have used more extravagantly."

"You seem so calm about it, now. It is not a feeling that you always portray." Grae knew that her statement was treading on uncomfortable ground. Honesty was the mood of the room.

"My life has been filled with darkness. It closes in on top of me like the lid of a coffin. I am not always aware of its timing. It is not a constant companion as my husband portrays, at times. I can pull myself out of the tomb when the sunshine of others shines on me. He prefers to have a sick wife. He prefers to hide her away. He wanted prosperity. My father made it possible. As hard as he worked, Squire David Graham could not have created all his grandeur on his own. There were not enough hours in his day. He wanted children. His lineage must be carried on. His guilt for forsaking his firstborn must be quenched. I gave him children. He did not want to feel love. I suppose he found it too painful." Grae drank in Martha's words. It was good to hear truth. Martha looked Grae straight in the eyes. "Was she so wonderful that no one else could even come close?"

Grae could not conceal the gasp that rose up in her throat. She heard in the woman's voice the years of pain that haunted her daily like a ghost in her house.

"Ama was wonderful. Loving and caring, wise beyond her brief lifetime. She would have been very unhappy with the life that Squire has built for himself." Grae was almost surprised at her own words. Somehow, she knew it was the truth. "Ama would have wanted him to take all the love he had for her and shower it on their son. Then, build a life with another woman who would show her men unconditional love. I think his darkest guilt is that he knows he let her down. He let his pain and pride overshadow any good he had inside; he let his life be ruled by fear."

"Does he ever change?" Martha's question surprised Grae. "I know that my life will not be long. He will outlive me. Does he remarry?"

Grae was afraid to answer the questions. She knew that she shouldn't divulge that kind of information. "Martha, I cannot tell you that. It is dangerous for me to speak of the future."

"Yes, I imagine it would be. There is a reason we cannot see into our own futures. If you knew what was going to happen in your life, you would not live it." Martha rose. "I am tired. I think I will go and rest for a while." As Martha made her way to the doorway, Grae searched her mind for something appropriate to say. Martha turned as she walked out of the room. "I am glad that we had this talk. I am pleased that you were honest with me."

After Martha left, Grae picked up the book that had fallen to the floor. It was *Sonnets from the Portuguese* by Elizabeth Barrett Browning. As Grae flipped through the pages, a piece of paper fell out. She picked it up and turned it over. She let out a small sob. It was a pencil drawing of Ama with the words "My Love" written at the bottom. It would be a hard thing for any wife to find, especially one who knew for a certainty that the words would always be true.

"I can keeps your mother upstairs. But, you young'uns better get busy. Massa David goin' to be home early, I bet. He will be 'spectin' somethin' if Miss Margaret wants to stop here." Gracie had already been lecturing everyone that morning on how they needed to be quiet as they decorated the house.

"Aunt Margaret will make him stop in Draper. She will come up with some excuse."

Bettie was giving her full attention to the careful placement of the hearts. A young male slave was on a ladder trying not to tear any as he repositioned them multiple times for her.

"What time are your guests arriving?" Grae had not been given any duties yet. She was the last one to come down for breakfast. The General had pawed her face to get her awake. She was still exhausted.

"We have told everyone to be here by three. We want to have an early dinner. Winter is a hard time for folks to be away from their farms," Davy said as he entered the room and overheard her question. "Some will need to return home before it gets too dark to care for their animals. It is not safe on our roads these nights. Deserters are everywhere."

"Don't they have slaves to tend to them?" The youngest Graham daughter, Bunt, asked the question of her brother. Grae realized that this child of privilege couldn't comprehend life without slaves.

"Now, Bunt, you know that not all of our family's friends are as prosperous as we are. They must work hard without the good labor of slaves."

Grae thought that about how Davy's phrasing was compassionate and condescending at the same time. It was as if he indeed was a cross between his two parents in his thinking. His thoughts must engage in a great wrestling match at times.

"Who is that coming?"

Mary Bell moved toward one of the front windows to look out. Grae came up behind her and saw a wagon with two slaves approaching. "It is slaves from Aunt Margaret's house."

"Do you think something is wrong?" Grae wasn't sure what their arrival indicated.

"Oh, goodness, no! I am surprised they are this early. They are bringing most of the pies and cakes for the party. One of Aunt Margaret's girls is the most wonderful baker. I think she lived up North for a time and learned in some big city bakery."

"She worked as a free person." Davy had joined the viewpoint from the front door.

"Free? Why is she a slave then?" Grae's question came out before she thought it through.

"She came south to visit her mother. As I understand, it was supposed to have been a secret visit to the Crockett farm. But, one of the overseers caught her out on a road near Draper. She didn't have papers indicating her freedom so he thought she was a runaway. Aunt Margaret heard the story. She knew the girl's mammy on the Crockett farm. The old woman was getting on in years, so Aunt Margaret bought the daughter and arranged with the Crocketts for visits to occur. She got to spend time with her mother and help care for her until she passed."

"But, she's still a slave?"

"It's all that can be. Her word is not proof enough for her freedom." Davy opened the door. "I must go and check on the hog."

Grae closed the door behind him as a cold wind blew past her. Slaves had been working all night cooking a whole hog on a spit in a pit in the ground. It was a long, slow process. Grae remembered about the endeavor from previous visits.

"How sad it is to live in a time when a person's word means nothing just because of the color of their skin." Grae's words were soft, but strong.

"Who are you talking to?"

Grae turned to see Martha coming down the staircase. A panic came over her. Martha wasn't supposed to come downstairs. "Good morning, Missus Graham!" She said these words very loudly. "I thought you were resting in your room this morning." Grae's voice got even louder.

"I am not deaf, child. You do not have to shout. I thought that I should get up and enjoy some of this time with my children before Mister Graham comes home and ruins the day." Martha had progressed to midway down the stairs. Grae started up them to block her way.

"Oh, you are so funny!" Grae faked a laugh. Martha gave her a strange look.

"I was not trying to be humorous! Why are you yelling? What is going on down here?" Martha craned her neck to try to see into the foyer below. Grae moved closer to her.

"Did you know that Violet made me a new dress? It is just amazingly beautiful. Why don't you come upstairs with me and see it? Gracie is so proud of her." Grae could hear scurrying in the rooms around the stairs. Martha wasn't listening to her.

"Let me pass. I want to know what is going on in my house."

Grae's mind raced trying to find another distraction.

"Miss Patsy, what are you doin' comin' down them stairs? We decided this mornin' that you was goin' to get some rest in case Miss Margaret come to visit on her way back home." Gracie appeared out of nowhere behind Grae at the bottom of the stairs.

"There's something going on in this house, and I want to know what it is." Martha's voice was strong and defiant. Grae liked it.

"Now, you know that mornin' always be a busy time in this here house. We doin' some extra cleanin' and polishin' in case Miss Margaret come callin'. You know, she is gonna worry Massa David to death to stop and see her Martha and these girls. Why, I bet you told her about our old friend here who is a-visitin'."

Martha turned her attention to Grae. The look of aggravated concern left her face replaced by a smile. "I did tell Margaret, but not the whole secret." Martha winked at Grae. Her attention reverted to the commotion she heard. "Perhaps I need to come and supervise the work to make sure it is done properly."

Grae knew it was time for her to move out from between the two women.

"Now, are you tryin' to say that ole Gracie don't know how to take care of this house?" A long pause hung in the air. "Somethin' Patsy need to tell me?" There was no backing down in Gracie's eyes. Slave or free person, she was a strong force.

"Well, no, I just thought…"

"You just thought you gonna' be the fancy lady of the house today, hmmm? Put ole Gracie in her place as your slave?"

Grae could see exactly where the slave woman was going with her speech. Guilt was a constant, powerful force in the Graham Mansion.

"No, now, Gracie, you know that I do not treat you…"

"Well, I thought I knew, but it seems that this mornin' you think you know better than old Gracie. Maybe you plannin' to ship me off to the old slaves' home."

Gracie turned in Grae's direction a moment and gave her a wink. She was a sly one. No wonder she had survived in the Graham home so many years.

"No, you know you are my family. As long as I am breathing, this is your home. I know that you always keep things going smoothly, I guess I…well, I just do not know what I was thinking." Grae saw a look of confusion pass over Martha's face. "Perhaps, Mister Graham is right. I have these spells of…"

"Now, you listen right here. That man ain't never right when it comes to my Miss Patsy. Don't you dare get that notion in your head agin. We done talked about that. You just need to keep trustin' ole Gracie. She know what be best for you. She thinks you need to rest up 'cause Miss Margaret be a handful. You know she gonna' come flyin' into this house like a cyclone. You and her will have a good visit, laugh and carry on with those girls while Massa David be a-steamin' with you all havin' such a good time."

Martha nodded and turned to go back up the steps. "Could you have someone bring me some tea?"

"I will do that. You go on back up there and calm yourself down. Gracie will take care of everythin'."

They watched as the mistress of the house climbed back up the stairs. When she was out of sight, Gracie turned to Grae and smiled.

"That be how it is done."

"You most certainly know how."

"I made it my job a long time ago to see to it that Miss Patsy know it is best for me to be watchin' over things in this house. She keep her eye on things, I know. But, she don't really haves to as I done already seen to it before she ever even think it usually. She got way more to worry about than any woman, black or white, ever need to bein' married to that man. She don't need him sayin' she don't know how to mind a house. I make sure everythin' done so he can't do no complainin'. Today, that came in handy. Miss Patsy don't cross me. I be like her sister. We fuss and carry on, but she know no soul look out for her better than this one right here." Gracie pointed her finger to her own chest. Behind that tough exterior, there was real love in the woman's eyes.

Grae knew that there wasn't much that Gracie wouldn't do for Martha, or Martha's children. It had nothing to do with who owned whom. Despite her youth, Grae knew that you couldn't buy that type of loyalty and devotion. It came out of love. It had no price.

The level of excitement and commotion was growing in the Graham household by mid-afternoon. The daughters had finished supervising the hanging of the decorations. All of the food was ready. Every table in the downstairs seemed to have some food item on it. The smell was intoxicating. Grae had no idea how Gracie had explained the aromas that had obviously risen upstairs. Everyone was dressed in his or her finest outfits. Martha was being encouraged by Violet to get dressed up for the visit of her favorite sister-in-law. The fact that forty or so of their closest friends were stopping by as well was not mentioned. Everyone seemed to be holding his or her breath.

"Theys coming! Theys coming!" A small, but fast, slave boy came running from across the road. He was dressed in a hat, coat, and shoes. That was a rare sight. Grae soon realized why. He was one of Gracie's grandchildren. They seemed to have it a little better than the rest. They had the better jobs on the farm. They were trusted.

A flurry of activity blew through the house. The guests had arrived over the previous hour. Grae tried to stay out of the way for fear she would see someone who might recognize her from past trips. Her interaction with the local community had been limited, especially on the journey five years earlier. All it would take would be for one person to question her identity. No matter what Squire David believed himself, he would not tolerate someone in his home that would bring his credibility into question.

"It is so exciting!" A teenage girl standing next to her was giggling with anticipation. "I just love surprises. Nothing interesting ever happens around here." Grae gave her a polite nod as she thought how this young woman would love to hear her story. "Davy Graham is so handsome. I bet his father was years ago, too. I wish there were more sons in this family. All our young men are off in that horrible war. We just do not know if they will even make it back. We could all end up as spinsters. Everyone knows that Nannie Tate just has Davy wrapped around her little finger. If she wasn't so nice, I would just hate her."

Grae was sure that she had mistakenly walked into the closet and ended up on the wrong southern plantation. "Have you seen Scarlett?" Grae's sarcasm needed an outlet. The young woman would never know the difference.

"Scarlett? I do not believe I know any girl by that name. Who are her family?"

"The O'Haras. You know, they have that beautiful plantation called Tara." The girl had a blank look on her face. "Oh, my goodness! What is the matter with me? I am thinking of a family I know further south. I was visiting there. I am such a silly girl. I forgot where I was." The girl seemed in deep thought, but finally released a smile and a giggle in Grae's direction.

"Everyone be quiet!" Bettie was walking around the house. She was dressed in her finest, which included a large hoop skirt that seemed to hit everything and everyone she came near.

"Are you going to have your mother come down before they get here?" Grae pulled Bettie aside and whispered to her. "In case your father is, well, you know, grumpy about it when he arrives."

"You have a valid point there. At least she can enjoy the initial surprise. Good thinking, Sarah. Why don't you go retrieve her for us?" Grae wasn't prepared for that instruction. She stood in front of Bettie for a moment, thinking about the consequences. "Please, we need to hurry. They are not far away." Grae nodded and made her way up to the stairs.

"That gown is just lovely." An elderly woman took hold of her arm as she passed by the closet. Grae wondered if she could just step inside it and wait the rest of the time out until her departure. She didn't think that the next few hours were going to be completely filled with the joy that was anticipated.

"Thank you. It was made by Gracie's daughter, Violet. She is a very talented seamstress."

"I have heard that. I must see about getting her to make some dresses for my granddaughter. After this dreadful war business is straightened out, I am going to send her to Atlanta to a finishing school. My sister, Melanie, lives there."

Grae did a double take as the woman said her sister's name. "Does she live at Twelve Oaks?"

"What did you say, dear?"

"Nothing, ma'am. I must get upstairs and retrieve Missus Graham before Mister Graham arrives."

"Yes, get poor Martha and let her enjoy the surprise. This affair will not be all pleasantries for her, I am sure." The woman gave Grae a firm nod and moved so she could pass.

Grae wound her way through the people. They were amazingly quiet. As she climbed the stairs, she wondered where The General was. He was not in her room when she awoke that morning. Grae couldn't resist peeking into the room she occupied in the present. A quick glance told her that Clara was quietly playing with a doll in the corner that was near Bettie's bed. There was a pallet beside the bed, closest to the wall, where Clara slept at night. It had not really been hard to conceal her presence from Squire. He never entered his eldest daughter's room. They never allowed Clara to go outside unless he was off the property. Everyone kept their mouths shut because they all were concerned what might happen to the poor child if he was to learn she was there.

Grae knocked softly at Martha's door and opened it. Gracie was standing behind Martha. She was adjusting Martha's dress as they viewed it in the mirror. The scene reminded Grae of a time not so long ago when she and

Martha stood before that same mirror. It was right before Grae had last departed 1859.

"Oh, do come in!" Martha turned to face Grae. "Oh, your dress is lovely. That color is beautiful. It shimmers."

Grae herself was amazed at how beautiful a gray dress looked on her. Her hair had grown longer. It was all one dark color, finally. No more glimmers of green shouting out from her locks. She chose to wear it down since she arrived in 1864. It was pulled back with a ribbon. Soft curls framed her face. She thought that it might conceal her appearance from anyone who might think she looked familiar.

"My girl, she do beautiful work." Gracie smiled with pride as she looked at Grae's dress. "If she were up North somewhere, she would be makin' her a fine livin'."

Martha furrowed her brow at the comment. "If Mister Lincoln has his way, she may have that opportunity right here in the South." Martha seemed lost in thought for a moment. "Grae."

Hearing her name startled her. Gracie did not look the least bit surprised.

"Yes, Ma'am."

"Are there slaves in your time?"

Grae thought carefully about the question. It was too complicated to answer in the limited time they had. She needed to get Martha downstairs.

"That is not an easy question for me to answer. My world is very different from yours. But, I will say that slavery can take many forms. There are places in the world where slavery still does openly exist, but our country abolished the practice long before my entrance into the world. I would not say that it is completely gone, though."

"People do not own others for labor in this country in your time?"

"Not legally. As you probably can imagine in any time, things are done illegally. It takes a long time for viewpoints to change. This young country that you live in still has many things to learn about what freedom means."

Martha turned away from her, permitting Grae to quickly motion to Gracie that they needed to get downstairs.

"You are all ready, Miss Patsy, and I bet that Miss Margaret will be here any time. Let's go on downstairs."

"Yes, I am anxious to do just that. It smells as if we have gone all out for dinner. I do hope that Margaret will stay and dine with us. I would be delighted to have a pleasant family dinner."

"Where are you gonna' send Massa David then?" Gracie laughed and then covered her mouth.

"Now, Gracie, it is not your place to be speaking about Mister Graham that way." Grae's eyes got big at Martha's reaction to her devoted companion. "It is my place." Both women broke out in giggles. Grae just rolled her eyes.

"Let's go now."

Martha led the way. Gracie and Grae exchanged glances. They could hear voices as soon as they began going down the first flight of stairs.

"My goodness, the children are being way too..." Martha stopped in mid-sentence. Grae could tell that Martha saw the crowd of friends that were in her foyer. She thought she heard the woman first gasped, and then start to cry.

"SURPRISE!"

Shouts and clapping could be heard from below. Gracie and Grae stayed behind her. Martha was almost at the bottom step when people started coming up to her. It was a large group of people and very loud. Gracie eased down the rest of the way and moved through the crowd. Grae stayed behind Martha for a few steps. She would have missed what happened next if she hadn't had the bird's eye view from the staircase.

Amid all of the merriment, Margaret walked in. The old woman was immediately absorbed by the crowd and they opened a path to her sister-in-law. Hugs and tears were exchanged. While this was still going on, some of the group began to move down the hallway and the area in front of the door was vacant.

It was at that precise moment that Squire David Graham walked into his home. His look went from shock to anger to sadness in about five seconds. Then, something happened that Grae would not have believed if she hadn't seen it with her own eyes. As he was looking at his wife of twenty-nine years smile and laugh in all the merriment, a lone tear ran down his face. For a moment, she saw a glimmer of emotion cross his face. As if he could feel her gaze, his eyes travelled up to where she stood in the shadows. He did not scowl or change his expression in any way. He just simply nodded. It was an acknowledgement of understanding between only them.

Seeing his arrival, the group yelled "SURPRISE" again and the crowd's attention shifted to his direction. He broke the contact he had with Grae as he began shaking the hands of the men in the group. Grae could almost feel Martha holding her breath. After a few minutes of hand shaking and backslapping, Squire made his way to first his sister, and then, his wife. Martha still stood on one of the last steps of the staircase. For the second time in five minutes,

Grae again saw something that she would have not believed. She saw Squire kiss Martha on the cheek and smile. A round of applause ensued and their children quickly encircled them and began to lead them through the house.

Grae did not realize that Doctor Minson was standing a few steps behind her and on the opposite side of the staircase. As he came down the steps after the crowd began to follow the guests of honor, he startled her.

"He knows that she will not be here much longer. I doubt she is here to see another anniversary."

Grae stopped dead in her tracks and chills ran down her spine. She watched as Doctor Minson walked on down the stairs and out the front door. Despite the cold, he sat down in one of the porch rocking chairs and lit a pipe that he pulled out of his pocket.

Did Martha Graham have some other ailment that only her husband and doctor knew about? Or was Jay right? Was Martha murdered by the man who now sat casually on the front porch of her own home?

The party continued for several hours. Plates and plates of food were consumed. A couple of the gentlemen brought out fiddles and banjos and began to play. There was singing. There was laughter. The Graham children were pleased with their accomplishment. The Graham parents, to all appearances, seemed to enjoy the celebration. A good time was had by all.

When the last guest had left and the hum of the house grew quieter, Grae found Martha sitting in the front parlor. She was humming to herself. She was so glad to see her friend so happy until she saw that in the shadow of the room sat Gracie, holding her head in her hands.

"What's wrong?"

Gracie didn't look up. "It started about an hour ago."

Martha's humming continued.

"What started?"

"Miss Patsy, she thinks she is back in the time when she and Massa David were first married. Back to when they had Mary Emily." Gracie looked at Grae and stood up. "She was..."

"The niece they adopted. The little girl who died."

"Yes. It was an awful time. For some reason tonight, she has gone back to that time. I swear I just do not understand what happens to her. One minute she be fine, laughin' with Miss Margaret and the other ladies. Even Massa David was on the best behavior I have seen him have in years, many years. Then, somethin' just snapped in her. She turned to Miss Margaret and told her that she was worried about Mary Emily. Bettie was standin' there and she became scared at the way her mother was talkin' and she run and got me. Now, this poor woman, my poor Miss Patsy, she be hummin' to that baby. That sweet child been dead for more than twenty years and she be rockin' that child to sleep tonight." Gracie reached her hands up to the ceiling. "Why Lawd do you let her get this way? She never hurt one soul her whole life. Ole Gracie tired. See if you can find Davy. He can help me get her upstairs. She always goes easy with him."

Grae turned to leave and Gracie grabbed her by the arm. "Don't say not one word to Massa David. He was nice tonight. But he always lookin' for a reason to lock her away or let that voodoo doctor give her more of his crazy medicine." Grae nodded and left in search of Davy.

She found him in the barn. The slaves were cleaning up what was left of the hog. So many hungry guests had been at the party that it surprised Grae any food remained.

"You take the rest of that meat back to the slave house and share among yourselves." It appeared that Davy had been checking on the progress of the cleanup.

"Oh, but, Massa Davy, you be sure? I not think that Massa Graham like that too much." It was Gracie's husband who made the remark. He gave the other slaves who were there a look of caution.

"My sisters, our aunt, and I hosted this party. This hog came from Aunt Margaret's farm. She told me herself to give the rest of it to all of you. Father has no jurisdiction in this matter." Davy smiled at the men. Hesitantly, they all smiled back. "You and the women have all worked hard for days to make tonight possible on top of all the normal work. You will share in this celebration. Everyone have a good meal and rest. Sabbath Sunday is tomorrow. We shall all be blessed." Davy turned and found Grae standing just outside of the barn.

"I am sorry to have to disturb you. It is your mother. Gracie said to come for you."

Davy's expression quickly changed from a smile to a look of concern. "I was afraid of this." He grabbed his suit jacket from a nearby post. "Please, lead the way."

They walked in silence. Every step seemed to take longer than necessary. A silent fear grew inside Grae.

"We have overwhelmed her with this celebration. My sisters and I so wanted for our family to have one more special time together. We never know when it shall be our last gathering. My sisters are getting older. They will most likely begin marrying soon, once this dreadful war is over. Their lives might take them far away. And, as you have seen now, our mother's health is not as it should be."

Grae chose to remain silent for the rest of the walk back to the house. As they entered from the rear lower level, they passed many slaves cleaning up the winter kitchen, the hearth room, and dining room areas. Grae did not have to tell him where to find his mother as the first member of the Graham family they encountered was his father.

"The affliction is upon us again."

The anger that Grae expected to see on Squire's face was not there. It was replaced by a look of exhaustion. The physical exertion of the trip with Margaret and the night's activities bore a heavy load on the man's shoulders. At sixty-four years, he was no longer a young man. What Grae saw in that moment was a lifetime of mental anguish. She knew that much of it had been self-imposed, nurtured by his anger and ambition. But, there are moments in any person's life where true feelings could not be hidden. A life of extremes, including wealth, hard work, self-imposed mental anguish, and torment, upon him and the lives of others, was catching up with the rock-solid Squire David Graham. He looked broken.

Davy walked past his father and his sisters. The two oldest were pacing and wringing cloth handkerchiefs in their hands. The youngest was curled up in a chair, softly crying. Grae wondered how many times the children had endured such a scene. Bettie and Mary Bell did not meet Grae's eyes. She felt ashamed to be seeing the family's heartache. She considered going upstairs, but was stopped by Gracie.

"Please come."

Grae re-entered the parlor. Martha was still sitting in the same chair. She was no longer humming. Her eyes were bugged out and staring. Doctor Minson stood beside Martha. He appeared to have just given her an injection. The syringe was still in his hand. Gracie stood to the side, praying softly.

"Mother, can you hear me? It's Davy." He knelt in front of her, taking one of her hands into his own.

Grae noticed the wedding ring that adorned Martha's finger. It was a lovely, unique two-ring set. The engagement ring mounting was an arrangement of diamonds in a flower-blossom design with the center diamond elevated above the rest. An intricately carved small vine of delicate flowers was around the wedding band. Both rings were gold. Grae wondered why she never noticed them before.

"The medicine must have time to work. Her condition is as bad as I have ever seen it." As Doctor Minson spoke, Grae could see a look of anger growing on Davy's face.

"Leave us. You have done quite enough."

"I was only acting on your father's instructions. You have not been here during these months of my treatment. You do not know…"

"I know plenty." Davy rose and faced Doctor Minson straight on.

Bettie entered the room and stood beside her brother. "We do not agree with your treatment of our mother. Davy may not have been here, but my sisters and I have. We have seen what this medicine, as you call it, has done to her." It was the Bettie as history portrayed her, strong and defiant.

"So there it is. The truth is finally revealed." Everyone turned toward the doorway where Squire stood. "You think that I have let this man harm your mother. Is that correct?" No one answered. "ANSWER ME!"

The raising of his voice seemed to jolt the heavily medicated Martha. Her hands lying on her lap began to twitch. Gracie quickly knelt beside her and took a hold of them. She continued whispering prayers. Doctor Minson slipped past Squire. They exchanged nods.

"Bettie and I know the truth. We know why you married our mother. We know who came before her, before us. She has an illness, a darkness. But you just want her concealed." Davy's stance was that of a soldier. He may have been facing his toughest adversary.

"You know? You know! You two know nothing!" The look on Squire's face no longer contained compassion. "What is this mockery of what you think you know? Why did you hold such an evening of merriment if you think it was nothing but lies?"

"For her...for us." Davy's answer was simple. "Our time together as a family is short."

"And your father, the monster, doesn't deserve any happiness, correct?" Squire shrugged his shoulders. "Why should it be different now than it has ever been? My life has been filled with misery. I thought I had two sources of pride, my children, and my business. I see that is not so."

"You have them listed improperly. Your business has always been before your children...all of your children." Davy's jaw was square and tight with his last words. Grae saw understanding pass over Bettie's face.

"What is he talking about, Pa?" Mary Bell came into the room. She had been so quiet that Grae had forgotten her presence.

"Ask him. Your brother, the Major, knows everything. He seems to think he knows what my life was like even before his birth. One day he will know that everything is not as it seems. I will be gone by then."

Mary Bell did not seem to know how to react to her father's words. Grae wished to be absorbed into the wall where she was standing.

"And you. You seem to be here for all of my tragedies." All eyes went to Grae as his rage shifted direction. "Why do you keep returning to my life?"

A look of fear crossed Gracie's face. It matched the confusion that was on the faces of Davy, Bettie, and Mary Bell.

"I do not understand you, sir." Grae bowed her head.

"You do not understand. I think that you understand perfectly. It is I who does not understand how this all works. I do know one thing for a certainty; you will never be rid of me." Squire walked over and stood in front of Grae. Slowly, she raised her head. "I will always be with you like the blood coursing through your veins." Grae's whole body trembled. Squire looked at his children and left the room.

"Has he gone mad as well?" Davy came over to Grae as she slowly sank to the floor. "He must think you are someone else. I am so sorry. We have dragged you into the embarrassment of our family. It is inexcusable. His actions toward you are horrid."

Grae looked up and saw the compassion on Davy's face as well as the embarrassment, confusion, and fear in that of his sisters.

"I am fine…He is distraught…Stop worrying over me. Tend to your mother." The Graham children returned their focus to their mother. Grae rose from the floor shaking all over, like a dog. She knew it was a strange reaction. She couldn't stop herself. She had never felt so terrified. She needed to shake Squire David off. He was almost under her skin.

With Gracie on one side and Davy on the other, Martha was pulled up from her chair. Her eyes no longer were bugged out, but they had a glazed look that reminded Grae of how overly drugged people looked in her time. Whatever Doctor Minson had injected into Martha, it was quick, potent, and lasting. It amazed her that this man who called himself a physician, had not returned to check on his patient. She realized how fortunate Jay was to return to the present when he did and not be further caught up in this doctor's questionable practices.

Though her movement was sluggish, Martha followed the prompting of her caretakers. Her feet shuffled across the floor like an elderly person's. Grae had no idea how they would get her up the many steps. She soon found out that Martha's slender son was stronger than he appeared as he lifted his mother up and carried her up the steps. Gracie followed looking as if she was ready to catch them both.

"I am so sorry, Sarah." Mary Bell focused her attention toward Grae when they had made the turn on the staircase and were out of sight. "I do not know what my father was talking about. It is certainly his exhaustion from the trip and the party as well as his concern for our mother. Our family really is not as bad as..."

"Mary Bell, please do not continue this ridiculous speech. Sarah did not read our story in a novel. She has now seen with her own eyes and heard with her own ears the inner secrets of our family. We cannot sprinkle them with sugar and serve them to her with tea." Bettie pushed Mary Bell out of the way. "Sarah, yes, we are embarrassed that you had to experience our family in this way. I would love to tell you that this is out of the ordinary. While tonight was an extreme view of the best and the worst of the Graham family, it is indeed just that, a glimpse into our messy closet. You probably should run quickly out of here at tomorrow's first light. But, I think that you are stronger than that and may very well see this as an adventure on your way to your Memphis home."

Grae knew from reading her journal that she liked Bettie Graham. This young woman had spunk beyond her time.

EIGHTEEN

Her room was cold and quiet as she closed the door. It was almost midnight and the glow of a half-moon shone into the room. Grae sat down on the bed and took off the heavy shoes. She would have just gotten under the covers was it not that her dress was so new and pretty.

"Sleep has been impossible. I have never seen such a party in this house."

The General had managed to paw the blanket away from the pillow on the bed opposite Grae's and had tunneled himself between the pillow and the blanket. He was completely hidden. He looked very warm.

"I cannot even describe what tonight was like. It was almost as bad as seeing Joseph Baker murdered." The General poked his head out from beneath his cocoon. Grae had gotten his attention. "It was like a rollercoaster of emotion. I saw Squire shed a tear at Martha's happiness and a few hours later, I saw him as hard and hate-filled as the night that we buried Ama. I felt like I had been set down into the middle of a movie and no one gave me a script. I am really afraid that if I am around him much longer, he will find a way to have me killed in a convenient accident."

"Okay, you are scaring me now. Tell me what happened."

Over an hour passed before Grae was finished. She thought that The General would wear a hole in the quilt on her bed he paced so much. He sharpened his claws. He could not be still. He even made strange cat sounds during some of her descriptions of how the good doctor had treated his patient. She had to tell him to be quiet for fear that someone would hear him.

"Perhaps you now understand why I say this house has so many lives. It was empty for a very long time before your grandfather moved in. I know that it has become a refuge to you and your family, but I'm not sure that anyone should be living here. You can see that there have been happy hours here, but they are so overshadowed by the sadness. It is in the very foundation that it stands on. The lives of those who passed through are buried here, in more ways than one."

The General moved closer to Grae and she stroked his fur. "For all the travelling talents of you and your mother, it was your grandmother who was truly the sensitive one."

"Granny Belle?"

"Yes, she could feel things. As much as she loved the house and its history, I know it disturbed her. I once heard her tell your grandfather that there was one room that literally made her sick to her stomach when she was in it."

"Which one was that?"

"Martha's room. The same room where the initials are etched into the window glass."

"Really? Did she ever tell anyone else that?"

"It's doubtful. Think about it. People don't want to believe such. If they can't see something, it doesn't exist. No one wants to think that the process from death to eternity might not be the smooth transition that people are taught to believe. No one dares to believe that a life can be so troubled in its natural state that it just might be afraid to go on to the next life. It scares people."

"I hadn't thought of it that way. There has been a lot of bad stuff happen on this property."

"Grae, you don't know the half of it. Your family, as dysfunctional as it is, may be the happiest family that has ever lived here."

"Maybe we will survive then."

"You might."

The General made the long jump between beds and settled back into his place. "You know that the little girl in your room is really in that room now?"

"Yes, Clara. How did you know?"

"She played with me today. I ran after her ball. I play with her in your room sometimes."

"You come in the Mansion?"

"Yep. Your grandfather lets me in when you all are gone during the day. Clara always acts as if she is scared of me. I bet she won't when we return."

"How come?"

"She knows me, now."

The General yawned and sunk back under the blanket. Grae wished that she had the power to take her

411

friend home in another form. She longed to see this friend, as he really should be in her time.

She couldn't open her eyes. The feeling scared Grae until she rubbed them and realized her eyes were matted shut. She had slept that hard. As she sat up in bed, she remembered all that transpired the night before. It amazed her that this journey, these journeys, had gotten her so close to this family. She stepped into their lives as one of them, like she was born into them.

Stretching, she looked around for The General. He must have slipped out when one of the slaves brought in the pitcher of water that stood beside the basin along with the clean clothes.

As Grae prepared for the day, she thought of her own family. They were not missing her, as she was not truly gone from their time. She had been in 1864 for almost a week and it seemed like forever. So much had transpired that she forgot about the fountain pen she brought on the journey. She supposed that it was her time token for this trip, as the broach and small knife had been on previous journeys. She opened a drawer on the small table where she had tucked the pen for safekeeping. It was still hidden, safely there.

The door to Bettie's room was open as she passed by, so Grae decided to peek in on Clara. Her initial scan of the room didn't find the little girl, so she stepped into the room and looked more closely. Clara wasn't on her little pallet beside Bettie's bed or even under it. She quietly walked over to the closet. Grae knew that the story was that the child was kept in the space after she passed. The Graham girls were afraid of what their father would do if he found out. Grae slowly opened the door. Clara was huddled in the corner facing the wall. The child was trembling. Grae bent down and touched her.

"Clara, you are burning up." The girl slowly turned around.

"I am cold."

"Come out of there and get in bed."

"No, he will see me. He does not like me." Her voice was barely over a whisper.

Grae rushed back over to the bed where she found a thick blanket folded up on the end. She grabbed it and wrapped Clara in it.

"I am going to go find you something hot to drink. Have you eaten?" Clara pointed to a bowl of half-eaten oatmeal in the corner. "I will be right back."

As Grae closed the door, she turned and found Martha standing in the doorway. Her face showed exhaustion, but her eyes were clear.

"The girl is sick, isn't she?" Grae nodded her reply. "Go get Gracie. Tell her to bring Old Naomi."

As Grae approached Martha in the doorway, the woman reached out and took her hand. "I am sorry for what you saw and heard last night. I do not know what happens to me. The medicine it makes me unable to move." Martha took hold of the doorway to give herself support.

"Perhaps we should get you back to your room." Up close, Martha looked very gray.

"Yes, that would be wise. Then, you hurry and do as I have told you." Grae and Martha slowly walked back to Martha's room. The woman went to her bed and lay down on top of the covers. She looked relieved. "Go now. Help the child."

Grae began to walk toward the door when she saw a glimmer of light shine through one of the tall windows. It looked like a spotlight on one particular windowpane. Grae knew that in her time there were initials etched in the glass. She paused for a moment and thought about the date that was on the etching. She was sure that the year was 1864. She must try to remember to look later. She needed to focus on getting help for Clara first.

Downstairs, she found Squire and his son sitting at one end of the breakfast table. Doctor Minson was seated by himself at the other end. Grae thought it best not to enter that room. Davy saw her pass the doorway and nodded. Grae went downstairs to the kitchen. She found Bettie and Bunt eating at a small table where Gracie was sitting. The scene caught Grae by surprise. She could not recall seeing slaves sitting at the same table in the kitchen with their owner's families before. Gracie looked up from the potatoes she was peeling.

"Mornin' now, child. Little Naomi says you be sleepin' like the dead when she brought you water this mornin'."

"Yes, I suppose I was."

Bettie and Bunt looked up towards her direction. Both of their faces were filled with sadness.

"Miss Martha says for me to tell you to get Old Naomi." Everyone's eyes looked at Grae.

"Oh, is Ma sick?" Bettie started to rise from her seat.

"It's not for her. She looks very tired, but I got her back to bed." Grae looked behind her. "It's Clara. She is huddled in the closet. She has a fever."

Gracie got up and walked quickly out the back of the house to go find Old Naomi.

Bettie rose from her chair. "I think we should take her something warm to drink." There were two pots on the stove. Bettie reached for a small cup on a shelf nearby and began to fill it with the liquid.

"I am not sure that coffee is the best thing for her."

"This is tea. Winter or summer, Gracie always has a pot of tea on the stove."

While Grae found that unusual, she didn't stop to question it. They were about to leave the kitchen when Gracie returned with a very tall and thin older woman. She didn't remember seeing her before. The woman's hair was solid white and her skin was like fine tissue paper. She carried a small brown bag similar to that of a doctor. Gracie led the way upstairs. When they arrived on the main floor, Gracie and Old Naomi headed to the back stairs.

"You stay here and watch." Bettie's voice was trembling. "I do not think that Pa will come back upstairs, but we need a lookout just in case." Even though she didn't relish the job, Grae nodded.

"Wait." Grae took hold of Bettie's arm. "Do Davy and Doctor Minson know about Clara?"

"Davy knows a little about the situation. He knows that we are hiding her. Doctor Minson does not. We would have liked for him to examine her, but I am sure he would tell Pa." Bettie turned and left quickly, following the others. Grae walked back toward the dining room to have a better view of the doorway. As she did, Squire walked through it towards her.

"Here you are again." His tone was nonchalant. As did the rest of his family, he looked tired.

"Good morning, Mister Graham." Grae tried not to meet his eyes.

"My son has told me this morning that he believes I owe you an apology. Do you believe that to be so?"

Grae could feel his eyes staring at the top of her head. She briefly met his gaze. "That is not necessary, sir. This is your home. You have the right to speak within it." The words left a bad taste in Grae's mouth.

"Those are wise words you speak, but I shall agree with my son. You are his guest. I do not treat guests unkindly."

Grae fought the urge to return his serve with an overhead slam down the middle. Her years of tennis created powerful imagery in her head.

"I apologize if my words and actions offended you. We should not have conducted our private family conversation in front of a stranger…even if she is a familiar one." Squire nodded and headed for the back door. "It would be wise of you to tell me who you really are and why you are here." He did not turn around to say these words. "You would not want me to think that you have bad intentions by returning here. It would be tragic if something happened to you, accidentally, of course."

Grae's recent words with The General came back to her. If she wanted to return to her own time, she might just have to tell Squire David where she really came from. It was a risk. But, one she might be forced to take. The ball was in her court now.

"She is resting now." Gracie returned about a half-hour later. Bunt had found her brother and told him what was happening. They both went outside to monitor the whereabouts of their father. "That child is not gonna' make it.

I know them girls think they cans save her, but she done got them chains in her chest."

"What? Chains in her chest?"

"You never heard that before. Where you be from, girl? Oh, Lawd, never you mind, I forgots. That not be the words for it where you be from." Gracie poured herself a cup of her tea and sat across from Grae, in the kitchen where they had both retreated to. "When that child breaths, it sounds like chains rattlin' in her chest."

"Oh, she has pneumonia. We need to get her some antibiotics." As soon as it was out of her mouth, Grae realized she had messed up. Gracie was giving her a very strange look.

"Is that city medicine? Would that crazy Doctor Minson have some in his bag?"

"No, I do not think that he would."

"Well, yous better pray then. Old Naomi says it is too bad for her poultice to work on the sweet girl. It probably be the same thing that takes the rest of her family. I hopes my girls don't get sick now, too."

The Graham house was unusually quiet for the rest of the day. Bettie and Mary Bell stayed upstairs checking on Clara and Martha. The weather was fair for mid-December, and as Grae looked out the windows, she could see quite a bit of farm activity. Doctor Minson was out making rounds throughout the community. Davy said that the doctor would probably not return for several days. Grae hoped that meant that Martha would not be subjected to his treatments for a while.

Grae helped take down the hearts that still adorned some of the rooms. As she carefully stacked them in a small box, she wondered how long they would stay hidden again before some curious soul would find them.

As the afternoon changed into evening, Grae went back upstairs. The door was closed to Bettie's room where Clara was resting, so she chose not to disturb her. Instead, she wandered further down the hallway where she saw that the main door into Martha's room was slightly ajar. Grae knocked quietly, but did not hear a response. Looking briefly behind her, she decided to peek in and see if Martha was resting. She found that the woman was awake. Her back was facing the doorway as she was sitting in a chair near a window. It was the window where Grae thought she saw the etchings located. Grae took that as a sign that it might be a good time to ask about them.

"Hello, Martha." Grae's voice was soft, but it still made an echo in the large room.

Martha did not turn from her view. "Please join me."

A matching chair was next to Martha's. It had a high back with rich velvet upholstery in a beautiful royal blue. She smiled at the color. She did not remember the chairs from her last visit in 1859.

"Are you feeling better?" As Grae sat down next to Martha, she saw that her friend had a little more color to her complexion. Perhaps even sitting in the winter sun was good for a person's health.

"I feel like I have walked through a fog and do not know how I got here. Moments ago, I was a girl in my youth dreaming of a prince who would rescue me. Now, I am an old woman who realizes that a prince came, but he did not rescue me." Martha's choice of words did not need explaining. "Yesterday was a celebration of a day that I once thought was the best one of my life. I married a handsome, ambitious man. I was full of hope and expectations. Mine has been a privileged existence from birth. But, its greatest abundance was steeped in sorrow and darkness." Martha grew silent.

Grae decided to join Martha in the silence, but her gaze returned to the windowpane as the setting sun shone in. She rose and stepped closer to it. The etching was there with a date of February 24, 1864, almost ten months earlier.

"Did you do this, Martha?" Grae pointed to the section of glass where a list of initials was etched. They would still be there over two hundred and fifty years later to serve as a mystery for a future generation.

"Alas, I did." Martha looked down at her hands and began to work her wedding ring back and forth on her finger. "I find that Doctor Minson's treatments for my spells of darkness require my confinement in this room for long periods. I do prefer this to be my prison cell than the real one below us."

Grae knew that Martha was referring to the shackle room in the basement, near the stairs to nowhere.

"I do not know if these treatments are all the device of the good doctor or if my husband also fancies himself to be a doctor of sorts, as well. They tell me that it is for my own safeguard and the protection of my children. They know that the latter is a reason I will concede. My children's well-being is more important to me than that of my own. I must surrender to that argument."

"Confinement must be hard though. You are such a gregarious sort."

"Indeed, my friend." Martha rose and smoothed down Grae's hair as she passed her. "You have seen into my soul. You know my true heart. It can be lonely. There are some who come and keep me company at times. My lifelong companion and dearest friend, my Gracie, never forsakes her Patsy. My children, on turn, visit with a book in hand and read long selections of our favorite authors until long past the hour to turn down the lamps. It is a joyful time for my heart. My older girls and I discuss the passages at great lengths. We search for hidden meanings in the writer's words. My youngest is rambunctious and seeks out adventure. Our readings reflect these dreams. We imagine what it might be like to live in faraway lands. Lands with exotic scenery that contrast with our own. Where a lion or giraffe might walk out of the jungle to meet us or the large mammals of the ocean might swim near shore to visit."

Grae smiled at the vividness of Martha's descriptions and the joy that crossed her face as she shared them.

"Are they the ones you are honoring with your etchings in the glass window?" Grae was immediately sorry that she asked the question as she saw the light fade from Martha's face.

"I find that the time has come for more days of darkness than of light. The doctor says that this medicine will make me feel this way. The good doctor's diagnosis confirms my own, and what is to become of me. As if he were predicting the weather, he appears so very pleased with his portentous statements, especially when my husband is in attendance." Grae's mind grew suspicious of the doctor's goal. "After these dark periods, I find that I have a strong desire to write down my feelings. My diaries have always been like close friends. I share my secrets without fear of embarrassment. Those who read them years from now shall surely take pity on my poor life."

Martha returned to her chair. A deep sigh seemed to push her further down into it. A few minutes earlier, she seemed like a bird with wings spread wide in pride and enjoyment. What followed was a shadow of that self, downtrodden, and spent as she sank into her prison chair. "I record the stories of my family when my mind allows me. Sometimes, such as the day that I made my mark on the window, I can only remember fragments. I try to honor those I love. They are there in that glass, some of them."

"This treatment that Doctor Minson gives you, what does it include?" Grae knew these were questions that plagued Jay's conscious. She wanted to have some answers to ease his heart.

"I wonder that myself, indeed. He does not divulge his secret recipe for the powder that is mixed in my milk, or the injections that pierce my arms. But, I have heard him say that it is poison."

"What?"

"Yes, you heard correctly. He says that there are bad places within my brain. These cause the spells of darkness. They make me talk out of my head. A minister might call them demons and try to remove them with the Word of God. But, the doctor says that there are parts of my brain that are sick and these potions that he creates will kill them. Myself, I do not understand. How does the medicine know what is bad and what is good? It would seem to me that the poison could not distinguish the difference."

Grae considered Martha's words. Her mind drifted to her father and the treatments for his cancer. That was indeed the same logic used in her time. Give poison to kill the cancer cells, but she knew that good cells died as well.

Gracie entered the room. The young slave named Little Naomi was behind her. She carried a tray of food and drink that was almost bigger than she was.

"Ah, Miss Patsy, you has a fine young lady here keepin' you company. Shall I gets a plate of food for her to join you?"

"Our Grae would more enjoy dining with my young ones, I daresay. We have had a good chat, but I am tired. I doubt that there is anything on that tray that will make me want to eat." Martha did not even glance at the plates of food. It appeared to Grae to be as much variety as the anniversary food the night before.

"I will sits here whiles you eat. Ole Gracie will not budge."

Grae slipped out of the room as Martha's trusted companion was laying down the law. She went back to her room. There was a bulge under the blanket at the bottom of her bed. Grae poked it with her finger. She heard a screech as The General scurried out from under his hiding place.

"Why would you do that to me? What have I done to deserve that? You scared me to death." The General's claws came out as he pawed the air in Grae's direction.

"Oh, you have nine lives, what are you worried about?"

"My dear, I have been a cat for a very long time. I used up those lives a century or so ago."

"Just exactly how long have you been a cat?" The General opened that door of conversation and she was going to walk right in and make herself at home.

"I have been a cat since around, well, I guess about 1860."

"Well, that isn't long. That's just four years ago." Grae poured fresh water into the basin and splashed some onto her face. It was very cold.

"What? No. I have lived as a cat from 1860 until your time."

"Oh, well, yeah. That is a long time." Grae was going to have to pay attention if she wanted to learn anything. "So how old would you be in my time?"

"As a cat, well, I guess I would be around..."

"No, as a human. How old would you be if you were still human?"

"I know that is a trick question. Let me just say, older than you." The General rolled over on his back. "And before you start asking again, I do not want to tell you who I am. There is no point in it. I have resigned myself to this fate and have accepted it. There is no sense rehashing an old story."

"Don't you think that people in my time miss you?" Grae knew it was a dangerous, and probably hurtful, question, but it was going to take asking a challenging question for her to find out any other clues.

"I am sure that there are people who do. Just because I look like a cat doesn't mean I don't still have some of my human feelings. But, it is best that they, like you, forget it and move on. I think most of them have."

"Most?"

"I'm sure it has been harder for some."

"Such as?"

"Such as, we are not going to have this conversation."

"I think we already are. Isn't there any bargaining tool I can use to learn more on this topic?"

Grae watched as The General jumped off the bed and started his ritual of pacing. After a few moments, he jumped on the opposite bed and sat across from her.

"Actually, there is."

"Okay, I'm all ears."

"There's another one of those modern expressions that doesn't make any sense. I thought my nagging had broken you of that habit. You haven't been using as many."

"You are avoiding the subject again."

"Against my better judgment, I will make the following deal. But, remember that a promise is just that, it is a solemn vow that you must keep." Grae nodded her head. "I will tell you my story. I will tell you who I am in human form. But, in exchange, you must make me a sacred promise." Grae kept nodding. "When you return home to your time from this trip, you will take off that key and never wear it again."

"But, I don't…"

"No, no…there aren't any conditions that you can maneuver out of this promise with. The key stays off your person forever. Not around your neck, not in your pocket, not in your shoe, it stays away from you."

"Hmmm. I'll have to think about that."

"I figured as much. You are just like your mother. You just can't stand it."

Grae wondered if it would be considered rude if she asked to have her dinner brought to her room. She didn't want to endure a night of conversation with Squire. A light knock at her door revealed Mary Bell.

"Good evening, Sarah. We are so sorry that we have been neglectful of you today. We have been staying close to sweet Clara." Mary Bell stepped into the room. The young lady looked worried and tired. "I am happy to report that she seems a little better. We were able to get her to eat some broth and a few bites of bread. I fear for her. Her poor health mimics her fragile spirit." Mary Bell's words described precisely how Clara's spirit was in her time. She had moments of gaiety, but they were cloaked in frailty.

"Is she resting now?"

Grae rose from the bed and looked at her own reflection. Her hair was in a great need of washing. She longed for the shower that was just down the hallway in her time. She noticed that she was pale and wondered if her fitful nights of sleep were already catching up with her.

"Somewhat. Her sleep seems tainted with dreams that cause her to cry out. I cannot imagine how horrifying losing her family must have been for her. I have talked with Davy about having Doctor Minson examine her upon his return. He says he will. Our father will be angry." In the reflection of the mirror, Grae could see Mary Bell bow her head. "I suppose you find it strange that we are so afraid of our own father."

"It is not my place to judge." Grae adjusted her dress and washed her hands before turning toward her visitor. "He seems to be a gentleman who demands control."

"Yes…I see that you are ready. Let us join the family for dinner."

Grae nodded, trying not to show the dread she felt.

All the Graham children were present for dinner. The lively conversation that she had witnessed at previous meals was replaced by a tired silence. Platters and bowls of steaming food were scattered across the table, but no one began to eat. Grae looked from person to person.

"We are waiting on our father. He is upstairs with Mother." Davy's voice was guarded. A quick glance around the table revealed everyone's fear—Clara was upstairs.

"One of the slaves is in my room with her." Bettie seemed to have read Grae's thoughts. Grae nodded.

"We should each say a silent prayer before our meal," Bunt spoke up, "Since we cannot say it out loud."

"What can you not say out loud?" Squire David came barreling into the dining room. The look on Bunt's face was full of fear.

"She cannot say out loud the words that she heard the overseer saying to the slaves. His temper got the best of him." Bettie chimed in.

"I shall speak to him about it." Squire sat down.

"Pa, if you do that, he may treat Bunt poorly in the future. Can you just not make reference to her?" Bettie was a sly one. She gave Grae a wink.

"That is wise. I do not wish to have to fire him. He has been a good overseer." Squire nodded to his son. Davy said a short prayer. Squire's conversation hardly paused as he continued. "Bunt, you should keep your distance from such situations."

"I will. I have learned my lesson." Bunt smiled widely. A look of relief was evident. She began to eat.

"Your mother has agreed to stay in her room for a few days." Squire did not look up as he placed food on his plate. "She must have proper rest to prepare for the holiday and this birthday nonsense for Margaret."

Bettie looked like she wanted to respond to her father. Grae noticed that Davy made eye contact with her and shook his head.

426

"Pa, you said that you wished for me to go check on how things are going at Lead Mines. I am thinking about doing that tomorrow."

Grae glanced around the table. Bettie had a slight smirk.

"Very good. Glad to hear that. Check in with our man, John. We have rumors that the Union is eyeing our mines for an attack. They know what an important role our lead plays in the war."

"Indeed, they do, Pa. I will try to advise them on what to do if that horrid event should occur."

"John is doing a fine job for you, is he not, Pa?" Bettie's question made Grae realize who this "John" was. Bettie would later marry a John Robinson.

"Certainly. I am pleased that he honored my wishes and resigned from his military post to return and assist me with business affairs. It is a pity that my own son could not do so."

"Pa, let us not have this debate again. You know that I have a responsibility to my men, our men, and our country."

"You first have a responsibility to your family. I will not debate this further. The hour is too late and I am too tired. I will bid you all good night." Without acknowledging anyone else, Squire David rose from the table throwing his napkin on his half-eaten plate of food. He left the room before any conversation could be carried on further.

"You will be taking me with you tomorrow, brother." Her father had barely left hearing distance when Bettie began talking.

"Now, sister, why would you want to go there?" Davy's voice had a teasing tone.

"Why, if you go to visit John Robinson on your own, you will do nothing but distract him with idle talk." Bettie's smile was wide with the banter between her and her brother.

"And, if you go, you will just distract him with your devout devotion. John knows of your devilish ways."

"John thinks that I am a fine, upstanding, young lady of this community. He is not my only suitor."

"That may be the truth. But, we know that he is the only one that Pa would approve of, so that means the deal is set."

"There will be no deals in my life, David Peirce Graham. My union shall not be like our parents. I shall die a spinster before I marry for the family business."

Once again, Grae saw that feisty spirit she had read about in Bettie's journal. She wished that she could know the older version of this young woman. She imagined that Bettie would have a story of adventure to tell at the end of her life.

"We shall take our new friend, Sarah, with us. Have you ever seen a mine?"

"No, I have not."

Grae realized that she couldn't really recall ever hearing much about the Lead Mines of Wythe County. Learning about the history of the State and the Nation was commonplace. Learning about local history was rarer than it should have been.

"It sounds very interesting. May I go with you?" Grae directed her question to Davy.

"Well, I suppose it would be fine. It is not a safe place for young ladies, but a quick visit should do no harm. There are one hundred or so troops there guarding the mines, along with our men. I do not foresee an attack coming this close to Christmas, in this dreadful weather."

"Bunt and I shall leave you three to your plans. We will stick close to Clara. I must spend some time composing my holiday wishes to Harold." Mary Bell had remained quiet through most of the dinner. She seemed to be lost in thought. "Sister Bet, I will begin the list of those we shall invite to Aunt Margaret's party. When Ma is more rested, we can review our list with her."

"Indeed. Thank you for thinking of our sweet little friend. We must all include heartfelt prayers for her tonight as we prepare for our slumber. Her fragile soul is in God's hands."

They all were silent thinking about the sweet little girl who was hidden upstairs. It weighed heavy on Grae's heart, as she knew the outcome would end tragically.

NINETEEN

The sky was clear, but the air was cold on the morning of December 17, 1864. It was a Saturday. A month and day of the week, long associated with fun and festivities in Grae's time, but there seemed to be a frigid ominous feeling on this particular day.

"I am going to visit Lead Mines today. Have you ever been there?" Grae already was dressed when The General began his morning stretch.

"I believe I recall going there on a field trip. We didn't get to see much because of safety concerns."

The General had a long process of stretching. It included extending each limb individually before he stretched them in pairs. It amused Grae. She imagined it was a combination of human and feline movements.

"I had a friend whose father was the last superintendent of the mines. He gave my friend and me a peek in it once. I remember it was dark and cold." He yawned again, and then seemed to be more alert. "Why are you going to the mines? You should not be that far off the property."

"Davy is going to check on the operation and productivity. Of course, Bettie wants to see John Robinson. We are getting an early start. The sun is starting to rise."

"Grae, no, you shouldn't be doing this. The mines are at least fifteen miles away."

"Oh, don't be such a worrywart. It's been all doom and gloom since I arrived. A horrendous war. People arguing. Clara's sickness. Martha's depression. Threats from Squire. This sounds like fun."

"Your version of fun needs some education. Your fun is supposed to be in the twenty-first century."

"Grumpy butt, I am going to open this door and let you out. Go bother some mice somewhere. I will tell you all I learn about lead mining when I return."

The General jumped off the bed and walked toward the open door. Before he went into the hallway, he looked back up at her. "You think I am a fuddy duddy. You think I am always trying to stop you from having adventures. I want you to have a life full of them. I want you to explore to your heart's desire. But, I want you to do it where you belong. I was daring like you, once. I had bruises and a broken bone or two in my time. I healed. I tried to defy the laws of time outside of my own world, and well...my life as I knew it was over. Worse than that. I have been forced to live another being's life. I am scared for you. You cannot seem to see that you really do not have any control in this time. You are helpless and you do not know it."

The General slipped out the door and ran down the stairs. Grae stood at the doorway long after he left.

"Sarah, I know that you will be so surprised at who we will be picking up along the way."

Bettie was a chatterbox of excitement. They ate bowls of steaming oatmeal and drank strong coffee quickly. One of the slaves packed a large basket of food for them. Despite The General's dire warnings, Grae was excited to get out of the Mansion for a day of discovery.

"Oh, I am not sure."

Mary Bell loaned Grae a long coat with a hat, muff, and gloves. It appeared rather new. The jet-black wool was a stark contrast to the royal blue dress Grae chose to wear. It seemed appropriate to dress up a little for the day of excursion.

"Is it someone I have met?"

"I believe that my daughter is torturing her brother this morning, Miss Leedy." Squire's tone was slightly friendly. "I believe that you shall be stopping at the Tate farm. It would be a happy day if my son would make good on his intentions and unite our families."

"Pa, you are not vexed that Sarah, Nannie, and I will be going along today?" Bettie put her arm through her father's and rested her head on his chest. It was a classic move used by daughters for centuries to melt their fathers' hearts.

"It does not please me. But, I know that your adventurous spirit will have nothing less. Your companions will have to suffer along with you, if this is not a wise decision. It is a mine. It is a dangerous place. Accidents happen there." Squire shifted his eyes in Grae's direction.

"Time to go, my ladies." Davy was waiting by the carriage with a slave who would be the driver. Davy helped Bettie and Grae inside. Grae looked back at the Mansion as they drove out of sight. She thought she saw The General on one of the hilltops, watching. She knew that he would do nothing but worry until she returned.

Grae soaked in the landscape during the ride to the Tate farm. The sun's rise broke through low clouds of fog as they made their way over the narrow roads. Missus Tate greeted them. Nannie smiled brightly as Davy helped her into the carriage.

Riding the back roads of Wythe County with Gav, Grae had seen what was left of the Lead Mines. Her view in 1864 was quite different. She saw the railroad tracks that followed the river. In her time, those tracks were now abandoned and were the path of the New River Trail. The New River was the second oldest river in the world. Grae could see that the river curved around the Lead Mines property in the shape of a U.

"What are those tall stone things?"

Grae wasn't sure if Davy would know the word "pyramid," but that is what the four large structures looked like to her.

"Those are the furnaces. They are about four stories high." Davy was paying close attention to their surroundings. "Those buildings over there are stores and an office. The roads that you see on the other side of the tracks lead to the mines. We have cabins for the workers to stay in. The tents are for the soldiers who have been guarding the mines."

"Sarah, do you see those two huge cuts in the side of the mountain?" Bettie seemed eager to be part of the conversation. "John has told me that one is called the long-hole shaft and the other, the short shaft. They call those things that run down into the shafts to bring the lead back up, dinky trains. I just love that name...dinky." She smiled, and then laughed. Her spunk came out in any situation. "Way, way over there, you almost cannot see it, but there is a ferry boat that crosses the river at Thorns Ferry."

They arrived at the office building as a man was coming out.

"Why, John Robinson, you look like you haven't slept in days."

Grae laughed under her breath at Bettie's bold greeting to her love. She had to admit that her friend was right. Bettie extended her hand for him to help her down. The young man looked haggard and tired. The clean shaved handsome face she had seen just two days earlier at the anniversary celebration now had the stubble of neglect to accompany the dark circles his eyes wore.

"I have not slept. We must be on guard." John Robinson did not seem to be too happy to see them.

John was about six feet tall. Grae thought that his eyes were his strongest feature. The color reminded her of dark chocolate with slight flecks of gold. Her previous meeting with him at the anniversary party was brief, but he appeared very smart and polite. Grae had a feeling that she was going to see another side of him.

"I must say, Davy, I am surprised that you have brought these ladies with you. Not only are the winds on the verge of turning any carriage over, but you must know that we have a threat of attack here."

"A threat? Where did this knowledge come from? Surely, even the Union shall have some decency to hold back restraint during this holiday time."

"Major! You did not earn that rank with such silly talk. Has a few days home at your comfortable mansion stripped you of all memories from our days on the battlefield? A messenger has come as little as an hour ago to say that General Stoneman is sending a band of soldiers to assault our mines. You must know that we have been in high production for many weeks now. The Confederacy needs all the resources we can offer. Our work here is vital to the Cause."

"Tell me all that you know."

The five of them hurried into the mining office to get out of the bitter cold. The closer they had gotten to Austinville, the location of the mines, the stronger the wind. There was no snow in the air, but Grae knew that her grandfather's adage, 'when the wind blew so coldly, it was too frigid for snowflakes,' was a true statement for this day.

As they entered the small space, Grae realized that this was the first time she had been in any sort of true office during her travels. It was interesting to see what was used in the inner workings of commerce over two hundred years before computers and electronics made their dominance felt. It was very simple and plain, devoid of a woman's touch. A small wood stove sat in the corner with a pipe going into the wall. A beat-up desk with stacks of unorganized papers and logbooks stood with several old wooden chairs around it. Dirty tin cups probably held the remains of cold coffee. She hoped that no one offered her some.

Even if Davy and John wanted to conceal the details from the ladies in their presence from the details of the situation, it would not have been possible in such a small space. They remained silent as John gave the details of what had been learned from the messenger who arrived earlier.

"We know that Brigadier General John C. Vaughn, a wagon train of supplies, and roughly four hundred of his men are on their way here from Wytheville to help us. The messenger had some sketchy details regarding what Union General Stoneman and his soldiers have done so far in Southwest Virginia. It is a travesty. Apparently, around a week ago, Stoneman and his command of about six thousand soldiers left Knoxville, Tennessee, with the total destruction of the salt works, Lead Mines, railroads, telegraphs, bridges, and ammunition stores from Bristol to Wytheville as their objective. Our Confederate leader in Southwest Virginia, General Breckenridge, was based in Wytheville. He is now preparing to defend Marion from Stoneman's forces. We now know that the Federals captured Bristol and Abingdon, as well as two locomotives full of food, clothing, ammunition, and other supplies. It appears that Stoneman is moving at incredible speed given this horrendous weather." John paused as an older gentleman walked into the office.

"Hello, Kohler, good to see you." Davy extended his hand for a firm handshake from the man.

"Good to see you, Davy. I had no idea that you returned from the war. Has your father sent you to check up on us?"

"Well, sir, you know my father, he does like to know what is going on at any business that he has interest. But, he was concerned about potential Union attacks."

"As well he should be. It would appear that it is imminent. What were you thinking, young man, when you brought these young ladies here? Now is not the day for a leisurely ride in the countryside." Kohler looked at Bettie, Nannie, and Grae. He tipped his hat, but did not speak to them.

"We were not aware of the potential for attack. John, please continue with what you were telling me."

"The messenger said that there are conflicting reports regarding the occurrences of the last couple of days, but basically General Breckenridge predicted that Stoneman would attack the important salt works in Saltville first, and he would leave a formidable force of his men there. But instead, Stoneman's men marched on towards Marion and Wytheville for his first assault. General Vaughn and his band of six hundred men are being chased by Stoneman. Reports say that they are only ten miles ahead of the Union forces. Vaughn should be arriving here soon. Davy, we know these mines. We must advise General Vaughn regarding how best to defend them." John was obviously exhausted from work, lack of sleep, and worry.

"John, you must lie down for a few minutes. Is there a cot in the back?" Kohler shook his head affirmatively. "I will go and see how things are going in the mine. Kohler can stay here as lookout."

"Davy, there is no time for rest."

Bettie walked towards John as he spoke. "Listen to my brother, you are exhausted. Even fifteen minutes of rest would improve the clarity of your thoughts and actions. A short nap will invigorate you for what you must face."

Grae saw a glimpse of how she imagined the life of Bettie and John would be. Bettie would be the voice of reason that John would follow. They would be a source of strength for each other. John resisted no further. Bettie led him to the back room. Grae watched as John lay down and Bettie pulled a chair nearby to sit and watch over his sleep. She turned to Grae and gave her the most beautiful smile of contentment.

"Nannie, you and Sarah, must stay here with Bettie while I go and gather the men and arm them. We need to let the men know that our Confederate forces are not far away." Davy turned to leave.

Perhaps it was nervousness, but Grae could not control the sudden urge she had to relieve herself. She knew that she could not wait much longer.

"I...I need to, well, be excused." Grae's face was red with embarrassment.

"What?" Davy did not seem to understand her phrasing.

"I need to visit the outhouse." Grae finally blurted out the real words.

"Oh, yes, certainly. I will show you where it is, and then you must come right back to this building." Grae nodded, not looking him in the eye.

As she followed him outside, she was shocked at how quick it had become colder. Davy showed her to the outhouse, and then turned and left. As she opened the door to step inside, Grae looked back to watch where Davy was going. The entrance to the mine was clearly within sight.

Grae stepped out of the outhouse and took a deep breath. As cold as the air was, it was a refreshing change to the odor inside.

"It is certainly obvious that no women work here." Grae spoke the words out loud, and then looked around to make sure no one was within hearing distance.

As she adjusted her coat, she felt like something was sticking her under her dress. She reached under the high collar and pulled out the chain on which the key was hung. "It must have gotten twisted." She decided to leave it hanging on the outside of her dress and under her heavy coat to keep it from bothering her later.

"No one knows what it is. There is no reason to hide it."

On a distant horizon on the other side of the river, she could see a large group of men riding horses and pulling a long line of wagons towards them. The winter landscape offered a clear view. She thought the group must be the Confederate General and his troops. She must let Davy know. As Grae carefully walked down the rocky hillside, she caught a glimpse of a cat running into one of the mineshafts. It looked suspiciously like The General.

"He couldn't possibly have come with us. I'm sure I saw him as we were driving away from the Mansion." Grae kept walking toward the entrance where she saw Davy enter. As she passed the area where she saw the cat enter, she could not walk past. It appeared to be an open shaft. Grae wondered if it could be some sort of test area. She knew so little about mines that it was futile to speculate.

"General, General, was that you? Do you hear me?" Grae heard her voice echoing. It was pitch dark. As she carefully walked further in, she froze in place as she began to feel loose rocks shift under her feet. She desperately tried to grab hold of something, anything, but there was nothing there but slippery rock walls. As her eyes began to adjust, she realized that she was on the edge of a very deep hole. Panic set in as her feet flew out from under her. Everything started moving in slow motion like in a movie. She heard the sounds of rocks hitting the side of the shaft below her. The sound echoed back to her. She felt the chain of her necklace catch on something, and tightness formed around her neck. She feared that she would choke until she felt the chain break.

She tried to reach for the key, but it was already gone. It was falling in slow motion down to the bottom of the hole. Paralyzing fear came over Grae. As cold as it was, she felt hot with fright. She thought she heard someone scream, but realized that the voice was coming from her own mouth. Something hit her in the head. She tasted blood. Still, the screaming continued. The glimmer of the key flashed before her eyes. She thought she heard the rattling of chains and the soft cries of a child. As her body hit hard on the ground below, everything went black.

Historical Timeline

October 18, 1860 – June 21, 1862: "The Journal of Bettie Ann Graham" is written.

November 6, 1860: Abraham Lincoln is elected President of the United States of America.

April 12, 1861: Confederate forces fire the first shots of the Civil War upon the federal garrison at Fort Sumter, S.C.

April 17, 1861: The Virginia Convention voted 88 to 55 in favor of secession from the Union.

June 1861: Camp Jackson, located in Wytheville, Virginia, became a regional induction and training center for the Confederate States of America (C.S.A.), housing over 20 companies with 2000 troops.

July 21, 1861: Manassas was the first major battle of the Civil War.

Late July 1861: David Peirce Graham of Graham's Forge, mustered and organized the "Wharton Grays," Company B, 51st Virginia Regiment. David P. Graham is elected Captain; William Tate, First Lieutenant; John Robinson, Second Lieutenant; and William Painter, Third Lieutenant.

August 1861: The Wharton Grays joined and trained with Generals John Floyd and Henry Wise's brigades at Camp Joe Johnston at Bonsack's Depot.

August 30, 1861: William Alexander Graham, Jr., nephew of the late Jackey Graham and son of former Secretary of the Navy, Senator William Alexander Graham, Sr., enlists as a Lieutenant First Class, Company K, Second Cavalry Regiment North Carolina.

September 10, 1861: Floyd's Brigade was attacked by General William Rosecrans' forces at the Gauley River Bridge in the Kanawha Valley (present day West Virginia).

September 11, 1861: At the Battle of Carnifex Ferry, Floyd's Brigade escapes in defeat, primarily due to Floyd and Wise's poor leadership. This battle and the subsequent loss of the Kanawha Valley to the Union proved to be critical in relation to West Virginia's statehood. Second Lieutenant John Robinson resigns to return to Graham's Forge to make iron for the Confederacy.

December 14, 1861: "Grand Review" near Newbern, Virginia. Five regiments of Virginia Infantry (22nd, 36th, 45th, 50th, and 51st), the 20th Mississippi, the 13th Georgia, three batteries of artillery, and the 8th Virginia Cavalry made up a force of 3500 men.

February 10-18, 1862: Although the "Wharton's Grays" performed valiantly during the strategic Battle of Fort Donelson (Kentucky), General Simon Bolivar Buckner surrendered the fort to General U.S. Grant. General Floyd withdrew his troops prior to the surrender, a point of controversy which continues to present day.

Mid-March – May 3, 1862: Captain David P. Graham returns home on furlough while a few men of the 51st Regiment are bivouacked at Camp Jackson. According to "Bettie Ann Graham's Journal," General Wharton and Captain Forsberg frequently visited the Graham family at Cedar Run Farm. Colonel Wharton reorganized the 51st Virginia Regiment leadership. General Robert E. Lee appointed General Henry Heth as General Floyd's replacement as commander of the southwestern division.

May 17-18, 1862: 51st Virginia Regiment saw action at the Princeton/Lewisburg (West Virginia) engagement.

July 3, 1862: 51st Virginia Regiment saw action at the Mercer Court House engagement.

September 10, 1862: The 51st Virginia Regiment, as part of the Third Brigade, gallantly fought and won the Battles of Fayetteville and Cotton Hill (West Virginia).

September 25, 1862: After the successful Charleston (West Virginia) engagement, the ailing Captain David P. Graham resigns from active service and accepts the position of Post Commander at Yellow Sulphur Springs near present-day Christiansburg, Virginia.

November 8, 1862: William Alexander Graham, Jr. is promoted to Captain of Company K, Second Cavalry Regiment North Carolina.

January 1, 1863: President Lincoln issues the Emancipation Proclamation.

May 10, 1863: General Thomas Jonathan "Stonewall"

Jackson dies from complications related to pneumonia and wounds received at the Battle of Chancellorsville.

July 1863: Captain David Graham is promoted to Regimental Major and William Tate is promoted to Captain of the 51st Virginia Regiment.

July 3, 1863: William Alexander Graham, Jr., Second Lieutenant, Company K, Second Cavalry Regiment North Carolina, is wounded at the Battle of Gettysburg.

July 18, 1863: Toland's Raid or First Battle of Wytheville.

September 30, 1863: William Alexander Graham, Jr. is promoted to Major and is discharged to become the Assistant Adjunct General of the C.S.A. forces in Raleigh, North Carolina.

May 9, 1864: Battle of Cloyd's Mountain (near Dublin, Virginia).

May 10, 1864: Battle of the Cove (near Wytheville).

May 12, 1864: General J.E.B. Stuart is killed in action at the Battle of Yellow Tavern near Richmond.

May 15, 1864: Captain William Hanson Tate of the 51st Virginia "Wharton Grays" is killed in action at the Battle of New Market. William was Nannie Montgomery Tate's brother.

August 25, 1864: James Graham Tate of the "Wythe Greys," 4th Virginia Infantry, "Stonewall's Brigade," was killed in action near Shepherdstown, WV. James was one of Nannie Montgomery Tate's five brothers who served in the

Confederate Army during the Civil War.

November 19, 1864: President Lincoln is re-elected.

December 6, 1864: Congress passed the 13th Amendment to the Constitution abolishing slavery.

December 15, 1864: Squire David and Martha Peirce Graham's 29th wedding anniversary.

December 17, 1864: Stoneman's Raid in Wytheville and Lead Mines.

ABOUT THE AUTHOR

Rosa Lee Jude began creating her own imaginary worlds at an early age. While her career path has included stints in journalism, marketing, tourism and local government, she is most at home at a keyboard spinning yarns of fiction and creative non-fiction. She lives in the beautiful mountains of Southwest Virginia with her patient husband and very spoiled rescue dog.

To learn about other books by Rosa Lee, visit her website at www.RosaLeeJude.com.

Mary Lin Brewer is a Carolina Tar Heel by birth, speech pathologist and school administrator by trade, and the mother of two miraculously stable offspring now in their twenties. A repressed history buff and late-bloomer to all things ghostly, Mary Lin is the official voice of the historical and haunted Major Graham Mansion. She resides in Dunedin, Florida and Wythe County, Virginia.

To learn more about Major Graham Mansion, visit www.MajorGrahamMansion.com.

For more information about the series, visit www.LegendsofGrahamMansion.com.

Made in the USA
San Bernardino, CA
25 September 2016